W9-CVA-114

PRAISE FOR ANDERSON'S ZOMBIE P.I.

"A dead detective, a wimpy vampire, and other interesting characters from the supernatural side of the street make Death Warmed Over *an unpredictable walk on the weird side. Prepare to be entertained."*

— Charlaine Harris

"A darkly funny, wonderfully original detective tale."

— Kelley Armstrong

ZOMNIBUS

ZOMNIBUS

New York Times Bestselling Author
Kevin J. Anderson

WordFire Press
Colorado Springs, Colorado

DAN SHAMBLE, ZOMBIE P.I. ZOMNIBUS

Copyright © 2017 WordFire, Inc.
Death Warmed Over originally published by Kensington Books 2012
Working Stiff originally published by WordFire, Inc. 2014

"Stakeout at the Vampire Circus"
First published as a Kensington eBook; first print publication in *Slimy Underbelly* by Kevin J. Anderson,
Kensington Books, 2014.

"Road Kill"
First published in eBook form from WordFire Press (2012); first print publication in *Mister October: An
Anthology in Memory of Rick Hautala*, vol II, edited by Christopher Golden, Journalstone Books,
November 2013.

"Naughty & Nice"
First published in eBook form from WordFire Press (2013); first print publication in *A Fantastic Holiday
Season: The Gift of Stories*, edited by Kevin J. Anderson and Keith J. Olexa, WordFire Press, 2014.

"Locked Room"
First published in *In Shambles* anthology, Jesse Duckworth, ed., Harren Press, 2014.

"The Writing on the Wall"
First published in *Dark Discoveries* magazine—Issue #28, JournalStone Publishing, 2014.

"Role Model"
First published in *Fiction River: Fantastic Detectives*, Kristine Kathryn Rusch, ed., WMG Publishing,
2014.

"Beware of Dog"
First published in *Streets of Shadows* anthology, edited by Maurice Broaddus and Jerry Gordon,
Alliteration Ink, 2014.

All rights reserved. No part of this book may be reproduced or transmitted in any form or by any
electronic or mechanical means, including photocopying, recording or by any information
storage and retrieval system, without the express written permission of the copyright holder,
except where permitted by law. This novel is a work of fiction. Names, characters, places and
incidents are either the product of the author's imagination, or, if real, used fictitiously.

ISBN: 978-1-61475-537-1

Cover design by Janet McDonlad

Cover artwork images by Jeff Herndon

Kevin J. Anderson, Art Director

Book Design by RuneWright, LLC
www.RuneWright.com

Published by
WordFire Press, an imprint of
WordFire, Inc.
PO Box 1840
Monument CO 80132

Kevin J. Anderson & Rebecca Moesta, Publishers

WordFire Press Trade Paperback Edition April 2017
Printed in the USA
wordfirepress.com

Death Warmed Over

DEDICATION

To MIKE RESNICK,
whose sense of humor is always dead-on.

CHAPTER 1

I'm dead, for starters—it happens. But I'm still ambulatory, and I can still think, still be a contributing member of society (such as it is, these days). And still solve crimes.

As the detective half of Chambeaux & Deyer Investigations, I'm responsible for our caseload, despite being shot in the head a month ago. My unexpected murder caused a lot of inconvenience to me and to others, but I'm not the sort of guy to leave his partner in the lurch. The cases don't solve themselves.

My partner, Robin Deyer, and I had built a decent business for ourselves, sharing office space, with several file cabinets full of pending cases, both legal matters and private investigations. Although catching my own killer is always on my mind, paying clients have to take priority.

Which is why I found myself sneaking into a cemetery at night while trying to elude a werewolf hit man who'd been following me since sunset—in order to retrieve a lost painting for a ghost.

Just another day at work for me.

The wrought-iron cemetery gate stood ajar with a Welcome mat on either side. These days, visiting hours are round-the-clock, and the gate needs to stay open so that newly risen undead can wander out. When the gates were locked, neighbors complained about moaning and banging sounds throughout the night, which made it difficult for them to sleep.

When I pulled, the gate glided open on well-oiled hinges. A small sign on the bars read, *Maintained by Friends of the Greenlawn Cemetery.* There were more than a hundred ostentatious crypts to choose from, interspersed with less prominent tombstones. I wished I had purchased a guide pamphlet ahead of time, but the gift shop was open only on weekends. I had to find the Ricketts crypt on my own—before the werewolf hit man caught up with me.

The world's a crazy place since the Big Uneasy, the event that changed all the rules and allowed a flood of baffled unnaturals to return—zombies, vampires, werewolves, ghouls, succubi, and the usual associated creatures. In the subsequent ten years, the Unnatural Quarter had settled into a community of sorts—one that offered more work than I could handle.

Now the quarter moon rode high in the sky, giving me enough light to see the rest of the cemetery. The unnatural thug, hired by the heirs of Alvin Ricketts, wasn't one of the monthly full-moon-only lycanthropes: He was a full-time hairy, surly beast, regardless of the time of month. Those are usually the meanest ones.

I moved from one crypt to the next, scrutinizing the blocky stone letters. The place was quiet, spooky ... part of the ambience. You might think a zombie—even a well-preserved one like myself—would feel perfectly at ease in a graveyard. After all, what do *I* have to be afraid of? I can still get mangled, for one thing. My body doesn't heal the way it used to, and we've all seen those smelly decomposing shamblers who refuse to take care of themselves, giving zombies everywhere a bad name. And werewolves are experts at mangling.

I decided I wanted to avoid that, if possible.

Even undead, I remain as handsome as ever, with the exception of the holes left by the bullet—the largish exit wound on my forehead and the neat round one at the back of my head, where some bastard came up from behind, pressed the barrel of a .32 caliber pistol against my skull, and popped me before I got a good look at him. Fortunately, a low-slouched fedora covers the big hole. For the most part ...

In the broader sense, the world hasn't changed much since the Big Uneasy. Most people go about their daily lives, having families, working jobs. But though a decade has passed, the law—not to mention law *enforcement*—still hasn't caught up with the new reality. According to the latest statistics by the DUS, the Department of Unnatural Services, about one out of every seventy-five corpses wakes up as a zombie, with the odds weighted heavily in favor of suicides or murder victims.

Lucky me to be on the interesting side of statistics.

After returning to life, I had shambled back into the office, picked up my caseload, and got to work again. Same as before ... sort of. Fortunately, my zombie status isn't necessarily a handicap to being a private detective in the Unnatural Quarter. As I said, the cases don't solve themselves.

Days of investigation had led me to the graveyard. I dug through files, interviewed witnesses and suspects, met with the ghost artist Alvin Ricketts and separately with his indignant still-living family. (Despite Robin's best mediation efforts in the offices, the ghost and the living family refused to speak to each other.)

Alvin Ricketts was a successful pop-culture painter before his untimely demise, attributable to a month's worth of sleeping pills washed down with a full bottle of twenty-one-year-old single malt. (No sense letting it go to waste.) The ghost told me he would have taken more pills, but his insurance had only authorized a thirty-day supply, and even in the deep gloom of his creative depression, Alvin had (on principle) refused to pay the additional pharmacy charge.

Now, whereas one in seventy-five dead people returns as a zombie, like myself, one in *thirty* comes back as a ghost (statistics again heavily weighted toward murder victims and suicides). Alvin Ricketts, a pop-art genius, had suffered a long and debilitating creative block, "artistic constipation" he called it. Feeling that he had nothing left to live for, he took his own life.

And then came back.

His ghost, however, found the death experience so inspirational that he found a reawakened and vibrant artistic fervor. Alvin set about painting again, announcing he would soon release his first new work with great fanfare.

His grieving (sic) family was less than enthusiastic about his return to painting, as well as his return from the dead. The artist's tragic suicide, and the fact that there would never be more Alvin Ricketts paintings, had caused his existing work to skyrocket in value—until the ghost's announcement of renewed productivity made the bottom fall out of the market. Collectors waited to see what new material Alvin would release, already speculating about how his artistic technique might have changed in his "post-death period."

The Ricketts family sued him, claiming that since Alvin was dead and they were his heirs, they now owned everything in his estate, including any new or undiscovered works and the profits from subsequent sales.

Alvin contested the claim. He hired Robin Deyer to fight for his rights, and she promptly filed challenges while the ghost happily worked on his new painting. No one had yet seen it, but he claimed the work was his masterpiece.

The Ricketts heirs took the dispute to the next level. "Someone" broke into Alvin's studio and stole the painting. With the supposed masterpiece gone, the pop artist's much-anticipated return to the spotlight was put on hold. The family vehemently denied any involvement, of course.

That's when the ghost hired *me*, at Robin's suggestion, to track down and retrieve the painting—by any means necessary. The Ricketts heirs had hired a thug to keep me from succeeding in my investigation.

I heard a faint clang, which I recognized as the wrought-iron cemetery gate banging shut against the frame. The werewolf hit man wasn't far behind me. On the bright side, the fact that he was breathing down my neck probably meant I was getting close.

The cemetery had plenty of shadows to choose from, and I stayed hidden as I approached another crypt. *Benson.* Not the right one. I had to find *Ricketts.*

Werewolves are usually good trackers, but the cemetery abounds with odors of dead things, and he must have kept losing my scent. Since I change clothes frequently and maintain high standards of personal hygiene for a zombie, I don't have much of a smell about me. Unlike most unnaturals, I don't choose to wear colognes, fancy specialized unnatural deodorants, or perfumes.

I turned the corner in front of another low stone building fronted by stubby Corinthian columns. Much to my delight, I saw the inhabitant's name: *Ricketts.* The flat stone door had been pried open, the caulking seal split apart.

New rules required quick-release latches on the insides of tombs now, so the undead can conveniently get back out. Some people were even buried with their cell phones, though I doubted they'd get good service from inside. *Can you hear me now?*

Now, if Alvin Ricketts were a zombie, he would have broken the seal when he came back out of the crypt. But since ghosts can pass through solid walls, Alvin would not have needed to break any door seals for his reemergence. So why was the crypt door ajar?

I spotted the silhouette of a large hairy form loping among the graves, sniffing the ground, coming closer. He still hadn't seen me. I pulled open the stone door just enough to slip through the narrow gap into the crypt, hoping my detective work was right.

During the investigation into the missing masterpiece, the police had obtained search warrants and combed through the homes, properties, and businesses of the Ricketts heirs. Nothing. With my own digging, I discovered a small storage unit that had been rented in the name of Gomez Ricketts, the black sheep of the family—and I was sure they had hidden the painting there.

But when the detectives served their warrant and opened the unit, they found only cases and cases of contraband vampire porn packaged as sick kiddie porn. Because the starlets were actually old-school vampires who had been turned while they were children, they claimed to be well over the legal age—in real years if not in physical maturity. Gomez Ricketts had been arrested for pedophilia/necrophilia, but he was out on bail. Even Robin, in her best legal opinion, couldn't say which way the verdict might go.

More to the point, we didn't find the stolen painting in the storage unit.

So I kept working on the case. Not only did I consult with Alvin's ghost, I also went over the interviews he'd given after his suicide. The ghost had gone into a manic phase, deliriously happy to put death behind him. He talked about awakening to find himself sealed in a crypt, his astral form rising from the cold physical body, his epiphany of throwing those morbid chains behind him. He had vowed never to go back there.

That's when I figured it out: The last place Alvin would ever think to look for his painting was inside his own crypt, which was property owned by the Ricketts family (though a recent court ruling deemed that a person owned his own grave in perpetuity—a landmark decision that benefitted several vampires who were caught in property-rights disputes).

Tonight, I planned to retrieve the painting from the crypt.

I slipped into the dank crypt, hoping I could grab Alvin's masterpiece and slip away before the werewolf figured out what I was doing.

It should have been as quiet as a tomb inside, but it wasn't. I heard a rustling sound, saw two lamplike yellow eyes blinking at me. A shrill nasal voice called out, "It's taken—this one's occupied! Go find your own."

"Sorry, didn't mean to disturb you," I said.

"You can't stay here."

Zombies have good night vision, and as my eyes adjusted, I made out a grayish simian creature with scaly skin. I'd heard that trolls sometimes became squatters inside empty crypts whose original owners had returned to an unnatural life.

The troll inched closer. I carried my .38 revolver loaded with silver-jacketed bullets. I would use it if I had to, but a gunshot would surely bring the werewolf hit man running. I had enough silver bullets to take care of the thug, too, but that would open a can of maggots with the law, and I just plain didn't want the hassle.

The troll rubbed his gnarled hands together. "If you're interested in a place to stay, we have many viable options. Pre-owned, gently used postmortem dwellings. If you're undead and homeless, I can help you with all of your real estate needs. Edgar Allan, at your service. Here, let me give you a business card."

"This crypt doesn't belong to you," I pointed out. "I happen to know the actual owner. He hired me to retrieve some of his personal property."

"Then we have a problem." The troll looked annoyed. "Burt!"

From the gloom emerged a larger and more threatening creature. Trolls come in various sizes, from small and ugly to huge and ugly. At close to seven feet tall with wide and scabby shoulders, this one belonged in the latter category.

"Burt is our evictions specialist," Edgar Allan explained.

I held up my hands in surrender. "Now, no need for that! I came here for a painting, that's all. No intention of interfering with your rental business."

"Painting? You mean this one?" The little troll flicked on a tiny flashlight. Hanging on the stone wall was a painting, unmistakably in the cute pop-culture style of Alvin Ricketts: two large-eyed puppies ... gaunt zombie puppies. "Somebody left it here. Looks real nice on the wall, brightens up the place."

A plan began to form in my mind. "I have a suggestion that would benefit both of us." I glanced back at the door of the crypt, straining to hear the werewolf outside. I doubted I could slip out of the cemetery carrying the Ricketts "art" without the hairy hit man intercepting me. Werewolves can run much faster than zombies, and inflict severe bodily damage—the kind that's difficult to repair. If he got his paws on the painting, I would never get a second chance to retrieve it.

I also knew that Alvin Ricketts had no interest whatsoever in owning this crypt.

"What kind of suggestion?" the real estate troll said. "I can make a deal. Nobody beats my deals."

"What if I could get the legal owner of this property to sign over the deed to you, free and clear, completely aboveboard—in exchange for the painting?" (Which was rightfully Alvin's property anyway, but I didn't want to tangle up the conversation.)

Edgar Allan seemed interested, but narrowed his big yellow eyes. "If we handed over the painting, we'd never hear from you again."

"I won't take it now. *You* deliver the painting to my office tomorrow," I said. "Bring Burt for protection if you like." I nodded toward the huge troll. "I'll see to it that the crypt owner signs all the right documents. We have an attorney and a notary right there in our offices." I reached into my jacket and pulled out one of my business cards.

After making sure that I took one of his cards, the troll shone his little flashlight on mine. "Chambeaux & Deyer Investigations. What's the catch?"

"No catch. Just be careful. That's a beautiful painting—I'd hate to have it damaged."

The troll glanced back at the large-eyed zombie puppies. "You think so? I was wondering if it might be a bit kitschy, myself."

"I'm not an art critic. Tomorrow, in my offices at noon."

"We don't usually go out at that hour ... but I'll make an exception."

I slipped out of the crypt and back into the shadows, ducking behind a tall stone angel, then moving to a big flat grave marker. I intended to circle around as quietly as I could on my way to the wrought-iron cemetery gate.

Before I made it to the third tombstone, a furry mass of growling energy slammed into me and knocked me to the ground. The werewolf hit man grabbed me by the collar and yanked me back to my feet. He was a smelly, hairy, muscular guy, half-wolf and half-human. His claws dug into the fabric of my sport jacket.

"Careful, this is my only jacket."

The werewolf pushed his long snout close to my face. "I caught you, Shamble." I could see he was having trouble forming words with all those teeth in the way.

"Chambeaux," I corrected him. "Can't a guy take a peaceful stroll in a cemetery at night?"

He patted me down, poking with his claws. "Where's the painting?"

"Which painting?" Not the cleverest response, but werewolves aren't the cleverest of creatures, especially the at-will lycanthropes.

"You know which painting. I've been watching you."

"I know you were hired by the Ricketts heirs," I admitted, "and I'm sure your employers think they're very important, but I have plenty of other cases. As a private detective who specializes in unnatural clientele, believe me, I've got more than enough reasons to come to a cemetery."

Growling, the werewolf searched me again, though I don't know where he suspected I might hide a large rolled-up painting. My chest pocket?

I heard heavy footfalls and looked up to see the scaly form of Burt the troll. "There a problem here?" Burt was sufficiently intimidating that even the werewolf didn't want to mess with him.

I pulled myself away from the claws and straightened my jacket in an attempt to regain some dignity. "I was just leaving," I said, and looked pointedly at the werewolf.

"I was escorting him out," the hairy guy growled. "Name's Larry."

Burt loomed there, watching as the two of us left the cemetery.

After we both passed through the gate, I sized up the werewolf. Since Chambeaux & Deyer had accepted the Alvin Ricketts case only a month and a half before my murder, maybe it was connected to my own case somehow. "Say, Larry, you wouldn't happen to be the guy who shot me, would you?" No harm in asking.

"Yeah, I heard about that." The hairy hit man growled deep in his throat. "Do I look like the kind of guy who sneaks up behind someone in a dark alley and shoots him in the back of the head?"

"That wouldn't be my guess."

"Have you ever *seen* a werewolf victim? Look at you, Shamble. You could pass for human, if somebody doesn't look too close." He flexed his claws. "If I killed you, you'd have been a pile of shredded meat."

"I'll count my blessings, then," I said. "See you around." I touched a finger to the brim of my fedora in a brief salute and headed away from the cemetery.

CHAPTER 2

Sitting stiffly at my desk—these days I'm usually stiff, no matter what I do; the aftereffects of rigor mortis are a bitch—I pondered the loose threads of investigations under way, figuring out how the evidence tied together. I like the bustle and little distracting noises around the office: the ringing phone, the slam of file-cabinet drawers, the clacking of a keyboard as Sheyenne's ghost types up reports.

She floated into the office carrying two manila case files. "Caught you daydreaming again, Beaux." Sheyenne dropped the files on my desktop. "Did you solve my murder yet?"

"I'm working on it, Spooky," I said, and it was the truth. "Aren't you the one who tells me to focus on paying cases first?"

"Somebody has to—Robin sure doesn't." She shook her head. "You need to have a talk with her. She might as well walk around with the words *Ask me about pro-bono work* tattooed on her forehead."

"It's refreshing to work with someone who still has a heart."

I'm seven years older than Robin, and throughout our friendship I've thought of my partner as a sweet kid sister. Sheyenne, on the other hand, is much more than that. My girlfriend, or *former* girlfriend—but former in the sense that she's no longer alive, not former in the sense that I don't care for her anymore—was the same age as Robin, but I *definitely* didn't think of Sheyenne as a kid sister.

I look pretty good for a dead guy, or so I've been told: well-trimmed dark hair, striking eyes accentuated by bold eyebrows, just the right amount of "rugged." I used to wonder how I would deal with turning forty, but now it isn't an issue. Since I was killed a couple of months shy of my fortieth birthday, I can claim to be thirty-nine for the rest of my existence and not even have to lie about it.

Sheyenne sighed, a conscious gesture since she hadn't drawn a living breath in almost two months. She was semitransparent as she hovered in front of me, her face a little emaciated, her eyes hollow from her lingering death, but she was still gorgeous with those big blue eyes, great figure (though too ethereal now), full lips, and an easy smile that gave the impression she was just cheesecake—a part she had played well as a cocktail waitress and nightclub singer. But I saw right through that, and I knew she was smarter than me and my imagination put together.

After working ten years at various jobs in the business world, Sheyenne had gone back to college and was in her second year of medical school, working part-time at a nightclub to pay the tuition, when I met her ... not long before somebody killed her with toadstool poison. Horrible stuff.

As a ghost of the poltergeist variety, Sheyenne could touch inanimate objects when she focuses her attention, so she does just fine as our receptionist, office manager, and paralegal. General office work doesn't strain her brain too much. So Robin and I let her write her own job description—Sheyenne shows up for work on time and has no intention of moving on.

The biggest drawback is that, although she can touch most physical objects, the screwy supernatural rules prevent her from touching humans. Apparently that definition includes *me*, a former human. Something about auras that surrounded living, or once-living, beings.

So although Sheyenne and I can see and talk to each other, we can't have any physical contact. The best we can do is sit around and reminisce about what might have been, remembering the one night we had together while we were both still alive—a hot and steamy lovemaking session that gets better and better with each retelling, and with each week of missing it. Talk about unresolved sexual tension!

I slid the files she had delivered next to the other stacks of paper, including my own autopsy report. Sheyenne still hovered there. "I've been combing through your cases just to get myself up to speed." She tapped a ghostly fingernail on top of the stack. "The answer's in there somewhere. You pissed somebody off enough to make them kill you."

"I piss a lot of people off. One of my many talents." I shrugged. "Half of these cases aren't even wrapped up yet." I picked up the files.

Revisiting the numerous cases would mean burning the midnight oil, but these days I had all the time in the world.

"You want me to get you some coffee? I just brewed a fresh pot—it makes the offices smell good for prospective clients," she said. "Alvin Ricketts and the trolls are due to come in soon."

"Sure, bring me a cup. It'll make my desk feel more homey." And a coffee-mug stain left on a file showed that I'd actually been working on the case. You could always tell how much time I spent on a client by the number of coffee stains on the paperwork.

Just before noon, the artist's ghost manifested himself in our second-floor offices, wearing his preferred form: long ponytail, tie-dyed shirt, and paint-stained jeans. Because he'd died from a sleeping-pill overdose, his eyes always looked droopy, as if he were on the verge of dozing off. But he was wide awake, especially since we were close to resolving the case. Without hesitation, Alvin had agreed to sign over ownership of his crypt, and Robin had spent the morning preparing the deed and supplemental documentation.

Sheyenne greeted him; she particularly appreciated our spectral clients because at least she could shake hands with a ghost. Alvin looked around the offices, a broad smile on his face.

A few minutes later, Edgar Allan and Burt entered the offices, a study in contrasts: the little simian real estate agent and the burly eviction enforcer. Burt carried the rolled-up painting under his arm.

"We're here to do business," said the little troll.

Robin who had been on the phone in her office for the better part of an hour, now hung up and stepped out, her face filled with joy. I knew she must have won whatever she was arguing about—and Robin usually does win, because her sheer optimistic persistence makes her as formidable as any shambling undead legion. Noticing the trolls and the ghost, she brightened even further. "Hello! Thank you for coming."

Robin's the kind of person you simply cannot dislike—a spunky thirty-two-year-old African American, slender and pretty, with brown eyes straight out of a classic anime. She was raised in a nice house in the suburbs, with two white-collar, six-figure-salary professionals for parents. A perfectly normal upbringing, good schools, a scholarship. After getting her law degree, she discovered her purpose in life and became a fiery activist determined to help the downtrodden. And the Big Uneasy had created a whole new class of downtrodden that needed help.

Five years ago, when I learned she was hanging out her shingle in the Unnatural Quarter, I decided to watch out for her. Robin is enthusiastic and as determined as a bulldog on a letter carrier's ankle, but despite all the cases she has studied, she can be a bit tone-deaf to reality, since her worldview is more aligned with *Sesame Street* than *Lord of the Flies.*

Quite honestly, that's one of the things I like best about her. Robin believes in the power of theLaw the way a little girl believes in Santa Claus, and I've decided to do my damndest to keep her that way, because if she ever loses that sparkle, some key part of her is going to die inside. That would be worse than when I died for real....

Robin was frugal, too. She didn't believe in wasting money on fancy cars or jewelry or decorations—not when there were people who needed our help. Sheyenne had done her best in the past couple of months to give the offices a more comfortable but still businesslike feel. It had taken most of her powers of persuasion to get Robin to agree to a fresh coat of paint on the walls, but Sheyenne had kept costs down by doing the work herself. I'm not sure if our clients have noticed the clean walls yet.

Getting down to business, Robin took the painting from the big troll enforcer and unrolled it on the nearby desk so we could look at the mournful zombie puppies. Alvin Ricketts let out a long, happy sigh. "Ah, just look at the pathos, the myriad levels! Doesn't it just speak to you ... right here?" He touched a fist to his ghostly sternum.

"It's cute," Sheyenne said.

Robin spread out the legal forms on the signing table. "I have the property deed to the real estate in Greenlawn Cemetery, the plat marking the location of the crypt, and the ownership-transfer documents for Mr. Ricketts to sign."

"Can you prove clear title?" asked Edgar Allan.

"Right here." Robin handed over the title documents, which the troll studied meticulously. "I don't specialize in real estate law, but the cemetery forwarded the proper paperwork this morning. I'd still advise you to buy title insurance."

"Seems to be in order." The little troll looked up at me, blinking his yellow eyes. "Pleasure doing business with you."

After the signatures were duly notarized, Edgar Allan handed out business cards. "In case you're ever in the market, I've got some underground deals that aren't in the regular listings."

Alvin's ghost rolled up the painting. "Now that I have my masterpiece back, I can start the auction tonight! No more waiting around. I want the world to see my work."

"Spoken like a true artist," Sheyenne said, then adopted a brisk tone. "However, we are running a business here. Remember that our contingency fee is one-third of the auction realization, plus expenses."

"Of course! I can't thank you enough!" Alvin bobbed out of the office with his treasure.

Robin was happy to see justice done, and I was glad to have another case solved. Now I could get back to investigating my own murder.

O   O   O

Unlike most people in real-world offices with real-world desks, I don't have vacation photos on the walls or framed certificates of completion from the Acme Detective School or the Crime-Solving Award (Honorable Mention). After Sheyenne painted the office, I just didn't see the point in putting that stuff back on the walls. That part of my life ended when my life ended. I did keep a novelty coffee mug Robin had given me years ago with *The cases don't solve themselves* printed on it.

I sorted through the pending and recently closed case folders. I started to read the first case summary, an investigation of black-market blood sales from Basilisk, the nightclub where Sheyenne had worked.

If Sheyenne was right and something in one of those files had gotten me killed, the pieces would come together if I just had enough time to ponder them. Who had wanted me dead? Sure, I had some unhappy clients—every business does—but dissatisfied customers usually just file a complaint with the Better Business Bureau. And had killing me been enough to satisfy the vengeful person, or was that just the start? It really tied my guts in knots, metaphorically, that *Robin* might be in danger too. As the token living human in our offices, she's the only one who still has everything to lose.

I needed to solve this.

The main door burst open, and a terrified-looking man ran in. He whipped his head from side to side. He wore a dark overcoat, gloves, a black floppy-brimmed hat, and oversized wraparound sunglasses like the ones old ladies wear after cataract surgery. He had parchment-pale skin. I didn't need to see the pointed tips of fangs that extended past his lips to determine that he was a vampire. (I *am* a detective, you know.)

Once inside the office, he yanked off the big sunglasses, blinking furiously, as jittery as a rabbit trying to climb an electric fence. "You've got to help me! I need protection!" He reached into the pocket of his overcoat and hauled out a sharpened wooden stake. "I found this—somebody's trying to kill me!"

CHAPTER 3

You'll be safe here." I came out of my office and extended my hand to reassure the skittish vampire. "I'm Dan Chambeaux. Come in and tell me more about what happened."

Humans tend to shrink away from a zombie, but unnaturals aren't so prejudiced. The vampire clutched my hand and shook it. (The rest of him was already shaking.)

You know the type: bald with black horn-rimmed glasses; intense but not threatening. He looked like the illegitimate love child of a bunny and a hamster, but without the fur. The sort of man who held a long, lit cigarette as an affectation, but never took a drag; he probably practiced the gesture at home with a pack of pristine cigarettes. I could imagine him in a bar ordering martinis—the fruity kind, not the manly kind.

He glanced over his shoulder, stepped farther into the protection of the lobby. I closed the door behind him so he'd feel secure. "I'm sure we can help you, Mr. ...?"

"Sheldon Fennerman." He removed his hat and gloves. "Fennerman with one *n*. Actually three *n*'s, but only one at the end. Would you like me to write it down for you?"

"I can figure it out," Sheyenne said, drifting up to him. "How about some coffee? I'm making a fresh pot."

Fennerman's expression melted into one of pure wistfulness. "Ah, I used to love coffee. Caramel macchiato, extra foam ... sometimes when I was really in need of a pick-me-up I'd add another shot of espresso." He heaved a deep breath, let it out. "But now it just upsets my stomach."

"How about some water, then, Sheldon," she said in a soothing voice. "May we call you Sheldon? We like to consider each of our clients a personal friend."

He brightened a little. "I knew this was the right place to come. I'll take sparkling water, no ice, with a twist of lime." Jittery and restless, the vampire paced around the office, adjusted a potted ficus, straightened our only framed picture on the wall (a sunny scene of whitewashed houses on a Greek island—the landlord had given it to us when we rented the office space). "You have very minimalist offices, might even call them austere. I could help you with that. I'm an interior designer."

"Maybe after we take care of your emergency, Mr. Fennerman—*Sheldon*, sorry." I gestured him across the foyer. "Come into the conference room. What trouble are you in?" My heart went out to the guy. His eyes were red and bloodshot, and not for any demonic reason. "You don't look like you're sleeping well."

"I haven't slept much at all, and I *hate* being awake during daylight." He shuddered. "I was never a night person during my life, and this is still awkward to me. I can't get used to the shifted sleeping schedule. I'm drowsy as early as four *a.m.*, and I'm wide awake well before sunset. Ever since these threats, I've been hiding out at Transfusion, the darkened all-day coffee shop for insomniac vampires ... and I can't even drink coffee!" He groaned. "No one should have to live like this."

Robin came out to greet the new client, and I introduced her. "We work cases jointly," I said, "from different directions."

Robin's a lawyer, and I'm a private investigator—separate specialties, but our work is related more often than not. Since neither of us could afford the rent, we'd joined forces—like the Three Musketeers minus one. All for one and one for all. We share office space to cut down on overhead, though technically we're two separate business entities, a legal firm and a detective agency (it's all in the fine print on new client disclosure statements). Because we had set up shop in the Unnatural Quarter, Chambeaux & Deyer got sarcastically corrupted to "Shamble & Die"—though in my case, it should be Die and then Shamble.

Robin already had a yellow legal pad tucked under her arm. "We're here to help you with your troubles, Mr. Fennerman. Can I join you for the intake meeting?"

"I need all the help I can get." He hurried into the conference room, and Robin took a seat across from the vampire, while I folded myself down into the chair beside hers.

Sheldon Fennerman laid the stake on the table and pushed it across to me, glad to be rid of the thing. "I found this on my doorstep when I came out at twilight yesterday. It's meant for me—a clear threat."

I picked it up, inspecting the sharp tip. "Freshly made, never been used."

"Do people reuse stakes?" Robin asked.

Sheldon continued, "And someone spray-painted *Die Vampire Die!* on a boarded-up window across the street."

I looked at Robin, narrowed my eyes. I had heard about this kind of harassment of unnaturals. "My first guess would be Straight Edge."

The purist blowhard group wanted all the monsters to go away. Straight Edge made no distinction among vampires, zombies, werewolves, witches, litches, necromancers, sewer dwellers, ghouls, or anything else. Just another group of bigots, the type who can't feel superior unless they manage to define someone else as less than human. In this case, at least the "less than human" label was accurate.

"If they've targeted you, personally," I asked, "why did they spray-paint on the windows across the street?"

Sheldon fidgeted. "It's Little Transylvania. A lot of my neighbors are vampires. It's not hard to find us on the block, especially with the window glass blacked out. The landlord offers good terms, and sometimes he even sublets the rooms during the day when we're asleep in our coffins. They're zoned as dual-use properties."

He rustled in his overcoat pocket and withdrew a rumpled piece of paper. "I found this graffiti in the alley just behind my brownstone." He pointed to the phrases with a trembling finger. *Eat Wood* and *Feel My Shaft.* "More threats against vampires."

"Well, that's not the only possible interpretation." I considered the stake and set it back down on the table, careful to turn the point away from the vampire. "If it's any consolation, Sheldon, the Straight Edgers are mostly talk. Bullies, but cowards."

The vampire was still jumpy. "But I know they've already succeeded! Six vampires around my neighborhood have vanished without a trace. Six of my friends. I can give you a list of names. We were very close, but they're all gone now! Someone must have driven a stake through their hearts."

"Have you seen any of the bodies?" I asked.

"If they turned to dust, who would ever find the bodies? It's a perfect crime."

"Not all vampires turn to dust," Robin pointed out. "Only the ancient ones, from long before the Big Uneasy."

"But they left their coffins behind!" Sheldon insisted. "Why would any vampire do that? Either my friends left in a hurry, or they're dead. Those haters are going to kill us all—and I'm next! But why me? I haven't done anything wrong. I'm just an interior designer. I'm no threat to anyone."

"Well, you are a vampire," Robin said.

"Not much of one. I was a *vegan* before the transformation, and now I only drink soy blood." His face wrinkled in an expression of disgust. "Nasty stuff ... then again, so was tofu turkey. But a person with strong convictions is willing to put up with things like that. I don't drink human blood. The very idea curdles my stomach."

Even though Sheldon Fennerman may have been a hypochondriac when he was alive, I took his concerns seriously. "Some people have an irrational hatred for what they don't understand. It's best to be cautious."

"You can offer me protection?"

I looked up, raised my voice. "Sheyenne? How is my schedule for the afternoon?"

She appeared at the conference table. "Just your appointment at Bruno and Heinrich's. I can clear it for you."

"I'll still take the appointment," I said. "Sheldon, why don't we go to your place, right now? I'll assess your home security situation, make sure you're safe for the time being. Then I'll gather information and try to track down who's been harassing you."

Robin said with a smile, "My services are available, too, if you need legal help."

"I'll open a new case file," Sheyenne said. "And we have to work out the financial arrangements."

I lifted my sport jacket and fedora from the coat rack and tucked my .38 in its holster. "All right, Sheldon. Let's hit the streets."

He reached out to pump my hand. "Thank you, thank you!" After applying extra sunscreen from a squeeze bottle in his pocket, he pulled on his gloves and floppy hat, turned up the collar of his overcoat, and adjusted the wraparound sunglasses. "I'll feel safe with you, Mr. Chambeaux."

CHAPTER 4

Every unnatural should have a Best Human Friend, someone to rely on, someone to talk to, someone who doesn't take any crap from you or give you any crap in return.

My BHF is a rough-around-the-edges beat cop, Officer Toby McGoohan. We've known each other since college, well before the Big Uneasy, well before I got killed. After only a month, McGoo was still getting used to the changed situation with me. To his credit, he was trying.

Three blocks away from our offices, while Sheldon scampered to keep up with me, I spotted McGoo in his blue uniform, surrounded by a crowd of curious bystanders. Most of them were zombies, mingled with a few human deliverymen, day workers, and just plain curiosity-seekers. They had gathered around a wrecked storefront whose large plate-glass windows were smashed.

Seeing the commotion, Sheldon hunched down in his overcoat. "Maybe we should cross the street. I don't want to get mixed up in anything."

"That cop is a friend of mine, don't worry." In fact, this was a good chance for me to introduce him to McGoo. "I can call in a favor, ask him to keep an eye on your place."

"All right, I suppose … if you think it's a good idea."

In the middle of the gawkers near the vandalized business, Officer McGoohan waved his hands and shouted at the top of his voice. "Back off! Give me room to breathe here—some of us still require oxygen in our lungs!"

When he walked his beat, McGoo tried to be prepared for everything. He carried a service revolver loaded with regular bullets on his left hip, and one with silver-jacketed bullets on the right. He had a spray can of Mace and a spray can of holy water, along with a bandolier with wooden stakes, both blunted and sharpened.

Right then, though, I could tell McGoo needed a little help with crowd control. When too many zombies gather in one place, people tend to get nervous *Night of the Living Dead* flashbacks. Nobody needs that kind of mob mentality.

I could lend a hand a lot faster than official backup would ever arrive. The police force was stretched thin in the Quarter, and not many of the beat cops wanted to be there; it was a bottom-of-your-career assignment.

McGoo never had a bright future on the force, and he was his own worst enemy. Neither a tactful nor an overly sensitive man, he didn't know when to keep his mouth shut. His biggest mistake was in thinking that everyone shared his rough sense of humor. Years ago he had told a series of inappropriate, non-politically-correct jokes, pissed off the wrong person, and got himself transferred to the Unnatural Quarter (a "punitive promotion") not long before Robin and I set up shop.

My BHF may be rough around the edges, but when you boil it down, McGoo is a decent cop who does a good job and actually *likes* walking the beat. He has no aspirations of becoming a high-and-mighty detective or putting up with the political garbage of the top brass. He considers administrative meetings to be more grueling than a shootout. I'm glad to have him around.

Basic law enforcement is problematic in a city where even the laws of science don't always hold true. Police work and the justice system don't function quite the same around here. Worse, the laws themselves aren't always defined—which is why Robin based her career on solving problems and setting precedents.

Even though the Unnatural Quarter has its rough parts, like any inner city, most citizens, natural and unnatural, try to color within the lines. We don't have to put up with anarchy just because all Hell has broken loose. The vast majority just wants a normal existence and struggles to live within a shaky framework of laws, abstaining from outrageous behavior and doing their best to get along.

Businesses sprang up that catered to the specialized clientele: commercial blood drives commissioned fresh supplies for vampire customers; processing plants developed seasonings and treatments to make chicken "taste just like human"; restaurants and bars served the proper food choices.

It's an odd sort of détente, but in the worldwide uproar after the Big Uneasy, the unnaturals realized that if they didn't settle down and behave themselves, the rest of humanity would go on a full-blown crusade to wipe them out. The worst characters were arrested, tried, and sentenced, and the real man-eaters were executed (by whatever means appropriate for their type). But daily life, etc., went on.

Even so, not everybody behaves.

While Sheldon kept his distance from the crowd of spectators, I yanked on a few stiff shoulders and pulled the unnatural bystanders back. "Hey, give the officer some space to work! He's trying to do his job." I hustled them out of the way. "Move along, nothing to see!" I hadn't gotten close enough yet to know whether there was anything to see.

Recognizing me, McGoo looked relieved. "Thanks, Shamble."

When the crowd dispersed, I saw that the wrecked place was the Hope & Salvation Mission, a charity operation run by a kind old woman who wanted to save the undead. The windows were smashed, the door ripped off its hinges, the siding splintered. Even some of the bricks had been crushed to powder. Somebody, or something, had made a mess of things. Something huge.

I groaned. "Who would want to do something like this?" Hope Saldana was a sweet, good-intentioned lady, and everybody liked her, both naturals and unnaturals. But not all unnaturals could resist their urges, and I was worried about what might have happened to her. "Was anybody hurt?"

"Mrs. Saldana is shaken up, but not harmed," McGoo said. "Got her in protective custody until we figure out what happened here. It's like a tornado hit the place!" He shook his head. "Imagine the strength of the guy who did this."

"Or woman," I said.

"If a lady did this, I wouldn't want to be her blind date."

I ran my eyes over McGoo's face, his square jaw, rounded nose, bristly brown hair, and five-o'clock shadow that hit by noon every day. "You're assuming she'd *want* to date you."

"I always assume that, until I learn otherwise." He put his thumbs in his waistband and regarded the scene. "I responded to a call about a disturbance, but the damage was done by the time I got here. Witnesses saw a huge, hulking monster, all hairy and warty, with glowing eyes, long fangs, and a cranky disposition." With his foot, McGoo scuffed some of the broken glass on the sidewalk. "Around here, that doesn't narrow the field of suspects by much." McGoo looked hard at me. "You're my inside man now, Shamble. Any clue what the perp might be or where I should start looking?"

By now, the crowd had dispersed like a puff of smoke from an amateur wizard's spell; Sheldon Fennerman hung back under an awning for shelter. I stepped up to the mission's broken window, looked inside, and saw minimal damage to the interior of the building. "Can't imagine why anyone, or anything, would want to do this to a Good Samaritan who's trying to help down-and-out unnaturals. Could be just a random act of vandalism."

McGoo gave me the same expression of scorn and skepticism he'd used when I told him I dated a centerfold model once. "Random act of vandalism? *Riiight.* I'll put that in my report—case closed. Let's go have a drink."

"I'll see you at the Goblin Tavern later." I gestured Sheldon forward, and the vampire shuffled toward us with great reluctance, pulling his hat down. "I've got a favor to ask—new case."

McGoo was not impressed. He made a rude sound. "Sure, add more duties to my job description. I've got nothing else to do here."

I ignored his sarcasm. "This is my client Sheldon Fennerman. He's been receiving death threats, and I'm assisting him with personal security."

McGoo became more businesslike. "What kind of death threats? Credible ones?" He talked as if Sheldon wasn't right there listening to every word.

"Mr. Fennerman says other vampires in his neighborhood have disappeared, and he suspects they've been murdered. Heard of any troubles down in Little Transylvania? Missing persons reports?"

"Not that I know of. Why does he think he's a specific target?"

"Inflammatory graffiti on the walls, sharpened wooden stakes left on his doorstep." I noticed that Sheldon was shivering. "Could be Straight Edgers."

"Straight Edgers?" McGoo rolled his eyes, made a skeptical assessment of Sheldon, and finally addressed him directly. "So, you're an undead guy who can turn into a bat, has the strength of ten men ... and you need *Dan Shamble* to protect you from a bunch of juvenile delinquents? Can't you just do the evil eye?" He raised the first two fingers of his left hand, crooked them, and toyed with the air. "Use your Bela Lugosi thing and glamour them?"

"I'm, uh, not very good at that," Sheldon said. "Never was."

"I believe Mr. Fennerman has good reason to be nervous, so I'm looking into the matter. I'd consider it a personal favor if you kept your eyes and ears open. For old times' sake."

That sparked a smile. "Will do, Shamble. Scout's honor." His smile became a sneaky little grin. "And I've got something for you—for old times' sake. What goes 'Ha-ha-ha ... *plop*'?" He didn't give me time to answer. "A shambler laughing his head off!"

"You're not funny," I told him, although that one was better than most of his jokes.

He cinched up his lips. "You don't appreciate deadpan humor."

Lately, McGoo had adapted his off-color jokes so that various unnaturals were the butt of the humor. In his early career, he had been reprimanded for his clueless non-PC ethnic jokes; nobody in regular human society took offense if a zombie felt insulted, however. Not so long ago, when I was still human myself, McGoo's jokes had seemed hilarious. And now I was one of his targets.

Did you hear the one about the zombie PI, dead set on solving his cases?

McGoo read the reticence on my face. "Yeah, I miss the old days, Shamble, when we were just everyday guys, you and me. But now that you're, you know, *dead,* it's awkward talking to you." He looked serious again. "Did you get the ballistics and autopsy report I sent over? Any clues?"

My own autopsy report. "I read through it, but nothing rang any bells."

I'm not a squeamish person, but I had a tough time even looking at the crime scene photos: my body sprawled facedown in the alley, blood pooling all around my head. Some bastard had done that to me...

"If I come up with any leads, I'll let you know." I stepped closer to my client. "Right now Mr. Fennerman's my priority."

Sheldon gave me a thin-lipped smile, and his tiny fangs protruded. We headed off to his place.

CHAPTER 5

It would be hard to say what section qualified as the "seedy" part of the Quarter. Unnaturals have different sensibilities about that sort of thing. Many haunters, underground dwellers, sewer jockeys, and walking dead don't mind ramshackle appearances, piled garbage, or thick shadows; in fact, some landlords charge a premium for particularly run-down buildings, on the assumption that it "adds atmosphere."

Whatever the definition, I knew we had found the seedy part of town. Sheldon Fennerman lived there. Definitely an odd location for a decorator.

He led me to an old brownstone, and we went down three steps to his front door, several feet below sidewalk level, as if the underground tunnels were starting to swallow the building. Stout iron bars fronted Sheldon's door; another set covered each of the two painted-over windows. Looking back and forth, convinced we were being followed, Sheldon told me to stay close. He dug in his overcoat, fished out a crowded key ring. The keys rattled as he held them in his shaky hands. He worked one dead bolt, then the next, then three more until he had unlocked all five of them. I heard a click, and he pushed open the door. "Quick, come inside!"

"Nothing to worry about, Mr. Fennerman. Anyone who comes after you has to get through me first." I realized that would have sounded more reassuring if I myself hadn't been gunned down in an alley.

After I followed the vampire into his apartment, he slammed the door, hooked the chains, and threw all five of the dead bolts. "Home, sweet home." At last, Sheldon let out a huge sigh of relief. "It's not fair.

Hoodlums, vandals, and murderers can just break in wherever they want, but vampires have to be *invited* into someone's home."

I frowned. "I thought the by-invitation rule applied only if the person is actually a homeowner. Vampires can enter rental properties at will." Robin had done an analysis six months ago for a breaking-and-entering case.

Sheldon groaned. "Now, that's a nuance I wasn't aware of. Something else to worry about!"

The vampire's apartment was a dim place with burnt-orange shag carpeting and blocky dark-stained Mediterranean-style furniture. Although Sheldon was a recent inductee into the ranks of the undead, I got the impression that he wanted people to think he had been turned into a vampire back in the early 1970s. A framed poster on the wall showed a kitten dangling from a branch, with the encouraging words *Hang in There!* For an interior decorator, he had an unusual sense of style.

"Let's do a quick security sweep, Mr. Fennerman."

"*Sheldon*, please."

"Of course, Sheldon. Looks like you've already taken most of the first-step precautions I'd recommend. How many exits do you have?"

"Just the front entrance and a small back door that leads to an alley."

"Could be a point of vulnerability. Bad guys would rather break in through a dark alley than the front door in plain view. Let's check your windows."

I made a full inspection of the premises and found no obvious weak points. The window bars were secure, and both the front and back doors had durable locks. "You've done a good job by yourself, Sheldon. No one's going to get in here easily."

"But I still don't feel safe! What about the sharpened stakes on my doorstep? Once, there was even a wooden mallet! And the disappearing neighbors? Somebody hates vampires, Mr. Chambeaux, but I have no idea who or why. Haven't they read *Twilight?*"

"I'll see if I can get any leads on who's behind this, and Officer McGoohan will keep an eye out when he walks the beat. I'll follow up on the Straight Edgers, even do a stakeout—if you'll excuse the expression—possibly tomorrow, depending on my other cases."

"Oh, I feel safer already," Sheldon said, beaming. "So many of my vampire friends—my book club buddies and dinner club companions—they've just vanished, one after another. No sign of a scuffle and no bodies. They must have turned to dust. And I'm sure I'm next."

"You're not next, Sheldon, because you hired me. I'm going to get to the bottom of this."

The vampire grew as warm and fuzzy as a werewolf under a heat lamp. "I knew I could count on you, Mr. Chambeaux. And now that you're here, why not stay for dinner?" On a small kitchenette table he'd set out a red enameled pot, two place mats, red linen napkins, and long forks at each place setting. "I love fondue, don't you?"

"Fondue?" I was more of a sandwich sort of guy.

"A very civilized dinner for special occasions. Just little bites. Bread and cheese ... bouillon, or hot oil—I can make whatever you prefer."

I figured that the best thing I could do for Sheldon right now was to start nosing around. "Thank you, but I've got a lot of cases to work on—including yours. I've got investigating to do." And a 3:00 appointment at the embalmer.

He looked crestfallen. "Of course. I should have realized. Everyone's so busy these days. I started a bridge club for my neighbor vampires, but it was difficult to keep them coming back. I guess they just weren't that interested in cards. My next idea was a book club to discuss the latest best sellers, but that didn't go well either. Maybe I should have chosen more literary books?" He let out a wistful sigh. "We had a dinner club, and I even tried to arrange ballroom dancing lessons for everyone. And outings! Did you know that groups can charter a leather-upholstered hearse for a guided tour of the Quarter? Tinted windows, of course. I thought that would be so much fun! But nobody showed up."

"You did all this for your neighbors?" I began to have my doubts.

"Someone had to act as the vampires' social director. Otherwise they'd get lonely."

I asked carefully, "And when did these other vampires begin disappearing?"

"Right after our first book club discussion. Another friend vanished before the next bridge night. Then, when I suggested a French-themed potluck, nobody came over at all! That got me so scared that I went out to each person's apartment—and no one was home. Some apartments were entirely empty. It's not natural, I tell you!"

"And how often did you have these get-togethers?"

"Not as often as I'd have liked, but I tried." His eyes were large. "Only four or five nights a week, but I was open to suggestions. And now they're all dead!" He moaned. "I should have done more."

I tried to reassure him. "When I come back to do the stakeout, I'll check with the landlord, try to get a look at the empty apartments." I

25

glanced at my watch. "Don't worry, Sheldon. I'll get to the bottom of this, and you'll be able to sleep easy all day long."

The sharpened stakes and mallets on his doorstep were a definite sign of mischief, possibly left by a group of teenage vampires with too much angst for their own good. But there was also the possibility that the missing neighbors had slipped away for their own reasons.

If I did find the answers I suspected, I wasn't sure Sheldon would want to know.

CHAPTER 6

Though it might not seem a manly sort of place for a private detective to frequent, beauty salons and spas are great places to pick up information. I'm not obsessed with fashion. I've never had a manicure, certainly not a pedicure. I don't buy my clothes because of photos I see in *Vogue: Undead*. I'm not too hard on the eyes, and Sheyenne still gives me that look now and then; I hope she does for a long time to come.

But a lot of basic things change after death, and there's a difference between looking pretty and simply maintaining yourself. Being "well preserved" takes on a whole new meaning, and it's a constant battle to stop the onset of decay.

In the month since coming back to life, I'd been getting weekly treatments at Bruno & Heinrich's Embalming Parlor, the zombie equivalent of a beauty salon. The proprietors—emaciated identical twins—were obsessive stylists who realized they had no talent whatsoever for interacting with warm-blooded human beings, so they became morticians by trade. After the Big Uneasy, Bruno and Heinrich found their true calling in life.

When I arrived for my 3:00 appointment, Bruno—or maybe it was Heinrich—greeted me with a ghastly smile. "Felicitations, Mr. Chambeaux. I'll be handling you today." He rubbed his fingertips together; he wore a fresh coat of matte-black nail polish. "The usual, sir? Or do you have special plans this week? We could do something more radical, more edgy."

"Just the usual," I said.

Bruno—yes, it was Bruno, I decided—looked disappointed. "Someday we'll get you out of your rut, sir. We could all do with a bit more flamboyance."

"Not all of us," I said. "Just top off the embalming fluid, check the hair and makeup, cover any discolorations."

"As you wish, sir."

When the physical body doesn't regenerate very well, little bits of daily damage begin to add up. Once you start to slide down that slippery slope, there's no getting back up again.

I had seen far too many people, both naturals and unnaturals, who let themselves go downhill, and I had no intention of turning into one of those decrepit necrotic shamblers who stagger around like drunken sleepwalkers with bad hemorrhoids and can't carry on an intelligent conversation. I wouldn't be effective at solving cases if I had pieces falling off me here and there.

Bruno gestured me toward a side room. "We've reserved your private chair, sir. I know you don't like to be disturbed during the process."

It's true that I like the private embalming chair, where I can mull over my cases while the embalmer does his work. But because I had just reviewed the files that Sheyenne had dumped on my desk, not to mention Sheldon Fennerman's predicament, I wanted more interaction. No telling what I might pick up if somebody happened to drop a juicy tidbit. "I'll be more sociable today, Bruno. Why not put me among the ladies?"

Bruno's artificially darkened eyebrows rose like ravens taking wing. "I'm sure they'd love that, sir. They talk about you after you're gone, you know."

Apparently, zombies can blush when the situation calls for it, because I felt a definite warmth in my cheeks. "Well, why make them wait? Now they can talk about me to my face."

In the brightly lit main salon, three makeup-plastered undead women reclined in their chairs while Heinrich flitted from one to the next, chatting and smiling while his clients gossiped in raspy cackling voices. The trio had been in their early sixties in human years, after which they'd added a few hard undead years. All three had the sinewy, rough look of heavy smokers, heavy drinkers, and heavy flirters. Heinrich did his very best, though the women still looked as if they had graduated from the Bride of Frankenstein School of Cosmetology.

"Well, look who's decided to join us today, honey," said the first, whose name was Victoria ("want to be my *Vic*-tim?" she had once said in a creaky attempt to be sexy). Zombie cougars on the prowl.

"He looks delicious," said the next, Cindy. ("Rhymes with *sin*, heh, heh." Well, not really.) "It'll be wonderful to have some masculine company here, instead of just us girls." She looked up quickly at Heinrich. "No offense, of course."

"None taken, love. My masculinity's not in question."

I eased myself into the chair while Bruno began to gather the tubes and tanks of fluid.

The third woman leaned over in her chair: Sharon ("I don't need clever wordplay to get a man"). "Got any plans, Dan? I'll be finished here long before these other ladies are ready for a public viewing. They need a lot more work done than I do." The other two looked at her with glares like wooden stakes, but Sharon ignored them. "You and I could go out for lunch or cocktails ... or just someplace for an afternoon delight."

"Sounds tempting," I said, feeling no interest whatsoever, "but my caseload is killing me. Mysteries to solve, bad guys to catch."

"Oh, you're not still obsessed with your dreary murder, are you?" Cindy-rhymes-with-*sin* gave a flippant toss of her head.

I wanted to get the bastard who had killed me, but more importantly I needed enough answers to be sure Robin wasn't in any continuing danger. What if the murderer had other targets on his list? And who had poisoned Sheyenne?

"Tragic," Victoria said. "I think about you every time the girls and I go to the Basilisk nightclub."

"My body was found in an alley a block away," I said. "Not at Basilisk."

Still, my death *might* have had some connection with the nightclub and the under-the-table blood-bank sales I had exposed. I'd been avoiding the place ... because of Sheyenne. "Anyway, I *do* work on more than one case at a time, ladies. Many clients to satisfy. Have you heard about threats being made against vampires? Wooden stakes left on doorsteps, anything like that?"

Cindy said, "Vampires ... not my sort of undead."

"I'll try anything," Sharon said. "I may be dead, but I'm not *that* dead."

"Any *thing* is right," Victoria cackled. "We've seen some of the creatures you've gone home with."

Heinrich gave a worried frown. "Vampires are some of our best clients during the night shift. They're so particular about their hair. And we do a brisk business in fang whitening."

"Not much for the tanning beds, though," Bruno said as he hooked up the heavy-gauge trocar to the cannula and started the pump to fill my vessels with fresh embalming fluid. He used a makeup brush to fuss over my face. He flipped my hair back and forth while he tsk-tsked at the entrance and exit wounds in my skull. "This really needs to be repaired, sir. If you will allow me? I can do wonders, both for your appearance and your self-esteem. That bullet hole is a distraction."

Previously, I had resisted doing much to cover it up other than wearing my hat lower. "Every time I look in the mirror, it reminds me that I still have to find the person who killed me."

"You don't need a hole in the head for that, sir. Tell the truth—how often do you look in the mirror?"

"Hardly ever."

"That settles it, then. Let me do my work. I *am* a professional."

Bruno opened jars of makeup and mortician's putty, then packed the front of my forehead, reconstructing the damage to my skull. I could feel the flow of fresh embalming fluid invigorating me.

"I could help you with your caseload, Dan," said Cindy, then added in a sultry, rasping voice, "as long as it's a *hard* case." The zombie cougars tittered.

Now, I don't mind flirting, especially when it helps people relax and answer my questions in an investigation, but that's where I draw the line. Ghost or not, Sheyenne is my girlfriend, so I smiled and said, "Thanks for the offer, ladies, but my caseload is already spoken for."

Taking my comment as a rebuff, Sharon said, "I don't think he *can* do anything, girls. Talk about dead wood!" They all laughed at that.

This time I didn't bother blushing. It didn't matter what they assumed. I was capable enough in the sexual department, but I wasn't in the market for a ZILF—especially those three.

Heinrich chatted about Alvin Ricketts and the art auction that night, which did interest me, but the ladies were unimpressed. They turned their predatory interest as the parlor door jangled open.

A boisterous man in a loud plaid sports jacket entered with his dark hair brushed back, a fine gold chain hanging at his neck just above a line of conspicuously woolly chest hair. "Ah, what beautiful ladies!" he said. "Could there be any better job than this?"

Brondon Morris was the representative of Jekyll Lifestyle Products and Necroceuticals, a profuse and avuncular snake-oil salesman who seemed to believe that everyone adored him, though no one did. He circulated among Unnatural Quarter businesses, supermarkets, parlors, and clubs, hawking JLPN products and distributing the toiletries that no unnatural should be without.

The zombie cougars cooed and fawned over the visitor. "Did you bring us any samples this time, Brondon?"

"Of course I did, ladies." He glanced up, recognized me in the embalming chair, and froze for an uncomfortable fraction of a second. I knew who he was, and he knew me; there was no love lost between us. He pointedly ignored me.

Humming loudly to emphasize how much he enjoyed his work, Brondon opened his case and pulled out tubes, bottles, and spritzers, handing them to the three zombie women. "Now, these samples are just for your personal use, ladies—skin creams, face masks, wrinkle reducers. I can't make a living if I give away all our products, and Bruno and Heinrich wouldn't be too pleased with me! I hope you'll tell all your friends about the quality of our line."

"We're dedicated customers," said Sharon. "You know we are."

Meanwhile, Bruno continued working on me, and Heinrich came back with a clipboard and a JLPN order form. Brondon continued, "We have a lovely new perfume that we're test-marketing right now."

"Is it from the new Zom-Be-Fresh line?" Victoria asked. "Fresh Loam?"

"Those products aren't ready for market just yet, I'm afraid. Two more weeks until the wide release. They're still undergoing laboratory testing."

"I'll help you test it," Cindy offered. "In fact, I'll help test any of your … equipment."

Brondon gave her a wide, sincere smile. "What a beautiful offer! I may take you up on that someday." He handed out shiny packets of nail cleaner, held up a small curved brush. "This is a useful new item, specially designed to scrub dirt from the fingernails of anyone who's just clawed her way out of the grave."

"Brondon, sweetie, do we look like we're fresh out of the grave?"

Wisely leaving the question unanswered, Brondon put the brush back into his satchel. Heinrich saved him by handing over the completed order form. "We're all very satisfied with JLPN products, Mr. Morris. And when your new Fresh Loam line comes out, we'll add it to our order. Your ads are generating a lot of customer interest."

"We're very proud of Fresh Loam, a whole new spin on our entire product line. One of the largest marketing campaigns in our company history."

So far, Brondon had kept his back to me, but now he looked in my direction, bent down to his sample case, and withdrew a small spray can. "It's a fact of life, Mr. Chambeaux, that zombies need deodorant more than the usual person. You're relatively new to the condition, but you'll realize it sooner or later. Our line ranks very high in customer satisfaction."

He came close and spritzed it in the air, but I flinched back. "No, thank you—I am who I am, and I prefer to smell that way."

"It's not about *you,* my friend. Because of my work among the unnaturals, I've gotten used to the smell, but you should be considerate to others who may be standing downwind."

"I'll keep that in mind, but I'm not interested."

"He's not interested in *anything,*" Sharon said.

"How about this? You're going to love emBalm!" He tried to hand me a small tube of lip balm. "No zombie wants chapped lips."

"No thanks."

Disappointed, Brondon tugged on the collar of his plaid sport jacket. "Is this just sour grapes for the … unpleasantness with JLPN a few years ago? Water under the bridge! We're a different company now—resurrected, if you will. Our new specialty products are designed to help unnaturals with all their hygiene needs."

"No sour grapes on my part, Mr. Morris. I stand by my investigative work, and the courts upheld it."

I had history with Jekyll Lifestyle Products and Necroceuticals. Case history. Personal history.

Four years into our partnership, Robin and I had worked on a class-action lawsuit against JLPN. The parent company had been a successful cosmetics and toiletries manufacturer for decades, but after the Big Uneasy, when much of the public shivered under the bedsheets in fear of monsters, the company's CEO—Harvard Stanford Jekyll—realized there was an entirely new pool of customers for a line of specialized creams, shampoos, toothpaste, deodorants, perfumes, everything an unnatural needed for a happy and productive unlife.

In a rather embarrassing incident, some customers experienced problems with a conditioning shampoo developed for vampires. Specifically, it made their hair fall out. Vampire Pattern Baldness. And once undead hair fell out, it didn't grow back. Vampires tend to be vain, banking on their sexual magnetism, imagining careers as cover models for bodice-ripping, jugular-puncturing romance novels. The shampoo users were distraught to watch their suaveness reduced with every stroke of a comb or brush.

So a group of newly bald vampires engaged the services of Chambeaux & Deyer. While Robin filed lawsuits, I did my detective work and discovered that two lots of the JLPN shampoo had "accidentally" been contaminated with garlic oil. After further investigation (impersonating a factory employee and surreptitiously copying confidential records, long after business hours), I found proof that the garlic oil was intentionally added by a disgruntled employee, who was later reprimanded and let go. The company pulled the vampire shampoo from the shelves, paid an undisclosed amount in damages—our cut of the settlement paid the rent for six months—and spent years recovering from the public-relations disaster.

Needless to say, I was persona non grata over there.

Brondon gave me an awkward smile now. "So let's bury the hatchet. How about trying some of our products? Free samples—in the spirit of goodwill?"

Even though most unnaturals used the stuff, I really had no desire to. "I appreciate the offer, but sometimes I do undercover surveillance. I don't want people to smell my cologne from a block away."

Brondon brushed off the insult and turned his attention back to the three zombie cougars, who basked in his presence. Because of his daily sales routine, I could think of few humans who were so entirely at ease among unnaturals. Brondon bent close and said in a stage whisper, as if he imagined that none of us men could overhear him, "I'll be at the Goblin Tavern later on tonight, ladies, if any of you care to join me for a drink...."

Victoria, Cindy, and Sharon fervently promised that they would see Brondon there, come Hell or high water—and nowadays, floods and the underworld were well within the realm of possibility. Brondon packed up his sample case, gave a flirtatious wave to the cadaverous women, and sauntered out of the embalming parlor.

Bruno unhooked the needle and tube from my arm. "There you are, sir. All topped off. Good as new."

"A reasonable facsimile, at least," I said, and I did feel refreshed. I took a quick glance at the mirror, touched a fingertip to the mortician's putty in my forehead. No sign of a bullet hole. Bruno had done a good job.

I paid him, gathered my hat and jacket, and headed back to the office.

CHAPTER 7

As I walked through the door, Sheyenne was arranging a stack of advertising flyers on the corner of her desk. I glanced down, trying to figure out what they were. "Another client?"

"A very dapper gentleman dropped these off, asking us to pass them out to our clientele. New business start-up in the Quarter. I figured we'd earn some goodwill by supporting our fellow entrepreneurs."

I picked up one of the flyers. It was for a glassmaker's shop that specialized in dark window tinting. *Black Glass, Inc. Opacity Guaranteed. Blocks out all harmful purifying rays of the sun—UV, infrared, and visible. We also repair mirrors.*

"Sure, go ahead and hand them out. I wonder if they install normal windows too." I thought of the damage that had been done to the Hope & Salvation Mission. "I might have a customer for them."

A few minutes later, Miranda Jekyll entered the office, cloaked in an aura of pomp and circumstance as if her very presence generated all the fanfare a person could need. She was dressed to the nines (or the tens, or however much she could afford), and she wasn't afraid to show it. Miranda's husband Harvey—Harvard Stanford Jekyll—paid for it all and resented every penny, especially now that he had filed for divorce, which only made her spend more extravagantly.

Her smile was as wide and dazzling as a great white shark's; her red lipstick made blood look pallid by comparison. Her cinnamon-dyed hair was intricately coiffed and cemented into place by more hair spray and styling product than a salon used in a week. A lawn gnome could have jumped through her enormous hoop earrings.

Harvey Jekyll insisted that their prenuptial agreement was null and void because now that she had become a werewolf, Miranda was no longer the same person who had signed the document. Therefore, she was not entitled to half of Jekyll Lifestyle Products and Necroceuticals. Robin had been fighting on Miranda's behalf for months, and I'd been working behind the scenes to gather leverage to use against Jekyll. After the vampire shampoo incident, Jekyll hadn't been on my Favorite Persons list to begin with.

Now Miranda swished forward with lupine grace, her back straight, head erect, hands slightly outstretched as if she meant either to embrace or claw whoever came within her grasp. "Sweethearts!" she announced, pronouncing it "sweet-hots," as if we were some kind of startlingly potent candy. "I've been *dying* to see you. I simply must have an update on my case."

I extended my hand in a businesslike gesture, but when she took it in her own, it was a caress, not a shake. Her pointed nails traced little patterns on my pale skin. "Mr. Chambeaux, it's always a pleasure to see you."

When Sheyenne offered her a beverage, Miranda fluttered her fingers in a quick dismissive movement. "I doubt you carry anything that I'd drink. Not to worry, I can stay only a minute. Considering how long it's taking your agency to solve my little problem, one might think I'm paying you by the hour. Oh wait, I am! But I don't resent it a minute, because it's my husband's money anyway. However, I simply *must* impress upon you how *desperate* I am to get out of this marriage."

"Come into the conference room, and we'll go over what we have so far," Robin said. "Is it all right if Dan sits in?" Technically, I wasn't supposed to be in a confidential attorney-client meeting.

"I hired you both, sweethearts, and I don't care whether this is solved in the courts or under the table … so long as it's solved."

I gestured Miranda into the conference room. "I'm sorry you're dissatisfied with our progress, ma'am."

"I didn't say *dissatisfied*—just impatient. I long to be free."

Sheyenne glided into the conference room, bringing the file; she set it in front of me, gave me a private wink, then left.

Robin sat down, serious. "If getting out of the marriage is most important, Mrs. Jekyll, your husband already wants a divorce, and you could sign the papers right now. Granted, you won't walk away with any of his fortune, but at least you'll have your self-esteem. You can be free to find true love, if that's your highest priority."

Miranda gave poor Robin a withering glare. "That would defeat the entire *purpose* of all those years I *endured* him, sweetheart. You simply must find a way to put him over a barrel in the courts. Or you, Mr. Chambeaux—catch him doing something very naughty … I'm sure he must be doing something. Aren't we all? If I can hold a big nasty club over his head, then we'll reach an amicable settlement."

Considering how bitter the relationship was, I doubted any settlement short of Miranda's slow torture and lingering death would feel "amicable" to Harvey Jekyll. Instead of pointing that out, I said, "I conducted intensive surveillance, Mrs. Jekyll, but my recent … setback created delays in several of our cases."

"Yes, yes—your death," Miranda said with a luxurious and dismissive brush of her clawlike hand. "I'm not an ogre, Mr. Chambeaux. Nobody expects the same sort of progress from a dead detective as from a live one, but that doesn't make me any less miserable. We've got to break the prenup, somehow."

Robin pulled out the inch-thick document and flipped through the pages. "Your husband's reason for breaking the agreement is nonsense. It won't stand up in court, despite his stalling tactics."

"Harvey's attorneys claim that the marriage itself has fundamentally changed, due to my transformation."

And everything *had* changed for her. Two years earlier, Miranda Jekyll had been scratched, infected, and transformed into a werewolf. Harvey Jekyll subsequently claimed, through his coterie of lawyers, that his wife was no longer human, therefore not the person who had signed the agreement, and therefore and whereas, he was no longer bound to the terms, yadda yadda, and she was entitled to nothing.

Miranda, not surprisingly, held a different point of view.

In the newly changed world, so many legal questions had no precedents for lawyers to fall back on. The courts were clogged, and few judges wanted anything to do with the societal headaches caused by the unnaturals.

Robin scrutinized the document that she had read many times before. "Granted, the original contract you and Mr. Jekyll signed many years ago is quite thorough and ironclad—"

"It should be," Miranda said. "Each side had seven lawyers at five hundred dollars an hour apiece, combing over every comma, period, semicolon, and exclamation point. Since when does a legal contract have an *exclamation point?* Well, this one has it."

"I filed motions for outright dismissal, Mrs. Jekyll, taking the stance that you are still the same individual who signed the contract. How can anyone disagree?"

"Harvey has photos of me as a werewolf. Show those to an all-human jury, and he'll have a ruling in an hour."

"You are exactly the same person, except for during that time of the month."

"Even then, I'm still *me*, regardless of whether I sprout hair and get more feisty—some men like that." Miranda tossed her head, and not a single strand of her hair moved. "Throughout history, men have put up with women turning into bitches for a few days every month. Never been cause for breaking a prenup before."

"Exactly!" Robin said with a grin. "I'm sure we can win this, if we get a sympathetic judge."

I looked down at the files. "Robin may be confident, but I'd feel better if I could dredge up concrete evidence of something that your husband wouldn't want displayed in open court." I pressed my lips hard together. "We always do our best to help our clients, Mrs. Jekyll, but ever since the JLPN class-action suit, I also have my own grudge against the guy."

She flashed her great-white-shark grin again. "Oh, that's no surprise at all. It's why I hired Chambeaux and Deyer in the first place! I was impressed with your work, even if it did cause severe financial losses to the company. Harvey deserved it."

I took out a stack of my old surveillance photos. Miranda had seen them before, but I decided we could all use a fresh look. "After you engaged our services, I spent weeks following your husband after dark, but I never found any evidence of him having an affair."

"No surprise. The man's a sexless little worm. He never wanted to have sex with me—*me!*" Miranda pointed to herself, accentuating her breasts as if her sheer animal desirability was self-evident. "I can't imagine him looking elsewhere for companionship, but who knows? In that twisted walnut-sized brain of his, maybe Harvey has needs, too, needs that I can't meet, though I couldn't imagine what they might be."

Now, Miranda was our client, and the client is always innocent, always wronged, and always on the right side of justice. But I'm not naïve, and I assumed that the sultry and vivacious woman was fooling around as well. Undoubtedly, her husband had his own private investigators trying to find dirt on Miranda. I just hoped that she was good at hiding it—and that

Harvey wasn't. In the matter of the prenup, it would all come down to which person had the better mudslinging campaign.

I spread out the photos and tapped them, focusing the conversation on business before Miranda could go into detail about her own sex life. "Here's a curious one. I followed your husband to the landfill outside the city, after dark. Some kind of off-books delivery or disposal. Shouldn't a big corporate exec have underlings for jobs like that?"

"Harvey has underlings to do *everything*, sweetheart. It's suspicious, but I don't see how that helps us."

"I plan to follow up and ask around." I pulled out more photos. Twice, I had tracked Harvey Jekyll to clandestine nighttime meetings with shadowy figures, once accompanied by his chief sales rep, Brondon Morris. "I have no idea what those meetings were. I could never get close enough."

"Could it be a sex parlor of some kind?" Robin sounded embarrassed. "Drugs? Gambling?"

"We can only hope," Miranda said. "You'll need proof."

"I will step up the surveillance, Mrs. Jekyll." As a zombie, I could put in long hours, day and night. "It's taken me a few weeks to … get back on my feet. Don't worry, I'm on the job now. The cases don't solve themselves."

"No, sweetheart, they don't." She reached into her handbag, which probably cost as much as a block of real estate in the Unnatural Quarter, and withdrew her checkbook. "I'm going to double your hourly fee this week in hopes that it encourages you."

She wrote out a check from her husband's account, blew us an air-kiss, and said her goodbyes.

CHAPTER 8

eated at my desk, I spent half an hour studying the homicide file McGoo had delivered to me (unofficially) four days after I awakened from the grave. "Here you go, Shamble—do your stuff. The cases don't solve themselves."

I was grateful, though intimidated. "It's not often a person gets a chance to catch his own murderer."

"Consider this a do-it-yourself project. Besides, it'll save me the work."

Fortunately for me, the medical examiner relied on virtual autopsies and high-tech imaging of suspected murder victims. (In my case, there wasn't much "suspected" about the murder.) My body had been buried intact, relatively speaking.

Now I reread the report, although I already had the words memorized: Classification of Death: Homicide. Cause of Death: Gunshot wound to head. Bullet entered lamboid suture of skull, completely penetrating brain and exiting forehead. Wound is consistent with .32 caliber bullet found at crime scene.

The slug had been embedded in a wooden door in the alley, having lost most of its momentum after passing through my skull. The bullet was damaged by striking the door (not to mention the back and front of my skull, which, according to McGoo, is quite thick). Even so, the lab had gotten good information:

Lead rim-fired bullet, five lands and grooves with a right-hand twist, consistent with a round from an antique Smith & Wesson No. 2 Army .32-caliber revolver. As best we could tell, the weapon was made around the time of the U.S. Civil War. No bullet casing found at the scene, but in that kind of gun, someone would have had to remove the casing manually, and only a stupid murderer would have left it on the ground. Anybody who could have killed *me* had to be reasonably smart, or lucky. Just for my own reputation, I preferred to imagine him, or her, as smart.

A lot of unnaturals had a fondness for antiques. Gun shops specialized in exotic pieces, and in the Unnatural Quarter it was easy enough to get hold of unregistered weapons of all makes and types. I just needed to figure out who owned a hundred-fifty-year-old Smith & Wesson .32 revolver.

Piece of cake.

O   O   O

Chambeaux & Deyer dealt with the usual gamut of cases: missing persons, divorces, civil lawsuits, recovery of stolen objects.

Seven years ago, Robin had won her first legal case dealing with unnaturals—securing a victory for a monster-literacy charity—before the two of us ever joined forces. A prominent werewolf millionaire had died as a result of a tragic silver-letter-opener accident (another story entirely), and the will left his entire fortune to the literacy charity. The jilted family contested the will, alleging that becoming a werewolf had rendered the old man mentally incompetent; they showed video evidence of his slavering, bestial antics to prove their point.

Robin argued that—notwithstanding the allegation that a werewolf was by definition mentally incompetent—the decedent was indisputably competent during *the rest of the month* when the moon wasn't full, and she entered lunar charts into evidence to prove that the moon had been in the gibbous phase at the time he signed the will. Based on her argument, the judge ruled that the monster-literacy charity was entitled to the full inheritance, as stated in the millionaire's will.

A few years before that, I had put out my shingle offering my services as a detective around what would later become the Unnatural Quarter. After McGoo got himself punitively promoted to this part of town, he threw me a bone and set me up with my first unnatural case.

He put me in touch with a forlorn family who was desperately trying to track down their uncle Mel. I treaded it like a regular missing persons case, even though Mel was one of the walking dead. He had died six months before the Big Uneasy, but his corpse was still fresh enough to rise up in the first wave of zombies after all the rules changed. When his family came to deliver flowers to the grave one day, they found the earth churned and a sunken hole left where Mel had battered his way out of the coffin and clawed himself back into the light of day.

They followed the muddy footprints out of the cemetery, but lost his trail on the way to the Quarter. So they hired me to find him. Standard detective work. I remember the blond-haired niece in particular, her lower lip trembling, tears filling her eyes … so sad, so sincere, not even twenty years old. "Uncle Mel is lost—I just know he's homeless somewhere! We've got to find him."

And that's what I did. I knocked on doors, I asked around the Quarter, I showed Mel's funeral-notice photo to anyone I met (though the photo wasn't going to be a very good likeness, since he'd been ripening in the grave for half a year). I finally found the unkempt-looking zombie sleeping in an alley, covered with flattened cardboard boxes and newspapers, little more than a pile of ambulatory detritus getting snuggly with rodents and beetles.

Success. I had done my job.

Mel was perfectly alert, and he must have been a charming guy in life. When I told him that his family had engaged my services to find him, at first he brightened, then became dejected as reality sank in. "They don't want to see me like this."

"Oh, yes, they do. Trust me, it'll be all right."

I arranged the meeting, and I was as excited as any of them. Since he'd been in the ground for so long, Mel was too putrid for embraces, however, which made for an awkward reunion. With one glance at his rotting form, the young blond niece and her aunts and uncles immediately reconsidered their wishes. Within minutes, they glanced at watches, consulted day planners, pretended they had other things to do.

The niece put her thumb to her ear and pinky to her mouth to mime a telephone and quipped, "We'll call you, Uncle Mel."

The others gave him their best wishes. "Take care of yourself, Mel."

"So glad you're okay."

"If there's anything we can do … Well, you'd better call first."

Afterward, the family had not made contact with Mel again, and he was left alone, heartbroken. A painfully typical case: Family loses loved one, loved one rises from the grave, loving family wants risen loved one back in their lives, family gets a whiff and changes their mind.

I had taken the forlorn zombie to the Hope & Salvation Mission and asked Mrs. Saldana to give him a helping hand. She gave Mel some self-help books and arranged for him to get a job. He's actually quite happy now....

With a sigh, I realized I wasn't getting any more benefit from the autopsy report, no matter how long I stared at it. Dead end. For now.

I delivered a couple of case folders back to Sheyenne. She opened the metal file drawer, sorted through dividers, and slid the folders back in place. "When I was in medical school, I was planning to be a surgeon," she said. "Now I'm reorganizing office files."

"I know, Spooky. Life didn't turn out the way we wanted it to. Come to think of it, death didn't turn out like we expected either. But at least you get to see me every day now." As if that would cheer her up.

She made the *pfft* sound and ruffled some papers, then flashed me a flirtatious smile. "Small consolation, but it'll do. Anyway, death is what you make of it."

She retrieved several unsolved case folders from my office and set them on her desk so she could comb through the documents herself. "Meanwhile, I'll keep doing the real work here—though it goes above and beyond the job description of an executive administrator."

"You're a lot more than an administrator. Paralegal too. Sounding board. Customer service rep."

"Business manager," she added. "If I didn't help Robin and you go over the books, you'd never balance the accounts."

"That's beyond my detective abilities," I said.

A week after she died, Sheyenne's ghost had appeared in our offices and boldly announced that she was my new office manager, Robin's new paralegal, and yes, thank you, she was going to accept the job, even though we hadn't offered it. I didn't have the heart to turn her down, especially after what Sheyenne had been through—after what we'd all been through. And after the promises I'd made to her on her hospital deathbed.

Now she looked up from the files. "Don't forget, Beaux, you promised to find my murderer in your spare time."

She'd been killed four full weeks before me, and I'd been diligently trying to solve *her* murder when I got shot myself. Coincidence? Whoever had given her the toadstool poison could be connected to the bastard who shot me. Or maybe not.

"I won't forget about it, Spooky, honest. I just hope you don't quit your job after the case is solved."

"You can't get rid of me that easily—I thought you'd figured that out by now." She gave me a wink. "Still, could be hazardous."

"It's already been hazardous."

When she gave me that heartwarming-to-the-point-of-incandescence look with those blue eyes, I doubted I could ever forget her if I walked the earth for another two centuries. Nothing would make me happier than to put her killer, and mine, in the electric chair (or whatever form of execution was appropriate for their particular type). I just had to narrow down the suspects until I got the right one.

Alas, there was no shortage of people who wanted me out of the picture.

CHAPTER 9

Sheyenne checked the schedule and let me know about the last client of the day. "An emancipation case."

"One of Robin's, then? Am I supposed to be here for it?"

Sheyenne gave me that "Do you even have to ask?" raised eyebrow. "You know she likes to have you there for moral support."

"I thought she wanted me there for the muscle."

"Ha!" With a psychokinetic *pfft!,* Sheyenne fluttered a bunch of the papers on her desk. "That's what I get for telling you how cute you are, Beaux. Now you think you're Adonis."

Robin poked her head out of her office. "Is our five o'clock here yet?"

As if she had summoned the client, I heard painstaking, shuffling footsteps out in the hall: a long drag, then a footfall, a long drag, then a footfall, followed by slow, ominous rapping at the door.

"I wasn't expecting so much suspense," Sheyenne whispered to me. She opened the door.

Standing in front of us was a decrepit, half-unraveled bundle of bandages and rags that swaddled a short brown man. He was so desiccated that he looked like a child's doll made of beef jerky. As he lurched forward, three moths flew up from among the bandages. I could hear his bones creaking.

The mummy spoke in a crisp businesslike British accent. "So sorry I'm late. My sundial is notoriously unreliable on cloudy days." With several ancient scrolls tucked under his elbow, he shuffled into our offices, dragging his left foot. He extended a skeletal hand to me. "Ramen Ho-Tep, at your service."

I took the grip, but didn't shake too vigorously, afraid I might break something off (which could lead to a lawsuit of our own). "Pleased to meet you, sir."

Robin greeted him with her dazzling smile. "Thank you for coming, Mr. Ho-Tep. Your case sounds very interesting. Would you mind if my partner sits in?"

The mummy regarded me. "Is he your slave?"

"No, and he's not an attorney either, but I value his insights."

"Brilliant," the mummy said. "By all means. I want many ears to hear the persecution I've suffered."

In the conference room, Ramen Ho-Tep thumped the ancient scrolls down on the table, and dust wafted up, along with tiny flakes of dried papyrus. Robin had already set out six enormous volumes of legal cases and precedents.

She wrapped up a half-eaten tuna sandwich from her late lunch and set it on a credenza next to a can of diet cola. "Sorry for the mess. I was just catching up."

"No worries," said the mummy. "You should have seen the state of my tomb when the archaeologists broke in."

"You speak English extremely well, Mr. Ho-Tep." I'm accustomed to unnaturals having slurred diction, and the ones with Southern accents are almost impossible to understand.

"I spent nearly a century lying in the British Museum," the mummy said. "One's bound to pick up something of the language, even though I wasn't actually aware. My body was loaned to the Metropolitan Natural History Museum shortly before the event you call the Big Uneasy ... and then I woke up. That was a most distressing day, let me tell you! For scientific purposes, the archaeologists had unwrapped half of my bandages, and there I was, naked under the bright lights. If I'd still had any blood flow, I would have blushed quite furiously."

Robin started jotting notes on her legal pad. "So, how can we help you, sir? I have the basics of your story, but I'd like my partner to be completely filled in."

The mummy rested his elbows on the table and leaned forward. The sinews in his jaw snapped and clacked as he talked. "Due to the woeful state of your public education system, your citizens have little accurate knowledge of ancient Egypt. Most of what they think they know comes from those silly mummy movies, although I must admit that Arnold Vosloo did a creditable job of it. Good special effects."

I didn't tell him I was a Karloff man myself. Old school.

His head twitched, as if he were trying to focus on his thoughts again. "I was the pharaoh of all Egypt, but I do not have an inflated sense of my own importance. You've probably never heard of Ramen Ho-Tep. I've nothing to do with the dried noodles, I assure you—in fact, I'm thousands of years older than prepackaged food." A sigh rattled out of his dry throat. "And now I'm merely ..."

He seemed dejected. "I ruled for twenty floodings of the Nile before I succumbed to a fever caused by the bite of a tsetse fly. I was entombed in a lovely pyramid in the desert suburbs. The workers were killed, of course, the records struck, curses laid down—the usual privacy and security measures, but insufficient. Robbers ransacked the tomb within a century or two, and much later a team of British archaeologists removed my body." Ho-Tep let out an indignant snort. "Apparently, if one calls oneself an 'archaeologist' rather than a 'tomb raider,' one receives far more respect. But the end result is the same.

"Now, being on display may sound glamorous, but it's quite dull, I assure you. Once I awakened, it became clear that I needed to explain the true ways of life in ancient Egypt. I am uniquely qualified for the job, but those"—he inserted a guttural string of Egyptian words—"from the museum wouldn't release me!"

Ramen Ho-Tep became more animated. His shoulders stiffened, his bones squeaked and bandages rustled, and he did look terrible to behold. Previously, I was skeptical about animated mummies who are supposed to be fearsome. I mean, how can anybody be afraid of something a banana slug could outrun? But now, as the mummy unleashed his true anger, Robin and I both flinched.

"I wish to be emancipated! I must be freed. I was Pharaoh of all Egypt! I was a god. I am not a slave—I am no one's property! And I should know, because I had a great many slaves of my own. Nevertheless, the museum insists that they own me."

Robin, as usual, grew incensed and indignant on behalf of her client. "We have laws against this sort of thing, Mr. Ho-Tep. Slavery has been outlawed for more than a century and a half." She turned to the law books stacked on the table, opened one of the thickest tomes, and riffled through the pages to where she had used a sticky note to mark a passage. "A wealth of case law has withstood every legal challenge."

The mummy unrolled his own ancient scrolls to reveal faded hieroglyphics. "I brought my own case law—*Egyptian* case law. Look at this clause here, under paragraph six, subclause B." He pointed to drawings that showed a sphinx, a bird, and squiggly lines that might have been water. "Right there, as plain as day: Shall I read it aloud? Bird, foot, round thing, another bird. How can opposing counsel argue? You need only show this to a qualified judge, and I shall be freed from captivity within the week."

"That might be a tad optimistic, Mr. Ho-Tep," Robin said. "The Metropolitan Museum will oppose the emancipation petition. They'll question your status as a human being, or they might claim that you're not capable of taking care of yourself. Or they could bring in an expert from the Health Department to testify that your moldy old bandages are a public health hazard, and therefore you can't be allowed to roam free." She gave him a look of great concern. "They'll try to humiliate you in front of a jury."

The mummy was furious. "This is not possible! I was Pharaoh of all Egypt!"

"Yes, you mentioned that," I interrupted, "but it won't necessarily impress a judge." In general, I prefer to give my clients a realistic view of their cases.

Robin chimed in, still optimistic. "Don't worry, we'll do everything legally possible to ensure your emancipation."

"Please hurry," the mummy said. "I've waited thousands of years. I simply can't bear it anymore."

o o o

After Ramen Ho-Tep shuffled back to the museum, Robin used a small hand vacuum to clean up the dust and debris he had left behind on the conference table, while I pitched in with a carpet sweeper to get rid of the larger pieces on the floor.

"I think I'll call it a day," I said. "I'm going to stop by the Goblin Tavern."

"I'll put in a few more hours here before I go upstairs," Robin said. No surprise. We both spent more time working than in our individual apartments above the office.

Sometimes I worried about her. She worked herself to the bone, gave 110 percent to her clients, felt every ounce of their pain, reflected their righteous indignation. She was always optimistic, utterly convinced that Justice would prevail and Truth would win in the end. How could I not love her for it? But I worried about her.

Robin and I—and Sheyenne—were a good team. Most of the cases were satisfying … except for the one that had killed me.

CHAPTER 10

Half of a private detective's job is simply keeping his eyes and ears open and going to places where people are willing to let their guard down and talk. That's why you see so many PIs frequenting bars and nightclubs. It's work-related. Really.

The Goblin Tavern is the sort of hangout you'd expect, a homey and dingy place where everybody knows your name, but they don't hold it against you. A long wooden bar lined with stools, some of them wide and reinforced for the larger customers; a handful of dark tables with splintered wooden chairs; an array of liquor bottles on the top and bottom shelves; three taps for beer; a medical-grade refrigerator for donated blood packs, soy blood, and a special stainless-steel locker for the good stuff.

Cobwebs were carefully cultivated along the rafters and in the corners; one big glass jar held pickled eggs in a murky fluid, right next to a nearly identical jar filled with preserved eyeballs; the two jars had different-colored screw lids, so customers wouldn't get confused. Shrink-wrapped packets of jerky, made from a wide variety of flesh, filled a cardboard box next to the cash register.

Ilgar, the goblin owner, hated the place and hated the customers. In his lair in the back room, you might catch a glimpse of him, hear the clack and chatter of his adding machine, maybe a muttered curse when the ledgers didn't add up to his satisfaction. He was rarely seen working the bar.

Because it's my business to collect information, I knew a secret about Ilgar and his tavern, but I kept it to myself. He was in very serious negotiations with an outside food-and-drink conglomerate, the Smile

Syndicate, that wanted to franchise the Goblin Tavern—a great relief for Ilgar, no doubt. The guys-in-ties were exploring the possibility of opening a chain of duplicate Goblin Taverns across the country, catering to curious humans who wanted a safe taste of the Unnatural Quarter, something like the Haunted Mansion in Disneyland, except with plenty of alcohol available.

Many humans are morbidly fascinated by the dark side of the city. Large, secure tour buses drive around the Quarter so that curiosity seekers can watch the monsters in their unnatural habitat. As part of the route, and the experience, the buses drop off the passengers for a drink at the Goblin Tavern, one of the highlights of the tour. Next year, the place was going to be a zoo, when the World Horror Convention was due to come to town.

Ilgar had a terrible time keeping bartenders and cocktail waitresses; he'd gone through three in one particularly bad week (two had quit, one hadn't survived). That changed when he found Francine, a fiftyish human woman who'd seen it all, had dealt with tough customers throughout her life, and didn't put up with any guff from rowdy unnaturals.

"I've waited on slobs, pigs, and jerks in human bars too," she once told me. "Certain people turn into assholes when they're drunk. Doesn't matter whether they're truck drivers or necromancers. I know how to spot 'em, and I know how to deal with 'em."

And she did. Francine settled right in at the Tavern, got to know the regulars. You might not think a human bartender could relate to the problems of unnaturals, but Francine had been through three marriages, a bankruptcy, a house fire, a drug-addict kid, and persistent plantar warts that made her feet so sore that she hated to stand all day (although she had no choice). As a career bartender, she was well practiced in listening to the customers' woes. She didn't try to offer solutions, just poured another drink and knew when to pick up a round.

I entered the tavern as night fell and took my usual seat at the bar. Even before she came over, Francine grabbed a pint glass.

There are stages of being a regular customer at any establishment. First, as the bartender gets to know you, she'll try to earn points by remembering you and your order. "Tap beer? Large?" Second, she goes to the next stage, asking the coy question, "You want the usual, Dan?" even though she knows what the answer will be. But we were past all that. As soon as Francine saw me, she pulled the beer without asking anything at all.

Yes, I come here that often.

My taste buds aren't as sharp as before, and I always have a funny aftertaste in my mouth, so the brand of beer no longer matters to me. And liquor doesn't affect me the same as it used to (Sheyenne might say that my thoughts are often fuzzy anyway). Even back in the old days, I never hung out at bars to get drunk, but for the social benefits. It's part of my job, although I haven't yet figured out a way to submit my tab as an expense that the IRS would allow. While death isn't a sure thing anymore, taxes still are.

Since it wasn't yet full dark, the Goblin Tavern remained fairly empty: a transition time, like changing shifts in a factory. The night crew began to rise up while the day lovers slunk back to their well-lit homes; others, not caring whether it was night or day, remained up for twenty-four hours.

Francine brought the beer. After only a cursory glance at my face, she said, "Looks like you had some work done."

"Just a touch-up." I self-consciously put a finger to the mortician's putty that filled the hole in my forehead.

"Looks good."

"I'd feel better if I knew who did it to me."

Here at the tavern I hoped I might bump into someone or something useful for one or more of my open cases, the Jekyll divorce, the mummy emancipation case, Sheldon Fennerman's missing vampire neighbors, the Straight Edge hate group, a black-market blood ring I had uncovered over at Basilisk ... not to mention Sheyenne's murder, or my own. It was like herding caffeinated cats to move all my active cases toward a resolution.

My mind liked to juggle the various puzzles at the same time. One piece might lead to another clue in a different case, then to another. Running a private investigation agency poses a mental-organization and time-management problem that's rarely discussed in detective fiction. Life isn't like a TV show, where the private eye works on one crime exclusively from start to finish, beat after beat after beat, until the whole case is neatly solved by the end of the episode. I have a lot of things going at once, at different paces.

Officer McGoohan came in and swung up onto the stool on my right. "Hey, Shamble."

"Hey, McGoo. Fancy meeting you here."

He looked around the tavern. "Nothing fancy about it."

"Tough day?"

"Isn't it always?"

Francine pulled McGoo his own beer and set it in front of him. He returned a quick nod of thanks and slurped the foam off the top. He and I have been meeting here regularly for years. The comfortable place is a vortex of normalcy in the chaotic Quarter, so long as you can ignore the more bizarre patrons.

McGoo sniffed, frowned at me, then got up and moved to the stool on my left—his other usual stool. "I love you, man, but I don't love the aroma. I'm going to sit upwind."

"Yeah, you're a breath of fresh air yourself," I said. He knew I didn't smell any different from most people. It's part of his schtick.

"Hey, Francine," McGoo called across the bar, "how can you tell when you get a letter from a zombie?"

Francine rolled her eyes at him. "I don't want to know."

"It has a tongue attached to the stamp!"

We were supposed to groan. I fought back a smile. "Sorry, I've been having trouble moving my facial muscles lately."

"Well, you *are* a dead guy, and you're a private detective." He elbowed me. "So I guess that makes you a stiff dick!"

I know he doesn't mean anything by his off-color comments. McGoo wants to be the life of the party, but has no idea how to do it. To an outsider, especially a sensitive and politically correct outsider, he comes across as abrasive and insensitive. But even though his jokes are in poor taste, I've never seen McGoo treat anybody with less respect because of their gender, ethnicity, or unnatural type. He knows it goes both ways and would have been perfectly open to dumb cop jokes or stupid Irishman jokes. Not many people tell those anymore; to be honest, I think Officer McGoohan misses it.

He and I met in college. We both got degrees in criminal justice. Afterward, I decided to go into private investigating, while McGoo went into the police force. I thought I was going to have it made with a big-ticket freelance job—the potential for lots of money, be my own boss, have all the freedom in the world.

McGoo wanted the prestige of the uniform, the respect of the public, being an important guy who stopped criminals and kept the streets safe. The satisfaction of a job well done was all he needed. Unfortunately, both of us were wrong, but by then we were stuck.

Early on, we each married a woman named Rhonda. We were too young, and both of us still considered the marriage to be one of the worst mistakes of our lives (although there was always room for us to make even bigger mistakes). One Rhonda was a strawberry blonde—mine—and the other a brunette—McGoo's; both were beautiful, both were bitchy. He and I spent a lot of time commiserating with each other, wondering if we had picked the wrong Rhonda. But either way, we would have ended up just as miserable. Both marriages broke up after less than three years, but our friendship had lasted for decades. Through life and death, you might say.

The door opened, and three cadaverous women shuffled in, dressed in gaudy clothes, their faces painted, their hair done up. I recognized Cindy, Victoria, and Sharon from the embalming parlor. Their body movements did not have the seductive grace they imagined; in fact, they looked like a trio of skeletal marionettes with tangled strings and an inept puppeteer.

"Oh, God, let's hope I'm never that desperate." McGoo took a long swallow of his beer. The three women regarded, then dismissed us as prospective prey and took seats at the far end of the bar. Francine went to take their orders.

"Any word on who smashed up the Hope & Salvation Mission?" I asked. "You sure Mrs. Saldana's all right?"

"She'll start patching up the place in the morning. No clues. We got some skin scrapings from the broken glass, but there were so many shamblers around—including a couple of ripe ones that dripped all over the crime scene—I doubt any of the tissue samples are uncontaminated." He looked over at me. "How about you? Your vampire client still afraid for his life?"

"I'm working up a supplemental security plan for him, but I think he may be overreacting. I'll talk with the landlord about the missing neighbors."

McGoo grew more serious. "Made any progress on your own case, or Sheyenne's? I really feel sorry for you, man. Scout's honor. If I can do anything to help, I will."

"I'll take you up on that, as soon as I figure out what to ask. I just gotta poke around. In the meantime, I'm turning up the heat on Harvey Jekyll for the divorce case. His wife is convinced he's up to something, and if I can find a little leverage …"

Back in my younger years, I didn't think of myself as a nosy person, but I fit in with lots of different people. I kept quiet, but within earshot of gossipy types who dished out juicy stories like rumor-mongering Typhoid Marys. I collected these details, thinking of them as tools for future use, rather than hand grenades to lob indiscriminately. If the information doesn't help me solve a case, then I do nothing with it. People—whether natural or unnatural—are entitled to their privacy, so long as they don't hurt anybody.

Being a detective isn't a fantasy profession like astronaut or pro football player or movie star, not something I had dreamed of doing since I was a kid. But I'm good at investigating, and the only way I can *stay* good is to maintain my personal social network of contacts, friends, even a few paid informants.

In order to have someone owe you a favor, you have to do them a favor first—earn the goodwill before you can spend it. I pay for McGoo's drinks most of the time, but that's just a minor gesture. After all, he's my Best Human Friend, and it gives him the opportunity to grouse about his minuscule cop's salary, although my earnings as a private detective, dead or undead, are just as minuscule.

As Francine delivered our second round, the door opened, and I saw the plaid suit jacket coming first, with Brondon Morris arriving half a second later.

The trio of zombie ladies at the bar perked up. "Brondon! We hoped you would come," cooed Sharon.

"I can help him come more than once," cackled Victoria.

Cindy patted the empty bar stool at her side.

Without the least bit of embarrassment, Brondon sauntered up to the bar and stood behind the women so he didn't have to choose one over the others. "Oh, barkeep!" He raised his hand. "I'd like a Scotch and soda, please."

He acted as if he didn't know Francine's name and she didn't know damn well that he drank Scotch and soda. I'd seen the sales rep in the Goblin Tavern several times, and I found it odd that he treated the human bartender with less respect than he gave the undead clientele. "And another round of drinks for these lovely ladies." He leaned closer to the cackling cadavers. "What's your poison? Lemon drops?"

"Margaritas tonight." Cindy lowered her voice to a raspy whisper that everyone in the bar could hear anyway. "Tequila makes me horny."

Based on that, I thought it might be best if she steered clear of the tequila, but that wasn't my call.

"You three look ravishing tonight." Brondon set his sample case up on the bar and opened it, removing tiny sachets. "I'd like you to try this. A towelette for just a sniff, not enough to give it away, but these are the first samples of our Fresh Loam scent."

The three women fawned over him. Over the course of the conversation, I watched Brondon "accidentally" trace his fingers over

Sharon's shoulders and give Victoria's arm a playful touch. He flirtatiously brushed against Cindy's back.

Next to me, McGoo shuddered and concentrated deeply on his second beer. "Guess the guy likes cold fish. I don't even want to think about what they might do together."

"You're being prejudiced, McGoo. Even unnaturals want love."

"Well, that guy's looking for love in all the wrong places, as the song goes. Hey, Shamble, do ghouls eat popcorn with their fingers?"

I was distracted by the interplay at the other side of the bar. "What?"

"No, they eat the fingers separately!"

I doubted Brondon had ever actually slept with any of the ladies, but he treated them as something special. It was all a game, which they seemed to enjoy as much as he did. They went home with perfume and toiletry samples, and he inspired goodwill with the core customers of Jekyll Lifestyle Products and Necroceuticals.

In my earlier surveillance, I'd seen Brondon tagging along with Harvey Jekyll, no doubt feeling special because the boss had invited him to party with the big boys, though I'd never figured out what sort of party Jekyll was attending. Brondon might be an opportunity for me to track down Jekyll tonight.

After he sipped one drink with the zombie cougars and saw no new customers around the bar, Brondon bade them goodbye to a chorus of disappointed pleas. He just laughed and waved, promised he would see them all again soon, then slipped out of the Goblin Tavern.

I decided to follow him. He might be nothing more than a JLPN lapdog, but you never know where things might lead. I finished my beer, put some money on the bar, and said, "Gotta go to work, McGoo."

"If you say so. I'm going to take my time here. Thanks for the beer." I left the tavern, turned left, and quietly shadowed the perfume salesman.

CHAPTER 11

For a zombie, it's hard to move quickly until the dead joints and muscles warm up. Still, it's not difficult to follow a human through the streets of the Unnatural Quarter, especially when he's wearing a loud sport jacket and trailing nose-curling fumes from a case full of clashing deodorants, colognes, and body washes.

By the time I left the Goblin Tavern, the city's night life was hopping. Neon signs glowed, and traditional shops opened up for unnatural clientele. Streetlights flickered ominously in an electric rhythm sure to trigger epileptic seizures; on side streets, many lights were burned out or smashed.

Brondon Morris walked with a jaunty stride, swinging his case, whistling a tune that only he could interpret. Going about his rounds, he certainly didn't look like a man engaged in nefarious activities. He dropped by an exclusive zombies-only bar, then a gentleman vampires' club, but when he stopped at a place just outside of Little Transylvania, I had to ponder my next move.

Basilisk: A Place without Mirrors.

The nightclub had powerful memories for me. I needed to go inside, even if following Brondon was just a pretext. I whispered a personal reminder, "The cases don't solve themselves." Whether or not I got any leads in the Jekyll divorce case by following Brondon, maybe I'd learn something about an even more important mystery.

Basilisk was where I had met Sheyenne.

After Brondon entered the nightclub, I waited a few minutes outside so he wouldn't suspect I'd been following him, then I pulled open the door.

Even my dulled senses were assaulted by the curling fog of cigarette smoke, incense, and scented black candles. Red lights filled the main room with a crimson glow, and the cocktail bar was brushed nickel, cold and unwelcoming, completely unlike the cozy Goblin Tavern. As advertised, there was no mirror behind the bar, no mirrors on the ceilings; even the brushed nickel appointments cast no reflections.

I heard an inane melody played on the piano by, appropriately, a lounge lizard. The microphone on the stage stood ready, but the spotlights were dark. Ivory would be performing tonight—she had no competition now that Sheyenne was gone. (I kept telling Sheyenne that even as a ghost she had a nice set of lungs—and that wasn't a euphemism for "nice pair of breasts," although that was true too.) Sheyenne couldn't get over her bad feelings about Basilisk, sure that she'd been poisoned in this place, though she had no proof.

I walked to one of the tables near the stage. The place was filling up, and the entertainment would start soon. I folded myself down into a chair as the lounge lizard plinked out a peppy tune.

I'd never gone inside Basilisk until a case brought me there. I remembered the night I first heard Sheyenne sing here, when she captivated the audience with a sultry rendition of "Spooky." I was still alive then, and so was Sheyenne.

I'd been investigating illegal blood-bank sales at the nightclub, fresh packets that had "fallen off the refrigerated truck" on the way to the hospital. I was hired to get to the bottom of it by Harry Talbot, the disgruntled owner of a licensed blood bar, who believed the competing black-market sales were cutting into his business. When I caught Fletcher Knowles, Basilisk's human bartender and manager, red-handed (so to speak), he was more annoyed than guilty. "Why get your panties in a wad about it, Chambeaux? I sell my stuff for almost the same price as Talbot does, but some customers prefer to be discreet. Would you rather they get back to basics and start feeding on people in dark alleys?"

Fletcher was balding, in his late thirties, with round John Lennon eyeglasses and a full goatee that he bleached very blond. He looked as if he should have been a barista rather than a nightclub manager. Fletcher got along perfectly well with unnaturals; he didn't care about their species or the color of their skin (white, brown, or gray) or their fur—it was all business to him. Basilisk was one of the more successful nightlife spots in the Quarter, and he lined his pockets with extra income from under-the-table blood sales.

Through word on the street, Fletcher already knew that Talbot had hired me, but he didn't see the situation as a problem. "Be reasonable. Nobody's getting hurt." He bought me a beer and told me to ponder long and hard about what I wanted to do, then made a halfhearted threat to have his goons beat me up if I didn't cooperate. Since I was still alive back then, the threat was enough to give me pause.

And then, as I was sitting at the table in front of the stage, trying to figure out how to keep both sides of the feud happy and me undamaged, Sheyenne came out to sing.

She was riveting: her eyes, her beautiful face, her gorgeous figure, and her bravery. I couldn't think of any other human who'd be willing to stand up and sing in front of a room full of stomach-turning, hungry, and potentially murderous unnaturals.

From the stage she hooked her eyes on me, clearly interested (maybe just because I was the only human customer in Basilisk that night). I bought her a drink during break. She sat down and talked with me.

Sheyenne was her stage name, she told me, derived from "shy Anne," because she'd been nervous when she first auditioned. She started out as a cocktail waitress, then did a short stint as an exotic dancer, but decided that wasn't for her. After working a few years in business and management, she had changed her mind and become a medical student, working her way through school, and she needed to earn money. I don't know what compelled her to fill out an application at Basilisk, but she told me the pay was twice what she could earn in any normal nightclub, though the tips were generally awful.

I told her I admired her, and that wasn't just a pickup line. I told her she was beautiful, and I meant that too. I came back to see her the next night, and the next. After hearing her sing, it seemed only right that I started calling her Spooky, and she asked if it was all right to call me Beaux.

Then I saw her outside of work, and we had dinner. One thing led to another, and after two weeks she invited me back to her apartment.

She was poisoned shortly thereafter, so we never really had a chance, although I like to imagine that our relationship could have grown into a lot more. Now that she'd come back as a ghost, she saw no point in continuing medical school—nobody wanted a ghost for a doctor. And not being able to touch her patients would definitely have been a drawback. I was damned glad to have her working for Chambeaux & Deyer....

Brondon Morris took me by surprise when he pulled up a chair and sat next to me at the table in front of the stage. "You're following me, Mr. Chambeaux."

I kept my composure, which is easy for a zombie to do. "I enjoy nightclub singing."

"You were at the Goblin Tavern too." He sounded more teasing than accusing.

"I believe I was on my second drink before you arrived. If I'm following you, then I'm going about it backward."

"Ah, you've got me there," he said with a grin.

I looked toward the still-dark stage. "My girlfriend used to perform here."

"Ah, yes, that human singer. What was her name ... Wyoming?"

"Sheyenne," I said.

"Yes, a poor lost young woman. She sneaked one of my Zom-Be-Fresh samples from an undead cocktail waitress, but she broke out in a horrible rash from using it." He laughed. "Then she got mad at *me*, even though I pointed out that necroceuticals are intended for unnaturals only, not for human use." He seemed embarrassed. "I apologized profusely, and JLPN compensated for her pain and suffering. The company is very sensitive about their public image."

"Tell that to all the bald vampires who used your shampoo."

The comment clearly annoyed him, but he maintained his pat smile. "I see why you're the private investigator and I'm just a salesman." He set his case on the chair and opened it. "I really wish you'd try our products. They're designed for undead men just like you." He pulled out a bottle of Zom-Be-Fresh. "Nothing to be embarrassed about."

"I keep myself clean, and I wear clean clothes."

"Yes, but to some people you still have a—how do I say it?—a *dead* smell about you, the way very old people have a certain odor."

"It's natural," I said, then realized the irony in my statement.

"Body odor is natural, but that doesn't mean we have to put up with it."

"Doesn't bother me," I said, then gave him a hard glance. "Why are you pushing it so hard, Brondon? You've got plenty of customers. What do you care about one more?"

"It's a matter of pride, Mr. Chambeaux. I started out as JLPN's research chemist, and I helped develop the whole line of necroceuticals, but the hard part is marketing. Even a brilliant idea will sit in a garage unless the public knows about it.

"I realized I'd come up with something remarkable for all unnatural customers, and I could see the need for it, so I decided to pound the streets of the Unnatural Quarter, knock on doors, get the word out. I sniffed out new customers, if you know what I mean. Over the years it's been my mission to see that these lifestyle products are widely distributed among all the unnaturals."

He seemed lost in his own story. "And because I was willing to do the legwork and gamble my reputation on this, Mr. Jekyll invested in me, gave me the financial resources. I knew that unnaturals would be skeptical, but I was sure I could win them over. That's why I provide so many free samples. My service to humanity"—he grinned again—"in all its forms."

"Thank you for being so inclusive," I said sarcastically.

I saw an opening and wanted to ask him more about his work with Harvey Jekyll, especially that secret meeting six weeks ago, or Harvey's furtive nocturnal trip to the dump, but then the piano player reached his crescendo, the stage lights blazed on, and the audience members began to applaud, whistle, and cheer. "Ivory!" A group of werewolves in the back howled.

With unexpected grace, an enormous well-endowed woman glided onto the stage, swaying, jiggling. She had ebony skin, fiery red eyes. Ivory's grin was wide enough to show her long white fangs to good effect, when she curled her pointed tongue to lick her lips, relishing the adoration of the audience. She wrapped both hands around the shaft of the microphone, grasping it and sliding her face close to it, as if it were a porn movie prop. "Evening, boys."

The werewolves howled even louder.

Ivory was a big mama with a big voice, a vamp in both senses of the word, and quite the diva. She advertised herself and her "services" in the Unusual Singles classifieds, as a BBV, or big-breasted vampire. I suppose there's a customer base for that sort of thing.

The words purred out of Ivory's throat and built in volume and power until she sang in a voice powerful enough to shatter glass. Maybe that's the real reason why Basilisk has no mirrors.

Back when Sheyenne had first taken the stage as a young human waitress in an unnatural nightclub, she had ruffled Ivory's feathers: The big vamp thought she was a *star*, while Sheyenne was just working her way through med school. But with her sincere delivery, Sheyenne's waifish crooning stole the show. There was no love lost between the two.

Sheyenne was convinced that Ivory was the one who had slipped toadstool poison into her drink, just to get rid of the competition. Normally, I would have considered that too extreme, but a vampire doesn't have the same standards about taking a life. I considered her to be a suspect, but the MO didn't make any sense. If Sheyenne had had her throat ripped out, I might have considered the vamp singer a more likely perpetrator. Surreptitious poison just didn't seem like Ivory's style.

I listened to the big vamp's first two numbers, then glanced to one side, surprised to see that Brondon Morris had taken his sample case up to chat with the bartender. I looked at the two of them, thinking hard.

I was killed only two blocks from this nightclub. Several people had heard the gunshot, but the shooter managed to run away without being seen. Fletcher Knowles himself was the one who had found my body. Convenient.

Sheyenne had worked here, and she'd been poisoned.

Could be a connection. I would definitely have to dig deeper.

From the stage, Ivory fixed me with her hot-ember eyes, one of those scary and seductive glamour gazes that can turn human victims into putty. Even I found it hard to resist, and parts of me began to stir. After all, I wasn't entirely dead.

After her first set, the vamp singer bowed to resounding applause and told the audience she would be back after her break. Customers shuffled toward the stage, wanting to talk to her but too shy to speak. Ivory glided through the crowds of admirers and stepped directly up to me; she ignored her fans, much to their disappointment. Some glowered at me, and I could sense their jealousy. Most of them couldn't understand why I wasn't grinning like a schoolboy from the attention.

Under other circumstances, Ivory would never have noticed me, but when she noticed my brewing relationship with Sheyenne, she decided to get me for herself. But it hadn't worked. With Sheyenne around, how could I look at anyone else?

"Hey, sugar. I haven't seen you around in a while." Ivory leaned closer, and her cleavage reminded me of a Venus flytrap about to swallow my head. She inhaled deeply. "You're less warm-blooded now than before."

I tapped my forehead where the mortician's putty still covered the scar. "Got shot in the head."

"Sorry to hear that, but I'm glad you came back to hear me sing."

"I came back for a lot of reasons."

She frowned. "Yeah, I heard about your poor little girlfriend. Never knew what you saw in that scrawny thing, when you could have had so much more." She traced her hands from her rib cage to her waist, then her hips.

"Sheyenne and I were happy enough while it lasted," I said.

Again, that mock sorrowful pout. "I heard she died, poor thing. I hope she's doing better now?"

"Sheyenne's just fine. And we're still seeing each other."

"Whenever you're ready to move on, sugar, I can meet you back in my dressing room."

"I wouldn't want you to disappoint all these adoring fans." I glanced at the crowd of men hovering around.

"Who says I don't have enough to share?" she said. "Stay for the next set—we'll talk afterward."

Without saying a word to the other fans, Ivory returned to the stage, and the lounge lizard played her intro. I got up and left quietly. No need to make a long night seem longer.

CHAPTER 12

Despite setback after setback, a determined person won't stay down for long—and Hope Saldana was a determined lady.

Early next morning, I stopped by the Hope & Salvation Mission just to see how the old woman was dealing with the destruction of her place. Even though McGoo had already told me she wasn't injured in the attack, I wanted to make sure she was all right.

Over the years, some unnaturals had grumbled about Mrs. Saldana's goody-two-shoes efforts to help down-and-out unnaturals, but she stuck to her guns and continued her missionary work. Her heart was in the right place, and she considered it her duty to help those who no longer had hearts, beating or otherwise.

When I arrived at the smashed mission, I saw Mrs. Saldana standing on the sidewalk out front, arms crossed over her pink flower-print dress. She guided the efforts of her assistant Jerry, a tall and lanky zombie, who was hanging a rectangle of plywood over one of the destroyed storefront windows.

Jerry was one of the first wayward souls that Mrs. Saldana had helped when she opened her mission. As the story went—and the old woman told the story whenever she delivered her sermons, since it made such a great example—Jerry had shambled up to her during a particularly bad jag, intent on eating her brain. But Mrs. Saldana accepted him, read him verses from her well-worn Bible, offered him hope and comfort, and talked him down from his slobbering hunger.

"God loves all His creatures," she said.

"Even a wretch like me?" Jerry had answered.

She gave him a sincere nod. "Just like the hymn says."

Jerry broke down and cried, and he'd been her inseparable helper ever since. His hunger hadn't abated, but he was working his way through a twelve-step program, and there were plenty of rats in the basement.

Now Mrs. Saldana took a step back to inspect the patch-up job. "That'll do, Jerry." She gave a brisk nod. "Bless you. Now we can continue our work."

The old woman had curly permed hair, gray but not yet old-lady blue. At first glance, she looked like everyone's favorite schoolteacher. No one I knew had ever heard Mrs. Saldana raise her voice or speak a discouraging word. She was an optimist, a caring person—and it pissed me off that anybody would do this to her place. Was it mere vandalism, or did someone hold a specific grudge?

Seeing the smashed-out windows, I unfolded one of the Black Glass, Inc. flyers I'd taken from our office. "Maybe you should give these people a call. It's a new company that specializes in repairing and replacing windows in the Unnatural Quarter. I'm sure they deal with regular transparent glass as well as opaque windowpanes."

She perused the advertisement. "Thank you, Mr. Chambeaux. I like to use local services if I can."

Her zombie helper looked at me, and the hammer in his hands slipped out of his rubbery fingers. The tool fell on his foot, but he didn't feel it.

Mrs. Saldana gave a schoolteacherly *tsk*. "Jerry, you just dropped a hammer. Pay attention. You wouldn't want to hurt somebody. You could get damaged too. We wouldn't want that, would we?" Embarrassed, the zombie bent over and picked up the tool.

"Anything else I can do to help out?" I asked.

Her smile reminded me of grandmother's kisses and the smell of apple pie. "It's not me you should be worried about, Mr. Chambeaux. It's those poor unnaturals who need my help. What a setback!" Dismay was plain on the old woman's face. "This damage caused a delay in today's services. I don't know how I'll serve breakfast to the needy ... although I think we can manage coffee. Jerry?"

"Coffee ..." he said, and shuffled inside through the gaping hole of the ruined door.

Mrs. Saldana smiled at me. "Come on in. Jerry is going to sweep up some of the mess."

Inside the front room, the old woman used a thumbtack to put the Black Glass flyer on a corkboard she had mounted on the wall. The rest of the board was crowded with snapshots of unfortunate unnaturals she had helped—a toothless grinning werewolf, two ghouls who wore angelic expressions on their faces, and rotting Mel, my very first case as a PI in the Quarter. A sincere handwritten note in blocky letters, written with thick clumsy lines, as if a child had used a brownish-red crayon: *Thank you, Mrs. Saldana! We love you and the Hope & Salvation Mission.*

In the main room, ten beige metal folding chairs sat in front of the small lectern where Mrs. Saldana delivered her sermons. Each folding chair held a well-thumbed Bible and a stained hymnal. A rarely used piano had been pushed off to the corner. I remembered that Mrs. Saldana had tried to teach Jerry how to play, but he wasn't dexterous enough to keep up with any fast melodies. A card table held a tray of cookies as well as a large percolating coffeemaker.

From inside, the old woman turned around and looked out the damaged front of the mission, where plywood now covered one of the two windows like an eye patch. "I've got to get that door fixed, or maybe I should leave it off. This is a mission, after all—we're here to help people. We welcome everyone in need." She made up her mind. "Yes, indeed, the door to Hope & Salvation should never be locked."

"A locked door didn't deter whoever vandalized the place yesterday," I pointed out. "Do you have any idea who may be responsible?"

"I haven't the foggiest," she said automatically, and her lips turned down in a flicker of a frown; I caught the expression before she formed an accepting smile again. "Whoever it is doesn't know that God loves them. My life's calling here, Mr. Chambeaux, is to give comfort and assistance to poor unnaturals. They can't help who they are, but they *can* control their urges. They *can* be good people if they stay on the straight and narrow. If I find whoever did this, I shall have to show them love and understanding ... although I'm inclined to give them a stern lecture as well."

"Officer McGoohan is working on the case," I said. I didn't want her haring off in pursuit of whoever had done the damage. She might get hurt.

"Yes, indeed. Such a nice policeman. Always so helpful. I've given him all the information."

I nodded. "He's a good man, ma'am, but he is overburdened. He and I help each other out on cases, so maybe I can give him a lead." I thought about the people harassing Sheldon Fennerman, wondered if they might have something to do with the vandalism here. "Have you had any dealings with a purist group called the Straight Edge, ma'am? I'm starting to wonder if they might be involved somehow."

Mrs. Saldana's brow furrowed. "Most unpleasant individuals. Straight Edge claims I shouldn't treat the unnaturals as God's children. They came here and talked to me twice, treated Jerry like dirt."

On the other side of the room, the lanky zombie had picked up a push broom and plodded across the hardwood floor, sweeping aside glass fragments and wood splinters. He looked up when he heard his name and let out a low growling groan at the mention of the Straight Edgers.

Now my interest was piqued. "Were they trying to scare you out of the city?" I couldn't imagine her closing the doors and giving up on helping the needy.

Her face grew pinched. "Oh, much worse than that, Mr. Chambeaux. They gave me posters to put up here in the mission—here!—proclaiming that unnaturals should just crawl back into the dirt, or wherever they came from, and *decompose*. How dare they treat my patrons that way!"

"It's the way they think, ma'am." I liked these people less and less.

"Not just that. They expected me to join Straight Edge! They assumed that we must be on the same side because I'm human. What they asked me …" She swallowed hard—I could see her throat clench. "It was horrible!"

"What did they want you to do?"

"They expected me to set up a trap for my own flock—for the wretches who come in here for hope and comfort, including Jerry!" She gestured to the wall of lovely photographs of her success stories. "I refused to do it, of course. They were quite angry, but I quoted Scripture right to their faces. They weren't even familiar with the Bible!" She snorted. "No, indeed, I don't like them—but I pray for them. I sent them back to their little clubhouse headquarters. Did you know they've opened a new office, just down the street? Right here in the Quarter! You should go there and talk to them, Mr. Chambeaux. I doubt they'd even deny trashing the mission."

"A new office?" Some detective I was! "Can you give me the address?" I wasn't surprised the purist group had a base of operations in the Unnatural Quarter, but I'd never had any face-to-face dealings with them.

"Of course." She wrote it down on a small notepad printed with pink flowers. "And this attack occurred the very day after I had my little tiff with them. I don't need to be a detective to connect the dots."

Kevin J. Anderson

"That's a big coincidence, Mrs. Saldana, but there's one thing I don't understand: Whatever caused this monster mash was definitely not human. Look at the damage! What sort of unnatural would ally itself with the Straight Edgers? No monster would want anything to do with them."

Jerry shuffled by with his push broom, sweeping around my feet, then disposed of the dust and debris beneath the unused piano.

"The Lord works in mysterious ways, Mr. Chambeaux," Mrs. Saldana said with a solemn nod. "And so does Satan."

CHAPTER 13

When I arrived at the Chambeaux & Deyer offices a short while later, the pig was already there.

She was an enormous white sow the size of a riding lawn mower, with large dark brown spots on her hide. Her flat upturned nose snuffled around the worn carpeting with the sound of an asthmatic vacuum cleaner, rooting under Sheyenne's desk, snorting the edges of the room as if we kept truffles under the baseboards. Her name was Alma Wannovich.

Fortunately, we're accustomed to unusual clients. By now we had gotten used to the big sow, as well as her equally large but currently less noticeable sister, a heavyset black-gowned witch who wore a midnight-blue scarf spangled with gold stars and crescent moons. Her wiry black hair stuck out in all directions like a panicked steel-wool pad.

"Good morning, Mavis," I said to the witch, then to the sow, "Good morning, Alma."

Mavis Wannovich tangled her fingers together in a gesture of desperation, though she didn't exactly fit the traditional damsel-in-distress mold. She turned to me without waiting for Robin to explain why the two sisters had come into the offices. "Ms. Deyer just received a letter from the publisher, and they deny everything! They refuse to help at all. They claim we don't have a case. How can they say that? Just *look* at Alma!"

The sow blinked her dark eyes at me, then grunted.

I did my best to sound reassuring. "You just let us handle that. Robin will know how to respond."

Robin stood with a pencil stuck behind her ear, preoccupied with rereading the letter. She looked up at the dejected witch, and I could see the wheels turning in her mind. "Don't be surprised or disheartened. I told you to be prepared for a blanket denial in response to our demand letter."

Mavis lovingly patted the sow's broad head, scratching her behind the ears. She tossed one end of the starry blue scarf over her shoulder. "We'll try to be strong."

Robin continued, "This is just standard procedure. Every publishing house has boilerplate letters, and they respond to complaints with categorical and vehement denials. It doesn't mean you have any less of a case just because they say so, but they hope you'll give up. We are not going to give up."

The sow grunted and snorted as if reciting a long paragraph in pig language. Mavis interpreted. "I know we have to pursue this case, Ms. Deyer, but my sister and I are just two witches trying to get by. We don't have the money for a protracted legal battle."

"Don't you worry about that a bit. If necessary, we'll finish your case pro bono."

"She means on a contingency fee basis," Sheyenne interrupted, rising from her desk. "One-third of the monetary award, plus costs, but only if we win."

"We'll fight for Justice," Robin said. "Alma has been wronged, and you have been wronged. The publisher's mistake caused your suffering, and I won't stand for that." Robin put her arm around the witch's shoulders. "Come and sit down, and we'll talk about the next step."

With a wan, stiff-upper-lip smile, Mavis trundled toward the conference room with a swish of her black gown. The door to the room wasn't wide enough to accommodate the large sow and the large witch at the same time, so Mavis let the pig walk in ahead of her. After they invited me to join them, I moved one of the chairs away from the long table so that the pig would have a place to stand.

Alma was Mavis's sister, just as largely built, although she'd had blond hair (with occasional black roots, which might be the reason for the dark spots on the sow's hide now). The two witches had bought a new book of obscure spells released by Howard Phillips Publishing—"We Love Our Craft." But due to an unfortunate typo in the incantations, one of the spells had gone horribly wrong: Instead of turning the two rather homely witches into svelte Aphrodite look-alikes, the spell backfired and transformed Alma into a fat sow. She'd been that way ever since. All of Mavis's attempts to reverse the spell had failed.

I remember how distraught the witch was when she first led the large pig into our offices, weeping. This was exactly the type of case that got Robin's passion. "A spelling error in a book of spells is a clear example of gross negligence," she said. "Look at the damage it caused! The publisher hasn't even offered to correct their mistake. We have to stop this before others suffer the same fate."

"I don't think the book had a very large printing," Mavis admitted. "We had to special-order it."

"They could at least have used a spell check," Robin said.

I offered, "Let me make some calls, put you in touch with witchcraft troubleshooting organizations that could help you find a reversal of the spell."

"Sheyenne will get you a list of support groups, too," Robin added.

Once the Wannovich sisters became our clients, I did some investigating, discovered that Howard Phillips Publishing specializes in collectible editions of arcane works, and they have offices here in the Quarter. So far, their largest seller has been an annotated but abridged edition of the Necronomicon bound in alligator skin (they had announced, but never published, an extremely limited numbered edition bound in human skin). Recently, the company had begun to offer publishing services, for a substantial fee, to print and distribute the memoirs and ruminations of unnaturals. Everybody, it seems, wants to write their life, and death, and life story. Most of these memoirs were available only in e-book formats and print-on-demand. Despite their fancy logo, Howard Phillips Publishing was little more than a vanity press.

Robin passed me the response letter, which was written in flowery legalese on formal stationery. The publisher's legal department—probably one guy in a back room somewhere—insisted, "Witchcraft is a dangerous hobby, and every practitioner should use appropriate caution. The spells in our spell books are intended for entertainment purposes only. The publisher accepts no liability for any misuse or inadvertent accidents that may occur as a direct or indirect result of our books. We make no warranties, express or implied, about the accuracy of our content. Any damages are the sole responsibility of the user."

"Reads like a form letter," I agreed and handed it back to Robin.

"We'll file a suit against them," she said. "In order to protect other users, our first course of action will be to demand that they withdraw all copies of this spell book from the market until the typo is corrected. In fact, I can probably get an ex parte injunction by showing irreparable harm to the user—i.e., being turned into a sow."

"But how long will all that take?" asked Mavis. The sow let out a squeaking snort, then sat on the carpet.

"I'm afraid it's going to require some time. First, we have to serve the complaint, and they have thirty days to file an answer. If they don't agree to take the book off the market, I have to file papers and go through written discovery, after which we take depositions, move for a trial date." A glint appeared in her deep brown eyes. "As another possibility, we can go directly to the media. Obviously, one interview with you and your poor sister, and our case is won." Robin leaned over to gaze at the mournful sow, and she put both her hands on the table. "But we are going to win this one. We're going to *win!*"

"I believe you, but my sister's a sow!" Mavis's lower lip trembled, and I could see she was about ready to unleash a hurricane of tears and sniffles. "I always wanted to work in publishing. I even applied for a job at Howard Phillips, offered to help with proofreading. They never responded. And now ... my poor sister!"

Alma nuzzled up against Mavis's dark skirts. The witch straightened her back, and her expression darkened. As she rose from her chair, Mavis's black gown seemed to grow more voluminous, her hair standing out like a big curly thundercloud. "If we can't find a way to fix this, then I want to nail that publisher to the wall!"

Robin sounded cheery, "We can help you with that, too, if you like."

CHAPTER 14

fter I ushered the witch and the sow out of the offices, walking them down the hall to the elevator, Sheyenne was opening the day's mail at her desk. She tore open an envelope and looked at the results with a disbelieving grumble. "You gotta love the post office." She held up the paper. "This letter to me—important chemical results—took weeks to be delivered, even though I filed all the change-of-address forms as soon as I came back from the dead."

Sheyenne had experienced a lot of trouble getting her mail forwarded. Since she was a ghost and gainfully employed, she used the Chambeaux & Deyer offices as her new physical address, but glitches still happened.

I plucked the paper from her ghostly hands. It was some kind of lab report, a spectrometer trace, tables of numbers and lists of complex compounds that I didn't understand. While working on other cases, I had seen blood tests and DNA matches for paternity suits, but these results didn't look familiar. "What is this?"

"Back at Basilisk I sneaked a bottle of Zom-Be-Fresh perfume that Brondon Morris was showing off around the club, but when I tried the stuff, it gave me a horrible allergic reaction—I had hives all over my skin, and they itched like crazy. I was miserable, and I told Brondon he shouldn't leave dangerous chemicals lying around."

"Funny, he just told me about that last night. If you stole the sample, he didn't exactly leave it lying around. And if you didn't follow the directions—"

She grimaced. "I know it's not designed for or marketed to humans, but JLPN is peddling that stuff all over town. I sure was sorry I tried it!"

I let out a wistful sigh. "Your skin looked just fine during our night together."

Sheyenne laughed. "It was dark, and the rash was mostly gone by then." We both paused for an awkward moment, reminiscing.

She turned her attention back to the chem analysis. "Brondon was panicked about a PR debacle, slobbered apologies all over me, but I sent the sample off to a lab anyway." She looked up at me, her eyes bright. "I had connections at the university through the med school."

I looked down at the sheet again. "These numbers make about as much sense to me as rap music. What does it mean?"

"Nothing." She frowned. "The perfume is perfectly harmless. No hazardous substances whatsoever." She drifted behind her desk, and with a poltergeist *harrumph* scattered some of the other envelopes, letters, and bills that she had placed there.

I wanted to wrap my arms around her waist, let her rest her head on my shoulder and stay that way for about an hour ... which is tough to do when you can't touch the other person. "At least now you know there was nothing to worry about."

"I would have pestered the lab about it, but I was too busy with other things ... like dying in a hospital bed." She hung her head.

"Sorry," I said, not really sure what I was apologizing for, but just generally sorry about everything that had happened. Even though I can see her ghost every day, the pain is still fresh, a sick burning in the center of my chest like the indigestion after eating three chili dogs and two pepperoni pizzas.

"Thanks, Beaux," she said. "That was a rough time."

"An understatement."

After we met at Basilisk, we spent more and more time in each other's company, growing close, and then we had our one night together. It should have been a lot more than that.

We'd gone back to her apartment. She and I each had that unspoken hunger, the magnetism that almost never happens, where two people click with a spark that both can see but nobody else notices. Pulse increasing, throat dry, accidental touches and then not-so-accidental ones, and a rising heat where you both know that this might not be the smartest thing in the world to do, but it's best not to ask too many questions.

I've had one-nighters before. In my line of work, you bump into a lot of desperate people, and more than half the time they're women. Sometimes they're pulling strings to encourage me to work harder on their cases; other times the ladies want to show their gratitude in some way besides just paying the bills.

With Sheyenne, though, it wasn't like that. Usually, when I hooked up with someone, client or otherwise, I'd have a queasy feeling afterward. Not guilt, really, just a general disappointment in myself. What I had with Sheyenne *did* feel good afterward—good enough that I didn't want to ruin it. Something that could have been a real relationship.

And so I did the instinctive thing, the male thing ... the wrong thing.

I knew that Sheyenne's parents were killed when she was just a teenager by a man in a business suit talking on a car phone, having an argument about a Chinese to-go order. She'd had to be strong, raise herself. She got a succession of jobs, always learning, never giving up on the chance to make something of herself. She seemed to take her independence as a badge of honor.

When I asked whether there was anyone who could have helped her out, she had said, "Problem is, when somebody helps you, they think you owe them. I wanted to avoid that."

So I didn't want to scare her off by being clingy and obsessive, didn't want her to think I had fallen head over heels for her, because surely that would spook her. So I retreated and kept myself busy, trying not to think of her too much. I stayed away for four days.

How could I not realize that she must have assumed I'd abandoned her, brushed her off—"Slam bam, thank ya, ma'am. Don't worry about breakfast in the morning."—when of course I thought about her every moment for four days?

When I thought I had waited long enough, I called her, but I got the unexpected message that her phone had been disconnected. Bad sign. I stopped by Basilisk, and Fletcher Knowles said that Sheyenne hadn't shown up for work in two days. Ivory insisted she hadn't seen the girl, suggested that she must have run off somewhere. The big vamp singer didn't seem terribly disappointed.

Finally, I went back to Sheyenne's apartment. Though no one answered my knocks, neither the polite one nor the louder one, I thought I heard a groan from inside. Using an old private investigator's trick, I pulled out the lock-picking tools I always keep in my pocket. I fiddled with the lock, but she had installed heavy dead bolts for additional security (a good idea, considering the part of town), and the reinforcement was too much for me. So I tried another PI trick and threw myself against the door, attempting to break it down. I nearly dislocated my shoulder, but I couldn't smash the dead bolts.

By now, I was positive I'd heard another groan, a weak cry for help inside the apartment. So I turned to my last and best trick and went down to the manager's apartment, slipped him a twenty, and talked him into letting me inside. He didn't seem convinced about any emergency, wasn't happy with Sheyenne at all. Apparently, she'd been late on her last month's rent.

I made him get his priorities straight.

After he used his key to unlock her door, I pushed my way inside to see Sheyenne lying on the floor, already on death's doorstep. Her skin was pale and grayish, her eyes half-open, her breathing heavy and wet, her pulse thready. She had vomited several times. I could see she had tried to crawl across the floor, but couldn't get anywhere.

"Call an ambulance!" I yelled to the manager, who seemed more worried about the mess on the floor than about the dying young woman. I picked Sheyenne up and carried her down the stairs and out the front door to the sidewalk. The paramedics arrived a few minutes later and rushed her to the hospital.

She'd been poisoned—a high concentration of the alkaloid toxin distilled from the "death cap" toadstool, *Amanita phalloides*. Even if the poisoning had been caught early, the mortality rate was greater than 50 percent ... and no one had found Sheyenne in time, because *I* was stupid and stayed away to give her space. By now the toxin had done its work: severe liver damage, renal failure ... nothing the doctors could do to save her.

It was long and painful, a horrible, lingering way to die.

I never left her bedside in the hospital. Sheyenne wavered in and out of lucidity, but she always knew who I was. "I thought you wouldn't call me back, Beaux. Thought I'd ... spooked you."

"Never," I said. "Just waited too long." Then I let out a long sigh. "I wish I could find some way to help you, Spooky."

Shadowy hollows surrounded her eyes, but her smile was the same. "You're doing it, just by being here. I've got no one."

"You've got me."

"I wish I could stay with you, Beaux. But someone wanted me dead. You're the private detective. Find out who did this to me. For me, please?"

"I promise I'll solve this case. I'll find your murderer, if it's the last thing I do."

"You're so sweet," she said in a breathy voice. "Have a good life."

She died an hour later, but I never forgot my promise to her.

One of her last acts in the hospital had been to scrawl a note, a holographic will, granting me custody of her meager worldly possessions—nobody really cared, since she didn't have any living relatives. When her ghost did not appear immediately after her death, I thought she was gone for good.

Weighed down with grief and anger, I went to her apartment to clear out Sheyenne's stuff and was surprised to discover that her snotty building manager was already intending to sell her possessions in order to recoup his lost rent. I had no intention of letting him do that, and we ended up in a shouting match. As a favor to me, Robin drafted and signed an impressive-looking legal document that spooked the manager, and I hauled out the boxes myself, put them in the storage unit that we retained for holding old case records.

Feeling lost and alone, I dropped all my other cases to work on hers, to track down who might have poisoned my Sheyenne. But my other cases didn't forget about *me*, and I should have paid more attention to the fact that a cocktail waitress/nightclub singer/med student wasn't the only one with enemies in the Quarter.

Less than a month after she died, there I was late at night, minding my own business—or Sheyenne's, actually—when one of those cases caught up with me in a dark alley not far from Basilisk. I'd taken the same shortcut back to the office that I always do. Someone came up behind me, put an antique Civil War pistol to the back of my head, and fired a round through my skull.

Unfortunately, it wasn't one of those cartoon villains who likes to gloat and gab and explain every little bit about his dastardly plan. No, this time it was just the gun, then the bang....

Now, as I stood in front of her desk reminiscing, Sheyenne crumpled the chemical analysis report and tossed it across the room with a swirling breeze of ghostly annoyance. "So much for sticking it to JLPN. I was so sure there'd be some contaminant or hazardous component, something that was a factor in my poisoning. But I know the lab guy, and this is for real." She looked fiercely determined. "I have half a mind to manifest before Brondon Morris, chew him out, and give him a wedgie in front of his zombie ladyfriends."

"You're a ghost," I said. "He knows you can't touch him."

"Oh, I can still make him miserable."

No doubt she was right. "I really think I could have loved you, Spooky," I said, startling her.

"Oh, Beaux, under normal circumstances you would have forgotten about me in a few weeks," she teased.

I didn't think so at all, but maybe Sheyenne needed to say that just to make the regrets glide down easier, like a $300 bottle of wine. Maybe I'd be smart to do the same thing, but it was damned hard to see that beautiful woman in my office every single day and never be able to touch her....

CHAPTER 15

Lunchtime. I've never been, nor do I intend to become, one of those disgusting ambulatory corpses with a sweet-tooth for brains. Even though I don't need to eat as often as before—undead metabolism is all out of whack—lunch isn't something a man should give up. I liked to do things out of habit just to pretend that my life was normal.

The big sign in the front window of Ghoul's Diner, my favorite lunch counter, said in bright orange letters: *Yes, We Serve Humans!* The diner was a warm and cheery place, crowded with unnaturals who liked to sit in the booths or take a stool up at the counter with elbows propped on the speckled countertop.

At the grill in back stood a sweaty grayish creature who looked decidedly unwell. Albert Gould, the proprietor, had skin with the sheen and consistency of sliced ham left too long in the sun. I had talked with him face-to-face a few times. Albert could be an unsettling fellow for anyone with a queasy stomach. Cockroaches scuttled around in his spiky hair, and thin whitish things dripped in and out of his nostrils as he inhaled and exhaled. At first I thought they were boogers; then I realized they were maggots.

Albert concocted variations of the daily special, catering to different types of clientele. Zombie special, vampire special, werewolf special, human special (although the humans who dared to eat there rarely became repeat customers). He served platters of sliced, discolored mystery meat, sometimes on a bun with all the condiments, other times spread out on a blue plate pooled in gelatinous gravy made from a mucus roux.

The smells inside Ghoul's Diner were rich and ripe. Conversation buzzed among the booths; a cash register rang up sales. From the back, a gush of steam and spray of water rose from where a reptile-skinned dishwasher blasted globs of food off the plates, then stacked them back on the shelves.

Esther, the diner's lone waitress—a harpy who never provided good service, but always received excellent tips because the customers were afraid to annoy her—chatted with two necromancers in a corner booth. She seemed to have no interest in her other customers.

I took a seat at the counter beside a bespectacled hunchback who was poring over stock listings in the newspaper. The folded front page had a headline story, *Elvis Found!*

I'd heard the story on the radio: A zombie came back to life, insisting he was Elvis Presley. Over the years, there had been many Elvis sightings, people who claimed the King had never died. This one was different, because the guy was unquestionably dead, and he had submitted flesh scrapings for DNA testing to verify his identity.

"Can I borrow the front section?" I asked.

The hunchback shrugged, a languorous rolling movement that made me a bit seasick. "Help yourself."

I turned to page two, found a story about the previous night's art auction, in which the Ricketts zombie puppies painting sold to a private collector for two hundred thousand dollars. Sheyenne had received the call that morning while I was at the Hope & Salvation mission; she calculated that Chambeaux & Deyer's one-third commission would be enough to pay off my outstanding funeral expenses and also provide ample operating cash for the business.

Below the story, a quarter-page ad gushed about the imminent release of JLPN's new Fresh Loam product line, posting a toll-free number for a full range of free samples.

Seeing me at the counter, Albert shuffled around the kitchen wall and stepped up to me, swaying on his feet. I could smell the aroma around him, but I wasn't one to complain.

"What's the lunch special today, Albert?" I asked.

"Lunch special," was all he said.

"Different from yesterday's?"

"Lunch special."

"Sounds good. I'll have that—the zombie special. And a cup of black coffee."

Next to me, without a word, the hunchback turned the page of his newspaper and studied the classified ads.

Albert shuffled off without acknowledging me, but I knew my order had lodged somewhere in what was left of his brain. He returned a few minutes later with a mug of coffee that sloshed on the counter when he set it down. Ghouls weren't known for their social graces or their dexterity. Neither were zombies, but I was glad to be on the high-functioning end of the spectrum. I lifted the cup and took a sip of coffee. It tasted flat and bitter at the same time; maybe it was me, maybe it was the coffee.

Now that Sheyenne had compiled my old cases, I took the time to ponder them while I waited for the food, mulling over what person, event, or bit of data might be connected to my own murder.

Back at the corner booth with the necromancers, Esther the waitress let out a howl of laughter loud enough that two werewolves at another table perked up before returning to their conversation. I glanced over, and one of the bald, sallow wizards looked at me. He could move one eye independently of the other, but when I met his gaze and didn't flinch, the eyeball drifted back to the harpy waitress.

The necromancers' guild didn't like me either. About five years ago, an ambitious rabbi had brought a clay golem to life by placing an Amulet of Animation (where do they get these names?) on the golem's chest. When a necromancer stole the amulet—thereby rendering the golem lifeless—the rabbi hired me to get it back. Pure detective work.

Robin, meanwhile, got on her legal high horse over the crime and as soon as I identified the perpetrator, she demanded that the DA file murder charges against the necromancer, because by stealing the Amulet of Animation, he had robbed the golem of life. The rabbi added his two cents to the case, insisting that the Amulet itself was an extremely valuable object, and he wanted grand theft added to the charges against the necromancer.

It seemed an open-and-shut case. Everything was going fine until I succeeded in stealing back the Amulet. (Definitely not an evening I would like to repeat; necromancers are abysmal housekeepers.) I retrieved the Amulet, and Robin presented the evidence to Judge Gemma Hawkins, who took one look at the mystical artifact and determined that it was mere cheap costume jewelry made of plastic and tin with gold paint. Worth about ten bucks. Grand theft charges dismissed.

Also, once the Amulet of Animation was restored to the golem's chest, he came back to life again, good as new. So the judge dropped the murder charge as well: no victim.

But Robin refused to let the case go—Justice had to be served. She submitted a succession of post-trial motions. She filed a suit on behalf of the golem for personal injury and negligent infliction of emotional distress, which the judge dismissed because she could not rule that the golem was a "person." Next, Robin demanded monetary damages to reimburse the rabbi for the lost value of the golem's services during the days when he was no longer animated. In exasperation, Judge Hawkins relented; she reprimanded the necromancer and made him pay a small fine, which Robin then appealed for a higher amount.

I had the easy part. All I did was break into a necromancer's lair in the middle of the night and steal a sacred object....

My blue plate special arrived. Sliced grayish meat swimming in an unappetizing sauce that had already congealed enough to form scabs. When Albert set down the plate, one of the maggots dropped out of his nose and into the gravy.

Not what I had ordered. "I think you gave me the ghoul special, Albert."

He looked down, focused on the food. "Sorry." He took it away.

Next to me, the hunchback was reading the sports scores.

"How did Notre Dame do?" I asked.

He slowly turned and looked at me through his round spectacles. "Do you have any idea how many times I've heard that joke?"

"Sorry, I'm a detective, not a comedian."

When Albert brought back the correct plate, I concentrated on my lunch, cutting a chunk of meat and popping it into my mouth, chewing as I considered the cases again. Somehow I couldn't believe that the rabbi or even the necromancer had any motive to shoot me. One down. Only about ninety-nine more cases to go through.

I finished my lunch in a hurry, paid the tab at the cash register, and returned to the counter to leave a two-dollar tip for Esther, even though she hadn't spoken a word to me. Maybe that was why I *did* leave her a tip.

I left the diner and headed out into the streets. I had work to do that afternoon.

CHAPTER 16

That afternoon I turned my attention to investigating Miranda Jekyll's case, revisiting my previous surveillance of her husband back when I was a living, breathing private eye. I had no doubt the man was scum, but so were a lot of people. It isn't always illegal. I had to catch him at something else.

The corporate president and CEO hadn't left his offices in two days, except to be transported in his black limo back and forth from the factory and the Jekyll mansion in a high-rent, guarded area outside the Unnatural Quarter. Earlier in the case, I had shadowed Jekyll for weeks to catch him going out on his extracurricular expeditions. (He was a singularly uninteresting man.)

This time, I wanted to get my ducks in a row before I started shooting.

Robin was preoccupied in her office writing a brief, so I told Sheyenne where I was going, then borrowed the keys to Robin's car.

Since I live and work in the Quarter, where most of my clients are, I rarely need to drive. However, the municipal dump is on the outskirts of the city, so I drove.

Even though I'm a zombie, my driver's license remains valid—a landmark case that Robin herself had pushed through the court system. However, I was required to reapply and take another driving test shortly after returning from the grave. I memorized the traffic rules and passed the written part of the test, but no one should have to go through an actual driving examination more than once. Parallel parking had always been a challenge for me, even when I was alive.

The Department of Motor Vehicles driving-test administrator was a rotund balding man who perspired profusely and seemed very uncomfortable to have to sit in the front seat with an undead applicant. He rolled down both windows and breathed as if he were either aroused or hyperventilating.

I performed my hand signals by the book, drove properly on one-way streets, executed a perfect Y-turn, and, with a generous amount of open curb, managed to parallel park. I left more than the preferred gap between the tires and the curb, but the DMV test administrator called it good enough and marked on his clipboard. If he failed me, he knew I would just reapply, and he was anxious for the test to be over. I got my renewed license.

Robin owned a rusted-out Ford Maverick two-tone (three tones, if you count the rust as a separate color). The original paint job was a brilliant lime green that had faded to a color more akin to snot. The engine puttered and snickered, but the muffler wasn't too loud, and at least the car ran. Sheyenne decided to dub the Maverick the "Pro Bono Mobile."

I drove out of town. The landfill's euphemistic name—the Metropolitan Pre-Used Resource Depository, according to the sign—was a reflection of some deluded city councilman's idea of beautifying an eyesore without actually changing anything but the name. Sanitation trucks from all over the city, both the Unnatural Quarter and the natural populated areas, poured their refuse here until high mounds of bagged garbage, loose litter, discarded furniture, and cast-off machinery formed an exotic artificial mountain range. Foul-smelling organic stuff belched and burbled as it rotted. Dried paper and cardboard whispered around in updraft circles as if stirred by a witch's broom.

For some mysterious, and therefore suspicious, reason, Harvey Jekyll had come out here late at night, alone and secretive, and I'd followed him. He must have delivered something that he didn't want a sanitation engineer, or even his own henchmen, to know about. And that made it very interesting to me ... although shady company dealings would not necessarily help Miranda Jekyll get a good divorce settlement.

Nevertheless, I wanted to find out what he'd been doing. Since I had no particular desire to wade through the mounds of piled garbage, I went to the man who might have some idea what Jekyll was up to.

The dump manager lived in his own double-wide house trailer parked in the foothills of the ever-changing debris landscape. The trailer had plywood for windows, sheet metal for an awning, and two old and bent folding lawn chairs so that he could sit outside and watch the rot.

After parking in the dirt clearing in front of the trailer, I climbed out of the Maverick and slammed the creaky car door. Three large flakes of rust broke off the driver's side door and fell to the ground; rust was basically the only thing holding Robin's car together. I knew what Sheyenne would have said: If Robin didn't do so much work for free, Chambeaux & Deyer would be able to afford a decent company car. Maybe our cut from the Ricketts art auction would be enough to upgrade.

I called out, "Hey, Mel, you in there?" I heard movement inside the trailer, and the door swung wide open with a bang because one of the hinges was loose and the air-piston door stop had broken off.

A hulking zombie—one of the putrefying kind—stepped onto the front step, swayed, caught his balance, then got his other foot on solid ground. "Dan Chambeaux! How are you, bud?"

"Just great, Mel." I don't know how he could be so cheery with his body falling apart like that. "How's life treating you?"

"Just as good the second time around as it was the first. Let's see where karma takes me this time."

I've mentioned Mel before: He was one of my very first cases, when his family hired me to find him, but then decided they didn't want him back after all. Mrs. Saldana had helped Mel get his job as landfill manager, and he loved the work. I had stopped by to see him often over the years.

Sometimes on my visits he'd invite me inside, and we would sit, holding highball glasses filled with ginger ale—not because Mel couldn't afford real booze, but because in life he'd been a recovering alcoholic. Even though dead, he didn't want to fall off the wagon, just on general principles. On a bowed shelf above his sofa, sandwiched between two wooden bookends, was an array of old used paperbacks, self-help books that he read with great interest.

Now that I'd also come back from the grave, Mel and I had more in common. Seeing me, he reached out and pumped my hand. I cringed at his strength. "Careful, Mel! Don't do any damage—it's hard to fix."

"Sorry, bud. I just like to have visitors. We zombies gotta stick together. We're blood brothers—or we would be, if anything was still pumping."

"I guess we're embalming-fluid brothers." He grinned at that. "I've got a few questions to ask you about a case. Maybe you could help me?"

"Feel free to ask anything, bud," Mel said. "You already helped me out so much. It's what friends do for each other."

Before I could inquire about Harvey Jekyll, I heard a loud rustling from the garbage embankment. Bloated black plastic bags were nudged aside, and I saw a huge rodent with bright beady eyes tunneling its way out of the pile like a gigantic mole—a rat the size of a German shepherd.

"Holy crap, Mel! What is that thing?"

Mel whistled to the emerging rat and slapped the thighs of his stained pants. "Here, boy! Come on." He was grinning. "That one's Spot, I think. Or it could be Fido. The third one's Rover. I haven't named the other ones yet."

"Other ones? How many are there?"

"It's a *dump*, bud. There's bound to be rats. And it's a big dump, so why wouldn't we expect big rats?"

The gargantuan rat waddled forward, enormously fat, no doubt because of all the garbage available to eat. Mel patted the brown bristly fur on its head, scratched behind the pink ears. The rat turned to regard me, snuffling, its whiskers twitching.

Two other enormous rodents followed the first out of the trash tunnel. Mel laughed and patted all three. "No, no treats for you today."

I didn't think monstrous mutated rats were an aftereffect of the Big Uneasy, but I couldn't be sure. "This is … unsettling, Mel. Why do they grow so big?" I had never much liked rats.

"Oh, probably because of the toxic waste dumped out there. I try to bury it deep, but sometimes the containers leak." He shrugged. "And then what are you going to do?"

I sensed there was more to the story, but wasn't sure I wanted to know the answer. Mel lowered his voice, kneeling down so that he could keep scratching the three giant rats that jostled around him for attention like eager puppies. "Every private citizen who comes here pays a dumping fee. I get all sorts of people and all sorts of trash. You never know what you'll find. Manna from heaven, or just garbage from the city."

The big zombie picked up a broken pipe from the ground, cocked back his arm, and flung it twirling out into the mounds of garbage. "Fetch!"

The three huge rats bounded after the pipe, scampering up the piled trash bags.

He took a seat in one of the wobbly lawn chairs in front of his trailer. "This is a place where people dispose of things, whatever they want to hide. Including bodies. And if somebody slips me an extra 'discretionary fee,' then I'll make sure no one ever finds whatever they want to get rid of."

I took a seat in the other bent folding chair. "I'm trying to track down something that was delivered here a little while before I was killed. Do you know Harvey Jekyll? Big corporate exec who runs Jekyll Lifestyle Products and Necroceuticals."

"Oh, yeah!" Mel beamed, showing crooked brown teeth. "A big shot from the factory in the city. He's been here. An uptight fellow, doesn't seem to like being around zombies. Now that I think of it ..." Mel scratched his head a little too vigorously and a clump of dark hair came off on his fingernail. "I can't picture him being comfortable around anyone."

"So you've seen him come out here?"

"Sure, bud. It's just business ... but none of *my* business, if you know what I mean."

I perked up, leaned closer, not sure the rickety lawn chair would support me. "What does he drop off? Can you show me where it is?"

Mel looked very sad. "You know I love you, bud, but he pays me to hide 'em, not share 'em."

I reached in my pocket, felt around for my wallet. "Maybe I could pay you more."

"I doubt it, but that wouldn't be fair or honest anyway. It upsets karma. If I break a trust like that, then who else can trust me?"

I decided to use the guilt card, embalming-fluid brothers and all. "Come on, Mel—who found you sleeping in an alley and brought you back to your family? Who put you in touch with Mrs. Saldana?"

His shoulders slumped. "You did, bud. And I guess I owe you."

"I can't even say for sure if this is important," I said. "But I've got to know. I'll leave your name out of it."

Mel gazed off into the garbage ridges around the trailer. "Okay, every once in a while Mr. Jekyll delivers a drum or two of toxic chemicals, experimental mixtures from his factory. Needs to get rid of the junk, but doesn't want to fill out all the paperwork. It all smells like perfume to me." He sniffed under his arms. "I put on JLPN deodorant every day. He gave me a lifetime supply. Want some?"

"Never use the stuff." Now I understood why Jekyll would come all the way out here, by himself, late at night. "Thanks for the conversation, Mel. You've helped me fill in a few blanks."

"Anytime, bud. Care to come inside for a non-drink?"

"Not this time. Other things to do." I wanted to go back to Sheldon Fennerman's apartment, talk to the landlord about the missing vampires, keep an eye on his place. "I've got a stakeout to set up before sunset."

"Suit yourself. You know where to find me." He shook my hand, then settled back into the folding chair.

I climbed into the rusty Pro Bono Mobile and started the engine (after two tries). The tires crunched as I executed a perfect three-point Y-turn—the DMV test instructor would have been impressed—and drove away from the dump.

CHAPTER 17

Here in the Unnatural Quarter, the best time for a stakeout (and suspicious human activity) is the lazy middle of an afternoon, in the hours before sunset—when the night dwellers haven't yet begun to stir and when daytimers are still at their jobs. If Straight Edge was going to do something stupid at Sheldon Fennerman's place, this was the likeliest time of day for it.

I arrived at the brownstone, knowing the skittish vampire should have been sound asleep inside. I made sure his front door was locked, checked the bars in place over the windows. As I guessed, the place was plugged up tighter than a constipated yak. Safe enough.

I walked around the block with a slow shuffling gait. In this neighborhood, an aimless zombie was by no means unusual, and I wasn't going to attract any attention. I passed through the garbage-strewn side alley, saw the clumsy spray-painted letters—*Eat Wood* and *Feel My Shaft*. I still wasn't convinced they were meant as threats against vampires.

I exited the alley, turned left on a connecting street, and went back up the block until I came back around to Sheldon's front door again. Still quiet, nothing happening. Time to talk to the landlord.

I knocked on the door of the brownstone next door. A lumpy, troll-like man answered the door, or maybe he was actually a troll; he lived in a shadowy apartment, the closest thing to an underground lair that a one-bedroom flat could be. When I flashed my PI credentials and asked about his previous vampire tenants, he shrugged his knobby shoulders. "Gone. No notice, no forwarding address."

"Did they actually move away, or did they just disappear?"

"Don't know." His yellow eyes shone like flashlights with weak batteries. "The tenants left a few things, not worth much. Nothing I could sell, nothing I could eat."

"Fly-by-nights? Did they owe you any back rent?"

"No. Vampires are good tenants, always pay on time. They left me their security deposits. Just moved out, I think."

In the back room of the flat, behind a closed door, I could hear a whimper, muffled screams, the sounds of a struggle. The troll shot an annoyed look over his shoulder. "Gotta go now. I'm fixing dinner." He tried to close the door in my face, but I got my shoe in the crack first.

I pushed with enough force to knock the troll backward and barged into the apartment. He yelped, "Hey, you can't come in here unless you've got a warrant!"

I swiveled my head down. "Do I look like I'm official law enforcement?" Seeing my expression, the troll scuttled away from me. He looked like a reject from a gargoyle-figurine factory.

The struggles and garbled whimpering came from behind a closed bathroom door. I popped the door open and saw a redheaded beanpole kid, no older than twenty, with duct tape over his mouth and his wrists tied, shoved into the corner. The bathtub was a large, deep whirlpool model, outfitted with extra heaters. It burbled, filled not with bubble bath, but with hot deep-frying oil.

The beanpole kid tried to yell through the duct tape, straining so hard I thought he might burst a blood vessel. He wore a bright red T-shirt with a straight white line down the middle, like a guide mark for a chainsaw murderer to cut him in half. I'd seen the stupid logo before, which meant he was a member of Straight Edge.

"You can't just go grabbing people for snacks," I said to the troll.

He stood just outside the bathroom door, sheepish. "A guy's gotta eat."

"This one wouldn't taste good anyway—too bitter."

I untied the kid's wrists. Even while I was rescuing him, the redhead seemed terrified of me; he looked as if he'd rather insult me than thank me for saving his life. I decided to keep the duct tape over his mouth for now.

The troll sagged his warty shoulders, sullen. "That processed-chicken stuff doesn't taste like human, no matter what the ads say."

"Consider it a restricted diet." I yanked the duct tape off the redheaded kid's mouth in one big tear, and he howled in pain; on the bright side, he wouldn't have to shave for a while.

"I *hate* you disgusting things!" the kid wailed at both of us and bolted out of the apartment in a gangly gallop of long arms and legs.

The sullen troll made his way to the small kitchen. "I guess I'll just get something out of the freezer."

O O O

Back on patrol, I shuffled around the block two more times, still not convinced that Sheldon Fennerman had anything to worry about.

In the month since returning from the grave, I had easily fallen back into my regular routine. Nothing much had changed from when I was a living, breathing private investigator—a sad commentary on how bright my life had been before....

After my death, the difficult transition period was probably tougher on Robin than it was on me. Poor kid, she'd been miserable.

I had completely missed the drama of my funeral, being dead at the time. I didn't have to listen to the graveside service. I didn't have to deal with undertakers, select the casket or flower arrangements—Robin took care of all that. Later, she told me that just getting through those few days was a harder battle than any legal case she'd ever fought.

My BHF McGoo helped her out, offered her a shoulder to cry on, and by then Sheyenne's ghost was also there. Without me in the office, Robin threw herself back into her cases, filing more briefs and appeals, appearing in court, speaking with a fiery vehemence on behalf of her clients. I would have loved to see that.

But I slept through it all.

When I finally woke up and clawed my way up through the soft dirt, I pushed aside the newly laid sod and stood there in the graveyard trying to figure out what the hell had happened. I felt like a fraternity pledge who had been given a roofie and been forced to endure some sort of bizarre hazing ritual.

I heard a stirring nearby and saw a grasping hand thrust out from another fresh grave, like in a scene from a classic horror movie. I bent down and started to dig, helping my new friend out of the ground. Together, reanimated and disoriented, we figured out what had happened, brushed each other off, exchanged names in an awkward sort of camaraderie. (Unfortunately, I hadn't been buried with any business cards in the pocket of my funeral suit.) Then we headed back toward the city and tried to rejoin what we remembered of our former lives.

When I shambled back into the office, Sheyenne's ghost let out a little squeal of delight. I was a bit surprised to find her still working her job, since she'd come there to be with me. Robin burst out of her office, still puffy-eyed and haggard-looking; one glance at me and, I swear, she fainted dead away. Nobody was expecting me to return from the grave. At one in seventy-five, statistics weren't in my favor. Then again, as a murder victim, I had a better-than-average chance of getting back on my feet.

Robin recovered herself and shook her head in disbelief. Tears streamed down her face. "I can't believe you're back!" She ran toward me, ignored my mud-encrusted suit jacket, clumpy hair, and pale skin, and threw her arms around me anyway in a big enthusiastic hug. She was sniffling.

I wrapped my arms around her. "I'm back, don't worry. There's still so much to do, and I couldn't break up the team, could I?"

"We're too good together, Beaux," Sheyenne added. "And now there's more than one ticked-off unnatural trying to solve a murder case."

Even though I was disoriented, I wanted to reassure Robin, so I lurched toward my office, leaving a trail of dirt clods on the floor. "How long have I been gone? Any leads? I want to get right back in the saddle."

Robin kept crying for half an hour. It was only later that I learned she hadn't really shed any tears before that, too worried about holding it together.

They had buried me in my best formal suit—okay, my *only* formal suit—and after clawing my way out of the dirt I needed to get it cleaned in order to look respectable. (In fact, it still hung in the closet in its protective plastic bag from the dry cleaner; my sport jacket was all I needed for daily use.) Robin had hired only the very best undertaker for me, and the embalming job was top-notch. Sure, my skin had a waxy tone, and shadows hung under my eyes, but I looked good for the most part, and I intended to stay that way.

Using official company stationery, we sent out a formal notice to all our clients, explaining that "despite my recent setback" I was back on the job and intended to devote the same attention to each one of my prior cases. Even though I was fundamentally different now, I belonged in the Unnatural Quarter. If anything, now that I was one of them, unnaturals would be less reticent to engage the services of Chambeaux & Deyer. I got back to work—business as unusual, you might say....

It was late afternoon now, and Sheldon would soon be stirring from his coffin, if he wasn't already awake with his off-kilter sleep schedule. On my fourth circuit of the block, I came around the corner and startled two young human men in front of Sheldon's brownstone. Both wore the same red T-shirts as the troll's hostage. One kid had descended the steps to the vampire's barred front door, while the other stood at the front wall wielding a can of black spray paint. He had managed to write *Bloodsucker, Suck My* when I called out, "Hey, stop!"

The two turned, startled, and I recognized the type. They weren't burly, muscle-bound skinheads who would bash in your head for so much as thinking a liberal sentiment. No, these were sneering misfits, big heroes when they discussed grand plans in their mothers' basements, but they rarely had the guts for face-to-face confrontation.

I lurched forward. "That vampire's under my protection!"

The two young men bolted, and one of them gave me the finger. Hooting like nervous hyenas, they dashed around the corner. I could have run after them, but my main priority was to make sure Sheldon was all right.

I went down the steps to the front door and saw that the would-be bullies had left two fresh oak stakes thrust between the bars. Sure that Sheldon must be awake from the ruckus and probably cowering inside his apartment, I knocked on the door. "Sheldon! It's Dan Chambeaux. You're safe now."

I knew it would take at least an hour to talk him down again.

CHAPTER 18

The red fondue pot was still on the table, and this time I didn't feel right about declining Sheldon's invitation. He was a nervous wreck, although vindicated now that I'd caught the vandals in the act, which proved he hadn't been imagining his peril. (I still wasn't convinced, however, that the Straight Edgers were capable of true violence, such as successive vampire slayings—and vampires weren't easy to kill.)

With frenetic movements, Sheldon went through the ritual of making melted cheese for fondue. At first, I thought he was still jittery from the threats, then I realized he was just excited to have company. After he had grated and heated three different cheeses, added kirschwasser and nutmeg to the fondue pot (I wasn't surprised that he skipped the tradition of rubbing the pot with garlic), he sliced chunks of stale bread and green apples, then sat across from me.

We set about committing fondue.

Sheldon chattered about his life, both before and after becoming a vamp. He talked about books he'd read, Broadway shows he'd seen. Ever the polite host, he asked about my life and hobbies—subjects I rarely discussed with clients. I didn't have much to say. While Sheldon talked about himself at novel length, my answers were more like short stories or vignettes.

By the time we used up the chunks of bread and wiped clean every smear of melted cheese in the pot, Sheldon had relaxed again. I realized that this was the best meal I'd had since I'd died. I tried to take my leave, but the vampire insisted we play a game of cribbage first. I fidgeted. "I haven't played since I was a boy, don't even remember the rules."

"Don't worry, I'm a good teacher." Though I tried to refuse again, he remained persistent, and I did feel sorry for the guy, after all.

One game turned into two, and he kept talking all the while. I thought of his vampire neighbors whom he had coerced into coming over for a dinner party, or to play cards, or to have a book club discussion, just to be polite; then they'd receive another invitation from Sheldon, and another, and another. I was pretty sure I had solved the case of the disappearing neighbors, though I didn't have the heart to explain it to Sheldon.

After the second game of cribbage, I finally convinced him that I had another appointment. "Remember, Sheldon—I'm an undead private investigator, and I have more people to help, just like you."

He looked forlorn as he stood at the front door. "You could always send them over here for a game or ..."

"You'll be all right, Sheldon," I assured him. "It's full dark outside, and the Straight Edgers don't dare go out in the city at night. Too many unnaturals abroad who don't appreciate their opinions. You have nothing to worry about."

Mrs. Saldana had given me the address of the new Straight Edge headquarters here in town, and now that I had seen them harassing Sheldon (not to mention rescued one of them from the troll's hot-tub deep fryer), I intended to pay them a visit first thing in the morning. But I needed to get something from Robin ahead of time.

O O O

I may be undead, but I do try to take care of myself and keep my body in shape. Three times a week I work out at the All-Day/All-Nite Fitness Center, a gym designed for unnaturals of all circadian rhythms. I have a membership and a locker there with worn sweats that smell mustier than my normal clothes.

In the locker room I changed quickly. I've never been one for exhibitionism among other naked guys in a gym, the sidelong glances to see whose is bigger and taking smug reassurance that at least yours is average or better.

In the showers behind the lockers, I heard the water running, and steam wafted up like fog on an old English moor. Long strips of cloth had been draped over several of the clothes hooks on the wall, a few frayed ends trailing on the floor. Over the spray, I could hear a cackling old

Mayan mummy soaping himself up and singing in the shower. Mummies enjoy the temporary rehydration they get from the water. This one's name was Ralph, and I'd seen him before sans wrappings—not a sight I wanted to repeat. Many unnaturals are shriveled up and desiccated in plenty of unappetizing ways.

In the bathroom in front of a mirror, a fully transformed werewolf stood with a white towel wrapped around his waist; he was using a blow dryer the size of an aircraft engine to blast the fur all over his body. We nodded to each other in a brusque guy greeting, then I exited into the workout room.

One section of the gym has free weights, resistance machines, pec presses, leg presses, and racks with every possible workout attachment. Treadmills and recumbent bikes line a mirrored wall, with an equal number on the opposite side of the room facing a blank black wall for the vamps, who have no use for mirrors. Though it was still two hours before midnight, I counted fifteen patrons using the equipment, getting in a workout before the night life got into full swing.

In a gym, you become accustomed to the regulars and recognize one another. Sometimes you know names, while other times you just think of the other patrons as "the guy who always hogs the bench press," or "the one who doesn't wipe down the recumbent bike after he's done with it," or "the chick in pink Spandex," or, worse, "the chick who should *never* be seen wearing pink Spandex."

I intended to work out alone, since Sheldon had given me a week's worth of conversation, but when I saw an acquaintance using a treadmill on the mirrorless side of the room, I decided to be sociable after all. She might actually have some information I could use.

She was big, buff, and athletic, and would have been intimidating even if she weren't a vampire. As usual, she had the treadmill set to its maximum incline and speed. If you had to bet, you might have guessed her name was Butch, but you'd be wrong. Her honest-to-goodness birth name was Tiffany, and she was damned proud of it.

I got on the treadmill beside hers, powered it up, and began at warm-up speed to loosen the stiffness in my knees. Tiffany gave me a businesslike nod. "Chambeaux." She wasn't even panting. The treadmill's maximum setting seemed a stroll in the park for her. "Healthy body, healthy mind."

I was proud of myself for working out three days a week. Tiffany, on the other hand, was one of those exercise addicts who never missed a night; nevertheless … I couldn't argue with the obvious results. I gradually increased my treadmill's speed as I got warmed up.

Our workout routines coincided often enough that Tiffany and I were cordial, but I didn't know very much about her. Looking at her physique and her "you want a piece of me?" demeanor, I realized she might be a very good person to have on speed dial. I might need to hire extra muscle if this business with the Straight Edgers got ugly. "Tiffany, have you ever considered doing freelance security work?"

"Me, a security guard? When you mix monsters and security guards, it never ends well. Why do you ask?"

"Just a case I'm working on. A human-supremacist group is harassing a vampire client of mine."

Tiffany looked as if she'd swallowed a mouthful of gangrene-tainted blood. "Straight Edge jerks."

"Have they ever bothered you?"

She reacted as if I'd insulted her. "Bunch of pussies. They're all about juvenile scare tactics, like throwing eggs at windows or toilet-papering houses. Show them a little fang, and they pee their pants and run away." She chuckled. "They should piss holy water with all their self-righteousness, but it smells just like regular piss. Who's the client?"

The treadmill program accelerated, and I had to work hard to keep up. "Sheldon Fennerman."

Tiffany lit up. "I know him. He helped me with the interior design of my place. Sweet guy." Her expression darkened. "Just the sort of person those bullies would pick on. Assholes … but I wouldn't worry about it too much. The Straight Edgers are about as dangerous as a dog turd on a jogging path."

"You don't think they'll follow through on their threats?"

"Somebody needs to take them out behind the woodshed. If they ever caused real harm, it would be by accident. Don't lose any sleep over them."

I continued to run on the treadmill, keeping up a good pace now. "I don't sleep much anyway."

CHAPTER 19

The men's locker room was empty, now that Ralph the Mayan mummy had finished his shower, and the werewolf was gone, although he had left drifts of long brown hairs on the floor, in the sink, and on the countertop. I took a quick rinse-off just to freshen up, dried myself gently so as not to slough off any skin, and dressed in my street clothes.

As a convenience to the All-Day/All-Nite patrons, a variety of JLPN shampoos, cream rinses, and body washes were provided in the showers. By the sinks and mirrors, I found spritzers of deodorant and small bottles of colorful colognes and aftershaves, each with a splashy sticker announcing *Coming Soon: New Fresh Loam Scent!* I declined to use any of it. Who was I trying to impress, anyway?

I had a long night ahead of me. I considered heading off to Harvey Jekyll's mansion, where I could crawl into the bushes and keep an eye out for nefarious goings-on, but I doubted Jekyll would be so obvious. Or I could return to Basilisk, talk to the bartender and Ivory to ferret out more information about who had poisoned Sheyenne. Or who had shot me.

When I emerged onto the main thoroughfare in Little Transylvania, I immediately spotted the plaid sport jacket. Since I knew Brondon Morris went about his nightly rounds, it was no surprise to see him out here, but I didn't expect him to be walking with another man of smaller build in a low-slouched hat and a trench coat with the collar turned up.

Instead of being his usual cheery self, handing out samples and greeting customers, Brondon was definitely sneaking around. The two men scuttled down the street, hugging the night shadows, which were plentiful. When they turned down a side alley, they acted like two lungfish crawling out of the mud, scurrying across dry land, then ducking into a brackish pool on the other side.

Very interesting.

After my workout, I was limbered up, and thanks to the shower and reasonably clean clothes, I had no particular smell about me, so I was able to follow them without being noticed. Halfway down a dark street, Brondon paused, holding up his hand, and his friend froze. I melted into the shadows beside a rusty drainpipe and an overflowing Dumpster. In the pale light of the waxing moon, I caught a glimpse of the mysterious man's face between the slouched hat and the upturned collar.

Harvey Jekyll! I had struck the jackpot.

Though I prefer to achieve results through sheer detective prowess, I don't complain when dumb luck takes a hand. This opportunity had fallen right on top of me like a drunken lap dancer in a strip club.

Brondon and Jekyll moved off again, and I followed at a discreet distance. The two men haunted the back streets, going to places I never would have ventured when I was still alive—empty buildings and warehouses, long rows of storage units, a lot filled with old delivery trucks. Other than a few bats flying overhead, nothing stirred out here. The street was like a ghost town, and I had to drop back.

Far from the crowded main avenues, Brondon moved with a jaunty step, and Harvey Jekyll strutted along, anxious to be somewhere. Ahead, I watched the pair of figures approach a large boarded-up warehouse with a flat asphalt roof and painted letters peeling off a cinder-block wall:

CHANEY & SON
BODY SNATCHERS FOR HIRE

At first glance the place looked as if it had gone out of business long before the Big Uneasy, but as I studied it with greater care, noted the precisely arranged old trash along the walls and the weeds that grew up between stones and chinks in the wall, I suspected that this ramshackle look was a cultivated appearance. It looked too pat, too staged.

When I edged closer, I accidentally kicked a dented beer can, making a clatter. (Have you ever seen a graceful zombie?) The two men whirled, and I melted into the shadows. I held my breath, metaphorically speaking. Where was an easily startled alley cat when you needed one? Eventually the men moved on.

Brondon Morris and Harvey Jekyll walked up to a rectangle of plywood hung on hinges, a makeshift door. Jekyll rapped on it with his knuckles, and the hinged plywood swung open, spilling yellow glow into the night. Both men shielded their eyes from the glare.

A large figure loomed in the doorway, a linebacker-sized human wearing a business suit. Behind the door guard, I spotted dozens of men inside the warehouse. I heard a buzz of conversation. A party where no one seemed to be having fun.

The door guard recognized the two new arrivals and stepped aside to let them into the warehouse. Before closing the plywood door, the big suit scanned the darkness, though he couldn't possibly have seen anything with his eyes accustomed to the bright interior lights. He yanked the door shut.

I crept up to the Chaney & Son warehouse and discovered that the windows weren't just boarded up: They had been packed with insulation, so that I could hear only faint muffled voices coming from within, no actual words. I approached the plywood door, hoping to discern words through the crack, but again no luck. So I melted back into the dark and waited for hours, watching, just to see what might happen.

Just before dawn, the door opened again and three disguised men emerged, scuttled around the corner, and disappeared down another street. I didn't recognize them. Two more nondescript men left in a different direction, then another trio, and the rest came out by pairs. I counted twenty attendees at the mysterious meeting, but with all the hats and upturned collars, I had no idea which ones were Brondon and Jekyll when they left. The perfume salesman must have traded his loud plaid sports jacket for a trench coat.

The burly doorman was the last to leave. He turned off the lights, shoved the plywood door shut, then fixed two padlocks in place.

Miranda Jekyll would find this very interesting. I decided to dig into the background of the Chaney & Son building, see if I found any connections to Harvey Jekyll.

Preferably something illegal.

CHAPTER 20

Robin met me as soon as I came into the office next morning, wearing that cockeyed optimist smile of hers, along with a clean gray pantsuit; her dark hair was pulled back in a thick neat braid. She looked fresh and ready to take on the world, full of energy, even though I knew she'd been up most of the night.

In addition to sharing office space and splitting the lease, we each had a small apartment upstairs, a cramped place not much bigger than a coffin; we could have knocked down the adjoining wall to make the combined room as large as a walk-in closet, but the building owner wouldn't allow it. Robin and I spent most of our time at work anyway; I'd never been much of a homebody, either before or after death, and Robin slept on the client sofa in her office as often as she crashed in her own bed.

In law school, she had been able to pull all-nighters: study, write a term paper, go to class in the morning, take an exam, hang out with friends in the afternoon, and party at night. I remember when I was that young, and that alive. McGoo and I had done it ourselves when we were in college. My "all-nighters" were different now.

Triumphant, Robin held an envelope in her hand. "It took me two hours, but I made Judge Hawkins see the light. You've got your restraining order." She often walked a fine line with the judge. Intent and cheerfully obsessive, she didn't realize that she could become a downright pest. But she usually got her way.

Sheyenne appeared, floating right through the wall. "I flitted to the courthouse and picked up the order, Beaux. We thought you'd like to deliver it to the Straight Edgers yourself."

I gave them an impressed nod. "I was going to scare them regardless, but it's nice to be packing some extra legal ammunition."

I paused to jot down basics about the Chaney & Son warehouse on a scrap of paper from Sheyenne's desk. "While I'm gone, pull the county records and see what you can find out about this building—who owns it, how long it's been empty, anything unusual about recent permits. Harvey Jekyll's involved in some suspicious activities there." I patted the envelope from Judge Hawkins. "Meanwhile, I've got a restraining order to deliver."

O   O   O

Normally, I wouldn't have given a second glance to the Straight Edge headquarters—an unmarked, run-down storefront whose windows bore the remnants of painted letters from a now-defunct political campaign. It was the sort of place used by accountants for a few months during tax season, after which it would remain empty but hopeful for the rest of the year.

The only sign in the window, designed to look like a No Trespassing sign, said, *Humans Only*, and below that, *Unnatural* = *Undesirable*. What a witty bunch.

I yanked open the door without knocking—what good was a knock going to do me?—and startled four people who were stuffing flyers into envelopes and painting large placards. The panicky group leaped to their feet and whirled around. One scrawny, mean-looking young woman, who clearly needed a boyfriend, and three equally scrawny and awkward young men, who clearly needed girlfriends, stared at me. I recognized the beanpole redheaded kid I had rescued from the troll landlord's dinner tub and the two punks who had vandalized Sheldon's brownstone. They all wore red T-shirts with the line down the chest. None of them looked to be older than twenty-one. I wondered if these punks comprised the whole organization, or if they just worked the day shift.

"Is this the zombie massage parlor?" I asked in a bright voice, feeling quite chipper. "My muscles are stiff."

"I'll turn you into a stiff," the beanpole snarled, trying to sound tough. He had red marks around his mouth from where I'd torn off the duct tape.

"Already been there," I said. "You forgot to thank me for saving you from the deep-fryer hot tub. Didn't your mother teach you manners?"

The Jane Fonda wannabe spoke. "Get out! You're not welcome here. Can't you read the sign? *Humans only*."

"The legal definition of 'human' is being challenged in the courts. My partner has set some remarkable precedents already. In the meantime, why not be inclusive? Embrace diversity."

The young man who had sprayed graffiti outside of Sheldon's home now puffed up his chest. "You can rot in hell!"

"I'd rather not rot anywhere." I strolled into the main room, and the four Straight Edgers cringed, as if afraid I intended to eat their brains. The posters they were making each had a straight unadorned line on a field of red; not much of a logo design.

With my cell phone I took a quick group shot of the four young activists. "Got your faces, just to verify you were here in the office. Now I need your names."

"What for?"

"I'm going to enter you into a sweepstakes."

Graffiti-boy looked ready to blurt out the information, but the scrawny woman snapped, "Don't tell him anything, Scott."

"Jeez, Priscilla, I wasn't going to!"

Then I glanced at the remaining two Straight Edgers and did my best bluff. "You others don't need to give me your names. We can bring charges against Scott and Priscilla, here."

The bitter young woman paled, while Scott looked tangled in knots. "It's Todd and Patrick!" he blurted.

"You bastard!" Todd, the beanpole, snarled at Scott.

"We all stick together," Priscilla said. "We're Straight Edge."

"What do you *want?*" demanded Patrick, the young man who had planted stakes at Sheldon's front door.

"You've been harassing a client of mine," I said. "A vampire."

"And? You unnaturals are all the same to us," sneered Priscilla. "You should just go … away."

"Go away—or else!" Patrick picked up one of the placards and held it like a shield, as if the sharpened wooden end would scare a zombie. He needed to do better research.

"I'm also here on behalf of the Hope and Salvation Mission, which was recently vandalized—I suspect you had something to do with that as well."

"You can't prove it," said Scott.

"Monster lover!" Todd said.

The young woman made a scoffing sound. "If we wanted to scare that goody-two-shoes old lady out of town, we'd take care of it ourselves, not hire a monster to do it."

I had to admit, that made sense.

Now that the conversation had stopped being amusing, I pulled the envelope from my pocket. "This restraining order has been duly signed by Judge Hawkins. All Straight Edge members are forbidden from approaching within fifty feet of Mr. Sheldon Fennerman's residence, Mr. Fennerman himself, or the Hope and Salvation Mission."

"This is bullshit," Todd snapped, then looked uncertainly at the young woman. His face flushed so red that his freckles disappeared in the noise. "Isn't it?"

Priscilla plucked the paper out of my hands, using just her fingertips as if disgusted to touch any object soiled by a zombie. As she read the words, the others peered closer, all four of them pooling their knowledge to understand the legal terminology. The young woman didn't sound so confident now. "It's infringing on our rights of free speech."

"File a complaint. My partner would love to put Mr. Fennerman on the stand, with a full jury of unnaturals, to determine just whose rights are being violated."

Priscilla spat on the floor in disgust; then, like a series of popcorn kernels popping, her three companions spat on the floor, imitating her. Personally, I thought it was silly. I glanced down at the spittle and phlegm, shaking my head. "And you folks say that zombies are filthy."

They glowered after me as I walked out the door. I was sure they'd spend the rest of the day fuming, engaging in vociferous imaginary arguments with me once I was out of earshot.

Now that I'd gotten a good look at Priscilla, Todd, Scott, and Patrick, I held them in even lower esteem. I could see why Tiffany at the gym didn't take Straight Edge seriously. I wondered if other members were more competent.

CHAPTER 21

I left the Straight Edge headquarters feeling good about myself, head held high. When I told Robin every little detail about the confrontation, I knew it would make her day; she'd probably do her victory dance.

When I came out onto the street, however, I sensed an odd tension in the air, one of those silent humming sensations that make you perk up, like all the friendly wild animals detecting a forest fire in a Disney cartoon. This didn't feel like the thrill of fear, though, but of hunger and keen interest.

Across the street I spotted the black-gowned, bristle-haired Mavis Wannovich walking along painfully on swollen legs, as if her ankles had filed notice that they didn't intend to support her body much longer. The enormous spotted sow, Alma, trotted alongside the witch. Mavis looked from side to side, glanced over her shoulder, and walked faster. I could see that both of them were on the verge of panic.

Behind the Wannovich sisters, shambling quickly to keep up, came a trio of zombies, their sunken eyes bright, hands outstretched in a grasping gesture. All three were ripe cases, at a stage where no amount of makeup or visits to the embalming parlor would reverse the putrefaction.

Farther along the sidewalk, the door of an office-supply store opened and a tall female vampire emerged, raising her nose to the air and sniffing as if someone had rung the dinner bell. A hairy half-transformed werewolf grocer in a wifebeater T-shirt sat in a folding chair outside his tiny tienda; he perked up as well, and his gaze fixed on the sow lumbering down the street. Lifting himself off the chair with a smooth motion, he began loping toward the witch and her sister.

Mavis picked up her pace, but I could see her wince with the effort. The zombies, vampire, and werewolf closed in.

I knew what was about to happen, and I had to stop it.

In order to live peacefully together, unnaturals had learned to control their base urges and get along with one another, though they tended to gather in the monster version of ethnic neighborhoods. Werewolves no longer killed human victims each full moon, vampires gave up drinking all but voluntarily donated blood, zombies and ghouls foreswore eating human flesh.

Most unnaturals, though, had not given up pork. The most devout black sorcerer or vampire kingpin might manage to block the urge to quaff virgin blood, but he couldn't resist the smell of frying bacon. Or fresh pork on the hoof.

Trotting down the sidewalk, Alma sniffed nervously from side to side. She let out an alarmed squeal, which only taunted the ever-growing crowd of hungry followers. Her sister struggled to keep up, but I could see they were in trouble.

I drew the .38 from my shoulder holster. As a private detective, I'd been licensed to carry a concealed weapon for years, and after my death, no one had tried to rescind the permit or request that I turn in my piece (so far). As far as I know, I'm the only undead private investigator who went back to the practice. Robin wasn't sure the handgun permit was still valid, after my death certificate was on file; she offered to clarify the issue by sending requests to the Bureau for a ruling, or at least a special exemption in my case, but I told her not to bother—in fact, after I saw the fiery glint in her eye, I *insisted* that she not bother. "Let me apologize later if I get caught," I'd said.

For my work in the Quarter, I keep the revolver loaded with silver-jacketed bullets, which are effective on a fair number of creatures. And if I have to fire on a regular human, the bullet part works just fine, silver or no silver.

The crowd increased as more unnaturals emerged from their lairs, and when the frightened sow squealed again, I pointed the .38 in the air, fired off a loud shot, then a second. The gunshots brought all movement on the street to a halt. I wove my way through the decrepit shamblers, sternly shook a finger at them, and glared at the vampire and werewolf.

Mavis took one look at me and almost melted with relief. "Mr. Chambeaux, are we glad to see you!"

"Looks like you could use an escort back home." I swept my gaze around the hungry faces that had poked out of doorways and converged on the sidewalk.

"Yes, please!"

Alma grunted.

I raised my voice to the crowd and coolly pointed the gun in a slow arc. "If anyone lays a hand or claw on either of my clients, you'll have to deal with me."

Mavis gathered her courage and shouted to the onlookers. "And if that doesn't work, I've got a spell book back home that'll turn you all into pigs … or something even less pleasant."

The unnaturals groaned and grumbled, glaring at me because I'd spoiled their snack. The sow snorted loudly, and then, to express her displeasure, she urinated a big puddle on the sidewalk.

Mavis was scandalized. "Shame on you, Alma!" But the pig seemed perfectly content and waddled forward with her sister and me.

"You'd both better go directly home," I said under my breath.

"I agree," the witch said, walking close beside me. "Alma and I used to have quite an active social life, but now you see why we rarely go out anymore. My sister isn't even viewed as human, just a potential smorgasbord of pork loins, ham, bacon, chitlins, and chops. Just look what that spell-book mistake has done! I wish we could make everyone see how terrible Howard Phillips Publishing is."

"Ms. Deyer filed a ringing complaint," I said. "Much more stern than the last one. I read it myself. Very powerful stuff. We'll see some results." *Eventually.*

The sow nudged into me with enough force to knock me off balance, but I kept my feet. Mavis let out a little laugh. "Alma's sweet on you. She told me."

The pig turned her massive head toward me, blinking her eyes. "She's a charming person," I said, "but I have a strict policy of never dating clients."

Alma sounded disappointed, but Mavis remained undeterred. "With a little encouragement, a love potion perhaps, maybe you'd change your mind."

"Let's just get you both safely back home," I said, politely declining their invitation to come inside for tea. "And next time, don't go outside without your spell books. I won't always be there to protect you."

CHAPTER 22

After walking the Wannovich sisters straight to their door like a gentleman, I was glad to be away from the tantalizing pork smell—I'm not completely immune either.

Heading back to the Chambeaux & Deyer offices, I heard the don't-mess-with-me voice of Officer McGoohan at the next corner as he chewed someone out. McGoo didn't have any children, but he would have done a good job bellowing "You kids quit roughhousing and give me some peace so I can watch the game!"

In front of a boarded-up lingerie store that had been empty for years, I saw the unmistakable plaid sport coat that identified Brondon Morris. Four workers clad in dark-blue JLPN company overalls had been busy pasting posters across the storefront.

"You can't post those here," McGoo said. "It's an eyesore."

In a wheedling but cheerful voice, Brondon responded, "It's just an advertisement, Officer. You can't prevent us from trying to sell our products. That's a restraint of free trade."

McGoo's voice rose as he continued to shake his head. "Take it up with a Constitutional lawyer. Meanwhile, let's pretend I'm a member of the Keep the Unnatural Quarter Beautiful committee. I'm not letting you just plaster that crap wherever you want."

The broadsheets advertised the upcoming release of the new line of necroceuticals. Poster after poster showed grinning vampires brushing their teeth, zombies spraying their underarms with aerosol deodorant, beautiful witches shampooing their hair with thick suds that foamed an unsettling shade of green, a husky male werewolf holding a bottle of cologne while two female werewolves, clearly in heat, sniffed his fur. Each poster said: *Call Our Toll-Free Number for a Free Sample Kit!*

"We spent a great deal of money printing these posters for the advertising blitz, Officer," Brondon insisted. "We're entitled to our right to publicity."

I stepped up and caught their attention. "I've got a colleague who might listen to your case, Mr. Morris. She's interested in theoretical and moral issues." It wasn't a serious suggestion; I doubted Robin would take Brondon Morris as a client anyway.

McGoo brightened as he saw me. "Dead Man Walking!"

Brondon Morris blinked at me, then scowled. "Thank you, Mr. Chambeaux, but I'd consider it a conflict of interest, in light of your firm's prior work to destroy the reputation of Jekyll Lifestyle Products and Necroceuticals."

I shrugged. "Just offering to help."

McGoo was not going to back down, I could see it in his eyes. "Look, Mr. Morris, I'm not saying that you can't advertise your products, only that you can't put *these* posters on *this* building. Did you get permission from the owner?"

Brondon was flustered. "The owner of this building has been dead for seven years. I checked."

"Are you sure he hasn't come back from the grave? Barring that, find one of his heirs."

The JLPN workers stood looking bored, holding stacks of posters and waiting for further instructions.

Brondon tried a different tack. "It'll only be for a few days, Officer. I promise, we'll take every poster down right after the product line is launched. We've already had a great financial setback because our first twenty thousand broadsheets had an unfortunate typo." He pointed toward the nearest one stapled to the boarded-up window. "A proofreader missed it, and the entire first printing came out offering a Free Sample *Kid*—which generated entirely the wrong kind of excitement among unnaturals! JLPN didn't notice until after we had distributed hundreds of the posters. We had to pulp them all and start from scratch."

McGoo looked sympathetic, but only a little. He turned to me. "What do you think, Shamble?"

"I'm biased. Our paralegal tried a sample of the Zom-Be-Fresh stuff back when she was still alive," I said. "It gave her a horrible rash."

"Horrible rash? Hmm, you think JLPN products contain a toxic substance?" McGoo asked. "Maybe I should have the department look into that. If the company is distributing dangerous—"

"We apologized for that!" Brondon said with a sniff. "But we have always made it quite clear that JLPN products are designed for unnaturals only. We're not responsible for improper use."

I was having fun, but I decided I had yanked Brondon's chain enough. "No need, McGoo. We did a chemical analysis from a lab we trust, but it came back negative. Zom-Be-Fresh contains nothing on the list of toxic or prohibited substances. Sheyenne just had an allergic reaction."

"I'm allergic to a few fragrances in toiletry items too," McGoo confessed. "That's why I don't use deodorant."

"Oh, *that's* why," I quipped.

McGoo barked orders to the overall-clad workers. "Tear those posters down and keep this plywood clean and beautiful. You're welcome to get written permission from other storefront owners, Mr. Morris, but don't just go poaching any blank wall space you find."

Though fuming, Brondon directed the workers to do as they were told.

As we stepped back to watch the cleanup project, McGoo asked conversationally, "Hey, Shamble, why do zombies pierce their nipples?" From the stupid grin on his face, I knew I didn't want to hear the answer. "To have a place to hang the air fresheners."

Instead of laughing, I decided to change the subject. "Any luck catching the big lummox that wrecked Mrs. Saldana's mission?"

"Not yet. And there've been three other incidents since then, major smashup jobs, and another dozen storefront windows shattered—meant to look like the work of our big brute, but I'm not so sure."

"Why else would somebody be smashing windows? Delinquents?" *Maybe the Straight Edgers?*

McGoo shrugged. "So far no suspects and no good leads. I don't know how such a huge creature can hide. You want to go out monster hunting with me late tonight?"

"Not really," I said.

"Suit yourself. You must have other fun things to do."

"Just cases, McGoo. Always cases."

CHAPTER 23

At Chambeaux & Deyer Investigations, we consider taking any case that involves human/unnatural relations, and sometimes we're hired to take the human side.

Sheyenne ushered in the new clients for their intake meeting. "Dan, Robin, this is Brad and Jackie Dorset, and their children Madison and Joshua."

Nice-looking human family: urban (or suburban) professionals, mom, dad, and the requisite two kids, probably a golden retriever at home. However, the Norman Rockwell family portrait stopped there: All of the Dorsets looked gaunt and haggard, their eyes bloodshot, as if they hadn't gotten sleep or a decent meal in ages. Accompanying them was a freelance medium they'd hired, but I wasn't impressed; if the medium's efforts had been successful, they wouldn't be here.

Brad automatically extended his hand, not seeming to realize that I was undead. My cold grip startled him.

Robin stepped up, smiling. "We're very pleased to meet you, Mr. and Mrs. Dorset."

"And I'm here in a professional capacity," said the medium. "Millicent Sanchez." She was a middle-aged woman with beautiful golden skin, and she wrapped her dark hair in a colorful red-and-green scarf. Silver hoop earrings dangled from her ears, and a crucifix the size of a deck of cards hung at her throat; so many silver bracelets lined each wrist that they looked like Slinkys crawling up her arms.

I realized that I had seen her previously. How can you forget all those silver bracelets? "We met before, Ms. Sanchez, back when I was alive. The ribbon-cutting ceremony for new wing of the Metropolitan Museum?"

She brightened. "Ah, yes, of course! I was there to summon spectral members from the guest list."

The two Dorset children, around eight and ten years old, respectively, looked as anxious as their parents. "Could we please get on with it?" Jackie Dorset asked. "We, um, don't have a lot of time on the parking meter."

"We validate for the lot across the street," Sheyenne offered. "Remember that for next time."

We all took seats at the table in the conference room. When Joshua and Madison looked ready to burst into tears, their mother reached into her purse (which was large enough to double as a rucksack). She withdrew two handheld video games, and the children fell into contented, obsessive silence.

"Now then, what seems to be the problem?" Robin asked.

Millicent Sanchez took the lead. "The Dorsets are being haunted—and it's not a pleasant haunting, either."

Brad Dorset locked his fingers together and squeezed his hands, like a pumping heart. "He won't leave us alone! We can't get any sleep. He ruins every meal. He disrupts any gathering we have. Jackie and I can't even go out to a restaurant."

"We'll never be able to get a sitter again," the wife added.

"We don't need a baby-sitter," the two children said in perfect unison.

"Do you feel you're in any physical danger from the ghost?" I interrupted.

Brad and Jackie looked at each other, surprised by the question. Jackie said, "No, of course not—it's just Uncle Stan."

"He was something of a pest in life," Brad added, "and he's worse now that he's dead."

Robin jotted down notes on a yellow legal pad. "Tell me about Stan."

"We're his only family." Jackie sounded more sympathetic than her husband. "He sold used cars, he belonged to the Odd Fellows club. We used to have him over for dinner every Sunday because he didn't have anyone else."

"He was a widower, then?" Robin prompted.

"No, a lifelong bachelor," Jackie said.

"He was gay, I think," Brad muttered, which earned him a flash of indignation from his wife.

"He was not! He just never found the right person."

"He certainly found *us* again, didn't he?"

I could see this was an argument they'd had before.

"Stan was my mother's only brother," Jackie continued, looking at me. "We felt sorry for him."

"Sunday dinner became Sunday *and* Wednesday," Brad said. "Then he joined us on Friday evenings too. And then he died."

"Was it murder?" I asked. "Anything suspicious?"

Again, Brad and Jackie Dorset blinked at each other, baffled. Brad answered, "No, he slipped on a patch of ice and split his head open on a brick planter. Just like that."

"And he's been haunting us ever since!" Jackie cried. "At first he thought he could go on as if nothing had changed. He popped in for Sunday dinner, then Monday and Tuesday, and all week long. After his tragic death, we were glad to see him ... at first. But he's, um, not a very good dinner companion."

"Drank too much," Brad said. "He always was a little hazy and wobbly."

Jackie seemed embarrassed. "The coroner said his blood alcohol level was a little high when he slipped and hit his head."

"Very high," Brad corrected. "Uncle Stan could get insufferable when he was drunk. Then he died drunk—and now he's a rambunctious and obnoxious *drunk* ghost."

"I've tried to communicate," said the medium. "I summoned his spirit. I spoke with him the last time he appeared uninvited for dinner."

"I made lasagna," Jackie said, "an old family recipe, one of Uncle Stan's favorites."

"We told him to go away," Brad said. "But he wouldn't listen. He insisted that we were his family and that he was going to be with us always."

The two kids looked up from their video games and groaned. Madison was especially loud. "He's a creepy old man. I don't want him popping in and out of our house at night."

"I can see how that would be very alarming," Robin assured her. "We've found that in family disputes, the best way to solve things is through frank and open discussion. I've seen many cases of ghosts who hang on to their old lives and refuse to move on. Sometimes the families can get along well enough, but other times it's just tragic for all concerned. The adjustment can be pretty painful."

I remembered that Sheyenne had had a terrible first few days after she returned as a ghost. She tried valiantly to adjust, pretended to go on as if nothing had changed, but the loss never stopped tugging at her.

One day, not long before my own murder, Sheyenne had floated up to me with a troubled expression on her face. "Would you come with me back to my apartment? Just to have another look around, in case we find any clues?"

"I packed everything up and put it in storage," I said. "Your landlord's probably cleaned the place by now."

"I know ... but it's something I'd like to do." Her sad expression pulled at my heartstrings. "Would you go with me? Please?"

"For you, I'd go anywhere," I said, and it was probably true.

We returned to the apartment building where she had lived while going to med school and working at Basilisk to pay the bills. She drifted beside me up the steps to the entrance.

I had an odd déjà vu of the night we'd strolled here after our date, the two of us in light conversation, occasionally and then more frequently bumping against each other as we walked along, finally holding hands. Every unnatural in town had probably smelled the pheromones we exuded....

"I don't know if I can convince your landlord to let us in," I said. I had not made a good impression in my previous encounters with him.

"I had a spare key," Sheyenne said. "You can use that."

"What if he's changed the lock by now?"

"He's too cheap. Besides, the former tenant is dead—why would he bother?"

We went up the stairs to the second floor. The third step creaked, and I remembered it from before. We had laughed at it then. Odd how little details like that stick in your memory.

Her door was 2B ("Or not 2B?" I remembered my *Hamlet* joke from that night). The hall floor was covered with weathered peel-and-press carpet squares. Sheyenne bent down and lifted the corner of one with a ghostly hand to reveal her spare key. "I knew it'd still be here." She handed me the key, and I inserted it into the lock. Sheyenne, being a ghost, simply melted through the door, eager to see what she could find.

As I turned the knob, I heard startled yelps from inside. I pushed the door open, afraid Sheyenne was in trouble—and saw a terrified Korean family seated around a table playing dominoes. Parents, three kids, and an old grandfather.

"What are you doing here?" Sheyenne demanded.

Upon entering the apartment, I experienced a flood of memories, and not the good ones ... not memories of how Sheyenne and I had started kissing as soon as we passed through the door, not the memory of her low-lit bedroom down the hall. No, what I remembered was when the landlord and I had found her sprawled and dying on the living room floor, already jaundiced and emaciated, too weak to move from the toadstool toxin.

This Korean family playing a game of dominoes did not fit the picture.

The three children screamed—not an unexpected reaction when a ghost floats through the wall and a strange man barges through the door. The father and grandfather stood together, ready to defend their home; the mother gathered her children. One young boy grabbed a handful of domino tiles and hurled them at me. "Go away!"

"He's rented it already, Spooky," I said. Her landlord had wasted no time. "This isn't your place anymore."

"But there's got to be a clue in here. I know we missed something!"

I apologized to the terrified Korean family. "We're very sorry. We didn't mean to intrude. Wrong address."

Dying had been hard enough for Sheyenne. Then she had to confront the fact that all the everyday details of her life were quickly and completely erased.

Yes, I could understand why Uncle Stan would try to cling to his lost loved ones. But he didn't have to be obnoxious about it.

Although Brad Dorset looked skeptical about the suggestion, Robin continued, "I've had some successes with mediation in cases like this. While I'm not a family-practice lawyer, I am a specialist in unnatural law, and we do have many clients who are ghosts. I presume you brought the medium along so you could summon Uncle Stan?"

"I can go into a trance right here and call him." Millicent Sanchez extended her forearms across the table so that her silver bracelets rattled. "Whenever you're ready?"

Robin studied her yellow legal pad and double-checked her notes. "I have enough information for an initial discussion."

Turning her hands palm up, the medium touched thumb and forefinger together and began to hum deep in her throat, as if practicing some form of Buddhist meditation.

Before she could finish her formal summons, the ghost of a chubby man appeared behind her, put both thumbs at the sides of his mouth, and stretched his lips in an inane clownish gesture. "I'm already here. I come and go when I want to!" He let out an exaggerated huff. "And I'm very offended. Jackie, you were always my favorite niece. This hurts my feelings!"

Jackie Dorset hung her head, her lip trembling as she fought back tears.

"She's your *only* niece," Brad said.

"You were never good enough for her!" The ghost loomed over Brad. "Jackie should have waited for someone better." Uncle Stan stormed and wove around the room, fluttering papers, rattling the doorknob, setting up a spectral wind. "You're not getting rid of me—I'm family! You have to keep me around."

Hearing the ruckus, Sheyenne flitted through the closed door of the conference room and gave Uncle Stan a withering frown. "That's not acceptable behavior from a ghost." Stan huffed at her, and she was about to scold him further when the office phone rang and she whisked herself back to the receptionist's desk.

The medium said in a thready voice, "The family respectfully requests that you leave them in peace, that you move on. Travel toward the Light."

In response, Uncle Stan jangled her silver bracelets, then yanked off her scarf, flapping it in front of her face like a matador taunting a bull. Millicent Sanchez grabbed at the fabric, trying to snatch it out of the air, but Stan kept taunting her.

Jackie began sobbing. "Uncle Stan, stop it, stop it!"

"Sir, we'd prefer to keep this amicable, but if you persist in this unreasonable behavior, we will be forced take formal legal action," Robin said.

"Go ahead and try!" Stan chortled. "What are you going to do, send some charlatan with a Bible and a dowsing rod? Paint the house doors red?" He stuck out his tongue, gave a loud raspberry, and flitted past the kids—who looked up in shock and dismay.

"He deleted our high scores!" wailed Joshua.

"You can't make me do anything I don't want to do." Uncle Stan hiccupped, then farted—mere affectations, since no air traveled in or out of any orifice of a poltergeist. Then his ghost vanished with a popping sound.

The Dorsets looked shaken and hopeless. The medium grabbed her scarf and tied it around her hair again in an attempt to regain her dignity.

"That could have gone better," I said.

Brad Dorset rose from his chair, upset. He glanced down at his wife. "I know he's your uncle, but we've got to do something."

She turned to Robin. "Take whatever legal action is necessary, Ms. Deyer. Make him rest in peace, so *we* can get some peace."

Robin escorted them out of the conference room and to the office door. "I'm sorry about this. We'll do everything we can."

Sheyenne was at her desk, talking on the phone, her expression filled with alarm. She hung up. "Dan, Robin—you've got to get to the museum right away—they need you!"

"What's the matter?" I asked.

"It's Ramen Ho-Tep—he's taken hostages!"

CHAPTER 24

The Metropolitan Natural History Museum was a grand, ancient structure that belonged in an even larger museum itself. Strung across giant Corinthian columns, a fabric banner advertised *Special Necronomicon Exhibition, Limited Time Only: The Original Book and Its Influence Throughout the Ages.*

On either side of the stone steps, two immense pedestals held fearsome gargoyle statues. Real gargoyles loved to stand next to the statues, making faces and mugging for the cameras so that their friends could take souvenir photos.

Robin drove recklessly through the streets and pulled up in front of the museum, stopping so abruptly that the old Maverick shed more shards of rust. Her desperation to intervene with Ramen Ho-Tep became even more apparent when she parked the Pro Bono Mobile illegally close to a fire hydrant and didn't even seem concerned about it. We ran up the steps, swimming upstream against a flood of evacuating patrons. A harried teacher herded an unruly class of fourth graders out of the museum.

The kids looked fascinated. "Why can't we stay and watch?" cried one little girl. "That was interesting!"

"It's not supposed to be interesting. This is an educational field trip." The teacher ushered them along. "Go on, move."

Robin and I ran through the front door, where an alarmed-looking cashier tried to charge us admission. I took command. "No time. This is a crisis." I didn't know if the mummy had threatened anyone; we just knew it was an emergency, something that was life or death ... or other. "Where's the Egyptian wing?"

"South hall," the cashier blurted. "But it's being evacuated."

"We know." Robin pulled out her pocketbook, flashed her bar card from the Board of Professional Responsibility. "I'm the attorney representing Ramen Ho-Tep. I need to see him before the situation gets out of hand."

"You're a little late for that," the cashier said.

Robin and I were already running through the security scanner. Since we hadn't paid admission—and also because I was carrying my .38—an alarm went off, but the museum guards were otherwise occupied. Robin seemed very upset to be breaking the rules, so I said to her, "Don't worry, we'll pay before we leave."

Oddly enough, that mollified her.

We ran past the arachnid display, then the Sorcery and Alchemy Hall on our way to Ancient Egypt. In the central hall, we encountered the ambitious Necronomicon exhibit. The Metropolitan Museum had pulled strings and fought challenges in court for the right to display the thick tome. Two lawsuits claimed the book posed a danger to the human public, although the time to worry about danger had already passed.

Though we needed to get to Ramen Ho-Tep, I hesitated, feeling an eerie connection to the magical book. This very copy of the Necronomicon, bound in leather made from the cured skin of infants and penned in human blood, was the reason I had come back from the dead—the reason all the unnaturals were now alive and abroad.

More than ten years ago, every rational person would have laughed at the possibility. Not anymore.

The planets had aligned in some sort of pattern that only astrologers considered significant. The original copy of the Necronomicon had inadvertently been left out under the light of a full moon, and a virgin woman (fifty-eight years old but a virgin nevertheless) had cut her finger (a paper cut, but a cut nevertheless) and spilled blood on the pages—which activated some buried spell and caused a fundamental shift in the natural order of things, unleashing ghosts and goblins, vampires and werewolves, zombies, ghouls, and all manner of monsters. Even the previously existing ones had come out of the closet.

The Big Uneasy.

Any further explanation, scientific or otherwise, was above my pay grade. The world had been dealing with the repercussions ever since.

"Dan, quit looking at the exhibits," Robin called. "Come on—Mr. Ho-Tep needs us!"

We encountered a crowd at the entrance to the Ancient Egypt wing, but Robin pushed past the people. "I'm his attorney. Let me through!"

The large display chamber held papier-mâché replicas of a pyramid, a gaudily painted sphinx, a shelf filled with canopic jars, and a diorama of papyrus marshes with Egyptian mannequins.

And Ramen Ho-Tep, who held them all enthralled.

I heard the mummy's distinctive British voice. "Not one step closer, you wankers! I'll do it! I'm warning you—*I'll do it!*"

Patrons who had been evacuated—by only ten or fifteen feet—watched in horrified fascination, leaning forward to get a better view. Three uniformed museum guards stood tense, ready to tackle the mummy to the floor; if they did that, he would probably shatter into bone dust and lint.

Ramen Ho-Tep had not, after all, taken hostages, nor had he seized one of the guards' weapons. It was worse.

In front of the exhibit's open sarcophagus, the mummy sat cross-legged on the floor. I couldn't imagine how he'd managed to bend his dried-jerky muscles and petrified bones into such a configuration. He dangled a red can of gasoline in his clawlike hands, threatening to dump it on himself. One of the guards held a long canvas fire hose, ready to open the valve if Ho-Tep should succeed in igniting his bandages; I suspected the high-powered spray would damage the mummy as much as a fire.

One man in a clean dark business suit, a neat tie, and gold wire-rimmed glasses looked highly agitated. Ramen Ho-Tep seemed most upset with him. I recognized the human museum curator, Bram Steffords, who had been so proud to obtain the Necronomicon exhibit after reopening the Metropolitan Natural History Museum "in these exciting, though darker times." I had shaken the curator's hand during the ribbon-cutting ceremony, but I doubted he remembered me.

Steffords growled, "If you carry out your threat, Mr. Ho-Tep, I promise we will bring you up on full charges for destroying priceless antiquities. The museum will sue you for damages to yourself and to this exhibit, as well as lost revenue."

"I don't give a bloody damn about your revenue, or your antiquities! *I* am the antiquity! But I'm a *person*, not property!"

"We have the paperwork to prove otherwise, Mr. Ho-Tep. Now stop this nonsense and put down that gasoline!"

To solidify his threat, Ramen Ho-Tep unscrewed the fuel cap. Fumes wafted up, and the guards backed away.

"I've got this," Robin said to me and pushed forward. "Excuse me, excuse me!"

The mummy turned toward her. Behind the bandages on his face, his chapped lips twitched in what might have been a surprised smile.

In that moment of hesitation, Steffords yelled to the guards, "*Now!* Jump him!"

But Robin threw herself between them and Ramen Ho-Tep. "You'll do no such thing! This man is my client!"

Steffords looked at her. "And who the hell are you?"

"Robin Deyer, Esquire, of Chambeaux and Deyer."

I reached into my jacket pocket, withdrew a business card, and handed it to the curator.

"I shan't go back on display," the mummy said. "I'd sooner burn myself and let my ashes join the river of time."

"He's been going on like that for an hour," one of the guards said to me out of the side of his mouth.

"We can resolve this, Mr. Ho-Tep," Robin said. "Think about the loss to history. Please give me a chance."

"I've waited quite long enough, thank you. I shall no longer endure being a prisoner. I was Pharaoh of all Egypt, and I deserve to be treated with respect!"

"Ask him if he had a girlfriend or something," the curator said. "Maybe we can dig her up and add her to our museum display if he wants companionship."

"I wish to be a free man!"

"And I want to be the King of England," Steffords quipped, imitating the mummy's British accent. "But that isn't likely to happen, is it?"

"Bloody hell, don't you disrespect me, you insignificant grave robber!" Ramen Ho-Tep sloshed the gas can, and a few drops spilled onto his brown gauze bandages. Clutched in his left hand was a disposable butane lighter, but I saw, like everyone else did, that he was holding it upside down. The ancient mummy had no idea how to use a lighter.

Robin said in a plaintive voice, "Mr. Ho-Tep, you're only hurting our case. We have to make our appeal according to the law. The law is the safety net that holds society together. This is *not* a solution. If you strike that lighter, no one wins: You lose everything, the world loses your priceless knowledge, and I lose a friend."

The mummy's hand wavered.

"I'm going to set up mediation so both parties can discuss this matter as adults." Robin glared at the curator. "Mr. Steffords, I suggest that you and your legal counsel attend. After airing grievances, we'll see if we can't reach some kind of compromise. We all want this to work."

"The bugger's going to have to make some damned hefty concessions," the mummy said.

"And I'm tired of this melodrama," said Steffords. "Our artifacts are supposed to be on display, not on stage. This is a respectable museum, not vaudeville."

I relieved the mummy of his gas can, capping it gingerly.

"How about ten *a.m.* Tuesday?" Robin suggested.

The curator fidgeted. "I'll have my secretary check my schedule."

"Clear your schedule," I said. "Ten o'clock. Tuesday."

Robin looked at Ramen Ho-Tep. "Are you busy at that time, Mr. Ho-Tep?"

"My calendar's been open for thousands of years."

"We look forward to seeing you, then." She slipped her arm through mine, and we walked out of the south wing and made our way to the museum entrance.

And yes, Robin did insist that we pay admission before we left.

CHAPTER 25

As we drove away from the museum, pleased at having averted a tragedy, Robin suggested we make a surprise visit to Jekyll Lifestyle Products and Necroceuticals. "We might unsettle him." She gave me an eager smile. "And it'll give us something to report to Miranda next time she pops in."

"I like the way you think," I said. Maybe I would pick up a clue about why Jekyll had been sneaking around with Brondon Morris. "Besides, we're out together anyway. It's good for you to get away from the office."

"Visiting a chemical factory that makes perfumes, deodorants, and toiletries isn't much of an outing."

I had been inside the factory before—illicitly—while investigating the garlic-laced shampoo lawsuit. I'd posed as a worker on the chemical mixing lines and then, after hiding out at the tail end of a shift, I crept into the main admin offices after hours and got my hands on proof that the shampoo contamination was a matter of record and that JLPN was culpable. The company complained to the court about the evidence submission and appealed the ruling, but they never managed to pin burglary charges on me, although the judge found it unrealistically convenient that an "anonymous source" would produce the precise documents Robin needed to win the case and secure a large judgment.

When we pulled into the JLPN guest parking lot, Robin's car was definitely the oldest one there. A limousine sprawled across two spots, both of which were designated "For Harvard Stanford Jekyll."

Inside the fence, the mammoth industrial building was capped by a tall smokestack spurting purple and green fumes. The sign in front of the entrance said *Jekyll Lifestyle Products & Necroceuticals—We Bring Fresh Back to a Stale World.* Then, in smaller letters, *An Equal Opportunity Employer.* In front, a tan-brick administrative office building sat apart from the factory.

"It smells like a thousand mall candle shops crammed into a trash compactor and left out in the sun," Robin said as she got out of the rusty Maverick.

I saw a loading dock and many trucks parked in a line, ready to be loaded with the new line of necroceuticals for distribution in the Quarter. A flurry of workers used hand trucks and forklifts to haul crates out of the chemical factory; each box was stenciled with *Try our New Line!* The workers rushed around like turbo-charged termites. A few golems would have been great for heavy labor like this, but as far as I could see, all of the JLPN employees were human.

A delivery truck backed up to the big doors, and men hurried forward with pallets of new shampoos, deodorants, liquid soaps, perfumes. As soon as a fully loaded truck drove off, the next empty one backed up to the dock.

A lawyer on a mission, Robin walked briskly to the front door of the admin building, and I pulled it open for her, trying to formulate what I could accomplish by seeing Harvey Jekyll face-to-face. Robin didn't seem to have a plan.

At the foyer reception desk sat a neckless man with a crew cut, business suit, and honest-to-goodness mirrored sunglasses. He looked as if he'd been rejected by the Secret Service Presidential Protection Detail because he was too large and intimidating. I'd seen him before—standing guard at the Chaney & Son warehouse the previous night.

"How may I help you?" The neckless man looked at Robin, then frowned at me. "*He's* not welcome here. Human employees and guests only." He said it in the same tone that, in another time and place, he might have told Robin she wasn't welcome because of the color of her skin.

"That hurts my feelings," I said sarcastically.

Robin was more indignant. "That's an odd stance for a company giving unnaturals the opportunity to live normal and happy lives."

"I don't make the rules. No zombies allowed. No unnaturals of any kind. Security reasons."

"My partner and I have business with Mr. Jekyll," Robin said. "I am the attorney representing Mrs. Jekyll in their divorce, and we have some questions for her husband. His attorney may wish to be present."

With a flustered sigh, the massive receptionist punched an extension on the phone, spoke gruffly, frowned. He hung up. "Wait here." A moment later, the locked security door buzzed and clicked, then swung open by itself (on hydraulics—nothing to do with ghosts or haunted houses). "End of the hall. Big office. Can't miss it."

As we walked down the hall to Jekyll's office, I could hear a stereo playing, sparkly 1970s pop music, either the Carpenters or the Captain and Tennille. In my experience, most villains prefer dramatic classical music or Wagnerian opera. Maybe Harvey Jekyll liked to be in a happy mood.

As soon as we stepped through the door, Jekyll climbed to his feet. "What's this about you being Miranda's attorney?"

He was a small, pale-skinned man with a large head, even larger eyes (which reminded me of the zombie puppies in Alvin's painting), and no hair. All in all, the type of person who might keep a plain gold ring that he liked to call Precious. His scalp wrinkled like a shriveled apple when he raised his eyebrows. Goblin mothers probably warned their teenaged sons that if they masturbated too much, they would end up looking like Harvey Jekyll.

I was afraid Robin had let the cat out of the bag, but she didn't seem perturbed. "You filed for divorce, Mr. Jekyll, and your wife has retained my services to protect her interests in the settlement. You have been duly informed. I sent repeated inquiries and notices—at least sixteen—to your counsel by registered mail. I have the delivery confirmations." She looked around the room. "Are you sure you don't want your attorney present?"

He snorted. "If my lawyer was worth anything, the divorce would already be final." Ignoring Robin as if scraping gum off his shoe, Jekyll swung his gaze over to me. He leaned forward, noting the repaired bullet hole in my forehead. "You don't look much the worse for wear after being shot, Mr. Chambeaux."

"Amazing what morticians can do these days, but I'm still only fit for the scratch-and-dent sale." I tapped my brow, feeling the putty that Bruno had so skillfully applied. "Maybe you have an idea who shot me? Some personal involvement perhaps?"

The little man's face screwed itself into a scowl. "You've already cost this company enough money—both of you. I wouldn't squander the price of a bullet. You were a pain in the backside while alive, Mr. Chambeaux, and now you continue to harass me after you're dead? I don't take kindly to anyone slinging mud on my family name."

I shrugged. "I have nothing against your family name. It's *you* I don't like."

He had had enough banter. "Now, is there some reason you both came here, or were you just trying to ruffle my feathers?" He scratched his bald scalp. "I assure you, I have none to ruffle. And no secrets to hide."

Robin said, "Why do you refuse to allow unnaturals into your factory, Mr. Jekyll? Your sign out front claims that you're an Equal Opportunity Employer. How is an unnatural supposed to apply for a job at JLPN if he's not allowed on the premises?" I noted the glint in her eyes, sure she was weighing the possibilities of a discrimination lawsuit.

Jekyll pinched his lips together. "The statutes governing nondiscriminatory hiring practices define the acceptable labor pool as *human*. The rules do not cover unnaturals. I don't have to let them on my property."

"And yet your product line caters to unnaturals," I said. "A strange business choice if you dislike them so much."

He sniffed. "I have nothing against the unnaturals, but I am concerned about corporate espionage. It's only a matter of time before some monster entrepreneur decides to get into this highly lucrative market, and I have to protect JLPN trade secrets."

I realized that Jekyll probably did have good reason to fear the competition. A line of necroceutical products manufactured by an unnatural instead of a human would have an obvious advantage among the customer base.

On the office stereo, the Captain and Tennille finished singing "Muskrat Love," and now the Carpenters were "On Top of the World." I had a sneaking suspicion Barry Manilow would be up next.

Next to the stereo sat a strange device that looked like a bullhorn mounted on top of a toaster. Since 1970s easy-listening pop did not require special amplification, I wondered what the gadget did. I fiddled with the controls, mainly because I thought that would annoy Jekyll.

It did. "Don't touch that!"

"Why not?" I turned another knob. "What is this thing?"

"A prototype." He scuttled over and snatched the device from me and set it on a shelf behind his desk. "A portable ectoplasmic defibrillator, designed to scramble—and hopefully *erase*—any trespassing ghosts. Ghosts make the most insidious industrial spies, slipping in where they're not wanted, snooping around." He narrowed his eyes. "You can't be too careful. The prototype is still in the testing phase—I'm having trouble finding ghosts who will volunteer for the trials."

I was glad Sheyenne hadn't come along with us.

Since Robin didn't have a plan for this meeting, I threw a curveball in hopes that it would rattle Jekyll. I liked to see where the red herrings would swim. "For one of my investigations, I've been monitoring the activities of Brondon Morris. He may be involved in some unsavory activities, possibly even a conspiracy to overthrow JLPN. Thought you'd want to know."

Jekyll blinked, then chuckled. "Brondon would never do that! He's a very important person in this company, one of our most talented chemists, and by far the best regional sales manager."

I watched his expression carefully. "Are you familiar with a defunct company called Chaney and Son? Mr. Morris has been meeting with a secret group inside their boarded-up warehouse." I was just testing him, stringing him along.

"I know nothing about that," he said, but the alarmed look on his face said otherwise. "I'll speak to Brondon about it. If he's sneaking around with unsavory types, I wouldn't want his public actions to adversely affect our company image. This is a crucial time for JLPN with the release of our whole new line of products. We can't afford any bad press."

I reminded myself that *Miranda* was our client. Even if Jekyll and his lapdog were doing something illicit, such activities didn't necessarily affect the divorce settlement. The two men could have been participating in an illegal cockatrice fighting ring, or smuggling body parts to mad scientist laboratories. What mattered to me was finding a way to break the rigid prenuptial agreement.

Sure enough, after the Carpenters finished mellowing their way through a glycemic coma, Barry Manilow started in with "I Write the Songs."

"We'd better go, Dan," Robin said. Clearly, we weren't going to get any more information from Harvey Jekyll, but I think it was the music that made her anxious to leave.

"Say hello to my wife for me," Jekyll said. "You probably see her more than I do."

CHAPTER 26

Late the next morning, a pleading arrived by courier from Howard Phillips Publishing—a service copy sent to us with the original filed in court. Not unexpectedly, the publisher's legal department refuted Robin's demand for reparations and declined to remove the defective spell book from bookstore shelves.

As Robin read the letter, I watched her expression fall. Her lips pressed together, and then she got that determined *look* of hers. When I saw her like that, I always thought she could walk into an oncoming tidal wave and the waters would part just to stay out of her way. She handed me the letter so I could read it for myself.

"We at Howard Phillips Publishing categorically deny any culpability in the strange and unfortunate accident that befell Ms. Alma Wannovich. We contend that the plaintiffs, Alma Wannovich and Mavis Wannovich, failed to use our spell book in accordance with the clearly stated guidelines on the copyright page. We assert that all spells published by Howard Phillips are completely harmless. Although Ms. Wannovich's situation is unquestionably tragic, our good company bears no blame for the aforementioned misfortune. Any public allegation that attempts to cast Howard Phillips Publishing in an unfavorable light will be met with vigorous legal action. We are committed to defending our good name with all the means and financial resources at our disposal."

I handed the letter back to Robin. "Not good news."

"It's just the next step in the dance." Her fingers tightened on the stationery, wrinkling the paper. "The more strenuously a defendant denies the charges, the more culpable they tend to be."

"Should I deliver a copy of the letter to Mavis and Alma?" After the tense situation the sisters had experienced on the streets, I didn't think it was wise to call them away from the safety of their home unless it was absolutely necessary.

Robin set the letter on her desk and flattened the crinkles. "No, I'll call them. I think it might be time to try an innovative approach—and I've got an idea."

"All right, but if Mavis and Alma need a shoulder to cry on"—I thought of the large sow—"or to nuzzle against, I'll do my part."

While Robin talked with the Wannovich sisters on the phone, I decided to check on Mrs. Saldana down at the mission, as well as Sheldon Fennerman, to let them both know about the restraining order against Straight Edge. I grabbed my hat, took my phone and my gun, told Sheyenne where I was going, and headed out.

At the halfway-repaired Hope & Salvation Mission, patrons had returned to take advantage of Mrs. Saldana's generosity. She made soup and cookies and passed out blood bags donated to the mission by the blood bank (type B positive packs that were near their expiration date; vampires considered that the least flavorful blood type, but Mrs. Saldana liked to reinforce the subliminal message of "be positive").

Inside the mission, Jerry the zombie was practicing at the piano but not doing very well. A mangy-looking werewolf snoozed on one of the folding chairs. Two bald vampires looked with disdain at the selection of blood bags, obviously not tempted; I wondered if these two had been victims of the garlic-contaminated JLPN shampoo.

A parked truck sat in front of the mission, with large panels that held sheets of window glass. *Black Glass, Inc.* was stenciled on the passenger door. Out front, Mrs. Saldana spoke with an exceedingly dapper zombie dressed in a black frock coat, a gray checkered vest, and black silk top hat. His eyes were sunk deep in their sockets; long gray hair extended below the brim of the top hat. He looked like the Crypt Keeper in an old horror television show that was experiencing a resurgence in popularity now that it had been repackaged as a slice-of-life comedy. Rather than the usual smell of death one would expect from a zombie in his state of decay, a haze of pungent cologne hung around him. By now, I recognized the distinctive scent of Zom-Be-Fresh.

I walked up to them. "I just came to make sure you're all right, Mrs. Saldana. No further harassment?"

The old woman brightened. "None whatsoever, Mr. Chambeaux. We're getting back on our feet now, and I want to thank you for giving me this gentleman's contact information. He's doing a fine job."

The dapper zombie extended his hand. "Franklin Galworthy, owner of Black Glass. I appreciate you recommending us, sir. We're just a start-up company and can use the customers."

"Pleased to meet you." The cologne smell was so strong my eyes began to water. "How's business?"

Galworthy took off his top hat and wiped an emaciated hand across his forehead. "Quite busy. The brute that did *this*"—he gestured to where he had framed the smashed windows with new two-by-fours—"has caused a lot of damage across the Quarter. Smashed glass everywhere." His grin showed off an array of teeth that would have startled even Mr. Sardonicus. "And all those places need replacement windows. At the moment, I've got more work than I can handle."

"I hope you find that horribly destructive creature," Mrs. Saldana said, fluttering her hand in front of her face. "You're the detective, Mr. Chambeaux. Any leads?"

"Not yet—Officer McGoohan is on it. If I learn anything, I'll let him know."

"Give me two days and I'll have the mission fixed up, good as new," said Galworthy. "And if the brute attacks again, we'll fix it again! That's the best way to defeat vandals, I say—take away their fun."

With a flourish like a circus showman, he twirled his top hat, plopped it back on the straggly gray strands covering his cranium, and returned to measuring the window before he cut the glass.

I informed Mrs. Saldana that, thanks to the restraining order, she could have the Straight Edgers thrown in jail for contempt if they bothered her again. The old woman blessed me and gave me a sweet grandmotherly pat on my shoulder.

My cell phone rang. It was Sheyenne. "Beaux, you better head over to Howard Phillips Publishing—something's brewing. Robin wants you there to see what she's got up her sleeve."

I didn't like the sound of that. "I take it the witches weren't satisfied with the publisher's response?"

"Robin has a plan, whatever that means."

"Now I'm curious. Give me the address."

Leaving the mission, I tried to hail a taxi and, as is typical when you're in a hurry, I couldn't find one. It was the middle of the afternoon, with sunlight filling a crystal-clear sky. Since not many unnaturals wanted to be abroad in bright daylight, they had snatched up all the available cabs.

So I set off on foot, stopping at every corner, holding out my hand, trying to catch a taxi. It took me sixteen blocks, and by the time I slid into the backseat of the cab and told the driver where to go, I was only four blocks from my destination. Still, it saved a little time.

When the taxi pulled up in front of the publisher's building, I paid the driver, tipped him too much, and bounded out of the backseat. I easily spotted Robin looking professional in her business suit; she stood between the black-skirted Mavis and her sow-sister Alma. A TV news van had already arrived, and two men with cameras recorded the small spectacle. Another camera van pulled up just as I arrived.

The headquarters of Howard Phillips Publishing was a modern rectangular structure of stone blocks and steel with reflectorized windows. In order to afford a stand-alone building in the city, they must have been doing well with their spell-book reprints and annotated editions of the Necronomicon, which they claimed were authorized by Abdul Alhazred himself.

Two medium-height, middle-aged men with prominent lantern jaws pushed their way through the main revolving door. They wore white short-sleeved shirts and neckties that were identically askew. At a glance, I guessed that this was the publisher and his entire legal department, twins apparently. From Robin's research on the case, we had learned that the brothers were Howard Phillips and Phillip Phillips, respectively.

"What's all this?" said the one I determined to be Phillip. "Go away— you're trespassing. Shoo!"

The TV cameras turned toward him, and he quailed. The other brother, Howard, grabbed Phillip's shoulder and pulled him back toward the revolving door, but Robin seized her moment. She raised her voice and spoke for the cameras. "My clients, Mavis and Alma Wannovich"— she pointed to the witch and the sow—"have suffered grievous harm due to errors in spell books published by Howard Phillips. The results are obvious."

Reporters began scribbling notes. Others held out recorders to capture her words. The news cameras recorded every moment.

In a scorn-filled voice, Robin continued, "However, according to this letter, the publisher insists their books are completely safe." She waved the letter in the air. "All right, let's give them the benefit of the doubt." She patted Alma's head and flashed the nervous twins a shrewd glance. "If this spell is indeed harmless, as they claim, then we'll graciously withdraw our complaint."

Howard and Phillip attempted to retreat, but only succeeded in jamming themselves into the revolving door. "But it *is* harmless!" the publisher cried.

"Thank you, gentlemen. We accept your assurances, but now for the proof." Robin gestured, turned her attention back to the cameras. "Mavis will cast this purportedly innocuous spell on Howard and Phillip Phillips. The truth will be obvious to everyone in a minute." She seemed completely in her element. This was even better than arguing a case in front of a jury. "Be sure to have your cameras tracking this."

Mavis opened the spell book, turned it so the news crews could capture the cover and its prominent Howard Phillips logo. The sow shifted back and forth, barely able to restrain a joyful squeal. "Summoning the Fairness of Form," Mavis said and cleared her throat. She fixed her glare on the twins and began to incant the strange words printed in the book.

The reporters held their breath.

"Stop!" cried Howard. "There's no need for this!"

"But don't you want us to vindicate you?" Robin said with an innocent smile. "You *do* believe the spell is harmless, don't you?"

The reporters loved it. Mavis chanted louder.

Phillip, the "legal department" brother, was even more agitated. "Wait! We wish to reconsider our position!"

Mavis looked at Robin for guidance as to whether she should continue or not.

"We're listening," Robin said.

"My brother and I, uh, need to study the matter further. It's possible that there might have been a typographical error."

"The typographical error is indisputable," Robin countered. "We have copies of the original wording and a side-by-side comparison to the version you published."

"But it hasn't been shown the misprint caused any direct harm," Howard spluttered.

"Then by all means, let's continue and remove any doubt." Robin nodded at Mavis, and the witch held up the spell book.

Phillip the Legal Department raised his hands again. "That's not necessary. Without admitting responsibility, perhaps there are some reparations we could offer? A donation to your favorite charity, a revised edition of the spell book—"

"An office with a window," Mavis said quite clearly.

Howard and Phillip looked at each other, perplexed.

Robin picked up the conversation. "The Wannovich sisters believe that your company is sorely in need of experts to do spell-checking. They have generously agreed to dismiss the suit if you give Mavis Wannovich her own office and a position in Howard Phillips Publishing, at an appropriate salary."

"And my sister, too," Mavis said. "She needs an office of her own."

"But she's a *sow!*" cried Phillip.

"Only because of you," Mavis snapped. "And part of my job will be to research a reversal spell to restore her." She held the error-ridden spell book like a hand grenade from which she had pulled the pin.

The sow grunted. The cameras continued to record the scene.

"I think ... that's acceptable," said the publisher.

"I'll draw up a hiring agreement and a waiver of liability," said the legal department.

"With my input," Robin insisted.

"It's my dream job," Mavis said. "I've always wanted to work in publishing."

CHAPTER 27

iranda's random casual visits occurred so regularly that we could guess when she was going to come in. She disliked being bound by appointments anyway, believing that the rest of the world operated on her schedule, not vice versa.

That afternoon she sashayed into the office in a sparkly amethyst cocktail dress, her bright red lips curved in a smile. A heavy necklace of pearls the size of poodle eyeballs hung at her throat. Not one strand of Miranda's unnaturally (so to speak) copper hair had moved since the last time we'd seen her.

She threw Sheyenne an air-kiss at her desk. "I don't mean to be impatient, sweethearts, but ... well, I'm damned *impatient*. I simply must be out of this loveless marriage, but I don't see penniless as preferable to loveless. Please tell me you have news for me."

"As a matter of fact, we have made some progress, Mrs. Jekyll," I said. "It's a good thing you're here—we need your help filling in some answers so we can plan our next move."

She flashed a set of dazzling teeth. "I remember when I used to plan my moves with Harvey. Yes, even Harvey." She looked up, as if expecting us to be shocked that she'd once been attracted to her own husband. "But we haven't had sex in years. He finds me disgusting now."

Robin sounded scandalized. "Disgusting? But you ... you're"—she couldn't quite bring herself to say the word *beautiful*, and instead settled on, "a very classy woman."

"Ever since the Change, Harvey refuses to touch me. I'm a werewolf. I get hot flashes. I think it scares him. Some people have a furry fetish—

they *like* the animalistic energy. Wouldn't you?" She looked meaningfully at me, and I found the question too awkward for a response. She let it go, getting down to business. "So tell me what you found. Is he fooling around with another woman? I knew it."

Robin asked, "What makes you so certain your husband is having an affair?"

She rolled her eyes. "Isn't it obvious? He's not getting any from me, and he's a *man*." She gave Robin a pitying smile. "You're so very innocent, sweetheart. *Everyone* fools around. It's not unusual—it's expected. Harvey knows that *I* fool around, but he can't prove it. That's the important thing."

"And how does he know that, Mrs. Jekyll?" I asked her.

"Well, I didn't become a werewolf by *accident*, and I wasn't scratched while out doing charity work. I had an affair with a werewolf, a big handsome brute." She sucked in a long breath, then licked her lips. "Ahh, what a wonderful time! We tried to practice safe sex, but we got carried away. I got infected from one of his little love scratches. No wonder Harvey wants a divorce. He can't stand unnaturals, and he would never sleep with one." She clicked her tongue against her teeth. "His loss."

"If you are committing indiscretions, Mrs. Jekyll, I advise you to be extremely careful. I'm not the only PI in town, and if your husband gets photos that prove *your* infidelity, our entire case is sunk."

"Don't you two worry about me. I've had plenty of practice covering my tracks. Besides, I've got better investigators than Harvey does, because you're the best. Am I right?" She pointed to the manila file Robin carried. "Now, are you going to show me what you've learned? I have an appointment with my dental hygienist."

We described our recent meeting at the JLPN factory, and then I explained how I'd followed a disguised and nervous Harvey Jekyll to a secret nighttime gathering at the abandoned Chaney & Son warehouse. By now, Sheyenne had tracked down the information I needed.

"That warehouse is just a front," I said. "According to records, it's owned by a dummy corporation called Ramshackle Solutions, and all the names on the paperwork are fake. Despite the warehouse's run-down appearance, a lot of interior remodeling has been done in the past year—new wiring, light fixtures, plumbing, a sound system." I paused for effect. "Every one of the contractors turns out to be an employee of JLPN. The work orders were signed with an illegible signature—and Harvey Jekyll has an illegible signature. It's proof he's involved with whatever's going on inside that place."

Miranda wasn't as impressed as I had hoped. "Oh, that's just boys pretending to be important. I wouldn't be surprised if they wore furry hats with buffalo horns. They even have a secret handshake, a little sign they make when they think no one is looking." She licked her forefinger and scribed a line in the air, as if making some kind of invisible tally. "They think nobody can figure it out!"

Robin looked puzzled, turned to me, but I didn't get it either. Miranda let out an exaggerated sigh. "A *line*, sweetheart. A *straight* line. Up and down?" She waited. "The Straight Edgers, of course. Harvey joined them a long time ago, probably to get back at me for becoming a werewolf."

Now I remembered the vertical line on the red T-shirts the four losers had worn in Straight Edge headquarters. "I served a restraining order against the organization just this morning, but I can't imagine your husband would be involved with amateurs like that. The secret gathering I saw at the warehouse looked much more sophisticated."

"Oh, only the novices work in public view," Miranda said. "It's like a hazing. New recruits with big dreams, tiny brains, and even smaller cojones. The real Straight Edgers are a better organized bunch. Harvey funds a good portion of their activities with JLPN profits—which is very annoying, since currently half of that money belongs to me. He hopes to get promoted to Grand Poobah or whatever." She shook her head. "But I need something more salacious than a secret clubhouse if we're going to make him budge on the prenup."

The little cogs and gears clicked together in my mind. "Not necessarily. If we could come up with concrete evidence that Harvey Jekyll is involved with an anti-unnatural fringe group, think of all the bad press—and right before the release of his new Fresh Loam promotion. The manufacturer of the most popular line of necroceuticals secretly hates his own customers? That might twist his arm."

Robin looked scandalized that we would stoop to such tactics, but Miranda chuckled again. "I like the way you think, Mr. Chambeaux. If you need evidence, Harvey keeps all of his special little treasures in a locked desk drawer in his study at the house. I'm sure it's evidence you could use."

"Could you get access to those items?" I asked. "Slip inside his study, retrieve anything that connects him to the Straight Edgers?"

Miranda glanced at her gold watch. "Of course not, sweetheart. That's what I pay *you* for. I haven't been home to spend the night in more than a year. I'm staying at the Grand Plaza Hotel in the Full Moon Suite, and it's costing Harvey a pretty penny ... but he considers it worth the expense not to have me around." When she smiled, Miranda's teeth looked more pointed than when she'd entered the offices. "Now, I have to be off to my dental hygienist. Good work so far. I'll add a little bonus when I pay this week's invoice."

Robin seemed flustered. "But how exactly are we going to gain access to the evidence? Shall I file a discovery request to see documents or items in his study? I don't think we have grounds—"

"If you do that, he'll make sure that anything interesting is long gone," Miranda said.

I reassured her. "I'll come up with something."

Harvey Jekyll had made a point of how effective a ghost could be in corporate espionage. It might just be time for Sheyenne to do a little legwork.

CHAPTER 28

fter Miranda departed, but before I could lay out my plans to dig up dirt on Jekyll, the phone rang. When Sheyenne answered, I could hear a frantic voice on the other end. She said, "Mr. Fennerman? Stay calm, Mr. Fennerman. Yes, he's right next to me."

She handed me the phone, and I heard the nervous vampire's voice warbling over the line. "They're back, and they've ignored the restraining order! Please help!"

I said in the calmest voice possible, "What are they doing, Sheldon? Are you safe?"

"For now. They can't get in, but they're pounding on the door. They broke my windows. I can hear them outside! They're coming to get me."

"Did you call the police?"

"They put me on hold. Mr. Chambeaux, save me!"

"I'll be right there, Sheldon. Just hang tight."

I'd thought the morons would lie low for at least a day or two, but something must have egged them on. I tucked my piece in its shoulder holster and headed out. With the pistol I could scare the Straight Edge dweebs away for now, but they could always harass the vampire again. Since I did not intend to set up a new career as a doorman at Sheldon Fennerman's brownstone, I needed a more permanent solution, one that would make the Straight Edgers leave my client alone.

As I hit the street, I took out my phone and punched in another number. Time to call in reinforcements.

O   O   O

Splattered raw eggs left gooey starbursts on Sheldon's front door. Rocks had broken the black glass of his windows. The three young men—Patrick, Scott, and Todd—wearing red T-shirts with the white line down the front, lounged on the street corner as if pretending to be hoodlums, but they didn't look old enough to smoke. Priscilla, the shrewish young woman, stood beside them waving a new hand-lettered sign:

UNDEAD
UNCLEAN
UNWANTED

I was surprised they had the balls to be so overt; I'd thought they were nothing more than armchair terrorists. Maybe Jekyll himself had coerced them into this underhanded retaliation. It was common knowledge that Fennerman was a Chambeaux & Deyer client, under our protection, and Harvey could well have riled them up just to cause trouble after Robin and I visited him in his factory office. Maybe he'd even promised these kids their own secret decoder rings if they completed their mission.

The Straight Edgers recognized me as I approached. "Did you have trouble reading the restraining order I served you? Too many big words?"

"We're on a public street," Priscilla sneered.

"You're harassing my client. I can see the broken windows."

"It was an accident," Todd said. "We'd apologize and offer to pay, but we can't go within fifty feet of him."

"And the eggs?"

"We were delivering groceries," Scott said. "I tripped, and they went flying."

The Straight Edgers were so full of themselves they didn't seem to realize where they were. The unnaturals already despised them and their intolerant activities. Priscilla, Scott, Todd, and Patrick were close to being fatally clueless.

Hearing the ruckus, a few monsters had stepped out of their front doors or emerged from their businesses, looking with disdain at the demonstrators. Some of the unnaturals rolled their slitted eyes, viewing the Straight Edgers as ill-behaved children who needed a good scolding and a weekend of public service. Other creatures, though, seemed happy for an excuse to return to their baser natures.

"We have a right to free speech, man," Patrick said. "Our opinion is our opinion."

"And everybody has one," I said, stepping closer, in their faces. "Like assholes."

This confrontation had the potential to degenerate into one of those interminably stupid "I know you are, but what am I?" debates. The mood of the gathered unnaturals was getting ugly. Claws extended, fangs bared. I had already rescued the beanpole Todd from a troll's deep fryer; now maybe I'd have to intervene to keep these dweebs from becoming a Straight Edge smorgasbord—and that really annoyed me. I was here to protect Sheldon, not his harassers.

I looked up with relief to see the black-gowned bulk of Mavis Wannovich waddling toward us, accompanied by the huge sow, as if the two were out for an afternoon stroll. Mavis carried her spell book now, confident and unafraid. And thanks to an anti-glamour spell Mavis had worked on her sister, Alma now smelled like sauerkraut rather than delectable pork, which kept her safe from the unnaturals who had considered her a snack a few days ago.

"Ah, Mavis! Thank you for coming down to help." I raised a hand to greet her.

Both sisters seemed renewed, self-esteem bolstered by their new positions at the publishing house. "Delighted to be of assistance, Mr. Chambeaux. One small way we can repay you for your kindness."

The Straight Edgers hooted and jeered. "Ooh, he's brought in a pig as reinforcements. I'm scaaaared!"

"Throw water on the witch and see if she starts melting," Priscilla suggested.

Mavis glared at them with a gaze that nearly turned them to stone. "Just try it, you little snots, and we'll see who starts melting. Better watch out, or I'll turn to page sixty-two!"

While the sow stood guard, Mavis opened her spell book. I slipped down the two steps to Sheldon Fennerman's front door and rapped with my knuckles. "Open up, Sheldon. It's Dan Chambeaux."

"I'm not coming out! It isn't safe!"

"I've got your back, don't worry. I need you to watch this, trust me. It'll be the end of all your troubles."

The door opened a crack, and the vampire poked his face out. "Is it going to bring my friends back? All the other vampires in the neighborhood?"

"I'm afraid they're not coming back, Sheldon, but at least you'll be safe."

Undeterred, Priscilla kept pumping her sign up and down, but she didn't continue her insults. All four looked queasy, trying to summon nonexistent courage from one another. The angry unnaturals on the street growled, as if they didn't want to wait for what I intended to do. "Humans, go home!" yelled a man who looked very human, probably an un-transformed werewolf.

"Fresh meat," a shambler said in a voice that sounded like a rumbling stomach.

A tall, pasty-faced necromancer moaned, "Why can't we all just get along?"

A potbellied ghost drifted among the angry people, glaring at the scrawny punks. "You're not better than us!"

I brought Sheldon out into the daylight, and he hunched into his loose bathrobe, keeping to the shadows of his front step. I removed my fedora and placed it on the vampire's head to shield him from the sun. "Sheldon Fennerman, I'd like you to meet Mavis Wannovich and her sister Alma, two other clients of mine."

"Very satisfied clients." Mavis smiled. "Mr. Chambeaux and Ms. Deyer solved our problems in a most satisfactory way, and he's asked me to help."

"Thank you," Sheldon said, "for whatever it is you're going to do."

"We're going to protect you." Mavis leafed through the spell book, found the correct page, cleared her throat, and glared at the Straight Edgers. "It's only fair to warn you that this is a very powerful protective spell, although you bullies already deserve whatever you've got coming to you."

"You don't scare me," said Todd, looking even more scared than when I'd rescued him from the hot-oil hot tub.

"A pity," Mavis said. "I'm casting this spell over Mr. Fennerman's domicile and his person. Anyone who harms him, or even threatens to harm him, will regret it."

"W-what does the spell do?" Patrick asked.

I said to her, "Be specific, Mavis. They're slow learners."

The witch grinned at the cringing Straight Edgers. "Anyone who harms, or threatens to harm, Mr. Fennerman will experience severe gastric distress. This spell will transform your last meal into a clump of live cockroaches inside your stomach—cockroaches that will do their best to burrow their way out."

Meanwhile, the crowd of monsters had started out ugly and was getting uglier.

"Maybe you should hurry up, Mavis," I whispered.

The witch began reading the incantation, drawing designs in the air and—more for theatrics than magical efficacy—she threw a pinch of smoke powder and set off a tiny bang. Priscilla dropped her sign with a clatter, and the Straight Edgers scattered like crows startled from an old corpse.

Some of the unnaturals glared after them, as if sniffing blood.

"Are they really gone?" Sheldon had tears in his eyes. "Thank you, Mr. Chambeaux! Thank you, madam, and you ..." He nodded toward the sow, who grunted amiably.

"They won't bother you again," Mavis said. "Or if they do, they'll catch a stomach bug they won't soon forget."

I picked up Priscilla's discarded sign and brought it to Sheldon. "Keep this as a souvenir." The vampire was beaming with a smile so wide that I could see the full extent of his very small fangs.

"Would you like to come over for dinner, Mr. Chambeaux? Fondue again? Maybe some games?"

"Not right now. Thank you, Sheldon." I took my hat back. "I have to keep my other clients happy as well."

The skittish vampire looked crestfallen, then turned to Mavis and Alma. "Perhaps you ladies?"

"I love fondue!" Mavis said. Alma snuffled, sounding delighted. Sheldon opened his front door and ushered the sow and witch inside.

CHAPTER 29

Now that the Wannovich sisters and Sheldon Fennerman were all satisfied, we'd wrapped up two cases. Cause for celebration.

But I still hadn't solved my own murder, or Sheyenne's.

I'd made her a promise on her deathbed that I would find out who poisoned her. Every time I looked at her ghost, that pale image of the vibrant young woman who meant so much to me, I remembered the pain and suffering she'd endured as the deadly toxin destroyed her liver and kidneys, made her sink into a shadow of herself, and then death.

That was one case I didn't intend to file in the "Unsolved" drawer.

Sheyenne already had copies of her medical report and autopsy, and as a former med student, she was quite interested in the cause of her own demise. *Amanita phalloides*, the deadliest toadstool in existence. She read up on the toxicology, studied the symptoms, treatment, and prognosis. Back in the office, she was studying the file again.

"I didn't have a chance, Beaux. Whoever slipped me that poison wanted me dead, but she didn't care that I would spend days dying. She knew I wouldn't be able to prove who did it."

"She?" I asked.

"Ivory. If it was up to me, I'd have you deliver her a special toadstool quiche from me. Just to get even."

"I don't think poison works the same on vampires," I said. "And we need proof before we do anything so rash. Fortunately, thanks to Mavis Wannovich, I've got another lead." I smiled, drawing out the suspense. "She gave me the address of a potion supply shop, the best source for toadstool poison in the city. I'm going to have a chat with the proprietor, see if we can find out who purchased the toxin that killed you. Want to go along? The cases don't solve themselves."

I swear I saw a vivid flush of life come back to her cheeks. "Absolutely. I'll consider it a date."

"You're such a romantic."

O   O   O

Grandma Wong's Herbal Warehouse, Potion Ingredients, Botanica, Hoodoo Supply, and Other Exotic Items was a dingy hole-in-the-wall shop filled with more clashing odors than Brondon Morris's sample case. Bunches of dried herbs dangled from the rafters, along with shriveled body parts, both human and animal. Large glass containers held hemlock, deadly nightshade, delicate white flowers of jimsonweed, clumps of graveyard moss. Humanoid mandrake roots were submerged in an oily transparent liquid, twitching as if bored.

Small jars were labeled *Eyes of Newt;* it looked like caviar. Dark vials in a refrigerated bargain bin were marked *Special Today, Virgin's Blood.* Incense smoldered in two small pots, filling the shop with a pungent reek, but a stronger smell of burning weeds came from behind the counter.

The only person inside the shop was definitely not a grandma, and not a Wong, either. The clerk was a young, well-tanned human with a mop of shaggy straw-colored hair, blue eyes, and a vapid smile. His nametag said *Jimmy.* In an ashtray on the glass countertop smoldered a joint the size of an index finger. Not only did Jimmy sell exotic magical herbs, apparently he wasn't averse to sampling them either.

He grinned as we entered—me walking, Sheyenne gliding—but made no effort to rise from his chair. "Mellow day, friends." He drew a long, slow inhalation through his nostrils. "Got everything you need, you know, whatever … a revenge spell or a love charm. Even some excellent seasonings if you're, like, a gourmet cook."

"We're interested in toadstools—poisonous ones," I said. "I understand you're the best supplier in town."

Jimmy didn't exactly recoil (he was far too mellow for that), but he did react with a molasses sort of alarm. "You mean, like death caps?"

"Exactly."

"Nasty stuff, very negative, friend." He picked up his joint and savored a slow toke, then exhaled as he centered himself and calmed his thoughts. He saw me eyeing him, then made a good-natured invitation. "Have a hit yourself, if you want."

"No thanks."

"Oh, this is more than just pure weed. Plenty of special additives in the supply cases here, and I've experimented with a little of everything. Some real magical mystery tours! One even let me see with my eyes shut for a week. Made it really hard to sleep." He held up the smoldering joint. "But this recipe … awesome mix! All in the name of continuing education."

Sheyenne sounded impatient. "Can we get back to the poisonous toadstools?"

"Yeah, we sell that stuff here. How much do you need?"

"I'm more interested in who else purchased it … say, around two months ago."

"Toadstools are a popular item, sells better than nightshade or hemlock," Jimmy said. "Lots of negativity in the world, like I said. Customers of all types—warlocks, necromancers, amateur alchemists, even a few bartenders. And I remember these two witch sisters who bought some … one of them turned into a pig, I think."

"I know about them," I said. "They're the ones who recommended your shop. Can you tell us specifically who else bought the death cap?"

"We're trying to solve a murder," Sheyenne added. "It's very important."

Jimmy got that slow-motion shocked look again. "Murder?" He drew another drag from the joint and exhaled. "I have records. Like, you know, a ledger right here." He moved some papers from the top of the display case and pulled out a three-ring binder. "Death cap toadstools are a controlled substance. I have to keep the supplies behind the counter and write down who buys it, but … uh, I only get around to tallying it up once a month or so."

My pulse would have started pounding, if my heart were still beating. This could be the clue we needed. Excited, Sheyenne drifted closer.

Jimmy opened the binder and flipped through pages and pages, lists of ingredients, customers, dates. He found the toadstool page, but instead of the names, numbers, and columns as on the other pages, we saw only a scrawled, barely legible note: *My Hand Looks Funny*.

Jimmy gave an embarrassed chuckle. "Sorry, man, that was a day I tried a new recipe. Must have lost track …"

Sheyenne looked disappointed, and I was afraid she might go into a poltergeist flurry, creating an herbal storm inside the shop. "You better hope you don't get audited."

The comment distressed Jimmy enough that he had to take another hit to calm himself. He extended the joint to me. "Sure you don't want any, friend?"

Sheyenne and I left.

She was quiet as we walked along the street, each wrapped in our own thoughts. By now it was long after dark. "It'll be okay, Spooky. Even dead ends are progress in a way," I said. "Narrowing down possibilities."

"It's not a total loss," Sheyenne said. "At least I got to spend time with you."

I pulled the phone from my jacket pocket. "I'm going to call Robin and let her know where we are, see if she's heard anything." I dialed the number, and Sheyenne drifted ahead, preoccupied.

A dark sedan drove up the empty street, pulling alongside me. The car paused as the passenger window rolled down. Probably some lost tourist asking for directions.

In my ear, I heard Robin answer the phone. "Hello?"

"Hi, just wanted to let you know—"

I saw the barrel of the pistol extend from the open window, then the bright muzzle flash.

They say you don't hear the one that hits you, but I certainly heard this shot—and five more in rapid succession. The bullets slammed into my chest like a half-dozen linebackers, spinning me around. I tucked my head and tried to roll; my phone went flying.

Sheyenne screamed. "Beaux!"

The dark sedan roared off, tires squealing on the shadowy street.

I sprawled on the sidewalk, broken and tattered, like a rag doll owned by a psychopathic child. Then Sheyenne was hovering over me, yelling for help. It seemed like an odd reversal from when I'd hovered over her hospital bed during her last days.

I groaned. I hadn't felt this bad since I'd been killed.

CHAPTER 30

After the shooter fled, Sheyenne had the presence of mind to grab my phone from where it had skittered down the sidewalk. She shouted to Robin, explained what had happened, then rushed back to me. "Help is on the way!" She was terrified and distraught; being unable to touch me made the situation much worse for her. "I'll stay with you—Robin's coming. We're going to get you fixed up."

I lifted a hand, wanting to brush my fingers through her beautiful hair, but that wasn't going to happen. "I'm fine." I'm not good at telling bald-faced lies. "Did you see who did this? The license plate? The make of the car?"

Sheyenne was crestfallen. "Sorry, I was more worried about you."

I levered myself onto my elbows. "The good news is, we must've stepped on somebody's toes, or they wouldn't have bothered to gun me down. That means we're getting close to something."

Unfortunately, in the past few days I'd been digging into a lot of old cases, making phone calls, asking questions. Who knew which one had pushed the shooter's buttons? He, or she, might be my killer, or Sheyenne's ... or it could be a different person entirely.

The Straight Edgers might be infuriated because of the restraining order I delivered or the protective spell we placed over Sheldon Fennerman. I'd been in Basilisk asking questions, and if Ivory was involved in poisoning Sheyenne, she might have gotten nervous, especially after we went into Grandma Wong's shop. Or, I'd followed Brondon Morris and Harvey Jekyll to their secret meeting in the warehouse. For that matter, the heirs of Alvin Ricketts could have been vindictive now that he'd sold his zombie puppies painting for a large amount at auction.

Sure, I had more enemies than I could shake a stake at, but I had a gut feeling that Jekyll was involved—a conclusion I drew partly from circumstantial evidence and partly because I just plain didn't like the guy. Even if it turned out he had nothing to do with my murder, I still wouldn't have minded seeing him screwed in his divorce.

I slowly sat up on the sidewalk. Sheyenne fussed over me and uttered a string of frustrated curses because she couldn't lend me a hand and help me to my feet. By myself, I managed to stand up again.

I looked at the bullet holes that had torn through my sport jacket. "Son of a bitch, this was my only good suit." A private investigator doesn't require many jackets, but I need at least one without bullet holes.

The six slugs had passed cleanly through my chest. Fortunately, they'd missed my spine, which I really needed in order to keep myself upright. I poked my fingers into the large holes across my torso—it was like Frankenstein's game of connect-the-dots. Every bit of damage to my body was tough to repair, and I had vowed never to become one of those shamblers who fall apart with each jostle or hiccup.

I heard a puttering muffler and recognized the sound of the Pro Bono Mobile. Sheyenne reappeared down the street in the headlights of the oncoming car. She flitted and bobbed like a will-o'-the-wisp, guiding Robin to where I was standing, then she yanked open the passenger door for me so I could collapse inside onto the musty fabric seats.

"Dan, I heard the gunshots on the phone," Robin cried. "Sheyenne said—"

"Just get me to the sawbones, and we'll see how bad the damage really is."

O   O   O

In the month since crawling out of the grave, I hadn't had any occasion to visit the Patchup Parlor of Miss Lujean Eccles, but thanks to word on the street, every zombie knows where to go for an emergency bodily repair.

Miss Eccles operated her business out of an old Victorian home. A large dead oak tree stood out front, from which dangled a tire swing for the human and inhuman children in the neighborhood. Sheyenne's ghost had drifted ahead, passing through the Patchup Parlor's front door to alert Miss Eccles we were coming. Robin helped me out of the car, slung my right arm over her shoulder, and supported me as I stumbled up the tulip-lined path.

I had a hard time getting my legs to move right, and I felt clumsy and stupid—worse, I was acting like a shambler, and that made me both embarrassed and horrified. Wasn't death hard enough already? "I'm just disoriented, that's all," I said. "I'll get better."

"Yes, you will," Robin said. "Or else."

Miss Eccles clucked her tongue as she looked me over. "Oh, my, my!" She was a sweet, plump woman in her late fifties, with gray-brown hair piled in a beehive hairdo that looked like an ancient obelisk. "You look much the worse for wear!"

Robin hurried me into the front room, where I slumped onto an old Victorian flower-print sofa. "Can you treat him?" Sheyenne asked. "Somebody shot him because of me."

"We don't know why I was shot," I said. "Not tonight, and not the first time either."

I ran the ideas over and over in my mind. We'd asked questions of the clerk at Grandma Wong's, but he hadn't given us any names of toadstool customers. And how could anyone have had time to set up the shooting? Jimmy the stoner clerk was the only one who knew we'd asked the questions, and I'd been gunned down less than fifteen minutes after that. Unless Jimmy did it himself ... but I doubted he was in any condition to shoot straight. *My hand looks funny.*

Though he gave us no names, Jimmy had mentioned that bartenders sometimes purchased the death cap extract, but the only bartenders I knew were Francine at the Goblin Tavern—she certainly had no beef with me—and Fletcher at Basilisk.

Fletcher Knowles.

Less than two months before my death, I had butted heads with him about his black-market blood sales. The nightclub manager had an ongoing feud with my previous client Harry Talbot—maybe I'd gotten in the cross fire somehow.

Sheyenne had worked at Basilisk, and *she'd* been poisoned with the toadstool extract.

And Fletcher was the one who had found my body not far from the nightclub.

When I came back from the dead, after reading the ballistics and autopsy results, I had pressed Fletcher about antique Civil War–era guns, specifically a .32 caliber revolver. He rolled his eyes, stroked his blond goatee, and insisted he used only garlic spray and holy water to keep patrons in line....

Now, while Miss Eccles pulled off my ruined sport jacket, Robin worked to unbutton my shirt and expose my chest. Hovering nearby, Sheyenne winced to see the wounds. The bullet holes looked nasty, dark craters in my puckered skin, now leaking embalming fluid. Bruno was going to have to top me off sooner than my regular appointment.

Robin had tears running down her face, but she didn't say a word.

"What's the prognosis?" Sheyenne asked. "If I weren't a ghost, I'd try to fix the damage myself." Her voice hitched at the end.

"Oh, my, my—I won't pretend this isn't going to be a challenge, but I've seen worse," Miss Eccles said. "Don't worry. There've been great advances in restorative mending. When I'm done you'll barely even see the marks."

Before the Big Uneasy, Lujean Eccles had owned and operated a taxidermy shop. Examples of her best work covered the parlor walls—a stuffed raccoon, a moose head, a leaping rainbow trout, and, for some reason, a rooster. I think taxidermy was still her first love, but she filled a greater need by offering pseudo-medical services for the undead.

She switched on two Tiffany lamps beside the sofa and bent close to my wounds. "Lean forward, please." She studied the exit holes in my back. "We can use some wire and plastic braces to repair your ribs. The slugs missed your vertebrae, fortunately. I could have replaced part of your spine with a dowel or a broomstick if I needed to, but you wouldn't have had much flexibility."

"Are any of the bullets still in me?" I asked.

"No, through and through. Six neat holes in front, six in back—it's all very clean."

"What's the internal damage, though?" Sheyenne asked.

"Mostly soft tissue, it looks like," Miss Eccles said. "I'll use a bit of packing material, tight little stitches here and there. I'll reconnect what needs connecting, and you'll be as good as ... as you were. I've even got some scab-salve that really minimizes the marks."

I looked up at Sheyenne, thinking like a PI again. "We need to retrieve at least one of the bullets so we can run ballistics. See if it's the same gun that shot me the first time around."

"I'm on it," she said. "*After* I make sure you're all right."

Robin added, "We'll get even later." Her expression was hard and determined, much like Sheyenne's. "And we *will* get even."

Miss Eccles puffed out her rounded cheeks and blew out a tired-sounding breath. She lifted her head and raised her voice. "Oh, Wendy! Wendy, come in here, would you? Bring my kit. We'll need some of that biofill mixture, the heavy-gauge sutures, and the fine flesh-colored finishing thread."

From the dim doorway that led into the back rooms, I saw a waifish yet hideous figure, a distorted female form. She hesitated to come out into the bright light, but Miss Eccles clucked her tongue again. "No need to be shy, dear—these are friends. We haven't got all night. Can't you see this man needs our help?"

"Yes, miss," Wendy said in a rattling voice. The young woman lurched into the parlor.

Though I had seen many horrific examples of creatures restored to life, this one would have won numerous prizes, and Wendy wasn't exactly a testimonial to the quality of Miss Eccles's work. I could see why the girl didn't like to go out in public.

"This is my Patchwork Princess. I put her back together when no one else would."

Sheyenne said nothing, but her eyes held deep pity. Robin, on the other hand, was ashen beneath her dark skin; she looked away and then seemed embarrassed for having done so.

"The poor girl was a wreck when I got to her—literally a wreck," Miss Eccles said. "She threw herself in front of an oncoming train, and the damage was atrocious."

"Sorry," Wendy said.

"The dear thing was miserable, wanted to end her life. She never expected to come back, but then suicides have a greater chance of resurrection. So there she was, even more miserable than she'd been before. I couldn't let someone suffer like that! So I went back to the train tracks with two empty bushel baskets, picked up every piece I could find, and brought her back here."

"Thank you, miss," Wendy said. Her arms weren't attached right. Her head seemed askew, and she was a crazy quilt of tiny stitches. Triangular pieces of tan Naugahyde had been sewn in places where the skin was gone. "She did the best job she could. I'm grateful."

"I took her under my wing. The poor dear's been a great help to me, and now she realizes that life isn't so bad."

The Patchwork Princess tottered off into the adjoining room and returned with a carpet-bag, which she set on the end table atop a doily.

Miss Eccles opened it and withdrew spools of sewing thread, darning needles, a crochet hook, and flesh-colored thread as well as thicker twine.

"I'd like to assist, if I can," Sheyenne offered as Miss Eccles probed the tears in my skin. The plump woman nodded. "Boar bristle paintbrush." Sheyenne placed the brush in the taxidermy-surgeon's outstretched hand. Humming to herself, concentrating on her work, Miss Eccles used the brush to clean the bullet holes. "Knitting needle." Sheyenne handed her the implement, which Miss Eccles gently eased through the wound and out my back to clean the channel.

Wendy fetched a pot full of gummy packing mixture. While Sheyenne helped Miss Eccles fix my shattered ribs and stitch together the major muscles, the Patchwork Princess hunched in a chair next to the Tiffany lamp. She spread my shirt and sport jacket in her lap, and with clumsy but determined strokes used a needle and thread to sew up the bullet holes.

While Robin watched with fascination, Sheyenne gave her the details about what we'd learned at Grandma Wong's. "I'm sure this has to do with whoever poisoned me. We were snooping around, trying to find out who bought the death cap extract—and then Dan was shot."

"I'll tell Officer McGoohan," Robin said. "We need the police force working on this too!"

I groaned. "No, let me talk to McGoo. He's got his hands full as it is. Besides, I'm supposed to be a hotshot private investigator. If I can't solve this, who can?"

Miss Eccles packed the body cavity with the biofiller, topped it off with cotton, then used almost invisible stitches to close the bullet holes, front and back. Wendy's stitchery wasn't nearly as neat or accurate as the other woman's taxidermy work, but both finished at the same time. Wendy shyly handed me my shirt and jacket.

As I shrugged back into the shirt, my arms seemed to be working well enough. The marks on my chest weren't unnoticeable by any means, but not nearly as bad as I'd feared. Robin fussed over my buttons (even under the best of circumstances, my fingers didn't have their previous dexterity). When I put the sport jacket back on, I decided that the stitched-up bullet holes added character, like a badge of honor.

I made a point of looking at the Patchwork Princess to boost her self-esteem. "Thank you very much, Wendy. Looks like I won't need a new suit after all."

Her smile was crooked, but as bright as sunshine. Miss Eccles said, "You know where to come for a quick fix when the inevitable happens."

Sheyenne paid the woman and thanked her.

"The inevitable's not going to happen anytime soon, Dan," Robin vowed as the two escorted me out of the Patchup Parlor.

Sheyenne added, "And let's not make a habit of this bullet thing."

CHAPTER 31

The next day Sheyenne went on the ghostly warpath. She returned to the scene of the shooting before dawn, found three of the six bullets that had gone through my chest, and delivered them straight to Officer McGoohan. Robin had already given him an indignant report of what happened to me the previous night. It was immediately apparent that this latest batch of bullets did not come from the same .32 caliber weapon as the one that had shot me in the head. These bullets were from a .38, like my own gun.

Great—two people were shooting at me, or the same person using two different guns.

First thing in the morning, McGoo submitted the slugs for testing and came to our offices. He tried to act casual, but I could tell by his red face that he had hurried over. "What's the matter, Shamble—getting shot once wasn't enough for you?"

"I can tell you, it doesn't get better with practice."

He did not manage to hide his concern. "So, you all right? Getting shot isn't such a big deal for you, is it?"

I gave him the "Are you kidding me?" look. "I'm patched up, and you can hardly see the bullet wounds. Cosmetic repairs have come a long way since the Big Uneasy. Want to see?"

"I'll take your word for it. No need to strip," McGoo said, then he got serious. "Who the hell did you rile up now?"

"I wish I knew. I'm still trying to figure out who murdered me the first time."

He snorted. "Some private eye."

"The suspect list is getting longer by the minute. We were trying to track down the source of the toadstool poison that killed Sheyenne, and Harvey Jekyll knows that I'm breathing down his neck, and I delivered a restraining order to the Straight Edgers, and the Ricketts family is mad because I recovered the stolen painting that just sold at auction. Enough? I've also got half a dozen other cases if we want to cast a wider net."

"If you worked on one case at a time, the suspect pool would be more limited."

"Great idea, McGoo."

"After what happened last night, you'd have been safer with me chasing down a giant monster."

"How did the hunt go?"

He blew a sigh out through his lips. "Didn't see the big brute, but I checked out all the vandalism sites. A lot of them have broken windows, but not the additional extreme damage we found at the Hope and Salvation Mission. Funny thing ... most of the smashed windows are being repaired by a new company called Black Glass."

I remembered the dapper, perfume-drenched zombie with frock coat and top hat. "I've met him—Franklin Galworthy. He's fixing the Hope and Salvation Mission too ... but Black Glass doesn't have much competition in the Quarter. Who you gonna call?" Then I understood the implication. "You think he's taking advantage of the situation, smashing windows to drum up extra business for himself?"

"Could very well be. I don't think that guy could crush bricks with his bare hands or rip apart door frames ... but the rest of the damage could have been done by a copycat."

He shuffled his feet, not sure what else to say. I could see the deep concern on his face, so I let him off the hook. "I'll take care of myself, McGoo—don't worry. Let me know if the ballistics lab comes up with any match on the bullets."

"Scout's honor."

O O O

Robin was tense and preoccupied, pacing around the office lobby as if rehearsing a closing argument for a jury. Then I remembered that this was the day when she and Ramen Ho-Tep would meet with the Metropolitan Museum staff to negotiate a possible solution. The fact that I'd been gunned down didn't have any effect on the other appointments on our calendar.

In the conference room, she had spread out her folders and documents next to her yellow legal pad. Piled casebooks formed a small pyramid, and the mummy's rolled-up hieroglyphic papyrus sat adjacent to the law books. She had set a glass of water at each place, with a pitcher in the middle of the table.

Robin bit her lip, and I could see she needed some encouragement. "You'll do fine."

She gave me a hesitant smile. "I'll bring my A game, Dan. I always do. Will you be in there with me?"

"If both parties allow it. You know I've always got your back."

Ramen Ho-Tep shuffled in early, step-step-*draaaag*, step-step-*draaaag*. He had given himself plenty of time to get across town from the museum. The mummy coughed nervously, and a moth came out of his throat.

At precisely 10:00 *a.m.*, the museum curator entered our offices with two members of his legal counsel, the director of the museum board, and a young man whose purpose I couldn't ascertain, probably an intern. They swooped into our main reception area like a murder of business-suited crows.

Robin greeted them professionally. "Welcome, gentlemen. Our aim today is to reach a satisfactory and mutually beneficial resolution on this matter so that my client and I don't need to pursue further legal action."

"We have prepared a lawsuit of our own," said Bram Steffords, the curator, "and we have the full financial and legal resources of the museum at our disposal."

Ramen Ho-Tep lurched forward. "And I was Pharaoh of all Egypt! I have the wealth of my entire land, much of which you have on display in your museum. That's stolen property! I am the rightful owner! I—"

Robin held up a hand. "Shall we sit down and begin our discussions?" She turned to the curator and gave him a hard look. "Just so you know, Chambeaux and Deyer is taking Mr. Ho-Tep's case on a pro bono basis, and I intend to pursue it vigorously, for as long as necessary. He has no financial concerns in this matter."

From behind the receptionist desk, Sheyenne let out a groan that she almost, but not quite, managed to cover up.

The guys-in-ties from the museum took their places in the conference room, sitting motionless as if they were on exhibit themselves. Sheyenne did not offer them coffee or tea; room-temperature water would have to do. I sat next to Robin, slightly more limber than Ramen Ho-Tep, who also settled into his seat.

Robin laid out the facts of the case, most of which the museum's legal representative disputed. Growing impatient, she said, "Should this matter go to trial, I'll have Mr. Ho-Tep take the stand, and every member of the jury will acknowledge that he is a sentient individual who should be free, while the museum considers him mere property. He can speak for himself very well. *And* with a British accent."

Steffords's legal counsel said, "And we have bills of sale along with exchange agreements with the Egyptian Department of Antiquities, which grant us the right to retain Mr. Ho-Tep and other ancient artifacts for display in the museum. He is a primary draw for our patrons."

The curator added, "However, the Necronomicon exhibit is our most popular attraction right now."

"You must let me go!" the mummy insisted. "I will accept nothing less than the freedom that is my due."

"And where exactly will you go if you leave the museum, Mr. Ho-Tep?" Steffords snapped. "Find a little apartment? Get yourself dry-cleaned?"

Indignant, the mummy balled his fists, his bony fingers crackling like tiny pieces of broken bamboo rolled into a ball. "Beware, lest I unleash the Pharaoh's Curse upon you!"

The curator chuckled. "There's no such thing as the Pharaoh's Curse."

Leaning across the table, the mummy said, "Can you really be certain about that, since the Big Uneasy? Are you bloody idiots prepared to wager your lives on that assumption? *I've* nothing to lose."

The entire coterie from the museum blanched.

Robin intervened. "Please, let's not go down that path. Wouldn't you rather examine this problem and try to find an amicable solution?"

Ramen Ho-Tep and Bram Steffords made disbelieving sounds in unison, as if they were part of the same choir.

I had seen this type of enmity in custody or divorce cases, when the two sides are so bitter, so filled with animosity toward each other, that they won't consider any solution unless the opposing party loses entirely. They don't care whether possessions or children or common decency are thrown under the bus, so long as the other side *doesn't* win. It looked as if the mummy and museum representatives were reaching that point. Robin might need to redefine *win* for each side in order for this to work.

She looked down at the notes on her legal pad and laid out her argument. "Let's consider for a moment: What exactly does the museum require from Mr. Ho-Tep? And what specifically does Mr. Ho-Tep want out of his situation?"

"We want him on display for all of our museum patrons," said the curator. "That is nonnegotiable."

"And I want *respect*. When I was Pharaoh, the population of the Nile Valley bowed to me. I lived in glorious times, times that have been forgotten, and the world needs to be re-educated! Egyptian society formed the basis of all human civilization."

Robin's eyes sparkled. "That settles it, then! The solution is obvious."

Steffords frowned. "Not to me."

She said, "Mr. Ho-Tep is your prized Egyptian artifact, but you're not using him to full advantage."

The mummy crossed his bandaged arms over his bandaged chest. "I feel quite sufficiently used, thank you."

"I mean, what better ambassador for teaching museum patrons about daily life in Egypt than Mr. Ho-Tep? Instead of keeping him sealed in a display case and away from the public, wouldn't it be better to have him act as the docent in your Ancient Egypt wing? You could have story hour. Let him tell all the listeners about his reign and his culture."

The curator looked at his legal counsel, who shrugged. Steffords said, "He's never volunteered to do anything like that."

"You never asked!" the mummy retorted, then looked over at Robin. Because his lips were so desiccated and stiff, I couldn't tell whether he was smiling or not. (I should have taken the sample of emBalm that Brondon Morris had offered me.) "Yes ... I could tell museum visitors about Egypt. The real Egypt. In fact, I'd bring it to life, tell them about my home, my family, my mates. 'Real Housewives of the Nile.' I could make quite a show of it. Brilliant!"

Robin said encouragingly to the curator, "Mr. Ho-Tep could be the star of your museum, sir, not just part of an exhibit."

"But only twice a week," Ramen Ho-Tep interjected. "And I need to be treated with proper respect."

"What does that mean?" Steffords sounded exasperated.

"He gets a salary," Robin said, "and an actual job title."

Ho-Tep piped up. "And a name tag, just like one of yours, to pin right here." He tapped the bandages on the left side of his chest.

The museum men huddled together, whispering. Steffords said, "Mr. Ho-Tep must cooperate fully with our educational objectives. It goes without saying that he'll have to follow appropriate standards of behavior."

"I was Pharaoh of all Egypt!"

Bram Steffords yawned. "Yes, yes, we know."

"And I will need slaves," the mummy continued. "Armies of them, like the ones who built my pyramid."

"We can't offer *that* many, but we might find you an assistant or two."

"We could assign an intern for that purpose," the museum board member suggested.

When the conversation fell into a lull, and no one made any further demands or protests, Robin closed her folder. She distilled the copious notes on her legal pad into a basic agreement on a clean sheet of paper, which she passed around for signature. "This will do for now. I'll have our paralegal type up a more detailed memorandum of understanding to summarize this meeting, and we'll draft a contract outlining the specific terms to which both the Metropolitan Museum and my client will be bound. I don't believe we need to pursue any further legal action, if we are agreed on the general principles?"

She looked at the business-suited men, who all nodded slightly, then, seeing their fellows do the same, nodded with more vigor. Ramen Ho-Tep leaned back in his chair, looking pleased. He nodded as well. I had to smile: Robin made it seem so easy.

She ushered the men out, cool and professional, and as soon as they were gone, she threw her arms around the ambulatory mummy, giving him a hug. He squawked, "Do be careful! I just heard something snap!"

She backed away, brushing dust off her business suit. "Sorry, I'm just so pleased."

Sheyenne drifted close to the mummy. "You understand that when Ms. Deyer told the museum representatives this was a pro bono case, it was merely a bluffing tactic? If you have any spare treasures of ancient Egypt, we still expect to be paid for our services—provided you're happy with the results of our work."

Ramen Ho-Tep sounded pleased. "Indeed, I am absolutely delighted! I've no doubt I can slip a golden ankh or scarab from a display case to donate to your finances."

Robin seemed embarrassed that Sheyenne would bring up money at such a celebratory time, but I added, "Our fees allow us to keep our offices open, Mr. Ho-Tep, so we can help other unnaturals in similar situations." After our cut from the Ricketts art auction, we were definitely going to have a good month, for a change. A solid payment from the emancipated mummy would keep us in business for a good time to come.

"I understand completely. I was a benevolent pharaoh. I shall meet my obligation to you." When the mummy left, I noticed he no longer dragged his foot.

Robin threw her arms around me. Sheyenne said in a longing tone, "I wish I could do the same, Beaux." I settled for giving her an air-hug instead.

Then a set of metal file drawers rattled open, one after another, and manila case folders scattered out as if they were spring-loaded. Papers flew in the air. With a swirling blur, the ghost of Uncle Stan appeared before us. He stretched his lips in what was intended to be a fearsome grimace. His eyes bugged out. He swirled and did somersaults in the air, dove down into the file cabinets, and unleashed another eruption of papers. He appeared more inebriated than he had during his previous manifestation.

Sheyenne was outraged. "You stop that!" She tumbled into him, poltergeist against poltergeist, knocking Uncle Stan for a loop. They both slammed into the wall, passed through, and reappeared, still tussling.

When Sheyenne released him, Uncle Stan was astonished that anyone would stand up to him. "You're ruining everything!" His lower lip trembled, and I thought he was going to start blubbering. "Stop trying to turn my own family against me!"

With a final blast of poltergeist power, he scattered the papers of the Dorset file around the office, then vanished into thin air.

I said, "Never a dull moment."

CHAPTER 32

I helped Sheyenne retrieve the scattered papers and folders in the ghost's aftermath, but I let her do the organizing (since she understands our filing system better than anyone). Robin retreated into her office to start drafting the contract between Ramen Ho-Tep and the museum.

And I finally told Sheyenne my idea of having her do a little fieldwork on the Jekyll case. "You never know what we might find," I said. I didn't even have to twist her arm, metaphorically speaking.

"I've been a med student, exotic dancer, cocktail waitress, nightclub singer, paralegal, and administrative assistant, but I'm happy to add a few more titles to my résumé. Besides, Harvey Jekyll or one of his henchmen could have been the shooter last night."

Miranda had provided a detailed description of the Jekyll mansion's layout, so we knew where her husband kept his secret materials. Since she would never deign to make a sketch, that afternoon Miranda sent over a pristine copy of the house's construction blueprints, obtained from the county records office.

With a magnanimous swish of her hand, she unrolled the drawings onto Sheyenne's desk. "Here you are, sweethearts. Legally speaking, I can't imagine why you might be interested in the design and arrangement of my home, especially not the location of Harvey's secure and private study *right here*." With a sly smirk, she pointed to the appropriate spot on the blueprints. "I'll just assume you're remodeling your offices and wish to study prime architectural examples."

I began to speak, but Miranda raised one scarlet fingernail. "Not a word! As I said, I don't want to hear it ... at least not until you have something." She flounced out of our offices, leaving Sheyenne and me to study the blueprints.

Robin was uneasy. "I don't like the precedent, Dan. By law, any evidence you obtain in this manner is tainted and inadmissible."

I don't generally keep secrets from my partner, but Robin still didn't know precisely how I'd gathered the documents that proved JLPN's involvement in the vampire shampoo scandal. "Think of it this way," I said. "Miranda Jekyll is still the legal co-owner of that home, and until the divorce case is settled, she's entitled to fifty percent of the contents. Unless her husband succeeds in nullifying the prenuptial agreement, aren't we within Miranda's legal rights, if she asks us to enter on her behalf? And borrow an item that is fifty percent hers?"

Sheyenne added, "It's not technically breaking and entering if I just walk through a wall or a window, is it?"

Robin remained skeptical. "We're on very shaky legal ground here. It could jeopardize our case—and get me disbarred, not to mention thrown in jail."

"On the other hand, unless we secure this evidence, we don't have a case to jeopardize," I pointed out.

Not willing either to admit defeat or give us her implicit permission, Robin took a stack of files into her office. "I'm going to prepare a brief. I'll be unavailable for most of the night." She closed the door. "And don't you dare get shot."

Sheyenne and I glanced at each other and decided it was time to go.

O   O   O

I was no longer limber or athletic enough for the cat-burglar acrobatics I would need to break into Jekyll's mansion. I'd always solved my own problems and done my own legwork, so it was frustrating to be on the sidelines. Sheyenne had to take part of the risk without me.

As soon as full night fell, I parked the car under a thick overhanging willow two blocks away from Jekyll's tree-lined mansion, which was surrounded by a red brick wall topped with wrought-iron spikes. During my initial round of surveillance months ago, I had managed to snap a few photos of a man with little social life occupying himself with uninteresting activities at home. It hadn't been worth the risk.

Now, however, Sheyenne knew where to look, and she was our very best chance for getting what we needed.

Since this was her first covert mission, I needed to see what Sheyenne saw. We settled on a tiny video camera, the kind of thing that would have awed a 1960s-era James Bond, but was now everyday technology. Sheyenne's spectral presence made the grainy image fade in and out when I received it on my smartphone stream.

The sound from the speaker was fuzzed with static, but I could hear her voice. "Check. Beaux, can you hear me? Check."

"Loud and clear, but let's be a little less loud, please."

"Sorry," she whispered.

Fidgeting, I waited under the willow, well out of sight of Jekyll's security guards who patrolled the grounds, while I watched the images on my smartphone. Sheyenne could make herself mostly transparent and could pass through solid walls; however, the camera, while admittedly small, could not pass through walls and might catch the eye of an alert observer as it drifted through the air. She needed to be very careful.

She crossed the grounds and pointed the camera to show me a couple of business-suited Secret Service types standing at strategic points. Two Dobermans trotted the perimeter like angular shadows.

"Stay clear of the dogs," I whispered. "If they start barking, everyone'll be on alert."

"Don't worry, I've never had trouble with dogs."

Some ghosts drive dogs into a frenzy of growling and barking; other ghosts, like Sheyenne, could have worked at the animal shelter without causing any particular distress. Even so, I didn't want the Dobermans to chase the small floating camera as if it were a chew toy.

Sheyenne drifted to the east wing of the home, then levitated to a set of windows on the second floor that marked Harvey's private study. "I can just pop inside and take a look."

"Bring the camera," I told her.

"In a minute. I need to make sure the window doesn't have alarm wires before I open it and bring the object through."

She set the small camera on the outer windowsill, leaving me with an extreme close-up image of the English ivy that Jekyll's landscapers had planted along the brick walls. I endured five minutes of nerve-wracking silence, punctuated only by a woolly caterpillar munching its way through a leaf. Finally, the study window swung outward just enough for Sheyenne to slip the camera through and carry it into the study.

"He did have an alarm system," Sheyenne said into the microphone. "I went to the control box and tickled it, made all the lights go haywire."

"Be careful."

"Do you hear any alarms? Don't worry, I'm inside. Let me get to work."

She panned the camera for me, and I got my first view of Harvey Jekyll's study. It looked like a perfectly normal home office with a large desk, cherrywood file cabinets, comfortable executive chair in oxblood leather, Italian designer lighting, and a high-end stereo system beside a marble shelf filled with old CD jewel cases.

It was too much to hope that she would find secret Nazi flags, embarrassing transvestite outfits, or even some of the vampire pedophilia that Gomez Ricketts had been selling out of his storage unit. Sheyenne panned the camera across the CD spines: The Best of Hall and Oates, the Bee Gees, England Dan and John Ford Coley, the Little River Band, and more Barry Manilow.

Yes, this was Harvey Jekyll's study, all right.

Then I saw one of the bullhorn-on-toaster gadgets he had kept in his corporate office. A portable ectoplasmic defibrillator. "Be careful around that device," I said. "Jekyll designed it to protect against ghosts."

"I'm not touching any controls, just having a look around."

A folded newspaper with a half-finished crossword puzzle lay on the desk next to a calculator and a day planner. Sheyenne flipped through the planner, looking for anything suspicious. He had marked a tiny asterisk on the day when I'd spotted him and Brondon Morris going to their secret club meeting; several other dates also bore asterisks. Other than that, Jekyll had jotted down only a few dinner parties, a dentist's appointment, and a note to pick up dry cleaning.

"He wouldn't leave anything incriminating out in the open," I said. "Can you find the locked drawer that Miranda told us about?"

She pointed the camera down at a heavy secured lock. "It's pretty obvious. Let me do my poltergeist thing and see if I can jiggle the tumblers."

"Be careful," I warned.

"Don't be a worrywart." She worked for a few minutes, and finally the bolt popped down so she could slide open the drawer. Inside, she found a floppy purple head covering, like a dunce cap, and a foot-long golden measuring stick, some kind of ceremonial object.

Sheyenne figured out the significance. "It's a straight edge, Beaux."

From the bottom of the drawer she took a small velvet case that opened to reveal a thick silver ring. "Well, look at what I found."

Sheyenne pointed the camera close. A straight line had been scribed across the silver surface on the face of the ring, surrounded by the words Grand Wizard.

I felt cold as the realization sank in. Harvey Jekyll wasn't just dabbling with the Straight Edgers. According to this ring, he was their leader.

"Now, that's certainly something Harvey wouldn't want made public," I said.

Suddenly the camera jerked, and the sound pickup transmitted the door banging open, voices shouting. I heard a man say, "The desk alarm was triggered—somebody must be in here!"

The view from the camera swung wildly back and forth. I glimpsed Harvey Jekyll looking like a gnome in a fur-lined smoking jacket, flanked by two burly security goons. They charged into the room.

"Spooky, get out of there!" I yelled.

The crossword puzzle newspaper and day planner flew up into the air, twirling around as Sheyenne unleashed her inner poltergeist. The desk lamp flicked on and off. File drawers opened and closed, clattering as folders sprayed a geyser of loose documents. The guards shouted, to little effect.

Jekyll, though, staggered into the spectral whirlwind and dove for the credenza. He grabbed the ectoplasmic defibrillator and turned the end of the bullhorn toward Sheyenne.

The image from the camera shot forward as if I were riding a bullet, heading straight toward the widening eyes of Harvey Jekyll. Then the screen went blank, filled with static. The camera feed was gone.

"Spooky!" I called, but got no answer.

Even from two blocks away I could hear the commotion behind the brick walls. I needed to go there and help Sheyenne somehow, but I knew I'd never get past the alerted guards. Bright beams stabbed into the dark as security lights blazed around the mansion perimeter. The Dobermans howled.

Suddenly, with a gusting cold breeze, Sheyenne was there in front of me. "Better get in the car and head out of here, Beaux. They're bound to do a sweep in just a few seconds."

"What happened? The camera went dark. I thought ..."

"I had to distract them, so I threw it in Jekyll's face. I didn't want to forget this." In her ghostly hand she held up the Grand Wizard ring.

"I wish I could kiss you right now," I said. I settled for giving her a heartfelt wink.

"Ditto," Sheyenne replied. "But use your imagination and figure out how to thank me later. Let's get back to the office."

I started the rusty Pro Bono Mobile with a roar and a putter, and we raced away.

CHAPTER 33

hough Robin couldn't fault our results when we gave her the full report, she was less than enthusiastic to learn about the commotion we had caused.

"You couldn't have been more subtle?" she asked. "Sabotaging his home alarm system, opening a second-story window, tampering with the lock on the desk drawer, stealing private property!" She sounded very discouraged. "Jekyll is going to guess we were involved."

"I didn't leave any fingerprints," Sheyenne objected.

"More importantly, it'll never go to court," I said. "If he thinks we've got his Grand Wizard ring, I very much doubt he'll risk us making it public."

"Maybe he can't prove we were the ones who broke in," Robin said, "but we can't prove the ring belongs to him either. We have a Straight Edge ring—so what? He'll deny it."

"We have the running video of me taking the ring from the study," Sheyenne said.

Robin did not look happy. "And that video proves you broke in. We need to delete it. Besides, just because you found the ring in a drawer doesn't mean it's *Jekyll's* or what he was doing with it. He might say Miranda planted it there."

"Even so, we'd better set up a meeting with Mrs. Jekyll—preferably tonight—to discuss how best to leverage this." I suspected that for once, Miranda might make time for a scheduled appointment. "In the meantime we'd better keep the ring in the safe, locked tight."

○ ○ ○

An hour before midnight, I joined McGoo in the Goblin Tavern for a quick beer. It felt good to get back to anything that passed for normal. Sheyenne had managed to set up a meeting with Miranda Jekyll at Basilisk—a public place, for safety, and late enough to accommodate her busy social schedule.

In the meantime, I informed McGoo that Sheldon Fennerman was now under a protection spell, but more importantly I let him know what we'd (unofficially) discovered in Harvey Jekyll's mansion. The Grand Wizard's ring was safely locked away, but I wanted McGoo aware of the situation, just in case. No telling what Jekyll or his goons might try to pull, and I had no intention of being gunned down a third time.

To prevent Robin from having legal heartburn, I chose my words carefully. "This is hypothetical, McGoo. I'm not actually saying that Sheyenne *did* slip into somebody's private study, or that she *did* obtain a very interesting and incriminating object."

"I get it, Shamble. We're just talking in general terms." He slurped his beer. "But—also in general terms—you need to be damned careful. You're playing with fire here." He looked up. "Say, are zombies afraid of fire, like in *Night of the Living Dead*?"

"I'm no more afraid of fire than a lot of other things," I said. "Clowns, though, they give me the creeps."

"You know what kind of streets zombies like best, Shamble?"

"What?" He had suckered me into another stupid joke.

"Dead ends."

"That's not even remotely funny."

Before we could finish our first beers, the radio crackled at McGoo's shoulder, and he acknowledged, listening to the squelch of code words. He looked at me. "Another disturbance at the Hope and Salvation Mission. Mrs. Saldana says it's an emergency."

I swung off the bar stool and moved as quickly as I could. "The monster's back?"

"No, this is something else." He headed off at a jog, and I kept up with him, glad for the hours I put in on the treadmill at All-Day/All-Nite Fitness.

In front of Mrs. Saldana's mission, by the light of the street lamps, I saw glass shattered on the sidewalk, lots of it, enough for two large windowpanes. The old woman huddled against the brick wall in her ubiquitous flower-print dress, her face filled with revulsion. She pressed her hands together as if praying while she stared at a puddle of red and tan goo that looked like rejected by-products from a cat-food factory. Off to the side, a black silk top hat lay where it had fallen to the ground, next to a frock coat and checkered waistcoat.

From behind her, in the yawning gaps where the windows hadn't yet been replaced, I saw the equally frightened Jerry, her gaunt right-hand zombie. He shuddered in the shadows, afraid to come outside.

We hurried up to Mrs. Saldana, making sure she was in no danger.

"It's horrible, horrible! Right before my eyes, he just ... *melted!*" The old woman's teeth chattered together. Through the open window, Jerry handed her one of the worn Bibles, and she clutched it to her chest, rocking back and forth.

"Who melted? What happened?" McGoo pulled out his notebook. "Shamble, can you ID the vic?"

I glanced down at the shapeless goo. Broken window glass. Black top hat. Among the reek of soupy flesh and bone, I smelled the distinctive scent of Zom-Be-Fresh. "My guess is that it's Franklin Galworthy. He was here replacing glass for Mrs. Saldana." I nudged the hat with the toe of my shoe. "And he liked to wear a lot of cologne."

The old woman finally found her voice. "Yes, Mr. Galworthy was here working late installing the new window. He's been so busy lately with all those smashed windows around town, and he was working late. I had just stepped out to bring him some lemonade." She glanced down, and I saw a paper cup in a little puddle. "I dropped it. I'm sorry for the mess, Officer."

"Don't you worry about it, Mrs. Saldana."

Her voice hitched as she relived the nightmare. "Poor Mr. Galworthy! He groaned in pain, then squirmed, and dropped the glass pane he was carrying. Shattered all over the sidewalk. I thought he was hurt, and then ... this happened. The poor man!"

"Nobody came by and doused him with acid?" I asked. "You didn't see a warlock cast some kind of dissolving spell?"

"No, Mr. Chambeaux. Why would anyone want to hurt a hardworking businessman? He spent all day fixing windows."

Jerry finally shuffled outside, reassured now that I hadn't melted in front of Mrs. Saldana. He carried a shovel and a bucket. "I'll clean this up."

"Not until the detectives get here. This is evidence." McGoo wrinkled his nose. "But it is disgusting." He nudged the collapsed frock coat that

167

lay in the ooze and bent over to inspect it with great reluctance. In the pocket, he found two sample sachets of Zom-Be-Fresh, which he plucked out. "Samples from JLPN's new line. Looks like Brondon Morris gets around."

Remembering how Sheyenne had suffered a severe rash from using the necroceuticals, I wondered if this horrible meltdown might be the result of another JLPN glitch, just like the garlic shampoo. "Can I take one of those packets and a sample of the goo? Run a comparative analysis?"

"Help yourself." McGoo handed me one of the packets. "You'll probably get to it faster than the department crime lab. All you zombies are buddies, right?"

"You might say I've got some skin in the game."

The police radio squawked again. "Officer McGoohan, what's your 20?"

"I'm still 10-8 at the mission—what's up?"

The dispatcher rattled off an address. "Domestic disturbance, possible 10-10 fight in progress. You're the nearest officer available."

He grumbled something about the precinct being understaffed. "On my way. That's just a few blocks from here."

I turned to McGoo, my interest piqued. "I recognize that address—it's Straight Edge headquarters." I recalled the angry crowd around Sheldon Fennerman's apartment. "Things got ugly on the streets earlier today. The Straight Edgers insulted a lot of unnaturals. Maybe somebody decided to take the law into their own hands."

McGoo looked as if a hairball had caught in his throat. "Maybe I should let them deal with the problem themselves." He let out a weary sigh. "My job would be a lot easier if I didn't have to protect idiots from being idiots."

After making apologies to Mrs. Saldana, we hurried off to the next emergency. Before we'd gone a block, we could hear the screams—truly bloodcurdling screams—and loud smashing sounds, as if someone were playing Find the Breakable Object with a baseball bat inside a curio shop.

The lights were on but flickering inside Straight Edge headquarters. The front door had been torn off its hinges and hurled across the street, like someone tossing a playing card. I could hear nostril-burbling roars.

As we ran closer, McGoo yelled, "Stop! Police!"

In response, the broken body of one of the three Straight Edge boys—Scott, I think—sailed through the smashed window and tumbled into the gutter. His red T-shirt was now saturated with other shades of red.

McGoo yelped, drew his weapon, and charged toward the open door.

"Call for backup!" I shouted.

"What do you think *you* are, Shamble? You've got a gun, come on!" I drew my .38, and we both approached.

The head of another Straight Edger—beanpole Todd, with red marks from the duct tape still prominent around his mouth—rolled out like a bowling ball and stopped in the middle of the street, eyes wide open, as if disappointed that he hadn't scored any points in the game.

Inside the headquarters, we came upon a scene of further carnage. Priscilla lay dead in two pieces on the floor. Patrick had been dismembered, as if some malicious child had plucked off his arms and legs, like a doll.

A battering sound as loud as a bomb blast came from the back, and McGoo and I charged in pursuit, armed and ready. A huge shape had hammered its own opening through the brick wall, and as soon as we entered, the suspended ceiling collapsed. An explosion of mortar and cement dust flew up in the air, obscuring our view, but I could see the thing was enormous.

McGoo, due to his training, shouted another quick warning; I didn't bother—I just opened fire. My silver-jacketed bullets did no good; McGoo also fired his weapon. One of the ceiling panels tumbled down and doused him with gypsum dust.

The hulking creature lumbered out into the alley and the darkness, completely ignoring us. I scrambled over the rubble and emerged just in time to see the huge shape scuttle with freakish speed up a drainpipe. It swung over a roof ledge and bounded away.

McGoo stood beside me, eyes wide. His cap had fallen off at some point during the chase, and his hair was mussed and covered with gray gypsum dust.

In the back room, we found the headless body that obviously belonged to Todd's head, the bowling-ball wannabe. One of the Straight Edge signs—*Unnatural, Unclean, Unwanted*—mounted on a wooden stick had been thrust entirely through his skinny chest, pinning him to the linoleum floor.

McGoo looked down at the impaled headless body. "What a clusterfart. We're gonna be out here all night. Why did I ask to be assigned to this precinct again, Shamble?"

"You didn't," I said.

"Oh, right." He got on his radio and called in the crime.

CHAPTER 34

A crowd gathered as the police team decorated the area in crime-scene chic. The medical examiner pronounced the bodies dead on the scene (not an intellectual stretch), and evidence techs took photos from every angle. The body wagon arrived, staffed by three ghouls, who piled out at the blood-spattered Straight Edge headquarters, showing an inappropriate amount of enthusiasm. Under the circumstances, nobody complained.

One of the ghouls retrieved Todd's severed head, which was still lying in the street. The other two ghouls each carried a clipboard bearing a diagram of a generic human body. As they collected torn body parts and severed limbs, they made checkmarks on the diagram to make sure they had rounded up all of the pieces. In some cases, it wasn't exactly clear which item belonged to which Straight Edger, but back at the Medical Examiner's Bureau they would sort it all out, putting the puzzle back together.

A year ago, the ME had been reprimanded for doing exactly that—putting puzzles together out of severed body parts and then trying to reanimate them, in the grand old tradition. He managed to keep his job only after apologizing profusely and promising henceforth to engage in such work only on his own time.

"You want to go down and work with the sketch artist, Shamble?" McGoo asked. "You got a better look than I did."

"Just a glimpse. Big, hulking, ugly." I gestured to the blood splattered on the walls and floor, and the bodies that had been torn asunder by the creature's bare hands. "Find anybody who meets the general description, and I'll try to pick him out of a lineup."

While crime scene photographers documented the operation, the ghouls hauled away the last of the disassembled Straight Edgers in plastic bags.

Queasy, McGoo said in a boneheaded attempt at levity, "Got another one for you, Shamble. What's invisible and smells like brains?"

"You're making jokes? Now?"

"Defuses the tension. Come on, why."

I knew the answer this time. "Zombie farts. Got any more?"

"A million of 'em."

"Then keep them to yourself." I turned slowly, staring at the smashed door and windows, the sheer violence inherent in the attacker. This had to be the same thing that had wrecked the Hope & Salvation Mission. I was very thankful Mrs. Saldana had not been killed.

McGoo said, "Solve this one for me, Shamble, and I'll buy you a beer. Scout's honor."

I snorted. "This has to be worth at least two beers."

"All right. Just remember I'm on a cop's salary."

"And I'm on a PI's salary."

The body wagon pulled away, weaving from side to side as if the ghoul drivers hoped to increase their nightly business by running over a few pedestrians on the way back to the morgue.

The police radio squawked again. "Officer McGoohan, 10-16 Code 3! Zombie fight, two suspects in the middle of the street. Reporting party says it looks like they're trying to kill each other—again."

McGoo rolled his eyes, relieved to answer a less gruesome call. "Now, that's the kind of disturbance I can deal with. On my way. McGoohan out." He shook his head and turned to me. "Well, come on—if it's two shamblers fighting, that's your people. Maybe you can help."

"Not exactly how I expected to spend my evening. I do have other plans." By now, it was nearly time for me to meet Miranda Jekyll over at Basilisk.

"You're such a social butterfly, Shamble."

As we ran up the block, we could hear cheering and jeering. A crowd had gathered along the sidewalks on both sides of the street, laughing, making catcalls and suggestions.

Two decrepit male shamblers circled each other like boxers. They were rotted, hideous hulks to start with, not counting the further damage they were inflicting upon each other. They moved in a grueling, drooling slow-motion cage fight. One wore a sky-blue, wide-collared tux like something from a retro prom, but it was smeared with mud from the grave and discolored by leaking bodily fluids. The other zombie wore a too-tight Disneyland hoodie, also splotched with graveyard dirt stains and effluvia. (Who in the world would want to be buried in a Disneyland hoodie? Or a prom tux, for that matter?)

Disney Dude swung his left arm loosely back like a dangling maladjusted catapult and drove it upward until his fist slammed into the side of Prom Boy's face. The blow made a wet squelching sound and a crack that signified a dislocated jaw. Two teeth sprayed from Prom Boy's torn mouth like little white Chiclets. His eyeball bulged from the left socket, then popped out.

The audience let out a gasp, followed by more shouts and smattered applause. In retaliation, Prom Boy swung his fist in a vicious right cut that cracked into the side of Disney Dude's ribs, sinking into the flesh and splurting out a stain that soaked through the hoodie. Another round of cheers.

Disney Dude, with a motion like a pile driver, slammed his other fist into Prom Boy's face, smashing his nose and caving in his features.

"Go get him!" yelled a vampire from the sidelines. "Take him down, mess him up!" It wasn't clear which of the zombies he was egging on; the rest of the crowd hooted similar encouragement.

Another blow slammed into the side of Disney Dude's head, cracking his orbital bone. The eyeball drooped out so that it dangled by the optic nerve and blood vessels, staring down at the Sleeping Beauty Castle on his sweatshirt rather than at his opponent.

With a wordless growl, Disney Dude tried to claw the remaining shreds of flesh from his rival's cheek, but Prom Boy grabbed the fingers and snapped them back. With a vicious yank he pulled them entirely off his opponent's hand and tossed the fingers like Mardi Gras trinkets to the audience, much to their glee.

McGoo yelled at both shamblers in his gruff authoritarian voice. "Break it up! Aren't you two decomposing fast enough?"

Reeling, the two brawlers separated, swayed, and let out angry moans from the bottom of their throats. Their words were slurred and incomprehensible, but I think they both said, "He started it!"

We heard a feminine wail from around the corner, and I groaned. Was this night ever going to end? Someone ran toward the scene with a lurching, cockeyed gait—a young woman with long hair, tight dress, and mismatched body parts, her face a mass of scars. I recognized Wendy the Patchwork Princess from Miss Eccles's Parlor.

"What are you doing? Don't do this for me—I don't want it!" Wendy cried. The crowd parted as she tottered up, tears leaking down her cheeks. "You were idiots before, and now it's even worse!"

The two fighting zombies turned toward her with pleading expressions on their mangled, sagging faces. Each man self-consciously tried to put a loosened eyeball back into the socket so he could focus on her.

When they tried to moan explanations, Wendy jabbed a crooked finger at them. "I don't want your excuses! If you two don't get over me and move on with your lives—or whatever—I swear to you, I'll throw myself in front of a train again. And this time I'll let *you* pick up the pieces!" Her shoulders hitched up and down as she wept openly. The spectators muttered.

Running up behind the Patchwork Princess came the stout, matronly Lujean Eccles. "Oh, my, my! Wendy, dear, come with me. Stay away from those louts!" She wrapped an arm around the girl's shoulder. Like a protective mother bear, she glared at the fighting zombies, ignoring everybody else. "You should be ashamed. You've already hurt this poor girl more than she can endure." Miss Eccles shook her head and made a tsk-tsk sound.

"What's the problem here?" McGoo said. "I want an explanation from somebody."

I introduced him to the sawbones. Still holding the Patchwork Princess, rocking back and forth to console her, Miss Eccles spoke. "When she was alive, poor, dear Wendy was torn between two suitors. The men claimed to love her with all their hearts, but they just couldn't stop competing with each other. They told Wendy to choose between them, but she wasn't ready to do that." Miss Eccles shot a sharp glance at the reeling, embarrassed combatants. "She should have dumped them both when she had a chance."

Wendy continued sobbing, pressing her face against Miss Eccles's chest.

"These idiots challenged each other to an old-fashioned duel with pistols in the park to determine who got to have Wendy."

The Patchwork Princess lifted her head. "I never, ever agreed to it!"

Miss Eccles made a raspberry sound. "That didn't stop them. They shot each other, both died—and Wendy blamed herself. She couldn't bear the guilt, so she threw herself in front of an oncoming train." The woman again reprimanded the cringing zombies. "This is *your* fault. Look what you did to this poor girl!"

In a huff, she turned the Patchwork Princess around. "Come with me, dear. You needn't bother with them anymore. Sorry for the disturbance, Officer." She guided the crying, weaving Wendy away and threw a last glare over her shoulder at the mangled zombies. "She doesn't want anything to do with either of you, ever again!"

The zombies hung their heads in regret—or maybe their necks had simply been damaged.

"All right, that's it. Show's over," McGoo said. The zombies shambled off in opposite directions.

McGoo raised his voice, shooing the crowd away. "Nothing to see here. You all go home."

The crowd dispersed, and McGoo let out a long sigh of relief. "Some crazy night, eh, Shamble? What is this, a full moon?"

"Full moon is tomorrow night. *This* is just a warm-up," I said, then glanced at my watch. Miranda would be waiting for me. "I've got an appointment."

CHAPTER 35

iranda Jekyll had suggested meeting at Basilisk herself, claiming it was one of her favorite nightclubs. I doubted any Straight Edgers would set foot inside a place like that, so we'd be safe enough from any of her husband's goons.

I felt more uneasy about having Sheyenne join me there, but she was adamant. "I'm in this with you, Beaux. I slipped into Jekyll's study, I got the ring, I was there when you got shot—you obviously need my help." She had given me a mischievous smile. "I'll meet you at Basilisk."

Sheyenne hadn't been back to the nightclub since her death, and I was afraid the visit would be a traumatic experience, but she insisted she had to face it. She had her own reasons: The meeting with Miranda gave her an excuse to keep an eye on Ivory.

After leaving McGoo and the brawling shamblers, I headed across the Quarter to Little Transylvania, arriving at Basilisk only a few minutes late. I entered the dimly lit lounge and looked around, expecting to find Jekyll's wife waiting for me, impatient, annoyed.

Miranda wasn't there yet. Naturally. She hated to be on any schedule at all, and was pathologically, rather than fashionably, late. I should have known.

A semitransparent Sheyenne appeared next to me with an uncertain expression. I could practically see the flood of memories crossing her face as she looked around the nickel-appointed bar and the tables bunched close to the stage where Ivory would sing. I wanted to put my arm around her.

"This place …" Sheyenne said, fighting off a shudder. "Right now, I could really use a hug."

I reached out to air-pat her arm; it was the best I could do. "It'll be all right—I'm here. I won't let anything else happen to you."

"So many memories. How can I not hate this place?"

I forced a smile. "They're not all bad memories, are they? This is where we met."

She responded with a wistful expression. "No, not all bad, I guess. But given the choice, I'd rather still be alive."

"So would I."

At the bar, Fletcher Knowles gave me a cautious nod, then his eyes widened when he recognized the ghost beside me. "Sheyenne! You're back—It's good to see you." He bustled out from behind the bar. "Really sorry about what happened ... and then Dan got killed too. What a mess." Standing awkwardly in front of us, Fletcher shook his head. "Did he tell you I was the one who found his body in the alley? Small world." He let out a nervous chuckle. "Quite a testimonial to Basilisk, I guess— my customers keep coming back even after they're dead." He glanced at the still-empty stage. "Now here's an idea—I can make it open-mic night, if you like. These people would love to hear you sing again."

"I don't know, Fletcher," she said. "What would Ivory think?"

"*I'm* the boss. She can move over if I tell her to."

I wasn't convinced who would win in a shouting match between Fletcher and the big vamp diva, but Sheyenne wouldn't change her mind anyway. Eventually, the manager backed off. "Okay, suit yourself. Can I at least buy you a drink?"

Sheyenne looked uncertain, glanced at me, then back at Fletcher. "I haven't had one in a while. What do ghosts usually drink?"

"Oh, any sort of distilled spirits."

"I'll take you up on it—as long as you're buying for Dan too."

"No problem."

Fletcher pulled me a beer, then poured a double bourbon and water for Sheyenne. I said, "Let's go find a table close to the stage—if you're ready for that."

"Oh, I can't wait. When that bitch starts to sing, I want to be up close, right where she can see me." Carrying her drink, Sheyenne drifted across the room. We picked an unclaimed table up front. I looked around—still no sign of Miranda. Twenty minutes late now. I thought she would have been anxious to hear what we had found in her husband's study....

Taking care of business, I handed Sheyenne the Zom-Be-Fresh sachet and the goo specimen from the disintegrating puddle of Franklin

Galworthy in front of the mission. After I told her what had happened to the dapper zombie, she looked appalled. "I need you to contact your friend at the chem lab. There's got to be some clue here as to what made Mr. Galworthy dissolve."

Sheyenne took the samples, regarded the Fresh Loam sachet. "I'll call in a few favors again, but I'll bet it comes up negative."

The tone of background conversation inside the lounge changed as Ivory emerged from backstage. The big vamp came into the bar area, swaying in an exaggerated half-corkscrew walk to accentuate her assets. Each time she turned, her breasts swayed with the movement about a half turn out of sync, trying to catch up. Her smile was very wide to emphasize her full set of teeth and fangs, which sparkled as if she had recently endured a very expensive tooth-whitening process.

Sheyenne hissed under her breath, ready to claw the diva's eyes out. "That bitch poisoned me. I just know it."

"Play it cool for now," I said. "Can't prove it—yet."

Ivory came forward, smiling even wider when she recognized Sheyenne. "Hoping to steal the show again, sugar? Take my place?" The vamp's friendly tone sounded as cuddly as an iron maiden. "Good luck if you want to try."

Sheyenne had her spectral hackles up. "I was good at singing, but I didn't need it—I would have moved on soon enough. I have a lot of talents. You never had anything to worry about."

Ivory gave a throaty laugh. "I was never *worried* about a scrawny little waif like you, sugar. With that warbly voice?"

"Then you didn't need to kill me," Sheyenne said point-blank.

Now the buxom vampire laughed even louder. "You think *I* killed you? Why would I bother? The competition helps me keep my edge. I always have the whole audience in the palm of my hand."

Now the vamp turned to me, working the full glamour of her personality. "I'm so glad you're here to listen tonight, Dan." Ivory leaned forward to make sure I got a good view of her cleavage; the chasm was so enormous it could have been seen from two blocks away. "I'll do a special number for you, make you forget all about that willowy little ghost. It's not as if you can *do* anything with her now."

Sheyenne lifted her glass of bourbon and soda and threw it directly in Ivory's face. The big vamp spluttered. "You little bitch!" Ivory extended her clawlike nails, thrust out her fangs, and the audience gasped in shock. Instinctively, I lurched to my feet to put myself between the two, although a vampire couldn't touch the ghost anyway.

Just then I heard an edgy, cackling laugh. "I had no idea this was audience participation night, sweethearts." Miranda Jekyll had arrived and instantly became the center of attention. Ivory stormed off to regain her dignity and clean up.

"Sorry about the drama, Mrs. Jekyll." I gestured Miranda to the empty chair. "We've been waiting for you."

In a fluid movement, she slithered into the offered seat. "I eagerly await your report, Mr. Chambeaux, but first things first. Isn't *somebody* going to buy me a drink?" Though Fletcher was dismayed to watch the retreating diva, he hurried over to our table. Miranda looked up at him. "Ah, there you are at last. I'll have a gin martini please, three olives, very large, very dry, and very dirty."

The conversation in the nightclub grudgingly returned to normal. I noticed that the three zombie cougars—Victoria, Sharon, and Cindy—had also ensconced (or entombed) themselves at the bar, gaunt and skeletal, fully painted. Compared to those three, Miranda Jekyll looked ravishing. The trio of cadaverous women ordered colorful fruity concoctions and sat together, waiting for someone to hit on them.

Before long, Brondon Morris did. He entered Basilisk wearing a different plaid suit this time—I imagined he must have a whole closet full of them—and chatted up the three undead women, paid for their round of drinks.

When Miranda followed my gaze, she emitted a low growl from her throat. Jealous? Another piece clicked into place. She'd been quite open about the fact that she had her own affairs. Was she cheating on Harvey Jekyll with *that* man?

"Brondon Morris is a loathsome human being," she said as if reading my mind, not tearing her eyes from him. "A little turd in a bad suit."

All right, probably not an affair, then.

"Brondon isn't my favorite person, either," I said. "I know my own reasons. What do you have against him?"

"He's an ambitious opportunistic climber who wormed his way into JLPN and wants to be a big fish. He'll keep looking for ponds until he finds an empty one just his size."

"So you two don't have any sort of ... romantic history?" I asked.

She let out a peal of laughter that caused heads to turn. "Oh, sweetheart, please! I prefer a man with more hair on his chest." She drew a sharp red-enameled finger across the cocktail table, leaving a deep scratch. She gave me an appraising look, then addressed Sheyenne's ghost. "And someone who has hot blood pumping. You have nothing to worry about, sweetheart. Dan Chambeaux's not my type."

At the bar, Brondon drifted away from the three cougars and engaged in an intense conversation with Fletcher. He handed over several samples from his case before shaking the bartender's hand and turning with a generalized wave of farewell to the clientele in Basilisk, although no one but me was looking at him. Then he scuttled away.

Miranda's martini arrived, and she drank half of it in a gulp, as if to wash away her thoughts of Brondon Morris, or of garish plaid in general. "Now then, to business. You said you made some progress? What did you find in Harvey's study?"

I leaned closer, lowering my voice. "Something that might be useful in leveraging a settlement."

"My, I love leverage," she chortled. "What is it?"

I told her how Sheyenne had slipped into the study, looking in the locked drawer where Miranda had suggested. "Not only is your husband involved in Straight Edge, he's *very* involved. In fact, he's the Grand Wizard himself."

Miranda chuckled. "Now, isn't that an embarrassing little detail about a man who's launching a new line of products for unnaturals! Harvey, Harvey, you evil little man—Grand Wizard of the Straight Edgers! Threatening to expose that ring will make Harvey squirm, all right. Silly little boys with their silly little prejudices and silly little costumes."

I added, "Only a few hours ago, someone—something—broke into the Straight Edge offices and slaughtered four human volunteers. That's going to put the group squarely in the news. Lots of publicity."

Sheyenne wasn't so convinced. "Yes, but they were murdered by a monster. What if public sympathy shifts to the poor Straight Edge victims torn apart by intolerant unnaturals?"

Someone chose that moment to let out a piercing scream that turned our attention to the bar. Cougar Sharon reeled back in horror as Cindy's appletini glass slipped from her grasp and shattered on the floor. The grayish necrotic skin on Cindy's forearm and hand also slipped off the bone, like a thick floppy rubber glove. She put her other hand to her face and let out a scream, just before her jawbone fell off. Her fingers pressed into her cheek and sank through to the skull. Her other arm fell off. She collapsed onto the bar stool and kept falling to the floor in dripping, dissolving pieces.

Other patrons made sounds of disgust. Many backed away.

Next, Sharon's head lolled to one side. As she reached up to hold it in place, the head fell completely off. She managed to catch her hair, dangling her detached head for a moment as her face continued to contort and scream. Then the hair ripped off the scalp like a hunk of sod, and Sharon's head fell face-first to the nightclub floor. Her body slumped forward.

Victoria had an extra five seconds of stunned panic that turned to sad resignation as she also flash-rotted like a time-lapse video and fell into a pile of suppurating goo that mingled with her two companions, pooling together around the three now-empty cocktail dresses.

The zombie patrons of Basilisk were the first to flee. Vampires and werewolves, who were not usually squeamish, looked grossed out.

"We should get out of here, Mrs. Jekyll." I wasn't sure what was causing this gooey crisis, but I feared it might spread. First Mr. Galworthy and now the cougars. Could it be some kind of undeadly epidemic? And what if I was vulnerable too.

Miranda finished the rest of her martini in a gulp. "I believe you're right, Mr. Chambeaux." With remarkable speed, she flitted out of the nightclub in the crowd of retreating patrons.

Wearing a sour expression, Fletcher Knowles, went to the back room and brought out a mop and bucket.

Ivory stepped out onto the stage, freshly made up and ready for her set. In disbelief she watched her admirers stampede for the doors. She grabbed the microphone, but saw it was a lost cause. She shot an angry glance toward Sheyenne, as if the ghost had caused the disaster.

With pure showmanship, Ivory announced, "Thank you for coming. That's our show for tonight, but I'm here all week!" She ducked back to her dressing room at the rear of the club.

CHAPTER 36

Next morning, Sheyenne hand-delivered the chemical samples for analysis to her friend at the lab, asking for results as soon as possible.

After the uproar of the previous night, a divorce settlement—however bitter—seemed less important than zombies falling apart in the middle of their daily activities. What if the horrific affliction spread across the Unnatural Quarter? It could turn into a real zombie apocalypse.

Nevertheless, I had a responsibility to our clients. I checked to make sure that Jekyll's Grand Wizard ring remained locked in the office safe. I needed to figure out how to deliver an ultimatum to Harvey Jekyll, let him know the leverage we had, and convince the man it was in his best interests to reach a settlement with Miranda. Robin was far too innocent for that type of work.

My overture (I considered it negotiation rather than blackmail) had to come from an unexpected quarter. Maybe I could recruit Tiffany from the All-Day/All-Nite Fitness Center. Considering how much the tough vamp despised the Straight Edgers, she might do the job just to watch the Grand Wizard squirm.

I spent the morning trying to work out details in my head. Shortly before lunch, the telephone rang, and Sheyenne called for me. "It's Officer McGoohan. He sounds upset."

I took the phone. "What is it, McGoo?"

On the other end of the line I could hear his quick breathing, the rasp in his voice. "Shamble … that client of yours—Sheldon Fennerman, the vampire?"

"Yes, I was about to close the case." The vampire's problems should be over now that the Wannovich sisters had cast their gruesome protection spell ... and since the Straight Edge kids had all been torn limb from limb, they weren't going to harass him anymore.

"Don't close it yet." I heard him swallow hard. "You'd better get down here right away."

By the time I reached the vampire's brownstone, two other police units had arrived and uniformed officers were keeping the crowd back. I saw the trollish landlord chatting with the people on the street. "He complained that his neighbors had been killed, but I didn't believe him. Now how am I ever going to rent to vampires again?" He lifted his pumpkinlike head, stared around with beady eyes at the people. "I do have apartments for rent, if anybody's interested? Some of them zoned for dual use, daytime and nighttime. There's a move-in special this month. I—"

I went directly to the troll landlord. "Where's Sheldon?"

He flinched back. "I'm just trying to make a living here!"

One of the cops who worked with McGoo called me over. "Dan Chambeaux? Right this way—Officer McGoohan told us to expect you."

He led me around the corner to the alley behind Sheldon's brownstone. McGoo was standing there, his face drawn, expression gray. "Shamble," he said, and shook his head. "Sorry I told you to hurry—not much point. I was just upset. There's nothing you can do."

Sheldon Fennerman hung dead, suspended three feet off the ground. A long wooden stake the size of a laundry pole had been shoved through the center of his chest and directly into the crumbling brick wall of the alley. The nervous vampire had been pinned there like a piece of meat stuck on a fondue fork.

I reeled. "Oh, Sheldon ... I let you down."

McGoo took off his cap and wiped his forehead, then replaced it. "What could have the strength to do *that?*"

My throat was as dry as grave dust. "We both know what has the strength."

"But why go after a nervous little vampire who wasn't hurting anyone?"

"Why smash Mrs. Saldana's mission either? Why slaughter a bunch of Straight Edgers? What's the connection?"

I saw genuine fear in McGoo's eyes. "Unless it's just running amok. I've got to get that monster off the streets, Shamble—but I wouldn't want to meet him in a dark alley unless I'm carrying a bazooka."

I wondered if they made silver-jacketed heavy ordnance against unnaturals. Probably a special order.

I looked down at the ground again. Among the garbage strewn in the alley, I saw dozens of large cockroaches curled up on their backs, legs waving weakly in the air. They were bigger than any roaches I'd ever seen.

McGoo ground one under his heel. "Now, what's all that about?"

Remembering the special incantation that Mavis Wannovich had cast, I realized that her threat had been *literal*, not just a scare tactic. "Sheldon Fennerman was shielded by a protection spell: Anyone who harmed him or his apartment would get a stomach full of living cockroaches."

"Some protection spell," McGoo said.

"Well, it worked." I nudged one of the writhing, dying insects with the toe of my shoe. "It just wasn't strong enough to stop this brute."

At the other end of the alley, the morgue truck rolled up and the three ghouls bounded out again, ready for a new customer, but I didn't let them near Sheldon. Once the crime scene techs took all the photos and gathered the evidence they needed, they set about removing Sheldon's body with all the finesse of baggage handlers testing the durability of various brands of luggage. I shooed them away. Sometimes, you just have to do what's right. I wrapped my hands around the shaft that pinned the vampire to the wall. "McGoo, help me get him down."

We had to wiggle the pole up and down until it broke free from the bricks. As gently as possible, we eased Sheldon down to the ground and worked the stake out of his chest.

I bent down next to him. His face had a startled look, more fear and surprise than pain. He probably hadn't known what was happening when he bumped into the monster in the alley.

It couldn't have been a random attack. Why would the brute have carried a long wooden pole with him? He must have been coming for the vampire.

"I'm so sorry, Sheldon," I whispered, and closed his eyes. My heart felt more leaden than usual. I swore that one way or another I was going to get that hulking bastard—not just for Sheldon, but for myself as well.

Chapter 37

t Chambeaux & Deyer, we encounter many impossible things, not to mention clients. Even so, it strained credulity that we received the chemical results *in a day*. Full analysis of the Mr. Galworthy goo and the Zom-Be-Fresh sample found in his waistcoat.

I shook my head in amazement at Sheyenne. "Even the police department can't manage an emergency turnaround like that! How the hell did you get an analysis so fast?"

Sheyenne gave me a coy smile. "You have to know somebody. And I know somebody." I saw on the envelope a handwritten *"For Anne,"* with a little heart drawn next to it. "He was a fellow med student—Andy," she explained. "And he had a crush on me. Very sweet. Now he works in the analysis lab, so I asked a favor. He'd do anything for me—even now."

Anne and Andy? I tried my damndest to pretend I didn't feel a twinge of jealousy.

"Andy found out about my death too late. I should have thought to call him when I was dying in the hospital. He did come to my funeral, though. Spiky brown hair, heavy-rimmed glasses, tends to blush at the drop of a hat."

I remembered somebody like that at her funeral. Not many had attended, so he stood out. I'd never known who he was until now.

"And no, he's not a suspect," Sheyenne said, glancing at my expression. "Just a friend."

She spread the chem reports on her desk, and we studied the analysis. There had to be some connection, some smoking gun in all of the numbers in the columns. Andy had already typed his conclusions at the bottom.

"Dear Anne, This analysis found nothing on the list of harmful chemicals. A full roster of trace elements and proprietary substances, but I compared them with known toxins, caustic agents, acids. I can't identify anything that could have caused the cellular breakdown of the victims."

Andy had gone the extra step—bless him, he must have had one hell of a crush on her (and who could blame the guy?)—of comparing all of these detailed results with the earlier sample of Zom-Be-Fresh she had given him, the one that caused her severe skin reaction. The substance found in the packet of the Galworthy goo was a pre-release sample from JLPN's new Fresh Loam line. There were slight differences in the list of chemical additives from the earlier sample, as would be expected with a new formulation and fragrance, but nothing that should cause the undead to disintegrate.

"I don't buy any of this." I was sure Jekyll Lifestyle Products and Necroceuticals had something to do with it. I'd seen Brondon Morris with Victoria, Cindy, and Sharon more than once, and not long before their unfortunate demise. And dapper Mr. Galworthy of Black Glass, Inc. had used more than his share of JLPN colognes and deodorants.

But the results were right there on the printout. The chemical analysis offered no incriminating red flags, certainly nothing I could take to McGoo. Nothing we could use against Harvey Jekyll, even if he was the Grand Wizard of the Straight Edgers.

Nevertheless, something disastrous was happening out there in the Quarter. News reports were buzzing with ever-increasing alarm. In addition to the four zombies that had dissolved, a vampire and two werewolves had also collapsed to the ground and sloughed into piles of oozing skin, muscle, bones, and internal organs. So the disaster affected more than just zombies. Rumors spread about a horrific new plague infecting the unnatural population, a disease that struck indiscriminately and without warning. No one was safe.

Add to that the increasingly violent depredations of the massive creature that smashed buildings, killed Straight Edgers, and had now staked poor Sheldon Fennerman. The Unnatural Quarter no longer seemed a safe and comfortable place.

The situation is bad when even monsters are afraid.

O O O

I didn't have much chance of sneaking into the JLPN factory, but I could still keep an eye out from the perimeter fence. Zombies are good at lurking.

I borrowed the Pro Bono Mobile and puttered away, nursing the accelerator. Oily curls of blue-gray exhaust wafted up behind me, clearly visible in the rearview mirror. It was long past time for us to get an official Chambeaux & Deyer company vehicle, but Robin was attached to the old bomb she'd owned all through law school.

The large JLPN industrial compound was surrounded by the usual chain-link fence, with the usual No Trespassing signs, and capped by the usual rows of razor wire. The first time I'd infiltrated the factory, I'd been human, which made slipping inside much simpler. I'd dressed in a worker's uniform, complete with a counterfeit employee ID badge, and pretended to belong there—piece of cake.

However, JLPN's strict "humans only" employment policy made that approach problematic for a zombie, even a well-preserved one like myself. I gazed up at the tall chain-link fence and the shark's teeth of razor wire curled around the top. Back when I was alive, and ten years younger, I might have been able to clamber over while wearing thick clothes. But that murderous-looking razor wire would take a few good chunks out of me, and I had no desire to get damaged further. I'd already been shot six times in the past few days—that was enough, thank you.

So I kept watch over the activity from the outside. The day was dark and overcast, and the temperature had dropped enough that if I'd been warm-blooded, I would be shivering. The drizzle wasn't enough to amount to anything, but it did make the world a clammier place.

The factory seemed much quieter than it had been last week. Apparently, the new-release Fresh Loam products had been shipped and distributed to apothecary outlets and beauty parlors across the Unnatural Quarter. The shift whistle blew, and fifty human workers filed out of the factory, pulling on jackets and carrying lunchboxes, as they walked to cars in the parking lot. I stayed put, guessing that the interesting stuff would happen after the normal activities had ceased for the day.

Sure enough, in less than an hour, Harvey Jekyll emerged through a side door of the admin building and scuttled to the motor pool, where he climbed into a blue open-bed pickup truck. He backed up to the loading dock, climbed out, scurried up the stairs, and went back inside. With a clatter, he returned, pushing an unmarked metal drum on a hand truck, which he loaded into the back of the pickup. Wiping sweat from his wrinkled forehead, he brought out a second drum.

I was surprised that the head of the company would do the heavy work himself. Surely Brondon Morris would have been happy to lend a hand, though it might have stained his loud plaid jacket. After securing the pickup's tailgate, Jekyll swung into the cab and drove off.

I was smiling inside as I whispered, "Gotcha!"

Revealing that Harvey Jekyll was the Grand Wizard of Straight Edge might have been embarrassing for his company, and now I'd have proof of his secret dumping of hazardous chemical waste. That was more leverage than Miranda could possibly need.

As Jekyll's pickup passed through the automatic sally-port gate and headed off down the road, I ran back to the rusty Maverick, intent on following him.

CHAPTER 38

Robin's car wouldn't start.

Knowing Jekyll was getting away, I banged my fists on the dashboard and steering wheel (careful to avoid hitting the horn). I tried the ignition again, and the Pro Bono Mobile's engine made a valiant attempt, like a little dog trying to jump over a gate but unable to get enough oomph. I flooded the engine.

So I sat back and waited, counting out a full minute, forcing patience upon myself, even though Jekyll was driving farther and farther with every second.

Finally, I tried the key again, listened to the starter whir—and the engine caught. A belch of blue-gray smoke curled up from the exhaust pipe. Now I was on my way, and although Harvey Jekyll had a head start, I was sure I knew where he was going anyway.

Since he might have noticed me following him too closely, the forced delay worked to my advantage. The gloomy drizzle became a full-blown rain as I drove away from the factory, and the puckered old wipers did little more than smear water and smashed bugs across Robin's windshield. But I managed to see well enough.

I headed out to the Metropolitan Pre-Used Resource Depository, turned into the gate, and rolled forward along the dirt entrance road, where I saw a set of fresh tire tracks in the mud and gravel. Partway in, I pulled over in a small turnaround surrounded by piled garbage. Since I intended to surprise Jekyll in the act, I didn't want to drive too close. I switched off the car and pocketed the keys, hoping the old Maverick would start again when I needed to leave. Right now I wanted to creep up and use my phone camera to snap images of Jekyll illegally disposing of toxic chemicals. Although I couldn't prove what the drums contained, I doubted Jekyll had the required municipal permits.

Up ahead, I spotted the blue JLPN pickup truck parked next to Mel's trailer. The rain had slacked off to a halfhearted miserable mist. Big Mel was unloading the two drums from the back of the pickup while Jekyll supervised. I couldn't hear what they were saying.

While Jekyll fidgeted, Mel chatted away as usual, waving his hands. His folding lawn chair was out in front of the trailer door, with a book spread open on the seat. He'd been reading outside in the late-afternoon rain. Zombies don't mind the damp, even though the weather can be hard on books.

When Mel had wrestled the two chemical drums off the pickup bed and onto the ground in front of the trailer, Jekyll pulled out his wallet and extracted a handful of bills, which Mel pocketed—talking all the while. He wrapped his arms around the first drum and began to drag it off to one side.

Taking pictures of everything, I felt like a predator closing in on a long-awaited kill. A thrill ran through me. Illicit chemical drums, an obvious payoff—and not by a JLPN minion, but by the CEO himself! When added to the silver Grand Wizard ring, this was more than enough for us to force a decent divorce settlement. In fact, it might be enough to bring down JLPN, or at least oust Harvey Jekyll from the company. Unfortunately, that would probably put Brondon Morris in charge, which wasn't necessarily an improvement, and if we destroyed Jekyll Lifestyle Products and Necroceuticals, Miranda's divorce settlement wouldn't be worth much. I would have to be careful about this.

Nevertheless, I snapped more images. Mel continued his cheery, constant conversation with Harvey Jekyll as he moved the first big barrel. He paused to pop open one of the caps on the lid and sniff the contents. He gave a big, dumb smile.

Alarmed, Jekyll shouted at him, which startled Mel. The big zombie slipped in the greasy mud, and the drum rocked from side to side, nearly tipping over. Some of the fluid sloshed across Mel's chest.

While Jekyll looked appalled, Mel laughed it off. He brushed the stain from his shirt ... and his eyes flew open, as if a hard candy had lodged in his throat. Mel stared curiously at his hand—which drooped like a wilting flower. Then his fingers fell off. His skin ran like melted wax down his arm, and a hole began chewing its way through his shirt where the chemical had soaked in.

Dropping all caution, I stuffed the phone in my pocket and raced toward my friend. I didn't care about hiding any more. "Mel!"

Jekyll whirled in panic. Mel turned toward me with an odd, abandoned look on his face and collapsed in on himself, flopped to the ground, and disintegrated into a mound of shapeless tissue.

"You bastard, Jekyll! What did you do to him?" I'd already seen other victims melt down and knew it was too late for Mel. But now I had proof positive that Jekyll was behind the epidemic. I grabbed my gun from its holster and ran up to Jekyll.

For a little guy, he was surprisingly strong. He shoved the chemical drum over, dumping the fizzy blue chemical onto my legs, my shirt, my chest. I felt the cold sliminess of the strange fluid, and I knew damn well what it would do to me. I'd just watched Mel collapse and do his best blob imitation. Within seconds, my flesh would drip off, my bones would fall apart, and I would become an un-undead.

Although I didn't remember anything about being dead the first time, I had no wish to return to the grave. I couldn't stand the thought of putting Robin and Sheyenne through the grieving process all over again.

Suddenly I realized that I was not, in fact, disintegrating. The fizzy blue chemical might have stained my suit, but my undead body was still functioning as well as a few minutes ago. I was too stunned to be thrilled by the fact.

Jekyll dove into his pickup and started the engine. The tires spun, kicking up mud and gravel as he accelerated. I didn't have time to wonder why I wasn't joining Mel in the glop brotherhood—I had to stop Jekyll from getting away.

I placed myself in the middle of the dirt road, but Jekyll didn't hesitate. He gunned the engine and came straight at me. Being brave, or just stupid, I stood squarely in front of the truck, and the pickup knocked me flat into the mud. The truck roared over me ... but the tires missed my body. The undercarriage passed mere millimeters above my face, and the truck roared off, slewing back out of the dump and onto the main road.

I lay sprawled on my back in the soft muck, and eventually I pried myself out of the puddle, reminded of the last time I'd crawled out of the grave. I was drenched, muddy, and humiliated, but not overly damaged.

Saddened and angry, I sloshed over to my friend's shapeless remains that were spreading in all directions like a red-and-yellow amoeba. In my jacket pocket, the camera phone was mud-smeared but still intact. I looked for a clean swatch of fabric so I could wipe off the lens. I definitely had the evidence I needed against Jekyll—and I was going to nail him for a hell of a lot more than a divorce settlement.

On Mel's lawn chair I saw one of his self-help books, soaked by the rain. Mel had always tried to better himself, to do his best despite his circumstances. The book was titled *I'm Dead, but I'm OK*. He'd made it only to chapter two.

Poor Mel. What remained of my heart went out to him, just as when I'd seen Sheldon Fennerman staked to the brick wall of the alley.

Garbage rustled in the giant mounds surrounding his trailer, and I saw gleaming black eyes, pointed snouts, and spiky brown fur as three gargantuan rats emerged from hiding, whiskers twitching as they quested the air.

They came closer to the pile of ooze and let out plaintive squeaks. Rover, Fido, and Spot—he had named them, befriended them. These oversized rodents were misfits through no fault of their own, just as Mel had been. They looked at me now, as if expecting me to make everything better again, or at least to explain. I had nothing to say, not to giant rats, not to anyone.

I patted each creature on the head, trying to console them. "You'll do all right here for yourselves. You've got all the garbage in the world as your home."

But that didn't help Mel.

No matter what, I had enough cold evidence for a long list of criminal charges against Harvey Jekyll. McGoo wouldn't hesitate to take action, I knew that. He'd be perfectly happy to wrap up the prominent case of the melting unnaturals and get a gold star in his personnel file, although it would take quite a few stars to get him reassigned outside of the Quarter.

The chemical drums were still here just in front of Mel's trailer, but I wasn't going to touch them. I had no idea why the dissolving substance had left me intact while it had disintegrated Mel, but I didn't intend to give the stuff a second chance.

I wasn't going to give Harvey Jekyll a second chance either.

CHAPTER 39

I had visions of charging into the JLPN chemical factory with McGoo at my side, guns blazing. The two of us would rough up a few of the perpetrators, slap Harvey Jekyll in handcuffs, shut down the whole operation, and emerge as heroes to a crowd of cheering monsters.

But Robin stubbornly insisted that we do everything by the book so we'd wind up with a perfectly clean legal case that would stand up to a long and messy trial. She was a dear kid, but she could be incredibly frustrating.

After I called McGoo with the news, he rushed to our offices, eager to make the arrest. Bursting through the office door, however, he took one look at me and said, "Jeez, Shamble, you look like shit—and you smell bad too."

"You always say that. This time there's a reason." I needed to change out of the chemical-soaked, mud-spattered clothes, but I'd been in too much of a hurry to clean up.

I explained what had happened at the dump. Robin had already downloaded the photos from my phone (after cleaning it as best she could) and displayed them on Sheyenne's desktop screen.

McGoo scowled. "So Jekyll's got some chemical that dissolves unnaturals. Then why are *you* still here if you were doused with the stuff?"

I looked down at the splotchy stains all over me. "Hell if I know."

"I'm not complaining," Sheyenne said, floating close.

"There's enough evidence to warrant Harvey Jekyll's immediate arrest," Robin said. "We can get more answers from him during the prosecution."

McGoo was angry on my behalf. "Damn right he's going down. You want me to call in the whole force, Shamble? Or should we go in solo, just the two of us?"

"If it's *two* of us, then it's not solo."

"You know what I mean."

"We have to be involved," Robin insisted. "This is our case. We broke it. Chambeaux and Deyer needs to be there during the wrap-up."

"Miranda's divorce settlement is our case, Robin," I pointed out. "This is criminal activity, and the police should handle it."

"The district attorney has more than enough evidence to get a search warrant for the JLPN factory. I've already been on the phone to Judge Hawkins," Robin said. "After Officer McGoohan serves the warrant and we search the factory, we'll find all the proof we need to send him to jail."

"If we're going out again, I need to change clothes," I said. "Spooky, is there—?"

"Yes, fresh shirt and pants in your office, shoes under the desk. No jacket, I'm afraid."

"I'll survive." That might not have been the appropriate thing to say. I shrugged out of my sport jacket, touched the clumsily sewn bullet holes, decided I liked them. "But I will need this one dry-cleaned."

"I'll take care of it tomorrow," Sheyenne said. "Let's get the bad guy tonight."

I went back into my office and half-closed the door for privacy as I began peeling off mud-encrusted clothes. McGoo brought me a wet towel from the restroom. "Wipe yourself down at least. No telling what that chemical might do to you in the long run."

"Thanks." I realized I could have used a shower, too, but I didn't want to waste the time going upstairs to my apartment. Jekyll probably assumed I had dissolved out at the landfill like Mel (at the very least, he thought he'd run me over with the truck). He was sure to be spooked, although he wouldn't necessarily think he'd been caught, wouldn't need to panic. But it was only a matter of time. We had to catch him before it was too late.

I buckled my belt, straightened my slacks; the new shirt was a little tight, so I left the top button open. I looked cleaner, but I still felt soiled by the whole matter. I couldn't stop thinking of how Mel had collapsed into biological ooze before my eyes.

McGoo was waiting for me in front of Sheyenne's desk. "So are we rolling? Come on, Shamble, let's get him."

Robin fidgeted awkwardly. "To make sure this is done properly, I'm going with you."

"No, it's not safe," I said.

"I'm going." Again, I saw the determination in her that won so many cases, and I knew I couldn't stand against that.

"Let's not argue about it—we'll all go," I said.

Before we headed out the door, I made a call from Sheyenne's desk. "We need to tell Miranda Jekyll what's happening. Who knows how far-reaching the indictments will go? It is our duty to protect the client."

When Miranda answered the phone, I could hear loud music in the background. It was just sunset—she couldn't possibly be at a nightclub already. I heard someone talking and laughing, then the music swelled again. "Oh hello, sweetheart!"

After I explained what I had discovered, she gave a cool click of her tongue. "That Harvey! I knew there was something wrong with him. I'd love to see the look on his face when you march in and arrest him." She covered the phone, and I heard her muffled voice, then a sultry giggle before she came back on the line again. "I trust in your abilities, Mr. Chambeaux, and I can't wait to hear how it all turns out. But I have other plans tonight. Full moon, you know—and some of us werewolves only get to let loose a few days each month."

I couldn't believe what I was hearing. "Mrs. Jekyll, this could win your entire case, bring down Harvey Jekyll. You could end up with everything, or you could lose the whole company—depending on what happens."

"And I trust you to do what's best for me, sweetheart. Don't worry, I have an alibi with plenty of witnesses! I may stop by the factory later, but some friends and I are at a pre-moonrise party."

The music swelled, and Miranda hung up.

CHAPTER 40

egardless of how much hard detective work I invest in a case, now and then a major lead miraculously falls into place—as if the cases really *do* solve themselves. That's terrific when it happens, but sometimes the timing sucks.

We were heading out the door to go after Harvey Jekyll when the phone rang: Fletcher Knowles from Basilisk—and his voice sounded uncertain. "Hello, Mr. Chambeaux? I found something ... something you should be aware of."

"I'm busy right now, Fletcher. We're just about to close a very large—"

He interrupted me. "I had to call you now, before she wakes up. I think I found the gun that was used to murder you."

That stopped me in my tracks, just like the original bullet did.

He continued, "A big antique revolver—Smith and Wesson. That's what the ballistics report said, right?"

My voice was a low growl. "Damn right."

"I found the gun in Ivory's dressing room. She's been hiding it in one of her vanity drawers. But you need to get over here right away. It's sunset, and she'll be rising soon—you don't have much time."

I swallowed hard, thought about McGoo and the big arrest at JLPN, but I knew the choice I had to make. "I'll be right there, Fletcher." I hung up and turned to Sheyenne. "The gun that shot me is at Basilisk. Ivory's been hiding it."

"*That bitch!* If I wasn't a ghost, I'd rip her fangs out, then move on to other body parts. I was going be a surgeon, you know. Hmmm, maybe if I used pliers ..."

I looked at Robin and McGoo. "You guys have to take care of Jekyll. I need to do this—it could wrap up my own murder case, and Sheyenne's."

"We've got it, Shamble," McGoo said. "Scout's honor."

"I'll be there in spirit," I said.

"*I'll* be there in spirit," Sheyenne said. "I'm going with you, Beaux. That vamp poisoned me and probably shot you to keep you from snooping around."

"Happy to have you along." I wasn't going to prevent her from joining me anyway.

We all left in a rush. I don't know which of us was in the greatest hurry.

O   O   O

Basilisk was closed for business until well after full dark; the neon sign was switched off. Dusk thickened into downright gloom as Sheyenne and I arrived, and Fletcher opened the door to hurry us into the dim nightclub. "I wasn't sure what else to do, Mr. Chambeaux." Nervous, he locked the door behind us. I gave my .38 a reassuring pat.

Fletcher spoke in a hushed voice as he led us toward Ivory's dressing room in the back, a place to which I'd been invited many times, though I had studiously avoided it. "Ivory's my biggest star, the best vamp singer I've ever heard, and it's going to ruin business if we have to get rid of her. But if she did kill you ..." He shook his head. His face looked as pale as his bleached goatee.

"Why would you help us?" Sheyenne asked.

He shrugged. "It's one way to get you to come back and sing."

Her translucent face clouded with anger. "Fletcher, if you help put away the vampire bitch that killed both of us, then I'll come back and sing every Saturday night for free."

"I hoped you would say something like that." The manager led us down the hall behind the stage. "And you did me a good turn, too, Mr. Chambeaux, even though you didn't mean to."

"How's that?"

"Remember Harry Talbot, the blood-bar owner who hired you to shut down my under-the-table blood sales? He's actually a cool guy. Likes progressive-rock music, same as me. He turned me on to some excellent obscure bands."

"So you're not trying to drive each other out of business anymore?" I asked. Talbot had paid his fee to Chambeaux & Deyer and closed the case; I'd never heard anything more from him.

"Just the opposite! We're in business together, my nightclub, his blood bar. We're opening up another place or two. There's certainly a market for it."

We fell into a hush as we reached the closed door to Ivory's dressing room. Fletcher turned the knob and the three of us entered. The vamp singer had a small makeup table and a chair, a ring of bright makeup lights, but no mirror (which wouldn't have done her any good). The table was covered with small jars, brushes, facial primer, foundation, powder, pencils, a rainbow of eye shadows and blushes, and her signature glossy red lipstick. A vase held a dozen long-stemmed red roses. The walls were covered with photographs of Ivory nuzzling famous people.

Her double-wide mahogany coffin rested on a riser on the other side of the room. Ivory had spared no expense: This was the best coffin offered in any funeral parlor catalog, about ten times more expensive than the one Robin had bought for me.

Though the sun had gone down a full hour ago, the big vamp remained in her coffin. Nothing stirred in the dressing room.

Fletcher said in a whisper, "She likes to sleep late. I usually come in here just before dark to help her put on her face. Since she can't use a mirror, it's my job to prepare Ivory for her public. It sometimes takes an hour, and I have to tell her a dozen times how beautiful she looks, since she can't see her reflection."

"Where's the gun?" I asked.

Fletcher slid open one of the vanity drawers to reveal a Smith & Wesson revolver, a big gleaming thing that could have been in a vampire's collection since the Civil War. Ballistics would prove whether or not this was the gun that had shot me, but it was too much of a coincidence to swallow.

Sheyenne nudged the makeup jars and bottles. "And if I find a vial of toadstool poison, that would be the cherry on top of the sundae."

Hearing the unmistakable sound of a creaking coffin lid, the three of us turned like startled rabbits facing the same rattlesnake. The big-breasted vampire extended her hands into the air, stretching, then sat up, yawning and rubbing the fuzz of sleep from her eyes.

When she saw us standing there, she recoiled as if *she* were the rabbit and we the rattlesnakes. "What are you all doing here? This is my private dressing room. Get out!" She quickly covered her face. "You can't see me like this!"

Ivory did look a lot different without her makeup. She turned her gaze on the manager. Vampires are able to manipulate people with a seductive hypnotic glamour, but what she gave Fletcher was exactly the opposite. He shivered under the glare.

"We found the gun, Ivory." I took a step forward to intervene. "What did I ever do to you? What made you upset enough to kill me?"

The vamp looked baffled. "Kill you, sugar? What are you talking about?"

Sheyenne pulled the Smith & Wesson from the drawer. "I've always known you poisoned me, and this is the gun that shot Dan, right here in your dressing room. Did you kill him because he was investigating my murder? Were you worried he'd catch you?"

I pulled my own .38 from the shoulder holster. The silver-jacketed slugs would do the trick.

More annoyed than afraid, the vampire diva climbed out, indignant but embarrassed by her fresh-out-of-the-coffin appearance. "I didn't even *have* that gun when Dan was murdered, sugar. I just bought it two weeks ago."

"What do you need a gun for?" I asked.

"For protection! In case you haven't noticed, I'm the star here, and I've got my share of obsessive fans … though not as many as I'd like. Sometimes they don't take no for an answer, so I decided to get a gun for peace of mind." She turned her sultry gaze on me. "Although *you* never learned how to take yes for an answer, sugar."

I tried to stay on point. "Then where did you get the gun?"

"I wanted something big, sturdy, reliable. It was a private sale. Cash. Very anonymous."

"Ivory, if that's the gun that murdered me, I deserve to know who owned it."

The vamp considered that and agreed. "All right, but don't tell him I told you. He might cut off my supplies, and I can't have that."

"*Who?*" Sheyenne demanded.

"Brondon Morris. He sold me the gun."

CHAPTER 41

Leaving Basilisk, we rushed to the factory of Jekyll Lifestyle Products & Necroceuticals. McGoo would already be there with Robin, but he didn't know that Harvey Jekyll wasn't acting alone. Brondon Morris did some of Jekyll's dirty work; apparently, he carried more than product samples in his case.

When we arrived after dark, the company was locked up tight, and a thick chain secured the fence gate and sally port. I was stuck outside.

The separate administrative building was dark and quiet, but I could see lights and hear nighttime generators humming inside the industrial complex. Perfumey vapors wafted from the smokestacks, venting the chemical operations on the process floor.

Sheyenne rattled, tugged, and twisted the padlocks and chain with her poltergeist hands, then drifted back, dismayed. "I can only do so much, Beaux. How did Robin and Officer McGoohan get in? Do you think he called for backup?"

"I'm guessing McGoo won't want to share credit for the big arrest—he needs every brownie point for his personnel file." I looked around, but saw no sign of them. I pulled out my phone and called Robin's number. No answer. Maybe they had gone back to the offices in defeat, so I punched in that number, but the phone rang and rang until the voice mail kicked in. I tried one last call, to McGoo's private phone. Again, no answer.

"We've got to get in there," I said, very worried now. "Spooky, go scope the place out. Check the offices. I want to know where Robin and McGoo are—and if there's anybody else inside."

"Leave you here? I won't be much good in a fight if I can't touch Jekyll or Brondon—"

"Right now I'll settle for recon." She blew me a kiss, then flitted off through the fence and into the dark compound.

The bright lights from the factory windows told me something was going on in the main building. I regarded the fence, the razor wire on top. If my friends were in trouble, I wasn't going to stay stuck out here in the cheap seats.

Bracing myself, I grabbed the chain links with stiff fingers, poked the toes of my shoes into the gaps, and hauled myself up. This was not my favorite thing to do. When I lurched over the curled razor wire, the sharp metal barbs tore the fabric of my shirt and pants, and I didn't want to think what it was doing to my skin. I'd be seeing Miss Lujean Eccles for another patchup as soon as this was over. But if Robin and McGoo were in there and in trouble, I didn't care how battered I got trying to save them. As I let myself drop, I heard a ripping sound, then I fell free. I got to my feet, brushed myself off, and staggered toward the factory and the open loading dock door.

From my earlier infiltration of JLPN during the garlic-laced shampoo case, I was already familiar with the big chemical vats on the process floor, the tanks of fragrances, base chemicals, active agents, dyes, and fillers. Mammoth horizontal stirrers churned the huge cauldrons, and the mixtures were piped off to bottling lines that filled containers, pasted on labels, sealed caps, and boxed up the necroceuticals for distribution.

During daylight hours, the factory was a synchronized, bustling place, filled with workers. Now most of the machinery was turned off, but I could still hear the sighing, burbling sounds of fermenting mixtures and chemical reactions.

I also heard voices, a man and a woman.

Brondon Morris, wearing a green plaid sport coat, had forced Robin up the metal steps and onto a catwalk on top of a huge vat. I saw no sign of McGoo or Jekyll, and I felt cold inside, fearing that McGoo might already be dead somewhere. What if Brondon had simply shot him in the back of the head, as he'd done to me, then coerced Robin in here?

Her hands were tied behind her back, and that got me angry. Brondon jabbed a gun directly in her face, forcing her to take another step along the catwalk. His broad grin was just like the one he had worn when flirting with the three zombie cougars. He was going to make her jump into the vat.

He brandished his gun, which looked like a .38, the type of weapon that had gunned me down in the street after Sheyenne and I left Grandma Wong's shop. If that was the same gun, then this guy must really like to shoot me.

I drew my own revolver and lurched to the metal stairs before he could shove Robin over the edge. "I wouldn't do that, Brondon!"

He swung around, startled, and looked down at me from atop the giant cauldron. "Dan Chambeaux!" He let out a mocking laugh to cover his surprise. "You really do keep rising from the grave."

While he was momentarily distracted, Robin kicked him in the shin. It was the best she could do with her hands tied.

Brondon yelped, hopped on one foot, and swung the pistol back to her. "Stop that!" As fast as I could, I started running up the narrow steps along the side of the vat, although I knew I wouldn't get there in time. Brondon didn't know where to point the gun. He swung it back and forth. "I suggest you stop, Chambeaux! I've got plenty of bullets, and even if they don't hurt *you*, imagine what they'll do to your pretty little partner."

I had made it halfway up the stairs, but I stopped, held up my handgun. "Don't hurt her, Brondon."

He rolled his eyes. "Of *course* I'm going to hurt her! Haven't you been following the program? Toss your weapon across the floor."

"Why in the world would I do that?" I decided to see how far I could push it. Moving slower now, I climbed two steps higher and kept my gaze fixed on his.

"Because I'll shoot her right now if you don't." He pressed the barrel against her head, pushed hard, and Robin flinched back. "You've already seen what a bullet did to your skull. You choose—think fast! Three ... two ..."

"All right! Stop, I'll do it." I tossed my revolver over the metal stairs and onto the floor. It was the only advantage I'd had, but Brondon could easily kill Robin in an instant. Maybe if I could get him to soliloquize, as movie villains do, I could figure out something. I glared up at him. "I've unraveled your plot, Brondon. We know you sold your antique Smith and Wesson to Ivory after you killed me." I pointed to the pistol in his hand, using that as an excuse to advance another step higher. "Did you use that .38 to shoot me down in the street a few nights ago?"

"It's my new gun," he said, admiring the weapon. "I wanted something lighter and more stylish."

201

Robin's dark eyes widened as she put the pieces together. She hadn't known what Sheyenne and I learned from Ivory. "*You're* the one who shot Dan?" She had real, heartwarming murder in her glare. "Why?"

I had been just about to ask the same question.

Brondon looked at Robin, annoyed, but she kept her back straight and refused to be pushed around. "He was closing in on me. I had to cover my tracks before he unraveled JLPN's overall plan."

Under other circumstances it might have been funny. "I never liked you, Brondon, but I was never after you—in fact, I had no idea you were involved in anything until tonight. Harvey Jekyll was the one in my sights. I followed him out to the dump with his hazardous chemicals, and we found the silver Straight Edge ring in his study. We know he's the Grand Wizard."

Brondon looked like a gorilla with indigestion. "*I'm* the Grand Wizard. *I* created Straight Edge. Harvey's just a second banana, a wannabe with money."

Now I was even more confused. "What are you talking about?"

Brondon wore a strange expression, then smiled. "Oh yes, I forgot—I never did get a chance to go over all the details before I shot you from behind. I decided it was better not to gloat, not to explain everything."

"I wish you had. It would have made solving my murder a heck of a lot easier."

"I didn't know what you had discovered, but I couldn't risk having you blow the whistle. Our new line of necroceuticals was being released in the Quarter, and I had to take you out of the picture."

"Sorry to pee on your parade, Brondon, but I wasn't looking into the new product line at all. I don't even use the stuff."

Brondon blinked. "But you were following me! I saw you."

"Miranda Jekyll hired me to do covert surveillance on her husband. She wanted to catch her husband having an affair so she'd have leverage for her divorce settlement. I was following you just to get to him."

Robin said, "The cat's out of the bag now, Brondon—you might as well explain it. Isn't that what villains do?"

"I'm not the villain—I'm trying to save humanity."

"Strange way of showing it," I said. "With all those people dissolving horribly in the last couple of days."

"Do you still have graveyard dirt in your ears? I said I'm saving *humanity*, not unnaturals. The whole line of necroceuticals was designed for this purpose, and this purpose alone." Finally, the villain's soliloquy. I used the distraction of his ranting to advance another two steps toward the catwalk.

"JLPN is the most popular toiletry line for unnaturals. All the monsters use our body washes, shampoos, deodorants, skin creams, perfumes and colognes, toothpaste, hair gel ... and *every single product* is impregnated with a seemingly innocuous Compound X."

"What an original name," I said. "Compound W and Preparation H were both taken?"

Brondon sneered. "After prolonged use, Compound X saturates unnatural tissue. They don't even know it. It raises no red flags on any chemical analysis. But now ..." He spread his arms wide to indicate the factory floor and the bubbling cauldrons. Then he caught himself in the middle of his overly grandiose gesture, looked embarrassed, and trained the gun back on Robin to stop her from kicking him again. "With all of our advertising, the unnaturals will have to try the new and improved Fresh Loam line. And each new product contains a different, very special trace chemical."

"Let me guess: Compound Y?"

"No! *Compound Z!* And when that innocuous chemical reacts with its counterpart Compound X, it becomes a deadly dissolvogen! The contaminated unnaturals disintegrate like the filth they are. They'll drop like a plague of locusts flying through a cloud of insecticide. And because Compound Z is pervasive in the products used by all unnaturals for their personal hygiene needs, the monsters will be virtually extinct before they know what hit them. The streets will run pink with goo!"

I thought his crackpot plan was good enough to go on a website that listed top-ten nefarious schemes. Since I had never used any of his samples, my own body wasn't affected when I was exposed to Compound Z. But poor Mel ... and I even felt sorry for the three zombie cougars.

"If thousands of unnaturals melt into puddles on the same day, it won't be hard to follow the bread crumbs back to JLPN's product release," Robin said. "Even if you kill us, someone will figure it out. You'll go to the electric chair."

Brondon snorted. "Do you really think the rest of the human race won't applaud? Wholesome citizens will see this as a second chance, a cleansing after the Big Uneasy. How hard could it be to eradicate the few stragglers and take care of any new unnaturals as they arise? I'm betting that good people would say enough is enough and finish the job."

Even without asking, I had another reason to be disgusted with the man. "I watched you flirt with Cindy, Sharon, and Victoria, saw you pretend to be their friend—and then you made them all just dissolve. You murdered them."

Brondon shrugged. "Since when is it a crime to kill dead people?"

"I can make that case," Robin said.

"Decent people are sick of bleeding hearts like you. Getting all uppity about *human rights*. Who cares about a few monsters? Harvey Jekyll and I will be celebrated as heroes."

He tried to push Robin to the edge of the vat, but she held her ground. I wanted to lurch forward and strangle him, but I was still four steps from the top. I could never get to her in time.

Sheyenne's ghost reappeared, flitting onto the process floor. She saw us, absorbed the tableau in an instant, and swept up in front of Brondon Morris, looking as scary as she could manage. "I'm not going to let you hurt Dan again! You killed him once."

But Brondon knew a ghost couldn't touch him. "Go ahead and say boo all you want. I killed you, too, when you got to be a pain in the ass. And you're both still annoying."

Sheyenne's expression was outraged. Brondon looked at her and laughed. "You didn't know? After you had such a strong allergic reaction to the Compound X in the sample you stole, I tried to do damage control, but you just had to send the sample out for chemical analysis, didn't you? Then I found out you were Chambeaux's girlfriend, and I caught him digging into JLPN business, saw him surreptitiously following Harvey. I could put two and two together. I had to get rid of you both."

"Sheyenne had nothing to do with it!" I said.

"I poisoned Sheyenne's drink at Basilisk—toadstool toxin. Tasteless, effective, nearly always fatal in a high enough dose. And I had plenty of it here in my chemical labs for research. Toadstools do wonders for certain skin conditions in unnaturals. After I killed you both, that should have been the end of it. Imagine my surprise when you both came back!"

I lurched up three more steps until I was almost at the top—but I was still unarmed. Brondon pushed Robin closer to the edge of the foul-smelling chemical vat. As she struggled to keep her balance, I yelled, "The Compound Z in that vat isn't going to hurt Robin. She's human."

Brondon looked exasperated. "She can still drown!" He cocked the gun. "And that stuff's caustic in high concentrations. We've done hundreds of animal trials on bunnies and puppies just to make sure. All part of JLPN's dedication to quality control and safety before we go to market."

He pointed the barrel directly into Robin's face again. "Now, you're going in, one way or the other." He tightened his finger on the trigger.

The gunshot took me completely by surprise.

CHAPTER 42

I experienced a brief disorienting moment, like in a movie—I thought Brondon Morris had actually shot Robin. Instead, he spun around, grabbed his shoulder, and dropped his pistol on the catwalk.

Huffing and sweaty, McGoo stalked across the factory floor, his service revolver out. He was always a good shot.

Before I'd been killed, the two of us would often spend Saturday afternoons at the gun range, recreationally blowing holes in targets shaped like muggers, terrorists, werewolves, or hunchbacks. He always hit the bull's-eye—center of chest, center of head. My shots were all over the place—not much finesse, but good enough to take down an opponent, regardless.

Brondon's eyes bulged as he caught his balance and saw the cop. "You *shot* me!"

"Just winged you," McGoo said, marching closer, keeping his revolver pointed up at the green plaid sport jacket. "Got your attention, though, didn't I?"

Brondon opened and closed his mouth. "But ... but you're *human*!"

"And you're an asshole."

Even if McGoo hadn't heard all the details of the nefarious JLPN plan, he had enough information to conclude that Brondon Morris was, indeed, an asshole.

Despite his bleeding shoulder, Brondon bent over and grabbed for the .38 he had dropped on the catwalk. Robin's hands were tied, and she couldn't get the gun herself, but just as his fingers touched the pistol, she pushed him with her hip hard enough to knock him off balance.

He tumbled into the chemical vat.

I wanted to cheer for her. I lurched up the last step and ran across the catwalk as Robin swayed to keep her balance. She teetered on the edge herself, but I grabbed her just in time and pulled her back from the precipice, holding her safe.

Sheyenne flitted close. "Officer McGoohan was handcuffed in Harvey Jekyll's office in the admin building. I found him and unlocked his handcuffs, but since I can pass directly through walls, I got here faster than he could run."

In the murky liquid, Brondon squawked and flailed, trying to stay afloat. Robin was appalled at what she had done. "I'm sorry! I didn't mean to—"

"Yes, you did—and you did a good job," I said as I worked to untie her hands.

Even though Brondon was human, the caustic chemicals began eating away at the fabric of his green plaid jacket. He sank under, then resurfaced, thrashing and flopping. His hair curled and fell off in clumps, and his skin steamed and bubbled; huge blisters covered his cheeks and forehead.

I should have thought to keep watch on Sheyenne. Although the ghost couldn't touch people, she floated to the main controls and flicked on the powerful stirring unit. With a loud hum like a jet engine firing up, the beaters began to churn and chop the contents of the vat, creating a whirlpool.

Brondon reached out with swollen, steaming hands—and was sucked under. The beater made a loud *thump* as the motors strained to break the large chunk into more manageable bits. Then the stirrer continued to spin more smoothly.

Robin was shuddering and sobbing. "What a horrible way to die!"

"Don't feel too sorry for him," I said. "He meant to do that to you."

Sheyenne had a disturbingly calm expression on her face as she returned to us. I said, "I didn't know you were so ruthless."

She didn't look guilty at all; instead, she was indignant. "That man *killed* me. He put toadstool toxin in my drink! I suffered for days as the poison destroyed my body, one organ at a time. *Brondon Morris* did that to me—and he shot you too. More than once, in fact." She sniffed. "Believe me, that might have looked messy, but he got off easy."

Self-consciously, I touched the bullet hole in the back of my head and the putty-filled one in the front. I couldn't argue with her logic.

McGoo bounded up the metal stairs to join us all on the catwalk, looking around with wide eyes. "We're all right, McGoo," I said.

Still self-righteous, Sheyenne presented herself to him and extended her forearms, wrists together. "Are you going to cuff me, Officer? You saw what I did."

He peered into the churning, frothing vat as the beater kept working. A large rectangular swatch of green plaid floated to the top of the liquid, then was sucked under again.

After a long pause, McGoo said, "I didn't see anything. He must have slipped on the catwalk." He indicated a sign on the cinderblock wall next to a pile of pipes from a dismantled scaffold. *Warning: Hazardous Chemicals.* "Must be an internal problem at JLPN, insufficient safety precautions for the employees." He looked over at Robin. "Someone should file a workers' compensation suit."

We descended the stairs, glad to be down from the vat. I retrieved my .38 from where I had tossed it. Robin rubbed her wrists, flexed her fingers. She smiled at me. "Thanks, I knew you'd come."

On the side of the huge tank, a laminated sheet announced, *Safety First! This Facility Has Had ___ Days Without An Accident.* The number *121* had been written with a grease pencil that hung by a piece of twine next to the sign. With the side of my hand, I smeared out the *121*, picked up the grease pencil, and wrote *0.*

McGoo was still red-faced and panting as he looked around the process floor. He touched the back of his head and winced. "Jekyll's around here somewhere. He's the one who knocked me out."

"We'll have to send an emergency recall notice to all the stores and facilities that were about to release the new JLPN product line," Robin said. "Get word out on the radio, have the mayor make a speech and warn all unnaturals. They can't be allowed to use any necroceuticals that contain Compound Z."

"You'll do no such thing," said a nasal voice. "That would destroy all our hopes and dreams."

Harvey Jekyll walked onto the factory floor. A small bookish man with shrunken shoulders and large eyes, he looked more qualified to be a dungeon librarian than a corporate executive. "I'm afraid I can't let any of you leave here—even the humans." Jekyll's nostrils flared, and the wrinkles on his brow furrowed together. "I'm very sorry that Brondon didn't live to see our ultimate triumph. Do you know how hard it is to find a good, imaginative chemist who isn't profit-motivated?"

"You can find him right there in the vat," I said. "But you'll have to strain out the pieces."

Jekyll stepped forward, and I noticed how very small his shoes were; perhaps he bought them in the boys' department. He had small, feminine hands, too. If clichés about endowment were accurate, that might have been another reason why Miranda was so eager for a divorce.

"Brondon was a crusader for humankind," Jekyll said. "Under my auspices, he created products to make real human beings safe, to make us stand strong against the unnaturals." Then, as if a thought had occurred to him, he raised his chin and smiled. "However, his death does now make me the official Grand Wizard of Straight Edge. That's a silver lining, at least."

We all just stared at him. Two villain soliloquies in one night?

"Harvey Jekyll, you're under arrest for murder," McGoo said. "Turn around and put your hands behind your back. I'm taking you in."

"Oh, don't be ridiculous, Officer. Murder of unnaturals? No one will care, and once I eliminate *you all,* I can pin everything on poor Brondon. That way he can serve a final purpose." The mousy man strutted forward.

I laughed in disbelief. "You're delusional, Mr. Jekyll. It's three of us against you."

Sheyenne flitted up to the catwalk and drifted down to join us, holding the gun that Brondon had dropped. "Four of us," she said.

"Oh, that won't be nearly enough," Jekyll sneered. "One of Brondon's greatest achievements was creating a concoction that makes a normal human strong enough to fight even an army of unnaturals." He reached into his coat pocket and withdrew a capped test tube filled with emerald-green liquid. He yanked off the cork and downed the contents. From the grimace on Jekyll's face, I assumed the potion was as vile as its creator had been.

Jekyll's scrawny figure began to change.

CHAPTER 43

Jekyll's entire body swelled up as if someone had hooked an air compressor to his nether orifice and inflated him like a Thanksgiving Day parade balloon. His shoulders expanded, his chest puffed out, and his shirt split into frayed tatters. His previously bald head sprouted thick shocks of wiry black hair. His eyes became huge, and his mouth sprouted square crooked teeth.

It didn't take a private detective to figure out that *this* was the violent brute that had caused so much mayhem around the city.

Not one to call a committee meeting before making a decision, McGoo pointed his service revolver and shot Jekyll full in the chest. I didn't blame him—this thing had torn the young Straight Edgers to pieces and staked Sheldon Fennerman to a brick wall.

Despite being shot, Jekyll kept growing and kept coming toward us. McGoo had fired the revolver loaded with normal bullets, which he'd just fired at Brondon Morris, but I doubted the silver-jacketed ammo in his other pistol would have had any greater effect.

I drew my own .38 and started shooting. Getting into the spirit of the celebration, Sheyenne joined in with Brondon's gun.

The bullets didn't bounce off Jekyll's hide, but were simply *absorbed* into his swelling flesh like raindrops in a mud puddle. The monstrous creature's biceps bulged, and his fingernails turned into thick talons. Warts the size of hard-boiled eggs popped up on his leathery skin.

"That thing is ugly!" McGoo said.

No wonder the witches' protective spell hadn't been good enough to save Sheldon; this brute would have gotten over a bit of cockroach-enhanced indigestion without any trouble at all.

I'd caught only a glimpse as this creature had bounded out of the alley behind the Straight Edge headquarters, climbed to the rooftops, and sprinted away into the moonlight. The monster had bashed Hope Saldana's mission, probably because the old woman aided and comforted unnaturals; he had ripped the four Straight Edgers into little pieces, no doubt because they were incompetent.

Or maybe he had other reasons. I didn't see the point in psycho-analyzing a loose-cannon monster to figure out logical explanations for his actions.

And he had murdered Sheldon Fennerman.

With Jekyll's transformation complete and his muscles as hard as braided steel cable, the slugs we had fired into him popped out of his body and pattered onto the factory floor. Sweating bullets, you might say.

The huge creature slammed a meat loaf–sized fist into the churning chemical vat beside him, puncturing it so that noxious fluids spewed across the floor. Then he tore down the metal staircase that ran up the side of the vat, bending the framework and hurling it across the factory floor with a loud clatter.

I kept firing until my pistol was empty. When Sheyenne had also emptied Brondon Morris's gun, she dropped the weapon, and her ghost swooped into the Jekyll monster and passed entirely through his body, much to her frustration. Backing away, McGoo shot two more times.

His glowing eyes fixed on his first target, the monster came straight toward Robin.

I was not going to let this nightmare juggernaut harm a hair on her head. "Robin, get out of here!" I charged into monster Jekyll like a kid from a peewee football league trying to derail a locomotive—and I was about as successful.

I punched him hard in his cabbage-sized nose, which seemed like a good idea when I thought of it. Jekyll didn't care which victim he got his huge paws on first. Since I was within reach, the brute grabbed my right arm. I struggled, but couldn't break free.

With a merciless motion like someone tearing the wing off a roasted chicken, the monster yanked my arm out of its socket, pulled it free, and threw the limb aside like a used toothpick.

Sheyenne screamed.

"Dammit!" I reeled. That wasn't going to be easy to fix, but at least I'd bought them a second or two. "McGoo, get her out of here!"

McGoo hauled Robin toward the exit next to the dismantled scaffolding and the sign on the wall that politely cautioned JLPN workers about the hazards of chemicals. "Come on, we've got to get out of here!"

For some reason, I heard howling outside the factory.

Yanking my arm off wasn't good enough for Jekyll. He lifted me bodily and hurled me against the giant chemical vat. I slammed into the curved side, leaving a man-shaped dent like something out of a Looney Tunes cartoon, then sprawled into the gushing Compound Z chemicals that continued to vomit out of the tank. I was drenched and disgusted, but fortunately the dissolvogen had no effect on me.

Leaving me behind, Jekyll bounded after McGoo and Robin. Even if they managed to get outside, this huge beast would catch up with them in only a few steps.

I tried to pick myself up. Lopsided and off balance without my right arm, I slipped in the oozing, steaming liquid and fell on my butt. A severed hand—not mine—plopped out of the punctured vat into the puddle beside me. Well-manicured ... no doubt Brondon Morris's.

Across the room, reenacting a scene from a bad horror movie, my detached arm flopped about, the hand clenching and unclenching, trying to finger-walk along the concrete. That's the thing about being undead: After coming back to life, the pieces are very persistent.

McGoo threw open the door to get Robin outside, but before they could escape into the moonlit night, a Tasmanian Devil flurry of fur, muscles, claws, and fangs bounded into the factory, snarling and thrashing.

McGoo instinctively grabbed his other sidearm, the one loaded with silver bullets, and aimed at the vicious wolf-woman. But I saw the line of pearls that ringed the werewolf's neck like a very expensive dog collar. "Don't shoot, McGoo! It's Miranda—Miranda Jekyll!"

The she-wolf hurled herself upon the bloated monstrosity that had been her husband. Jekyll twisted from side to side and swung at her, but Miranda sank her fangs into the rope-cable muscles of his neck. Her she-wolf body was covered with hair, made out of solid muscle, more sleek and attractive than her normal form.

Jekyll knocked his wife aside with an arm the size of a bent telephone pole and sent her sprawling across the concrete floor. She landed on all fours, and her paws skittered on the sealed surface. She just barely managed to keep herself from tumbling into the Compound Z–laced puddle.

Now we could add spousal abuse to her case against her husband.

Ignoring Miranda, the brute lurched toward my two friends like a poor man's King Kong. Robin picked up one of the steel pipes from the scaffolding and brandished it to defend herself against the oncoming monster. "I have had a very rough night already!" She swung the pipe back and forth, but didn't manage to look threatening.

I finally got to my feet and went after Jekyll with weaving footsteps. Armless and off balance, I must have looked like one of those clichéd *Walking Dead* zombies.

My severed arm crawled toward the door, working its way toward the monster. It was disorienting to try to move a part of my body from ten feet away, but the arm couldn't wait for me to catch up. It had nearly reached him.

The chorus of howls outside grew louder—a whole pack of werewolves closing in.

Miranda bounded forward to join Robin and McGoo, her lips curled back, fangs bared. She plucked the metal pole out of Robin's hands and faced Jekyll. The monster would tear them all to pieces in just a few seconds.

"Harvey!" I shouted. "For all your big talk, you're just as unnatural as the rest of us!"

He turned his head to snarl at me. Jekyll wasn't expecting my severed arm to grab onto his ankle with a grip like a ferocious poodle. He roared, looked down.

In that instant of distraction, Miranda swung the heavy steel pipe with all her lupine strength, like a golfer trying to make the longest drive on a championship course. She cracked him solidly between the legs. And regardless of how massive and muscular the Jekyll monstrosity was, he did not have testicles of steel.

Six bristling werewolves bounded through the door, letting out angry howls—Miranda's friends from the full-moon party, I assumed. They loped forward, some walking on two legs, others reverting to a more animal form.

Preoccupied with his own agony, Jekyll didn't even notice. His groan sounded significantly higher pitched than before. He bent over and seemed to fold down and shrink in upon himself. With a long, miserable whimper, he curled into a ball on the floor.

"That worked better than Kryptonite," McGoo said, breathing hard.

"Bastard deserved it." Miranda growled and slavered onto the moaning man on the floor, who reverted to his former mousy physique. "I have wanted to do that for *years*."

Her werewolf friends prowled the factory floor, and Sheyenne circled, warning them to stay away from the deadly chemical puddles. I was surprised to see that one of the hairy man-wolves was Larry the lycanthrope hit man the Ricketts heirs had hired to harass me. Panting, Miranda smiled at the whole pack. "Thanks for coming, sweethearts." She had unlocked the fence gate to let her werewolf friends in.

Finally, in the better-late-than-never department, we heard sirens in the distance. Taking no chances, McGoo slapped handcuffs on Harvey Jekyll's wrists, although he had some difficulty prying the man's hands away from his crotch.

Robin looked at the torn sleeve of my shirt and the empty socket where my arm had been ripped away. "Oh, Dan, your arm!" She retrieved the limb from the floor and carried it to me—although I don't know what she expected me to do with it.

"My souvenir from the case," I said, taking it from her with my remaining hand. The arm kept twitching in my grip.

Sheyenne was distraught and indignant. "We'll get you to the Patchup Parlor. Miss Eccles can stitch you back together again. After what she did for Wendy, reattaching a severed arm can't be beyond her abilities."

"It's obviously still functional." I concentrated on my detached limb to make the fingers curl in the "OK" sign.

The sirens grew louder. McGoo went to stand outside the door, waving for the police. "How did they know to get here? I didn't call for backup."

"I did—after I set you loose," Sheyenne said. "I can use a phone, you know. Wouldn't be much of a receptionist if I couldn't."

By the time the cops rushed into the factory, guns drawn, the crisis was already over.

Miranda Jekyll paced and prowled around the factory floor, a mass of feral energy. "I wish we could plug that vat. Nasty stuff."

"It's draining into the floor grates," Robin said. "What if Compound Z gets into the groundwater?"

Miranda's snout curled. "The factory has holding tanks before any effluent is released into the sewer system. Environmental requirements." She growled in frustration. "This is *so* not how I intended to spend my full moon."

I held onto my right arm with my left hand. "Not how I expected to spend mine, either."

Robin, though, was smiling. "We won't have any further trouble litigating your case, Mrs. Jekyll. In fact, I have no doubt that all JLPN assets will belong entirely to you. Your husband is going to trial for multiple counts of murder, conspiracy, terrorist acts, attempted genocide, assault, felony property damage. Give me a few minutes—I can come up with plenty of other ideas for the district attorney."

Miranda sniffed, and her fur started to look less ruffled. "Thank you, sweetheart. I feel better already." Contentedly, she groomed the silky hair on her forepaw. Her werewolf friends let out a chorus of howls.

CHAPTER 44

I could feel the tug, and my shoulders rocked back and forth, but Lujean Eccles needed to make sure the stitches were tight. With my intact left hand, I gripped the side of her floral-print sofa for stability. Sheyenne passed surgical and taxidermy implements to Miss Eccles as she requested them. The sawbones pulled hard on the artificial sinew, then put her weight behind the effort, pressing on my right humerus until I felt the bone pop back into its shoulder socket.

"There you are, Mr. Chambeaux—as good as new."

I concentrated on the fingers of my until-recently-detached arm and was relieved to see them curl down to the palm and straighten again. Next, I tried the hand, turning the wrist from side to side. I bent the elbow and finally raised the arm. "Excellent work, Miss Eccles."

"It's nice to have a repeat customer." She began packing up her sewing kit.

"I'm not exactly glad to *be* a repeat customer."

Sheyenne hovered above the repaired arm, concerned. "Can you feel your fingers?"

"What can I do to help?" Robin asked. "Does it hurt?"

"Doesn't hurt … much. We're back in business." I held up my hand in a high-five gesture. Robin smiled and slapped my palm. Sheyenne did the same, although her spectral hand passed through mine. "I have good people to take care of me."

Wendy the Patchwork Princess tottered into the sitting room, carrying my old jacket, which was amazingly clean and patched up again. It still looked tattered with the bullet holes sewn up in clumsy stitches, but it smelled fresh, and there was no sign of mud or blue fizziness.

"Sorry it's not better," she said.

"It's just great, Wendy." I ran my fingers over the black stitches that held the bullet holes together. "It has character, and I plan to wear it every day. From now on, this is my lucky jacket."

"Lucky?" Robin said. "What kind of luck are you talking about?"

With her help, I shrugged my arms into the sleeves, straightened the collar, smoothed the lapels, and assessed my appearance in Miss Eccles's parlor mirror. "I may look like I came off the discount rack in the used-body store, but this is who I am."

"That's the way we like you, Beaux," Sheyenne said.

Maybe some flesh-colored upholstery tape would mask the stitches holding my arm back on, and makeup could cover the neatly sutured bullet holes across my torso. I resolved to remain well preserved, keep my regular appointments at Bruno & Heinrich's Embalming Parlor for a touch-up, and spend more time at the All-Day/All-Nite Fitness Center.

Lujean Eccles placed her hands on her ample hips, pleased with her work. "Don't feel bad about it, Mr. Chambeaux. Our scars tell stories of who we are and what we did. A person without marks hasn't done anything."

It was a good sentiment. "I'll remember that." I brushed off the front of my jacket and placed the fedora back on my head.

O O O

After Jekyll's crimes were exposed, the uproar among unnaturals was so great that all hell was about to break loose. The warning against JLPN's new line of Compound Z–saturated necroceuticals went out wide. All product stockpiles were impounded, every bottle taken from the shelves; every tube of toothpaste, jar of hair cream, pack of emBalm, or bottle of skin softener was recalled and incinerated, just in case.

Even so, because of accidental glitches or just plain obstinate stupidity, seventeen more unnaturals dissolved into puddles of goo. But it could have been much worse....

The Dorset family returned to our offices, more desperate than ever. The medium, Millicent Sanchez, looked frazzled, her hair in disarray, her eyes bloodshot. The family looked defeated, the children so skittish they could barely concentrate on their video games.

"Breakfast, lunch, and dinner—it's *constant* aggravation," Jackie Dorset said. "Uncle Stan wakes us up at all hours of the night. He heckles the children while they're doing homework. He chases away any guests we have over. There's got to be a law against spectral stalking!"

"And law enforcement to go along with it," Brad said. "Nobody will do anything to remove the nuisance."

"Changes in the legal system take forever to implement," Robin said with genuine sympathy.

"I'm just here as a courtesy," Millicent Sanchez announced, sounding miffed. "This is the first time I have ever abandoned a client, but I can't take any more." She handed her notes and records to Robin. "I've never endured such persistent harassment from a ghost. It's completely unprofessional. I have my other clients to worry about."

Brad Dorset gave a resigned sigh. "Uncle Stan's been vindictively haunting all of Millicent's customers, trying to ruin her business."

The medium pushed herself away from the conference room table. "Best of luck to you. No charge—just don't *ever* call me again."

As she reached the door, the needy ghost of inebriated Uncle Stan appeared with a gush of cold wind that blew the medium's skirt up past her waist in a very unsatisfactory Marilyn Monroe steam-grate parody. Millicent Sanchez squealed, swatted at the air. Even though the ghost couldn't touch her, she tripped and fell face-first to the floor in the reception area, much to Uncle Stan's glee. She scrambled out of our offices on hands and knees.

Robin lurched to her feet and barked like a drill sergeant. "I will not stand for this! There *will* be standards of decorum in these offices!"

Uncle Stan's puffy cheeks swelled out so he could let rip a very loud raspberry.

Just then Sheyenne appeared in front of the drunken ghost, cocked back her balled right fist, and punched Uncle Stan squarely in the nose. He reeled in shock, and Sheyenne drew herself up. "There's more where that came from. If you try to terrorize our clients, you'll have to come through me." She raised both fists now. "You've done enough harm. You should be ashamed of yourself."

Uncle Stan started blubbering. "They're my family, my *only* family. You can't keep me away from them! It's cruel and unusual."

"You're the one who's cruel and unusual," muttered the boy Joshua, then tried to concentrate on his game. Uncle Stan disrupted the game's circuits, and the unit died with an electronic sigh of doom.

But Sheyenne was on a tear of her own. "Ghosts like you give apparitions everywhere a bad name! *I've* had to accept my situation—now do the same. Just because *you* don't have a life anymore, it doesn't give you the right to ruin somebody else's life."

"We loved you when you were alive, Uncle Stan," Jackie said with a sniffle. "But you're dead now. Please move on."

"I'm not going anywhere," the ghost said, then his expression fell. "I've got no place to go. I just wanted to be noticed and not forgotten."

"Well, this isn't the way to go about it," Sheyenne scolded. "It's tough enough for unnaturals to be accepted in this world. We're fighting for our right to be treated as regular citizens, so we try to get along, be good neighbors, and *not* eat or attack one another. But you know what you are, with your spectral terrorism? A roadblock for all unnaturals trying to gain acceptance!"

Tears welled up in the ghost's red-rimmed eyes, and he grew maudlin in the way only a long-term drunk can. "I'm sorry. I didn't mean it."

Jackie Dorset was emotional as well. "It's not that we don't love you, Uncle Stan, but we need our own space."

Brad added, "After all, how can we miss you when you're always there?"

"But I'm lonely!"

Robin pulled her chair closer to the table, put her elbows on the surface, and assumed her professional mediating-lawyer position. "Now that we've finally opened a genuine dialogue, maybe we can find a middle ground? You don't need to be at opposite ends of the spectrum."

"We've always been willing to talk," Brad said. "If Uncle Stan would agree to a cease-fire."

Sheyenne hovered by Uncle Stan like a tough enforcer, ready to punch him in the nose again. She had knocked some sense into him already.

"Maybe ... we can pick one night a week when we'll be glad to see you, and we can all be good company to one another," Jackie said.

"You mean, like Sundays used to be?" Uncle Stan brightened. "And Wednesdays, and—"

"*One* day a week," Brad said sternly.

Stan looked crestfallen, then lifted his eyes. "And holidays. How about holidays? Those should be family times."

"Christmas and Thanksgiving only," Brad conceded.

"And Easter. We have to get together for Easter."

Jackie looked at her husband and grudgingly said, "Okay, Easter too."

"And Arbor Day was always my favorite—"

"No," Brad said.

Robin added, "Perhaps you're going too far, sir."

Uncle Stan let out a long sigh. "All right. Every Sunday, Thanksgiving, Christmas, and Easter."

"But you have to agree to leave them in peace for the rest of the year," Robin said.

The ghost blinked mournfully at the Dorsets. "You could still invite me over at other times, if you like. I mean … if we get along."

"Your own behavior will dictate that," Robin said. "This is a trial period."

"I'll change. I promise."

"I have resources for you," Robin added. "We can even line up some ghostly counseling services."

O O O

The office was quiet for a few days, which gave us time to wrap up the cases we'd been working on. Sheyenne was happy to close several files: the emancipation of Ramen Ho-Tep, the Wannovich sisters' lawsuit, the case of poor Sheldon Fennerman, and Miranda Jekyll's divorce.

Miranda paid us a hefty bonus. In addition, the Chambeaux & Deyer share of the proceeds from the Alvin Ricketts art auction arrived, and Ramen Ho-Tep paid his bill with a golden scarab brooch from his private collection. With the welcome influx of cash, we were able to clear all of our overdue bills and pay off the remainder of my funeral expenses. (They had been weighing on me like a bunch of old student loans.)

We also had more than enough to buy a new company car, though Robin spent the money on getting the Pro Bono Mobile fixed instead. I could have bought a whole wardrobe of expensive tailored suits, but I had already decided to keep my old bullet-scarred one. Instead, we put the extra money into the operating expenses account, saving for a rainy day. The Unnatural Quarter had a lot of rainy days.

Sheyenne packed up the finished paperwork and closed case files in a bankers' box and headed off to our storage unit. When Sheyenne was gone, Robin came in and sat on the corner of my desk. She had that concerned look on her face. "I worry about the risks you take, Dan. I tried to warn you, but you didn't listen."

"Oh, I listened. I just wasn't careful enough."

She sighed. "You're dead, and I still worry about you."

"Even these bullets can't stop me from getting back up and going to work. But I won't let it happen again—I promise I learned my lesson."

"Or maybe you should take up a safer profession?"

I laughed. "Like being a zombie accountant? I'm a private investigator—that's what I do. I can't change that any more than you could close your law books and walk away from the legal profession."

She smiled. "You're right. You know me, and I know you."

"That's why we're such a good team," I said. "I'm here for you, no matter what."

Robin came around the desk and threw her arms around my shoulders in a fierce hug. Fortunately, her fierceness didn't knock lose any of the stitches Lujean Eccles had used to reattach my arm. She felt warm and smelled good, and I let her just stay there for as long as she wanted.

CHAPTER 45

On the following Saturday, Sheyenne and I went to the Metropolitan Natural History Museum to see Ramen Ho-Tep's first public presentation. Despite his grudging acquiescence to the terms, the museum curator and his staff got behind the effort and provided substantial publicity. People flocked in to see the ambulatory mummy do his schtick.

"An afternoon at the museum," Sheyenne said. "When we were still alive, we might have called this a genuine date."

I grinned at her as we walked into the Ancient Egypt wing. "So why can't we?"

A smile crept across her beautiful face. "Other than the obvious physical limitations, you mean?" She arched her eyebrows.

If she had ever finished med school, she would definitely have caused an increased pulse rate among her male patients.

"I'm not that kind of guy, Spooky. I don't do that on a first date."

She laughed. "Yes, you do. Or did I count wrong?" As if we had rehearsed it, we both took in a deep breath and let out a sigh. That one night would have to do. Dead guys can't be choosy, and I would rather have a ghost of Sheyenne than any other real woman.

"We could go out for fondue," I suggested. "In honor of Sheldon."

"You'd have to invite Robin too. She's the only one who could really enjoy the food." Then her pragmatic streak came to the fore. "We could discuss cases, make it a tax-deductible meal."

"Sounds good to me."

A crowd of patrons, many of them school-aged children, had gathered around the exhibits and the artificial pyramid that held the ancient treasures. I glanced at my watch—we were just in time.

The museum intern designated as the mummy's personal assistant (though Ramen Ho-Tep insisted on calling him a slave) hovered around the periphery of the audience, straightening chairs, nervous about this big debut. Recognizing us, the intern pointed to two empty chairs near the front; as guests of the former pharaoh, we had special VIP passes.

Lujean Eccles was also in the audience, accompanied by the Patchwork Princess. The museum had consulted with Miss Eccles on how to spiff up Ramen Ho-Tep for his public-speaking debut. A smile brightened Wendy's crooked face when she noticed I was wearing the jacket she had stitched up. She waved, and I waved back.

The lights dimmed, and with great theatrical effect, the mummy of Ramen Ho-Tep rose from his sarcophagus and regarded the crowd, who oohed and aahed. The children's eyes were as big as saucers. The mummy was indeed ready for prime time: his bandages were freshened, the stains removed, the caked dust whisked off him.

Seeing us, he swelled larger with self-confidence. "I was a pharaoh of Ancient Egypt!" His voice boomed, sounding impressive. "I ruled the lands from the Nubian Desert and Kush in Upper Egypt, down to Thebes, and the Nile Delta and Memphis."

"Memphis?" asked a young boy. "Where Elvis lived?"

"No! *I* was the King." Ramen Ho-Tep crossed his arms over his chest. "I had thousands of slaves, and I was worshiped by my people. They gave me gold, lapis lazuli, myrrh, and pretty little paintings on sheets of papyrus. I was a giant among men, worshipped as a god." He stood barely five feet high, shrunken due to desiccation and dehydration. "My father was Nor-Man Ho-Tep, and before him was—" The mummy rattled off a string of names, none of which meant anything to the listeners.

When the audience started to yawn, the intern/slave scurried to the front and whispered, "Maybe you should skip the rest of the family tree, Mr. Ho-Tep."

"How did you get to be a mummy?" a girl interrupted.

"Let me tell you, young lady." Ramen Ho-Tep leaned forward. "When a great pharaoh dies, his body must be carefully preserved for the next life. I was taken to the House of the Dead by my priests and washed in palm wine and rinsed with water from the Nile. All my internal organs were removed—liver, lungs, stomach, intestines—and placed in canopic jars. That's why I feel hollow inside to this day. The embalmers pushed a hook up my nose to pull out my brain, since I wasn't using it anymore."

"Eww," said a chorus of audience members, mainly the adults.

"Do you need your brain now?" asked a boy.

"I really don't miss it."

Ramen Ho-Tep regarded the audience. "I had a beloved cat. As was tradition, and because I was Pharaoh of all Egypt, my cat was also mummified. Everyone needs a pet in the afterlife. His name was"—he uttered another mishmash of odd-sounding syllables, paused, then said, "It translates as Fluffy."

The kids giggled.

Ramen Ho-Tep reveled in the attention as questions came at him from the audience. Bram Steffords stood at the back of the room, looking haughty, but unmistakably pleased with the presentation.

"This is going to work out just fine," I whispered to Sheyenne. "Ramen Ho-Tep is in his element." Glancing down, I saw that her ghostly hand was resting on mine, though I couldn't feel it. Imagining that we were holding hands did produce a surprising warm swirly sensation in my stomach, though.

After the mummy had finished, and the audience members crowded forward to ask for his autograph on their program booklets, Sheyenne and I left the Ancient Egypt wing.

Now that I had time, I decided to spend a few minutes at the Necronomicon exhibit out in the central hall. I wasn't a scientist, nor an occultist (the two professions now had more overlap than anyone ever imagined), but this book's strange magical powers, not to mention a ludicrous set of coincidences and a rare planetary alignment, had changed the world.

If not for the Big Uneasy, I would have stayed dead after Brondon Morris shot me, and the cases wouldn't have solved themselves. On the other hand, without the Big Uneasy, without JLPN's scheme to eradicate the unnaturals, I probably wouldn't have been shot in the first place....

Near the rare books displayed in high-security vitrines, I saw the large black-gowned form of Mavis Wannovich, wearing her pointed black hat and the star-and-moon spangled scarf. She held a thick notebook in her hands, scribbling notations. Well behaved and very clean, her sow-sister Alma rooted around the displays, pressing her dark eyes close to the glass so she could read the information cards.

The witch looked up with a smile on her face. "A pleasure to see you, Mr. Chambeaux. Alma's here under a special dispensation—I've gotten her classified as a service pig." Then her expression fell. "Oh, I heard about Mr. Fennerman. I'm so sorry our protective spell wasn't good enough. I feel just terrible. That poor vampire!"

"Your protective spell worked, but it would have taken a howitzer to drive away that monster." After an awkward moment of silence, I added, "You're looking good ... much more relaxed."

Mavis self-consciously brushed down her frizzy black hair. "Thanks. Alma and I just had the most amazing spa and mud-bath treatment. Sometimes you have to pamper yourself."

"How are your jobs going?" Sheyenne asked. "Is the publishing house treating you well?"

"Oh, yes. Now that our dispute is resolved, Howard Phillips is a fine company, and they definitely needed someone to organize their records. Alma and I have our work cut out for us. In fact, I'm here taking notes for the special rerelease of our annotated Necronomicon. There were typos in the previous printing, if you can believe that!" She rolled her eyes. Alma let out a loud confirmatory snort.

"Any progress on reversing your sister's condition?" I asked.

"We'll get around to that, but we've both been incredibly busy. Howard Phillips has an entire room full of slush-pile manuscripts. They've fallen far behind, all those aspiring authors just waiting for a response ... Now it's my responsibility to go through the shelves, alphabetize the submissions, and begin responding. I give each book a fair assessment, don't pull any punches. And Alma can smell a bad manuscript from the other side of the room."

The sow circled, pressed her snout against a display case, and came back to us.

Mavis added with a happy sigh, "This is my dream job, Mr. Chambeaux—working as an editor, dealing with writers, seeing a book through the publication process, typesetting, proofreading, printing. I want to thank you and Ms. Deyer for the opportunity. And yes, we will eventually start testing spells to reverse the effects on my sister, as soon as we institute some solid quality control."

"If you're satisfied with our service, would you write us a short testimonial—just a few sentences?" Sheyenne said. "Did you receive our bill, by the way? I can print up another one, if you'd like."

"Oh yes, don't worry—the check is in the mail." Mavis beamed. "And Alma and I would be honored to write you a glowing recommendation." After pondering a moment, the witch added, "Now that I think of it, Mr.

Chambeaux, you've been through such enthralling adventures in the Unnatural Quarter. Have you ever considered writing about some of your more interesting cases, penning a memoir? The world would be fascinated to read it ... or at least a number of our special-edition subscribers would."

I frowned. "Never thought about it."

"Since Alma and I have such fond feelings for you, if you were to submit a manuscript to Howard Phillips Publishing, I would give it my fullest attention."

Sheyenne hovered beside me. "Not a bad idea, Beaux. You could handwrite a few pages a day, and I'll type them up. In less than a year, you'd finish a whole book."

I wasn't convinced, but seeing Sheyenne's enthusiasm, I decided not to turn her down right away. "I'll think about it."

CHAPTER 46

In rare cases, the wheels of justice turn swiftly, like a steamroller.

The evidence against Harvey Jekyll was incontrovertible, and he did not deny the charges of his toiletry-based attempt at genocide. In fact, he seemed proud of himself, expecting "decent humanity" to rally to his defense. He was disappointed.

Meanwhile, the unnaturals demanded revenge, some incensed enough that they called for Brondon Morris's identifiable body parts to be strained out of the chemical sludge from the factory vat and also put on trial. Such a demand would have made more sense if the pieces had been reanimated, but no such luck.

Instead, Jekyll had to face the music himself—and the music did not sound like Barry Manilow or the Carpenters.

In his final statement to the court, Jekyll said, "One day, you'll see I was right. When the last humans are cowering under their beds because the monsters have taken over the world, you'll all wish they'd used Zom-Be-Fresh."

Verdict: Guilty.

Sentence: Death.

Knowing the brutish monster that Jekyll could become, the warden and prison guards were terrified to have him in their prison. Worried that he might sprout huge biceps and fangs if some additive in the prison pudding or chipped beef interacted with the trace residue of his transformational potion, they reinforced the cell walls and installed extra bars across the door. And all the while, the prisoner just sat there, a scrawny bald human who looked as if he should have been spending the days stroking a white Persian cat on his lap as he plotted the conquest of the world.

But prison rules didn't allow him to have a cat.

O   O   O

After the trial wrapped up, Miranda Jekyll came to our offices to thank us profusely. She was lighthearted and aloof, completely free—and, in a way, scarier than ever. She was still dressed to kill, lavishly bedecked with jewelry, wearing a dress that had cost more than her imported automobile.

She was accompanied by a hunk—tall, dark, and handsome, exuding power and animal magnetism. He had long black hair that seemed to flow in a faint breeze every time he turned to show off his profile. His shirt was unbuttoned halfway down his chest. When he greeted us, he spoke in a luscious and exotic foreign accent.

Miranda introduced her male companion. "This is Hirsute, another once-a-month werewolf, my soul mate."

I shook the man's powerful hand. "Hirsute?"

"It's French, I think," Miranda said. She scratched her fingernails down his bulging sleeve. "He understands me like no one else ever has." Hirsute raised Miranda's hand, pressed it to his lips, and gave it a nibbling kiss. Her smile showed pointed teeth, and a purring growl came from the base of her throat.

"I'm just informing you that I won't be at Harvey's execution, sweethearts. I've got a scheduling conflict. I can't understand why the judge would pick a date so close to the full moon, and you know I always have other plans. Besides, I don't need to watch the little worm get fried. Thanks to you, I now control JLPN. I have more wealth than I ever expected to get in the divorce. And I have Hirsute."

Though Jekyll Lifestyle Products and Necroceuticals took a severe financial hit from the scandal, Miranda had no intention of declaring bankruptcy. Her husband had been a frugal man and had squirreled away substantial liquid assets. If he'd succeeded with his Armageddon of unnatural meltdowns, he would have lost his customer base, so he had established contingency accounts. Miranda announced she would put the money back into JLPN to rehabilitate the company image.

With her new fortune, she had also purchased a large game preserve up in Montana, as well as her own private jet. "Over five hundred acres of pristine wilderness," she said. "Completely fenced off, plenty of room to roam and hunt. Hirsute and I will fly there every month on the full moon, where we can tear off our clothes and just be free, running naked in the moonlight."

"Sounds idyllic," Robin said. "Maybe you should consider opening it for the use of all werewolves?"

"I'll think about that, sweetheart. *After* Hirsute and I tire of it."

Then Miranda and the hunky werewolf strolled off.

O   O   O

Given the furor surrounding the case, the judge put Harvey Jekyll's execution on the fast track. Since he was a human, there was no need for any convoluted or supernatural means of dispatching him. He would go to the chair, which was affectionately named Sparky, Jr.

Because we were instrumental in solving the case, Robin, Sheyenne, and I received invitations to witness the execution, though it wasn't exactly a social occasion. For years now, Robin had been a passionate defender of unnaturals, and her compelling speeches were vital in shaping public opinion; she had given brilliant testimony during Jekyll's trial. Knowing that the mousy corporate head was actually going to die, however, gave her many second thoughts. She wrestled with her conscience and got over it.

So did I. I had only to think about Sheldon Fennerman pinned to the brick wall or Mel dissolving into goo at the dump…. Worst of all, Jekyll had tried to kill my friends.

No, I didn't have any crisis of conscience.

Although Brondon Morris had actually murdered Sheyenne and me, we were satisfied to let Jekyll take the fall for it in the public eye. Behind the scenes, Jekyll might have been second banana to Brondon in many ways, but now he got to be the star of the show. It was sure to be an electrifying performance.

In the Pro Bono Mobile, we drove to the prison on execution day. Sheyenne rode in the backseat, although she could have drifted along at her own speed.

The main prison complex looked not unlike the JLPN chemical factory—Jekyll probably felt right at home. Outside the gate, a dozen human protesters carried signs in defense of Harvey Jekyll: *Execution Is Murder! Harvey's a Hero!* and *Straight Edge Can See It, Why Can't You?*

On the opposite side of the entry road, a large group of unnaturals had come for a tailgate party. They howled for Jekyll's blood, flesh, and bones. (They were willing to settle for any scrap.)

A van for Jekyll Lifestyle Products & Necroceuticals was parked near them, with a huge banner: *Under New Management!* Three volunteer workers—lawn gnomes, I think—were handing out free samples to the crowd. The unnaturals were skeptical, but most pocketed the samples for later use.

After we showed our credentials and drove through the prison sally port, we made our way to the warden's office. McGoo was already there and introduced us to the warden, who somberly shook Robin's hand, then mine, and gave a polite nod to Sheyenne.

McGoo wore his best uniform, clean and pressed. This was the serious part of his job, and he wouldn't have missed it for the world. "You ready for this, Shamble?"

"More ready than Harvey is."

"Right this way," the warden said. "We're on a schedule."

o o o

McGoo had brought popcorn, which I thought was in poor taste. He pushed the bag toward me as we turned toward the observation window that framed the medieval-looking electric chair. "Lighten up, Shamble. He's the bad guy, dead to rights."

"Dead to rights," I agreed.

Then he told another one of his stupid jokes. "You know why witches fly on brooms? Because vacuum cleaner cords aren't long enough."

We fell into a hush as the prison guards led Harvey Jekyll into the death chamber, where he got to see Sparky, Jr. The little man didn't resist or beg for mercy as they adjusted the seat to raise him, then secured the leather straps around his thin wrists and ankles. All the while, his owlish eyes looked at me through the observation window.

"I should have put the guy in prison back when he sold that garlic-laced vampire shampoo," I said.

Robin agreed. "If we'd shut down the company then, he never would have had a chance to plan this whole scheme."

"Brondon Morris still would have done it," McGoo said.

"After today, we can all rest easy." Sheyenne turned to me, suddenly concerned. "Do you think that's what'll happen? Is that why I came back as a ghost? Am I supposed to move on after I see justice done to my killers?"

"Do you want to leave?" My heart ached already, just looking at her.

"I'd rather stay with you."

"I'd like that, Spooky. Death wouldn't be the same without you."

Sheyenne looked touched, then gave me a wink. "Besides, you and Robin couldn't run the agency without me. You're not going away, are you?"

"Don't plan to."

The prison guards washed Harvey's bald scalp, added conductive cream, put damp sponges inside the metal cap, then tightened it onto his skull.

"Does that feel all right?" one of the guards asked. "Comfortable?"

"It's just fine." Jekyll did not take his eyes off me.

Unlike most traditional megalomaniacs, he didn't deliver a long, eloquent speech, or curse us with his dying breath, or proclaim his innocence. He just waited as the clock ticked.

Because so many unnaturals wanted to see (and preferably participate in) the execution of this toiletries version of Adolf Hitler, the judge had chosen a guest executioner by lottery, rather than using the regular one. One lucky unnatural was allowed into the control room to do the honors. The winner was a simpering, bug-eyed lab assistant with a small hunchback.

When the second hand had swept around the clock to the appointed hour, the warden nodded to him. "Igor, throw the switch!"

I won't dwell on the gruesome smoking and jittering blast that surged through Harvey Jekyll's body. It wasn't any more horrific than what he had done to *his* victims. The little bastard smoked, but at least he didn't dissolve.

When it was over, Jekyll sagged into a lifeless mass in the chair. His eyes were screwed shut, his lips pulled back to expose his teeth in a death grimace. After the physician pronounced him dead, guards unstrapped him from Sparky, Jr., lifted him onto a gurney, and covered his body with a sheet.

Igor came out, grinning with delight and full of manic energy. He pulled out a phone camera and asked to have his picture taken with each of us. We obliged, and Sheyenne requested a copy of the photo so we could hang it on the wall of Chambeaux & Deyer Investigations.

The warden shook our hands. "A job well done. Justice isn't always easy. Well worth the added cost in this month's electric bill."

McGoo clapped me on the shoulder, my damaged one, then apologized, thinking he'd hurt me. I let him believe that. I stood with Robin and Sheyenne, relieved, feeling the tension drain away. We had about five minutes of peace, in which we imagined a silly, happily-ever-after future.

Until Harvey Jekyll's body rose from the gurney. He sat up from beneath the sheet and pulled it away from his burned head. His eyes were bright and focused. "Well, that was unpleasant."

We all gaped at him. Statistics can really bite you in the ass. One in seventy-five return as zombies, with the odds favoring suicide or murder victims. Harvey Jekyll had been lucky. We hadn't.

The warden let out an annoyed sigh.

Robin looked frightened. "We're arguing the precedents, but the law currently states that even the most heinous criminal can be executed only once."

"That law needs to be updated," I growled.

The warden stood in front of Harvey Jekyll, extended his finger in a stern warning. "You're free to go, Mr. Jekyll. But I never want to see you in here again. I hope you've learned your lesson."

The prison guards went back to the lockers and retrieved a clean set of clothes for Jekyll and handed them to the small, newly undead man. Jekyll scowled down at his hands, flexed his fingers. "You've made me an *unnatural?* This qualifies as cruel and unusual. You'll be hearing from my attorneys, I assure you."

Trying to gather his dignity, Harvey Jekyll dressed, glaring at us all the while. His expression held more unspoken words than all of Robin's legal tomes combined. He left the prison, a free unnatural man.

Jekyll didn't need to threaten us. We got the message.

Working Stiff

The Cases of Dan Shamble, Zombie PI

STAKEOUT AT THE
VAMPIRE CIRCUS

1

The circus is supposed to be fun, even a monster circus, but the experience turned sour when somebody tried to murder the vampire trapeze artist.

As a private detective, albeit a zombie, I investigate cases of all sorts in the Unnatural Quarter, applying my deductive skills and persistent determination (yes, the undead can be very persistent indeed). Some of my cases are admittedly strange; most are even stranger than that.

I'd been hired by a transvestite fortune-teller to find a stolen deck of magic cards, and he had sent me two free tickets to the circus. Gotta love the perks of the job. Not one to let an opportunity go to waste, I invited my girlfriend to accompany me; in many ways her detective skills are as good as my own.

Sheyenne is beautiful, blond, and intangible. I had started to fall in love with her when both of us were alive, and I still like having her around, despite the difficulties of an unnatural relationship—as a ghost, she can't physically touch me, and as a zombie I have my own limitations.

We showed our passes at the circus entrance gate and entered a whirlwind of colors, sounds, smells. Big tents, wild rides, popcorn, and cotton candy for the humans, more exotic treats for the unnaturals. One booth sold deep-fried artichoke hearts, while another sold deep-fried human hearts. Seeing me shamble by, a persistent vendor offered me a free sample of brains on a stick, but I politely declined.

I'm a well-preserved zombie and have never acquired a taste for brains. I've got my standards of behavior, not to mention personal hygiene. Given a little bit of care and effort, a zombie doesn't have to rot and fall apart, and I take pride in looking mostly human. Some people have even called me handsome—Sheyenne certainly does, but she's biased.

As Sheyenne flitted past the line of food stalls, her eyes were bright, her smile dazzling; I could imagine what she must have looked like as a little girl. I hadn't seen her this happy since she'd been poisoned to death.

Nearby, a muscular clay golem lifted a wooden mallet at the Test Your Strength game and slammed it down with such force that he not only rang the bell at the top of the pole, he split the mallet in half. A troll barker at the game muttered and handed the golem a pink plush bunny as a prize. The golem set the stuffed animal next to a pile of fuzzy prizes, paid another few coins, and took a fresh mallet to play the game again.

Many of the attendees were humans, attracted by the low prices of the human matinee; the nocturnal monsters would come out for the evening show. More than a decade had passed since the Big Uneasy, when all the legendary monsters came back to the world, and human society was finally realizing that unnaturals were people just like everyone else. Yes, some were ferocious and bloodthirsty—but so were some humans. Most monsters just wanted to live and let live (even though the definition of "living" had blurred).

Sheyenne saw crowds streaming toward the Big Top. "The lion tamer should be finishing, but the vampire trapeze artist is due to start. Do you think we could …"

I gave her my best smile. With stiff facial muscles, my "best smile" was only average, but even so I saved it for Sheyenne. "Sure, Spooky. We've got an hour before we're supposed to meet Zelda. Let's call it 'gathering background information.'"

"Or we could just call it part of the date," Sheyenne teased.

"That, too."

We followed other humans through the tent flaps. A pudgy twelve-year-old boy was harassing his sister, poking her arm incessantly, until he glanced at me and Sheyenne. I had pulled the fedora low, but it didn't entirely conceal the bullet hole in my forehead. When the pudgy kid gawked at the sight, his sister took advantage of the distraction and began poking him until their mother hurried them into the Big Top.

Inside, Sheyenne pointed to empty bleachers not far from the entrance. The thick canvas kept out direct sunlight, protecting the vampire performers and shrouding the interior in a pleasant nighttime gloom. My eyes adjusted quickly because gloom is a natural state for me. Always on the case, I remained alert. If I'd been more alert while I was still alive, I would be … well, still alive.

When I was a human private detective in the Quarter, Sheyenne's ghost had asked me to investigate her murder, which got me in trouble; I didn't even see the creep come up behind me in a dark alley, put a gun to the back of my head, and pull the trigger.

Under most circumstances, that would have put an end to my career, but you can't keep a good detective down. Thanks to the changed world, I came back from the dead, back on the case. Soon enough, I fell into my old routine, investigating mysteries wherever they might take me … even to the circus.

Sheyenne drifted to the nearest bleacher, and I climbed stiffly beside her. The spotlight shone down on a side ring, where a brown-furred werewolf in a scarlet vest—Calvin—cracked his bullwhip, snarling right back at a pair of snarling lions who failed to follow his commands. The thick-maned male cat growled, while the big female opened her mouth wide to show a yawn full of fangs. The lion tamer roared a response, cracked the whip again, and urged the big cats to do tricks, but they absolutely refused.

The lions flexed their claws, and the werewolf flexed his own in a show of dominance, but the lions weren't buying it. Just when it looked as if the fur was about to fly, a loud drumroll came from the center ring.

The spotlight swiveled away from the lion tamer to fall upon the ringmaster, a tall vampire with steel-gray hair. "Ladies and gentlemen, naturals and unnaturals of all ages—in the center ring, our main event!" He pointed upward, and the spotlight swung to the cavernous tent's rigging strung with high wires and a trapeze platform. A Baryshnikov look-alike stood on the platform, a gymnastic vampire in a silver lamé full-body leotard. He wore a medallion around his neck, a bright red ribbon with some kind of amulet, and a professional sneer.

"Bela, our vampire trapeze artist, master of the ropes—graceful, talented … a real swinger!" The ringmaster paused until the audience realized they were supposed to respond with polite laughter. Up on the platform, Bela lifted his chin, as if their applause was beneath him (and, technically speaking, it was, since the bleachers were far below).

"For his death-defying feat, Bela will perform without a safety net above *one hundred sharpened wooden stakes!*" The spotlight swung down to the floor of the ring, which was covered with a forest of pointy sticks, just waiting to perform impalement duties.

The suitably impressed audience gasped.

On the trapeze platform, Bela's haughty sneer was wide enough to show his fangs; I could see them even from my seat in the bleachers. The gold medallion at his neck glinted in the spotlight. Rolling his shoulders to loosen up, the vampire grasped the trapeze handle and lunged out into the open air. He seemed not to care a whit about the sharp wooden stakes as he swung across to the other side. At the apex of his arc, he swung back again, gaining speed. On the backswing, Bela spun around the trapeze bar, doing a loop. As he reached the apex once again, he released, did a quick somersault high in the air, and caught the bar as he dropped down.

The audience applauded. Werewolves in the bleachers howled their appreciation; some ghouls and less-well-preserved zombies let out long, low moans that sounded upbeat, considering. I shot a glance at Sheyenne, and judging by her delighted expression, she seemed to be enjoying herself.

Bela swung back, hanging on with one hand as he gave a dismissive wave to the audience. Vampires usually have fluid movements. I remembered that one vamp had tried out for the Olympic gymnastics team four years ago—and was promptly disqualified, though the Olympic judges could not articulate a valid reason. The vampire sued, and the matter was tied up in the courts until long past the conclusion of the Olympics. The vampire gymnast took the long view, however, as she would be just as spry and healthy in the next four-year cycle, and the next, and the next.

A big drumroll signaled Bela's finale. He swung back and forth one more time, pumping with his legs, increasing speed, and the bar soared up to the highest point yet. The vampire released his hold, flung himself into the air for another somersault, then a second, then a third as the empty trapeze swung in its clockwork arc, gliding back toward him, all perfectly choreographed.

As he dropped, Bela reached out. His fingertips brushed the bar—and missed. He flailed his hands in the air, trying to grab the trapeze, but the bar swung past out of reach, and gravity did its work. Bela tumbled toward the hundred sharp wooden stakes below.

Someone screamed. Even with my rigor-mortis-stiff knees, I lurched to my feet.

But at the last possible moment, the vampire's plummeting form transformed in the air. Mere inches above the deadly points, Bela turned into a bat, stretching and flapping his leathery wings. He flew away, the medallion still dangling from his little furry rodent neck. He alighted on the opposite trapeze platform, then transformed back into a vampire just in time to catch the returning trapeze. He held on, showing his pointed fangs in a superior grin, and took a deep bow. On cue, the band played a loud "Ta-da!"

After a stunned moment, the audience erupted in wild applause. Sheyenne was beaming enough to make her ectoplasm glow. Even I was smiling. "That was worth the price of admission," I said.

Sheyenne looked at me. "We didn't pay anything—we got free tickets."

"Then it's worth twice as much."

With the show over, the audience rose from the bleachers and filed toward the exit. "The cases don't solve themselves," I said to Sheyenne. "Let's go find that fortune-teller."

2

As Sheyenne and I walked along the midway in search of the fortune-teller's booth, we suddenly heard screams—not the joyful yelling of riders on a rickety roller coaster, but loud, terrified cries. Bona fide bloodcurdling shrieks. The screams of children.

I was moving before I even knew it, and Sheyenne flitted along beside me. Five children came running toward us, eyes wide enough to qualify the kids as amine cartoon characters. They yelled wordlessly, pelting past us.

They were running from a circus clown.

I had seen him on the circus posters: Fazio the Clown, grinning with a painted smile so wide he could have swallowed a bloody feast and not even left stains on his chin. His very appearance was supposed to be joyful and comforting, but I thought it looked diabolical—as it did to the kids, apparently.

Fazio implored, "Wait! I just want to make people laugh!"

Pursuing panicked children was not how *I* would have tried to make them laugh.

Panting, the clown stumbled up to us in his big floppy shoes. "I don't know what's wrong with kids today." His face was covered with white greasepaint, and he wore a bright red nose the size of a tennis ball. His bald cap was wrinkled over the top of his head, and shocks of pink hair stuck out in all directions. His teeth could have used whitening (a lot of it) and orthodontia (a lot of it). He held out a bicycle horn and honked it in my face. "Does that make you laugh?" Then he giggled, an edgy Renfield-catching-a-whole-handful-of-flies laugh.

"Sorry, not today," I said.

Glum, Fazio hung his head and shuffled off with his floppy shoes.

We found the booth of Zelda the fortune-teller, a rickety affair made of plywood and two-by-fours painted bright blue, festooned with crepe paper and a stenciled sign that said: FORTUNES TOLD: $5. But the price had been crossed out and reduced three successive times to the bargain rate of $1.

At the booth, a customer forked over a dollar bill, so we kept our distance, watching the fortune-teller in action. Zelda had told me to be discreet.

The customer was a potbellied man in plaid shorts and black socks. (And they say unnaturals look odd?) Zelda wore a curly wig of platinum-blond hair, eye shadow and blush that must have been purchased in bulk and applied with a trowel; the five o'clock shadow had come in a few hours early on the fortune-teller's cheeks. Gold hoop earrings, gold necklaces, and gold bangles accessorized a dress with a high neckline, but still showed planetary-sized bosomic curves, which were obviously just stuffing.

Zelda shuffled a well-worn deck of regular playing cards, then laid five cards face-up on the wooden tabletop in front of the customer. "The eight of clubs is a good sign—it shows you have worthy goals and are determined to achieve them." The supposedly female voice was falsetto and unconvincing.

He laid down another card. "The king of hearts indicates that you will be happy in romance, lucky in love."

"But when?" the man asked, plaintive.

"Unfortunately, the cards have no time stamp," Zelda said. "Now, the third one … ah, the three of spades! A very significant card. You are destined to have great financial success, but it may take a while, so be patient."

The man took hope from that. He looked at the last card. "And the jack of diamonds?"

Zelda shook her head. "That, unfortunately, is a minor card. It merely signifies that your breakfast won't satisfy you for long and you should seek refreshment from one of our fine food booths." The fortune-teller gathered the cards and restacked them in the deck as the customer bent down to pull up his black socks, which had slid lower on his ankles, then he walked off.

Taking our cue, Sheyenne and I stepped up to the fortune-teller. Zelda shuffled the deck, gave me a skeptical look. "I charge extra to determine the fate of the undead."

"We're not here for a reading, uh, ma'am. You hired us—I'm Dan Chambeaux, private investigator, and this is my associate Sheyenne."

Her voice dropped at least two octaves, and she lit a cigarette. "Of course, Mr. Chambeaux—thanks for stopping by." Zelda eyed my gaunt form, looked at my complexion, frowned at the bullet hole in my forehead. "Your business card didn't say you weren't alive."

"Those are old cards. I need to get them reprinted."

Sheyenne joined in. "We have references available upon request."

I got down to business. "I understand your magic fortune-telling deck has been misplaced? You need us to find it?"

"Not misplaced—*stolen*. I'm sure of it this time."

Some questions beg to be asked. *"This* time?"

"It's my second deck gone in six months! I thought I must have misplaced the first one—it happens in the circus, packing up, tearing down, day after day. But real magic fortune-telling decks are hard to come by, so I kept careful watch on the replacement cards. It was the last deck the supplier had in stock, and I couldn't afford another. But it's gone, too. Somebody stole it ... somebody who's out to get me." He lowered his voice. "I predicted that, even without the cards!"

The customer is always right, as the saying goes; and also, the customer is sometimes paranoid. "We'll look into it, Mr., uh, Ms. Zelda."

"Aldo. My real name is Aldo Firkin. Zelda's just a stage name." He dabbed at the layers of peacock-colored eye shadow. "It's all an act."

"You don't say," I said. Sheyenne pretended to jab me with her spectral elbow, though I couldn't feel her touch. She sometimes has to remind me to show a proper professional attitude in front of the clients.

The fortune-teller frowned, plucking at the absurd dress. "You think I *want* to dress up like this? I'm not a natural-born transvestite, but I can't make a living otherwise. It's a stereotype we can't shake—nobody wants male fortune-tellers. What a sham! All these decades of fighting for equal rights, and I have to do this." He adjusted the ridiculous wig. "Now, about my stolen cards? I really need them back. I've been doing my best." With a burring rattle of laminated paper, Aldo/Zelda shuffled the regular playing cards. "But there's nothing magical about these. I'm just making it up. My other deck—now, those cards were *real,* the magic just barely starting to wear off."

His brow furrowed as he looked down at the old playing cards. "Oddly enough, my fortunes seem to be just as accurate with this ordinary deck. I must be really good at this." He tapped the deck, drew a card, looked at it, and smiled. "Ah, correctly predicted that one. Maybe there's real magic here!"

"Or maybe you're just telling people what they want to hear," I suggested.

Aldo grinned. "Ah, and that's the real magic, isn't it? Give cryptic fortunes and let the customer figure out the true meaning. 'You will lose something very valuable to you, but you will gain something unexpected.' That's one I told the fat lady a few months ago."

"Sounds like a bad horoscope," I said.

"Actually, it sounds like a *good* horoscope," Sheyenne said.

The gaunt vampire ringmaster walked by, still wearing his equestrian jacket; he kept to the awnings, shading his head with his black top hat to avoid the direct sunlight. Aldo waved. "Oscar! Come here—this is the private detective I was telling you about. Dan Chambeaux, meet Oscar Kowalski, ringmaster and circus owner."

The ringmaster gave a formal nod, and we exchanged a cold grip. "Dan Shamble?"

"Chambeaux," I corrected. "People always mispronounce my name. And I wouldn't expect a vampire to be named Oscar Kowalski. I'd think something more like … Bela."

Kowalski let out an annoyed snort. "Bela is a drama queen and a pain in the ass, but he does draw a crowd, and that's what it's all about." He lowered his voice. "I'm glad Aldo called you to look into the thefts. We've had a rash of them over the past two weeks." He shot a narrow-eyed glare at the transvestite fortune-teller. "But we need to be discreet."

Aldo sounded indignant. "He's a *private* detective, not a public one. And I couldn't wait any longer—I need my magic cards back."

"What other thefts?" Sheyenne pressed.

"Mostly minor items, low value," Kowalski said.

"My fortune-telling cards are extremely valuable!" Aldo insisted.

The ringmaster continued, "But it causes a lot of nuisance and unease. We like to think we're family here at the circus."

"I miss the Bearded Lady," Aldo muttered. "Harriet was like a mother to us all, really kept the circus tight-knit, like a family. Things were so much nicer before she went off to lead a semi-normal life of her own."

Kowalski shook his head. "We all miss Harriet, but there's not much call for everyday freaks after the Big Uneasy. People can see weirder creatures on any walk through the Quarter."

I got back to business. "We need to know what the other items are. All the clues should lead to the same suspect."

"I can get you a list—a long one," Aldo said, then considered. "But if you're investigating all of the thefts in the circus, then Oscar should pay your bill."

The ringmaster's shoulders drooped. "I'll pay *half* . . . provided Mr. Shamble—uh, Chambeaux—can help us all out. Most of the other items aren't worth much."

"If there's a thief running loose, maybe we should report it to Officer McGoohan?" Sheyenne suggested.

I explained, "I have a good friend on the police force. He'll take your problems seriously."

Kowalski cleared his throat. "That won't be necessary. We must count on your discretion, Mr. Chambeaux. People don't trust circus folk as it is, even here in the Unnatural Quarter, and I don't want to do anything to reinforce that stereotype. You probably don't like it when people consider all zombies to be brain-eating clods with speech impediments."

"Not at all," I said. "I work hard to stay well preserved."

Kowalski tipped his hat. "I hope you can resolve this quickly and quietly. The circus is your client."

"But find my magic cards first," Aldo insisted as he jotted down the list on a scrap of paper.

"If we find the thief, we should find all of the stolen items," I said.

Sheyenne and I read the list as we walked away. In addition to the magic fortune-telling cards (two sets, but I doubted we'd find the one he'd lost six months earlier), Aldo had listed a hammer (standard hardware store issue), glass milk bottle from one of the game booths, dagger from the knife thrower's act, three costume-jewelry necklaces from Annie the fat lady (hence a rope-length of jewelry), and a cold Reuben sandwich from a refrigerator in the Flag. I figured we could discount that last item.

We had no trouble finding the fat lady, mainly because she wasn't very mobile, but also because she was so large. In her open tent, Annie reclined on—and covered most of—a queen-sized bed. Plates mounded with chocolate chip cookies, brownies, and Danishes sat within reach of one hand; by the other side of the bed sat a tray of chicken wings and ribs. She had apparently been through several plates already, but despite the aftermath of her obviously enormous appetite, her face looked saggy. I didn't think the fat lady looked healthy at all, but since I'm undead, I'm not one to point fingers.

243

Annie's wide throat was round and somewhat tubular, like a pelican with a particular lucky catch of fish. She had permed gray hair and wire-rim glasses that made her look like the world's kindest, and largest, grandmother. An enormous floral muumuu extended all the way down to her ankles; sleeves covered the wrists where they met the gloves. Under her gigantic tent of a dress, her mounded belly stirred and squirmed in a disturbing way, as if her intestines were rearranging themselves before our eyes.

Annie gave us a twinkling smile. "Hello, dears! Come in and stare—that's what I'm here for. Would you like a cookie? I've got plenty." She extended the tray to us.

"No thanks, ma'am," Sheyenne said. "I'm ectoplasmic."

"And I'm on a low-carb diet," I added, even though it was just an excuse. My undead taste buds were no longer very discriminating, and Annie needed a constant stream of calories just to maintain her bulk. She consumed the rest of the cookies with methodical swiftness, as if it were her mission.

"We're from Chambeaux and Deyer Investigations, and we're here on a case." I set one of our business cards on the bedside table next to the chicken wings. "We've been hired to investigate certain items that have gone missing. If there's a circus thief, we'll catch him."

"A thief? Oh, my!" Annie held her hands to her face, licked a few crumbs from her fingers. "I refuse to believe members of my dear circus family are thieves." Her mounded stomach shifted and churned, and Annie let out an embarrassed giggle, placing her hands flat on her belly. "Just a bit of indigestion—it tends to get extreme in my case."

I held up Aldo's handwritten list. "According to this, you've lost several items of jewelry?"

"Oh, dear me, I may have misplaced a few cheap necklaces—I'm always doing that. When I manage to walk around, I can't see the ground, and if something falls ... well, I just give it up for lost. I wouldn't call them *stolen*. The circus people are my family. I'm like a mother to them since Harriet's gone. Someone has to watch out for everyone."

I tipped my fedora. "If you think of anything, please let us know, ma'am. Any clue would help."

Leaving the fat lady's tent, we strolled along the midway, and soon Fazio the Clown buttonholed us again. "I saw you two talking with that fraud fortune-teller! He's a fake—a complete fake. I doubt he could predict *yesterday* if he had a newspaper in front of him."

If you had asked me before the Big Uneasy, I would have said that all fortune-telling was fake. Now, though, I'd seen plenty of evidence of functional spells. "He's at a disadvantage if he lost his magic cards."

"Not the cards—the sham costume. Him in his stupid wig and his clumsy makeup! It's an embarrassment. Makeup is no joke. I work hard on my appearance, greasepaint over every inch of exposed skin." He tugged at his shocks of pink hair, straightened the bald cap, then tweaked the bright red nose. "It's a beautiful design, the perfect clown face—I've even got it trademarked. But Zelda, or Aldo, or whoever or whatever the name is, does it just to make a buck. It cheapens the art of face painting."

"And why do you paint your face?" Sheyenne asked.

"For a greater purpose, of course—to get a laugh."

Or a scream, I thought, remembering the terrified children.

"We're investigating a rash of burglaries, not makeup techniques," I said. "Any comments about his missing deck of fortune-telling cards?"

"I don't know anything about the first one he lost, and not the second one either." He snorted, then stormed off. "You should be investigating Aldo. His eye shadow is a crime!"

3

After gathering as much information as we could, Sheyenne and I returned to the Chambeaux & Deyer offices in the seedy, run-down section of the Unnatural Quarter (I realize that's not very specific).

Sheyenne began compiling a list of circus suspects and digging up dirt on them. She's good at uncovering details, whether they be sordid details, suspicious details, or just plain bookkeeping details.

A large part of my job is time management. Real life as an undead private investigator isn't like a TV detective show, where the PI works on one mystery at a time and solves it without other clients getting in the way. In addition to investigating stolen items at the vampire circus, I had several active cases.

My partner, Robin Deyer, came out to brief me on the legal battles she had fought during the day. As a lawyer, Robin makes sure that downtrodden and underrepresented monsters get a fair shot in the legal system. She's a young African American, as pretty as she is determined—and she is extremely determined. Her eyes had a faraway, preoccupied look because case subtleties ran through her head at all times.

I had taken her under my wing back when I was a human private detective. We shared office space, offered assistance on each other's cases, and enjoyed working together. After my murder, I think Robin was hit even harder by my death than I was. When I came back from the grave, she welcomed me with open arms (after she got over the shock and uneasiness). She made a special point to treat me just as she'd always done, and we quickly got back to our usual routine.

"Any word on the gargoyle case?" I asked.

For several weeks Robin had represented a gargoyle who was suing the Notre Dame cathedral for unauthorized use of his likeness. Comparing the gargoyle himself with photographs of several specific stone figures on the ancient cathedral, the resemblance was undeniable.

Her expression tightened. "I think we're going to lose that one. There seems to be an unbreakable statute of limitations clause in church law. Today, I'm neck-deep in that unnatural voting rights case."

Robin was tilting at a different windmill, challenging voter restrictions recently put in place for the sole purpose of denying unnaturals the right to vote. (No one seemed to remember that in some corrupt cities, dead people had done more than their share of voting over the years....) Both political parties insisted that the proposed voter suppression rules against unnaturals were disenfranchising their constituents, although neither side had been able to prove that unnaturals leaned toward any particular affiliation, as a rule.

After Robin described a brief she had filed and her court appearance schedule for the week, I told her about the vampire circus and headed to my office to take care of my own work. "I think I can wrap up the Amontillado case this afternoon."

"Good," Sheyenne called from the receptionist's desk. "We need to send them a bill."

Robin cautioned, "The outcome wasn't what the client expected. Maybe we should offer a discount—"

Sheyenne cut right in. "The client is a client, and a fee is a fee." If Robin had her way, she would do all cases pro bono, and Sheyenne often had to remind her about the facts of business. Even though I was undead and Sheyenne was a ghost, *Robin* still needed to eat, and we all had to pay the rent on the office space.

I suggested a compromise. "Give the client a coupon for his next case with us. We did solve the mystery, which is what he hired us to do."

A wealthy man had asked me to track down a very rare cask of Amontillado, more than a century and a half old, and I found the cask behind a brick wall, along with an animated skeleton that had been manacled there. In the years since the Big Uneasy, the skeleton had managed to break loose from one manacle by detaching his entire bony hand. With his wrist released, he was able to reach the cask, work the bung loose, and pour the extremely expensive sherry down his throat. Of course, since he had no throat, the rare Amontillado spilled all over the vault floor and dried up. When I found the very expensive and very empty cask I'd been hired to track down, the skeleton laughed and laughed at the joke, saying in a rattling voice, "I drank it all, I drank it all!"

Now I sat at my desk and wrote up the report, reducing the total number of hours billed on the case just to make Robin happy, and to make me feel better as well; Sheyenne didn't need to know.

It was full-dark outside by the time Sheyenne flitted through my closed office door. She carried a stack of papers, which could not spectrally pass through the barrier, so they fluttered to the floor outside. With an impatient frown, she flitted back out, picked up the papers, and opened the door to enter via the normal way.

"I ran down the usual suspects at the circus. Some very interesting background material."

I took the papers. "Anything suspicious?"

She arched her eyebrows. "Naturals and unnaturals all working for a traveling circus run by a vampire—isn't that suspicious enough?"

"I was hoping for something more specific."

"So many aliases, stage names, plenty of skeletons in the closet—and not like the one you found with your cask of Amontillado." She grinned at me.

"Speaking of that ..." I handed her the bill and final report, which pleased her very much.

She continued with her summary, "First off, Oscar Kowalski is not a very talented businessman. He's filed for bankruptcy twice since the Big Uneasy, barely scraped through, and seems to be in rocky circumstances right now."

I said, "I don't see how stealing a deck of fortune-teller cards, costume jewelry, and a cold Reuben sandwich would help his financial situation."

"Probably not." Sheyenne glanced down at her papers again. "Checking back along the circus route over the years, I found that two goblin roustabouts were arrested for petty theft, but they escaped and disappeared. Young twins. Their juvenile records should have been sealed, but Robin pried them loose because the law is still murky."

"Robin used a murky law to her own advantage?" I asked. "Good for her."

Sheyenne blew an imaginary breath through her lips. "The goblins were over eighteen years old—adults according to the letter of the law—but goblins live a long time, and those twins are still adolescents as far as *goblins* go. Still, nobody's bothered to change the law, so we got the arrest records. Not that it does us much good, if the twins are no longer with the circus."

Robin would probably decide to challenge that law, now that she'd noticed the injustice.

"What else?" I asked.

"Aldo—or should we call him Zelda?—is late on his child support, and his ex-wife is trying to track him down." She checked off items on her list. "Fazio got arrested for drunk driving in his clown car, but that was never prosecuted. Oh, and his clown license has expired."

I frowned. "I didn't know there was such a thing as a clown license. I find that very suspicious."

Sheyenne blinked her blue eyes at me. "More suspicious than all the other things?"

"He's a clown. I'm always suspicious of clowns."

4

With the information Sheyenne had uncovered about the circus personnel, I went back to the midway early enough to catch the nighttime monster matinee. While unnatural crowds started to gather inside the Big Top for Bela's performance, I stopped by Oscar Kowalski's office trailer just outside the main tent. I wanted to ask him about bankruptcy filings, late child-support payments, Fazio's expired clown license, and anything else that came to mind. Instead, I stumbled into another crisis.

"I refuse, Oscar!" Bela cried with an exaggerated and obviously fake Transylvanian accent. He raised his chin with an imperious air and flared the nostrils on his beak-like nose. "You must cancel the show. I can't perform under these circumstances—it is impossible!"

"Nothing's impossible, Bela." Kowalski sounded long-suffering and annoyed. He sat at his desk with an open, and messily scribbled ledger. "Nobody's canceling the show. You *can* go on, and you *will* go on."

"But it's been stolen!" Bela clutched at his throat, where I noticed the gold medallion was missing. (The far-too-clingy silver lamé bodysuit had previously demanded most of my attention.) "It's my Air Commander medal, given to me for being a Flying Ace in World War Two—or World War One, I forget which. If I don't wear the medal, then I won't have the confidence to transform into a bat at the climax of my show."

I interrupted, startling them. "You need a magic talisman to change into a bat?"

"Have you ever tried it?" Bela snapped, then whirled on Kowalski. "Have *you?* Most vampires are incapable. It requires the utmost concentration. My Air Commander medal is the perfect focusing aid."

"So it's like Dumbo's magic feather?" I said. "Without it, you wouldn't have the self-confidence to fly?"

Bela raised himself up, looked down his nose at me, and said with withering sarcasm, "Yes, exactly like that." He sniffed.

"It's all in his head," Kowalski explained to me. "Nothing magical whatsoever. The medallion's just a piece of junk."

"It is part of my act! I feel naked without it."

Again, I had trouble tearing my attention from the excessively form-fitting lamé bodysuit.

The ringmaster looked at his watch, closed his ledger with finality. "Sorry, Bela, but the show must go on. So follow that advice—*go on!*"

In a huff, the vampire trapeze artist strutted out of the admin trailer.

With a flicker of relief on his face, Kowalski turned to me. "Every week he's got some other excuse, imagines he's been cursed whenever he passes gas, threatens to quit the circus, but I doubt any rival show would have him."

"Are there other monster circuses?" I hadn't heard of any.

"No. Hence, my point. And I admit it takes a lot of concentration to turn into a bat, especially on the fly, but he doesn't have to be such an ass about it." He brushed down his jacket, looked at the watch again. "Now, I didn't expect to see you back so soon, Mr. Chambeaux. Come up with answers yet?"

"Even better—I've got a lot more questions."

"How is that better?"

"That means I'm making progress."

Kowalski stood from his desk. He looked tired as he reached for his top hat. "I can't talk with you at the moment. The show must go on for me, too, and if there's any unreasonable delay in the performance the lions start complaining."

"Don't you mean the lion tamer?" I asked.

"No, Calvin's easy to deal with, but the lions want their treats, and they can get quite demanding." He showed me out of the trailer and locked the door behind us.

With the audience crowded in the Big Top for the monster matinee, the midway was quiet and dark. I decided to lurk and snoop, two things for which a zombie detective is eminently qualified.

Since the Air Commander medal was the latest stolen item, I made my way to Bela's darkened tent. Though he considered himself the star of the circus, the vampire's mobile domicile wasn't much more than a place to shelter his coffin when he needed some quiet time—wide open and not secure. If Bela had gone to ground to take a nap, someone could easily have snatched his medal from the nightstand and run off with it.

I walked around outside Bela's tent, senses alert and scanning the ground for any unusual clues ... such as that playing card lying face-up on the ground not far from the tent.

It was the jack of diamonds, the same card that predicted a person would be hungry soon after breakfast. I guessed it came from Zelda's deck.

I kept plodding along, scanning from side to side. The circus seemed eerily empty, filled with shadows. I heard the audience cheer in the Big Top; Calvin must be in the middle of his act.

Spotting something ahead, I bent over to pick up another playing card, the six of hearts. With two dropped playing cards making a dotted line that led from Bela's recently burgled tent toward the general direction of Zelda/Aldo's trailer, I knew how to connect the dots.

As I approached the trailer, I heard raised voices, an argument in full swing. Aldo was shouting, so upset that he still sounded high-pitched and falsetto, and not in an attempt to maintain his transvestite identity. "What did you want with my magic cards anyway? It wasn't enough for you to steal my fortune-telling deck, so you had to steal my playing cards, too? And my makeup kit? You're trying to ruin me!" He had his wig in his hand, and a smear of cold cream had removed only the first few layers of eye shadow.

Fazio was still in full clown makeup, his bright red nose planted in the middle of his white-painted face, his pink hair sticking out in all directions. "You have nothing I'd even want to steal—certainly not your amateur makeup kit! You are a fake and a disgrace!"

Before they could come to blows, I interrupted, holding up the two playing cards. "Are these from the deck? I found them on the ground near Bela's tent—there's been another robbery."

Aldo grabbed the playing cards, as if he could make a good start with only two of the fifty-two. "Yes, there has—my cards and my makeup kit."

Fazio asked, "What other robbery?"

"Someone took Bela's Air Commander medal right before his trapeze act."

"Bela never goes anywhere without that gaudy thing." Aldo crossed his arms over his too-obviously padded chest, then turned to the clown. "Why would you steal the poor vamp's Air Commander medal?"

"I *didn't* steal it! And I didn't steal your damn cards, either! Or your makeup kit. I am a completely honest, law-abiding citizen."

"Then what about my Reuben sandwich?" Aldo demanded. Fazio hesitated just long enough for the fortune-teller to pounce. "I knew it— you took my sandwich!"

"Those may be two unrelated cases," I said. "And, Fazio, you're not off my list of suspects—I know you've been keeping secrets."

The circus clown seemed to turn even whiter than his greasepaint. "You ... know my secret?"

"Your clown license is expired, and that's enough to make me suspicious," I said, deciding not to bring up the clown-car drunk driving incident. "I can bring in the real police at any time, but for now I'll keep looking."

I stalked off among the dark trailers and tents. I hoped I could find the Air Commander medal in time to take it to the vampire trapeze artist before his act, just to give him a psychological boost. The crowd in the Big Top continued to cheer the lion tamer's show.

I paused at Annie's tent. Since the tent flaps were open, I looked in. The fat lady was inside, lying on her bed, and appeared to be asleep, covered by a mounded blanket. She looked like a mountain range under the comforters. More plates piled with cookies, brownies, ribs, and wings remained within easy reach; someone must replenish them all day long. I left her to rest.

I circled around, trying to keep an open mind but ready to find Fazio responsible (okay, I admit, I was guilty of clown profiling). There, outside the front of his tent, I found the red ribbon and gold disk—Bela's Air Commander medal, just lying on the ground. Not only was the circus thief persistent and random, he was also clumsy. Why steal things, then drop them all over the place like a cat losing interest in a mouse?

In the Big Top, the crowd cheered and applauded as Calvin finished his show. I grabbed the medal, deciding to confront the clown later. At the moment I had to get the Air Commander medal back to the vampire trapeze artist before he started his act.

I expected to feel a tingle of magic; if the Air Commander medal were really a spell-impregnated amulet, I should have been able to sense the power even with my numb fingers. Then the "gold" disk rotated as I dangled the ribbon, revealing *Made in China* stamped on the back; I suspected the disk itself was nothing more than coated tin.

But Bela somehow had it in his head that he needed this thing for his bat transformation, so I might as well be of service.

I raced to the Big Top at the best speed I could manage—joints and muscles tend to stiffen up postmortem, so it's a good thing I keep myself in shape. So many spectators were milling at the main tent opening—mummies, werewolves, ghouls, vampires, a very tall ogre—that I couldn't get inside, so I ran around to the side by Oscar Kowalski's office trailer. I pushed my way through a smaller stage entrance, holding up the medal. "Wait—I have to get this to Bela before he starts!"

But the ringmaster had already announced the performance, and the crowd drowned out my voice. Spotlights shone on Bela, high up on his trapeze platform, and the audience gave suitable gasps as the light swung down to illuminate the hundred sharpened stakes.

For all his prima donna behavior, Bela was a true showman. Even without the not-so-magic medal around his neck, he showed no sign of nervousness as he grabbed the trapeze and swung out over the yawning gap. As Bela began his act, Kowalski withdrew to the side of the tent, where he saw me holding the red-ribboned amulet. "I found it," I said, "but too late."

The ringmaster gave a snort. "He doesn't need the thing. It's all in his head, and I can't let him make excuses. The show must go on."

Above, Bela did a beautiful somersault loop, then caught the trapeze bar again.

"His ego needs to be taken down a notch anyway. He demanded a big pay raise. Does he think the circus is actually making any money? We're holding on by a spiderweb here."

I lowered my voice. "I know about the bankruptcies, Mr. Kowalski."

The ringmaster frowned. "So then you know I can't pay Bela anymore, but I can't have him leave, either. If he refused to do the show tonight, and I had to refund all these tickets …" He gestured to the audience. "I might as well bury myself six feet under without a book to read."

Bela swung back and forth on the trapeze, increasing his momentum and height as he set up for the climax of the show.

Kowalski looked up. "The fumble is all part of the act, you know. He better not chicken out tonight."

At the apex of the swing, Bela flipped himself into the air, spun three somersaults, then reached out to catch the returning bar, fumbled and missed—just as I had seen him do that afternoon. Bela wore a panicked look, his arms outstretched as he plummeted toward the pointy wooden stakes.

The audience gasped. A necromancer screamed in a high, womanish voice. Kowalski and I waited for Bela to transform into a bat.

And waited.

He flailed and thrashed in real panic. In the last instant, Bela squeezed his eyes shut, either in a last-ditch attempt to concentrate or to avoid seeing so many sharp wooden tips. And then he slammed into them. Since he'd been falling spread-eagled, Bela managed to impale himself on a goodly number of the one hundred stakes.

Kowalski gaped. The monsters in the audience screamed; some chuckled, thinking it was part of the show. But when Bela sizzled and fumed, his body boiling and flesh sloughing away to leave only a skeleton that crumbled to dust, people began running out of the Big Top. A few stayed and applauded.

"I have to manage this crowd!" Kowalski said as he bolted away from me. "The show's over—you saw it finish. Nobody's getting refunds."

Disgusted, I held up the Air Commander medal and called after him. "I found this by Fazio's tent—and I bet he also stole Aldo's deck of fortune-telling cards."

Then I had another thought, realizing that the uproar would let Fazio know that Bela was dead—and the clown *knew* he was responsible. If the amulet truly had no magic, I didn't know whether this counted technically as murder, but at the very least he had caused a deadly accident, messing with the vampire trapeze artist's head before a dangerous act. Fazio had some explaining to do, and I had to stop him before he fled the circus.

I pulled out my cell phone and called Officer Toby McGoohan, commonly called McGoo (by me, at least), and told him to roll the squad cars, that we had a death at the circus and a possible murderer to arrest. McGoo likes to hear things like that. He's my BHF—my best human friend—and we've helped each other on many cases. I knew I could count on him now.

First, though, I had to prevent the escape of a deadly circus clown.

5

I expected to find Fazio at his tent, stuffing valuables into a hobo sack so he could run far from the Quarter. That's what *I* would do if I were a killer clown cat burglar responsible for the death of a vampire trapeze artist.

I did find Fazio in his tent, but he wasn't packing up to leave. Instead he was wailing, outraged. "They stole my nose! The little bastards stole *my nose!*"

The clown whirled to face me, and I saw that the big red nose was indeed gone from the middle of his face. More shocking, though: The fake nose wasn't the only thing missing. Fazio's *real* nose was gone, leaving a cavernous empty sinus socket draped with a few shreds of rotted flesh. The makeup had been smudged around his eyes, and I could see the sunken hollow look, the grayish tone to his unpainted skin.

"You're a *zombie!*" I cried, demonstrating my detective abilities.

"Not just a zombie," Fazio insisted. "A clown, too. That's my true calling in life—and afterlife."

A zombie clown, I thought. Now *that's* scary.

Fazio moaned, covering the nose hole in the middle of his face. "All I ever wanted was to make people laugh." Then he looked up at me. "Why are *you* so surprised? You're undead, and you came back to keep solving cases. Why can't I still be a clown just because I'm a zombie? Maybe that's why I rose up in the first place—to make people laugh."

Actually, he wasn't making anyone laugh that I could tell, but I decided not to argue with him.

He touched his cheeks. "Put on enough greasepaint and a wig, no one can tell the difference. I still do my job." A wave of anger passed through him again. "And those little goblin bastards stole my nose! I thought we were done with them for good! Last time they were here, the twins stole everything that wasn't superglued down." He let out a huff. "In fact, we *tried* supergluing everything down ... which did prevent the thefts, but kept us from using the items at all. Bad idea. And then they stole the tube of superglue."

"Which way did they go?" I heard sirens wailing in the distance. McGoo responded quickly, especially when he knew he'd have a nice arrest on his record without having to do the footwork.

The clown sniffled again—which came out as a loud hooting sound without his nose—and pointed out the tent. "They grabbed the nose off my face and ran that way. Somebody must be hiding them."

"What would they do with a clown nose?" I asked. "Can you sell it on an auction site somewhere?"

"They don't *do* anything with what they steal—they just steal it. It's an illness. That's why you find so many things just lying around on the ground."

I bolted out of Fazio's tent, hoping to intercept the kleptomaniac goblins. The circus midway was full of attendees streaming toward the exits, chattering about Bela's spectacular (and, most agreed, *entertaining*) death. Some unnaturals still insisted it was part of the show and were trying to figure out how the trick was done.

Then I spotted another playing card lying on the ground and a necklace a few steps beyond that, then a baseball cap, and an eye patch. This was like a scavenger hunt. All of the breadcrumbs were heading toward the fat lady's tent.

I heard a scuffle and a squeal, and I put on a burst of speed; zombies can move quickly in emergencies, or when they're especially hungry. "Over here!" I yelled, hoping someone else would come running. I already knew Fazio was sounding the alarm among his circus friends, who were already alarmed after the death of the vampire trapeze artist (or maybe just because of the approaching police sirens).

The flaps of the fat lady's tent were down, but I yanked them open. I saw Annie struggling with her enormous dress, pulling down the fabric folds to cover her body—and the dress itself, or something inside it, was fighting back.

"Quickly, my dears, quickly!" When she saw me, a look of horror crossed her face (I often get that reaction). She did not look like a sweet granny now; her whole face was much skinnier, as if someone had deflated her. Annie still had many chins, but they hung like wattles around her neck.

As she struggled and thrashed with her recalcitrant dress, the fabric tore, and a goblin's smooth, ugly head poked out. The second young goblin also squirmed and broke free, ripping the dress to shreds as they both escaped from their unorthodox hiding place. Inside the tentlike flower-print fabric, they left behind a rather scrawny-looking Annie in a one-piece bathing suit. The goblins hissed and snapped, annoyed to be exposed.

Goblins are like small gray-skinned elves ... if those elves happened to be born from a mother saturated with toxic waste and poisonous thoughts. Their huge mouths were filled with needle-like teeth, and their glowing eyes could have been used as a plumber's utility light. As the goblin twins tried to scramble away, Annie wrapped her arms around them and pulled the creatures close to her in a motherly embrace.

There was hardly anything to Annie now. With all her loose skin, she looked as if she was wasting away, despite the numerous plates of ribs, cookies, etc., she consumed every day. Then I realized that if she had been hiding the kleptomaniac creatures, they might have eaten much of the food.

The fat lady's eyes were wide, her expression desperate. "You can't take my boys!" She yanked the goblins closer, practically smothering them. "I was trying to protect them, and they helped me when I needed it most! They're so sweet." She held out her hand, and one of the goblins tried to bite it. Annie giggled.

More shouts came from outside the tent. Fazio, the now-noseless clown, staggered in, accompanied by Aldo, who'd thrown on his wig while he ran, as well as the werewolf lion tamer, who still held his bullwhip, ready to use it.

The vampire ringmaster barged in right behind them, distraught. "The police are coming. What the—" He stopped when he saw the goblins. "What the hell are those two doing here? With all the arrest warrants—"

As the kleptomaniac goblin twins tried to bolt, Calvin cracked his bullwhip, and they skittered back into Annie's protective embrace.

"I won't turn them out into the cold," she said with a sniffle. "They're just misunderstood. They stole things, but they didn't mean anything bad by it."

"Nothing bad?" Kowalski cried. "They stole Bela's Air Commander medal. Without it, he didn't think he could turn into a bat—and now he's dead!"

Annie was disturbed by this. "But he started out dead."

"I mean he's really dead now!"

"Well, I'm sure they're very sorry," Annie insisted.

"The medallion was fake." I held it up so everyone could see the words *Made in China* stamped on the back. "No intrinsic magic."

Annie sounded defensive. "There—no harm done."

The clown and the fortune-teller looked at the strangely emaciated form of the fat lady. Aldo said, "What happened to you? You used to be so ... so ..."

"Fat," she answered.

"I was about to say *substantial*." Then Aldo remembered his priorities. "And what happened to my fortune-telling cards?"

"I lost weight, thanks to your magic cards." She sniffed, sounding glum. "When Harriet left the circus, I wanted to be in better shape to mother you all. It's quite a job! I wanted to be healthy, go on a diet, so I signed up for a guaranteed Gypsy weight-loss routine. Mean Cuisine. I lost four hundred pounds—and now I can't stop!"

Aldo scratched his wig, which was already askew. "What did my fortune-telling deck have to do with it?"

"I needed your cards, ones with real magic, and that's why I took your deck six months ago." She sniffed and made an excuse. "Well, you did leave them lying around a lot." When the fortune-teller glared at her, she turned away. "I just had to have two specific cards, the fat lady and the skeleton. I superglued the cards together, read the spell from the Gypsy diet book, and *this* fat lady started to look more like a skeleton. Worked like a charm!"

"Uh, it *was* a charm," I pointed out.

"But because of the superglue, I couldn't separate the cards again. Impossible to break the spell. And I realized I was going to lose my livelihood! Being a fat lady is all I am ... and believe me, there was a lot of me." She pulled at the excessive folds of her torn dress. "Everybody loved me when I was a fat lady. Everyone wanted to hug me, lose themselves in my expansive ... everything. I needed another fortune-telling deck, a fresh skeleton card and a fat lady card, so I could break the magic."

"So you stole my other deck, too!" Aldo said.

"The goblin boys did." Annie sounded ashamed. "You were much more careful after losing the first one, and I wasn't exactly nimble enough to slip into your trailer unnoticed. The boys came back to the circus, looking for shelter and hoping to hide from the police, and I just asked them to do me that one favor. Unfortunately, once they got started ..."

Officer McGoohan and four uniformed cops charged into the tent, all trying to fit through the open flap at once, as if they were performing their own circus clown act. Fortunately, because it was designed for a fat lady, the tent opening was double-wide.

McGoo's a rough, tough cop who gets himself in trouble more often than the criminals do, but he and I have gotten each other *out* of trouble enough times, too. "Shamble, tell me what's going on here."

I rattled off a quick summary. "Fat lady hiding kleptomaniac goblins in her dress, a vampire trapeze artist accidentally murdered because he couldn't change into a bat, deck of magic fortune-telling cards stolen—among other things."

McGoo nodded. "Oh, another one of those cases."

The goblins tried to bolt as the policemen rounded them up, and Calvin used his whip with great enthusiasm as well as precision. Even after the goblin thieves were handcuffed, they snapped with their needle-like teeth, trying to bite the hands that arrested them. Fortunately, among his other useful defensive items, McGoo kept a roll of duct tape on his belt, with which he secured the criminal goblins' mouths.

"Oh, my poor dears," Annie wailed. "They just need some love and understanding."

"They need a little time behind bars," I said. "Or at least doing community service." All in all, I doubted the stolen items added up to more than a misdemeanor.

"There are other arrest warrants for those two." McGoo was shaking his head. "And the fat lady was aiding and abetting."

"For petty theft," Kowalski said, troubled. "Bela might disagree, but he never liked to accept blame for anything. He did sign a waiver acknowledging the inherent risk in performing death-defying feats."

Kowalski stood next to Annie. "The circus is like family, and Annie is part of it. We're not pressing charges against her, and we'll return all the stolen items to their rightful owners."

"Except for my magic deck," Aldo grumbled.

"I can track down another one," I said. "Part of my services."

"And my Reuben sandwich."

"Can't help you there...."

Without asking permission, the clown and the fortune-teller worked together—a victory in itself—to open the trunks in the back of Annie's tent, moving aside the plates piled with cookies and gnawed rib bones. Fazio lifted out a bright red ball. "Here's my nose!"

Digging deeper, they also found what was left of the deck of magic fortune-telling cards. Aldo was dismayed as he counted through them to find the skeleton and fat lady cards torn in half, by which Annie had apparently broken the weight-loss spell; other cards were missing as well, probably strewn on the ground somewhere along the midway.

The former fat lady wept, still clutching at straws. "Maybe if everything's returned, there won't be any charges filed?"

"Suit yourselves." McGoo shook his head as the cops wrestled the still-squirming goblins out of the tent. "Those boys have already gotten themselves into enough trouble, more than just robbing circus folk. They'll probably serve a year in juvie, maybe get out early for good behavior. Or maybe not."

"Yes, they are quite a handful," the fat lady said. "Even I have to admit that." Looking longingly after the wayward goblins, Annie drew a deep shuddering breath, then turned to Oscar Kowalski. "I don't suppose the circus has any use for a *skinny* lady? At least until I fill out a little bit? The spell is broken, and I'm gaining weight again ... and it'll be even faster when the twins don't eat most of my food."

The ringmaster thought long and hard. "I could use someone who understands the circus—and business. I'm no good at handling the day-to-day paperwork, the administration, managing the employees. I'm a showman, not an accountant." He propped himself up, snatched off his top hat. "I never was much good at the business side of things. You'd think a vampire circus would *want* to be in the red."

Annie finally brightened. "I can help. I can be like a mother to everyone. And if I manage the money, it'll be like giving everybody an allowance!"

Fazio had reapplied his nose, although his makeup remained smeared. He looked at the remaining platters of food. "Annie, you wouldn't happen to have a banana-cream pie I could smash into someone's face? Just for the gag?"

"Sorry, dear, I only have cookies."

The zombie clown threw cookies at Calvin, but nobody laughed. Rather, the werewolf lion tamer caught them and munched politely.

Aldo came up to me, smiling. "Thank you for everything, Mr. Chambeaux. You did track down the cards, and the thieves. And if you can find a replacement deck ..." He held out his abbreviated deck of magic cards, shuffled them, and extended the pile to me. "Pick a card, any card."

I did, looked at it myself, then slid it back into the deck. "No, thanks."

Aldo frowned. "Don't you want to know your future?"

"I'm a detective," I said. "I'd rather figure it out for myself."

ROAD KILL

It's never a good thing to wake up in a coffin, unless you're a vampire—and I'm definitely not a vampire. I'm an entirely different sort of undead.

Now, vampires *belong* in coffins; they actually find them comfortable. Vamps go there regularly to get their sleep. I've even known several who kept everyday coffins and vacation coffins (fitted with tropical interior décor). Some are just stripped-down pine boxes, while others are luxury models rigged with stereo systems for music or audiobooks. Some coffins even have tingly massage fingers on the bottom.

The coffin I woke up in wasn't one of those types, and I sure as hell didn't belong here.

I'm a zombie, and zombies aren't so picky about where they rest. Sure, coffins will do just fine, but once we've clawed our way out of the grave, we don't need to sleep often, and when we do we're okay with sleeping on a sofa, or even just propped up in a corner somewhere. It doesn't really matter.

But I knew I hadn't taken a nap here on purpose.

I'm not just any zombie: I'm a zombie *detective*, and it's my job to figure out mysteries. I'm good at my job—though I try to avoid being part of the mystery itself.

The coffin was dark and cramped, with very little elbow room. I squirmed, thumped the sides of the box with my arms, managed to roll myself over onto my stomach—which did me no good at all—then had to exert twice as much effort to roll myself onto my back again.

I pounded the wooden lid with my fists. Yes, it's a cliché: I had become one of those things that go bump in the night.

I felt the entire coffin vibrating beneath me, accompanied by a low pleasant thrumming. No wonder I had dozed off for so long! But this wasn't a timed "Magic Massage Fingers" sensation. I realized the sound was road noise, the vibration of wheels.

I was in the back of a vehicle somewhere.

Worse, I was in a coffin in the back of a vehicle going somewhere.

I hammered on the lid of the coffin, felt around the edge. No safety latch there. That was a code violation, and I was starting to feel testy.

Coffins are supposed to have quick-release latches, otherwise it's a safety hazard. Ever since the Big Uneasy, laws had changed to protect the unnaturals. My partner Robin had hung out her attorney-for-hire shingle on behalf of the vampires, zombies, werewolves, ghosts, and other assorted "beings" that needed legal representation in the changing world. One of her early legal victories was to institute safety systems in coffins and crypts so that, in the event that a dead body came back to life, he or she could re-emerge without discomfort or inconvenience.

I got my hands in front of my chest, flattened my palms, and pushed up against the coffin lid. The planks creaked but remained fastened. Nailed shut. This was getting more annoying by the minute.

I tried to remember where I'd been and how I'd gotten there, but it was all a big blank. I'm better-preserved than most zombies, many of whom eat brains because they have a deficiency in that department (kind of like a vitamin deficiency). Me, I've always loved a good cheeseburger, but these days I rarely bother to eat except out of habit, or sociability. I don't have much appetite, and my taste buds aren't what they used to be.

My mind, though, is sharp as a tack … usually. Otherwise, I wouldn't be much of a detective. At present, I felt as blank and stupid as one of those shamblers who can only remember long strings of vowels without any consonants.

Moving in the cramped box now, I patted myself down and realized that I still wore my usual sport jacket with the lumpy threads where the bullet holes had been crudely stitched up. I managed to get my fingers up to my face, felt the cold skin, ran them up around my forehead and skull, felt a crater there—a bullet hole, entry wound in the back of my head, exit wound in my forehead.

Yes, everything seemed normal.

For many years, I'd been a detective in the Unnatural Quarter, a human detective at first, working on cases where unnaturals ran afoul of the law, or stumbled into curses, or just lost things from their original lives. I made a decent living at it, especially after I partnered with Robin, and the cases we dealt with were more interesting than typical adultery spying for divorce cases.

On the downside, I had ended up getting shot in the back of the head while investigating the poisoning death of my girlfriend. That would have been the end of any regular Sam Spade or Philip Marlowe, but the cases don't solve themselves, so when I came back from the dead ... I went right back to work.

I pressed hard against the lid of the coffin again, heard the boards creak, listened to the nails groan a little bit. That was some progress, at least. I kept pushing.

Even though zombies have the advantage of being able to sleep wherever they like, vampires are generally more limber. I was accustomed to stiff muscles and sore joints, however, so I kept pushing. I put my back into it. (What, was I going to get a bruise?) With steady pressure, I managed to coax the nails farther out. The boards splintered, and the lid finally came loose.

I nudged the top of the coffin aside by a few inches and let in some cool air. But I was still trapped.

A thick silver chain and a padlock had been wrapped around the coffin. Great. Silver chains and a nailed-down coffin—exactly what would be required to contain a vampire. Okay, B+ for effort, but somebody really needed to go back to the field guides and do a better job at identifying their unnaturals.

How could anyone have confused me for a vampire?

Then one or two of the pieces fell into place with a big thud. I wasn't supposed to be here—this should have been someone else! I'd been duped, or switched.

Finally, I remembered about the witness protection program.

At Chambeaux & Deyer investigations, we take all sorts of cases— from a monster in trouble who lumbers through our doors, to humans having trouble with monsters, to monsters having trouble with one another. There's never a dull moment.

Occasionally, we get cases punted to us from the police, usually because Officer Toby McGoohan, my best human friend, brings them to us. McGoo appreciated the extra help on his backlog, and we appreciated the business.

McGoo and I were old friends well before I got shot—a down-on-his-luck private detective and a politically incorrect, often rude, beat cop with no prospects for promotion, even in the Unnatural Quarter. Some friendships survive even death. If I could put up with McGoo's lousy jokes, he could put up with my cadaverous infirmities.

He showed up in our offices wearing his full patrolman uniform and blue cap, leading a man in a ridiculous disguise: a trenchcoat, a wide-brimmed hat, and a curly wig that Harpo Marx would have found too extreme.

"Hey, Shamble," McGoo said. I had long since stopped objecting to his nickname for me, a deliberate mispronunciation of my last name.

When he didn't introduce his companion, I nodded to the stranger. "Correct me if I'm wrong, McGoo, but a disguise isn't supposed to *draw* attention."

The man in the goofy wig muttered, "I didn't want anyone to recognize me." He looked around, then muttered to McGoo, "Are we safe here?"

"Safe enough. These people are going to help get you into the witness protection program."

The man took off the hat, silly wig, and trenchcoat, to reveal he was a slight-framed blond man, as scrawny and skittish as if he had stepped right off the "before" side of a muscle supplement ad. He was a vampire.

"Let me introduce Sebastian Bund," McGoo said, "former blood barista at one of the Talbot & Knowles blood bars. He's also a key witness in an important case involving the illicit blood market."

Scrawny Sebastian slicked back his blond hair, which had been mussed by the wig. "Thank you for your help ... as soon as you help."

Our receptionist at Chambeaux & Deyer is my girlfriend—and former client—Sheyenne. She's a ghost now, and I had been investigating her murder when I got killed, but we're still a couple. Many spirits linger because they have unfinished business, but even after I solved Sheyenne's murder, she remained, and she works for us now. Apparently her "unfinished business" now involved typing and filing in our offices. Chambeaux & Deyer couldn't have functioned without her.

"Could I get you some coffee or tea, or blood, Mr. Bund?" she asked, as she dropped the intake paperwork on her desk.

"Do you have any B-positive?" Bund asked.

"I think we just keep O in stock for the clients."

Bund shook his head. "Never mind. I can't stand the generic stuff. I'm fine."

McGoo pushed the papers aside. "There can't be any record of this. Everything off-book."

Sheyenne frowned. "Then how do we send our bill?"

"I'll take care of it, don't worry. I'll find a way to get it out of petty cash."

"If it's only petty cash," she countered, "then maybe the case isn't worth our time."

"We have a big petty cash fund."

Robin came out to meet the new client as well, looking friendly now, but when she sinks her teeth into a case, she's as hard to shake as a zombie with lockjaw. We went into the conference room together, so McGoo could explain the case to us.

Sebastian Bund had been caught up in under-the-counter blood sales, watering down the product, selling the extra out a back alley and using a seemingly legitimate blood bank to move his supplies. He would swap out rare and expensive types for more generic flavors. No one had noticed ... until one of the mislabeled packets was actually used in surgery rather than for unnatural consumption, and the patient nearly died.

The plot unraveled, arrests were made, and the operation was pinned on an ambitious gangster family led by Ma Hemoglobin. (Her real last name was Hamanubin, but nobody referred to her by that.) She had six sons, two of whom were vampires. Ma Hemoglobin and her boys ran blood-smuggling operations throughout the Quarter.

The District Attorney had vowed to bring them down. The owners of the Talbot & Knowles blood-bar chain (former clients of mine, I'm pleased to say) were eager to press charges.

"Unfortunately, each witness who would have testified against Ma Hemoglobin suffered an unfortunate demise," McGoo said.

"Is there such thing as a fortunate demise?" I asked. McGoo ignored the interruption; I think he was annoyed that he hadn't thought of the joke himself.

Several vampire witnesses had "accidentally" been locked in sunlit cells, and their ashes weren't in any shape to testify. Some of the human witnesses were assigned to vampires-only holding cells, and after the prisoner meals were "accidentally delayed" by several hours, the human witnesses were too drained to be of any use and "accidentally" contaminated with holy water during the resuscitation efforts so they couldn't even be turned into vamps themselves (thus, doubly prevented from taking the stand against Ma Hemoglobin). Another particularly important witness had vanished from a locked bathroom, and the only evidence was a brownish-green slime all around the toilet. There were rumors of sewer-dweller hit men who came up through the porcelain access to strike their target.

"Sebastian is the only witness left," McGoo said. "And obviously our traditional police protection methods haven't worked."

"Sounds like you need a zombie detective," I said.

"We need someone competent. Sebastian has to go into witness protection until the case comes up for trial."

Robin just nibbled on her pencil, deep in thought. "So you need our help to make sure he's moved without being seen."

McGoo nodded. "We've already got an operation under contract. He'll be taken cross-country in a coffin in the back of an eighteen-wheeler. We'll disguise the truck, make it look like it's hauling pre-packaged school lunches."

I cringed, and Robin shuddered, both of us remembering our own experiences with school lunches. "No one's going to mess with that cargo."

So, McGoo already had the general plan and his connections to the police force. We just had to work out the details.

Obviously, as the ominous voice always says in movie trailers, *something went wrong*. I wasn't the one who was supposed to be riding in the coffin. Somebody had set me up.

Once I pushed the loosened coffin lid to one side, I began to work on the silver chains and padlock. Fortunately, silver has no effect on me—that's an advantage to being a zombie, and I try to look at the glass as half full.

As a detective, I'm quite proficient, or at least marginally adequate, with lockpick tools that I keep in a handy travel pack in my pants pocket. My fingers were clumsy, but no more than usual. I worked with the tools until I sprung the padlock, removed the hasp, and shoved the chains to the floor.

Just as I sat up, the semi truck hit a bump in the road, which made the coffin thump against the trailer bed. My teeth clacked together, and then the hum of the road became smooth again. I knocked the lid to the floor and lurched up out of the coffin.

This was actually easier than when I had clawed my way up through the packed graveyard soil back when I first rose from the dead—not to mention a lot less dirty, too.

The truck rumbled along, and I stepped out of the coffin, flexing my stiff knees, stretching, brushing the wrinkles in my sport jacket. I looked around the coffin, but saw no sign of my fedora. I hoped it wasn't lost.

Even though my leaky brain had recaptured the basic story of Sebastian Bund going into witness protection, there were still many gaps. Once again, I felt around my head, but discovered no lumps. It's difficult to knock a zombie unconscious by bonking him on the head, anyway. There must have been something else, maybe a sleeping potion. I felt groggy, rubbed my eyes, still trying to get awake.

"Coffin" and "coffee" both derive from the root word "caffeine," I think—and I could have used a strong cup right now to help wake the dead. I needed to be alert, to judge whether I might be in danger.

Inside the trailer, other crates were stacked high all around where the coffin had been stashed. The crates were all filled with prepackaged school lunches; from the "Use By" dates stamped on the sides, they would not expire for more than a century.

I worked my way toward the front of the trailer, hoping I could find some way to signal the cab. The driver up there needed to know he had the wrong cargo. If someone had knocked me out and switched me with Sebastian Bund, then the star witness might be in danger.

The engine noise was loud, but I leaned against the wall and started pounding as hard as I could. (For a trucker hauling coffins filled with the undead, that would probably be unnerving.) If he had the window open, maybe he'd be able to hear me back here. I pounded harder and then, to reassure him, hammered out "Shave and a Haircut."

Faintly, from the cab, I heard him pound back on the door, "Two Bits."

I pounded harder, more desperately. He pounded back, and I heard his muffled voice. "Quiet back there!"

So much for raising the alarm. I guess I would have to wait until he stopped for a potty break—I hoped he had a small bladder.

I sat back down on the edge of the coffin, slipped my hands into the jacket pockets—and felt immediately stupid when I found my phone. That would have been a good thing to remember from the start. I didn't like all these lapses in my memory. Could a zombie get a concussion?

Since I had no idea where the truck was, possibly out in the middle of nowhere, I hoped that I'd get a signal. I was pleased to see at least one-and-a-half bars; that should be good enough.

I kept McGoo's number on speed-dial, and he picked up on the second ring. He must have seen the Caller ID. "Shamble! What are you doing awake already?"

"Trying to figure out where the hell I am." He didn't sound surprised to hear from me. "You sound like you know more about this than I do."

McGoo snorted. "I know more about most things than you do."

"I'd argue with that, but today I'll give you a free pass if you can tell me why I woke up in a nailed-shut coffin surrounded by silver chains in the back of a semi truck."

"Silver chains? There weren't supposed to be any silver chains."

I stared at the phone, then put it back to my ear.

"*That's* the part you find unusual? Why am I here in the first place?"

"It was your idea, Shamble, but if you don't remember your own brilliant solution, I'll take credit for it. The narcomancer said you might suffer some temporary memory loss as a side effect. It was a powerful spell."

"Narcomancer?" The word meant nothing to me, and I couldn't call any image to mind. "Don't you mean 'necromancer'?"

"*Narco*—narcomancer," McGoo said. "I suppose you've forgotten you owe me a hundred bucks, too?"

"I don't owe you a hundred bucks. But narcomancer … like in narcotics?"

"No, like narcolepsy. His name was Rufus. He's a wizard who worked a spell to put you to sleep—and putting a zombie to sleep is no easy task."

"Rufus?" The name still didn't ring a bell.

And suddenly, it did.

I recalled the man whose matted mouse-brown hair seemed to have a moral disagreement with combs. His wispy beard looked as if someone had been experimenting with spirit gum and theatrical makeup but had given up halfway through the job. His watery blue eyes were extremely bloodshot, and he seemed jittery. Although he specialized in putting people to sleep, he seemed to be an insomniac himself.

I remember him rubbing his hands together, repeating his name and grinning. "Yes, Rufus … are you ready for my special *roofie*? You'll snooze away the journey."

He began to speak an incantation—then everything went blank.

"It's all going down as planned," McGoo said on the phone. "We made all the arrangements for Sebastian to be whisked away in the truck to his new home, but we put you in the coffin instead, under a sleep spell—it was *supposed* to last for the entire drive—while Sebastian went by a roundabout route. A brilliant idea, actually. I suggested it."

"No, you didn't," I said. "That was my idea."

"I thought you didn't remember."

"But why would we *do* that?"

McGoo said, "Just to be safe. You were triggered to wake up if anyone tampered with the coffin. You were worried something bad might go down."

At that moment, an explosion hit the truck, blowing out the side of the trailer, scattering packaged school lunches everywhere, and hurling me out into the pitch-black night.

2

The squeal of the truck's air brakes would have made a banshee envious. The semi jack-knifed, its wheels smearing rubber along the highway like black fingerpaint. The truck groaned to a halt with a cough and gasp, and debris rained down everywhere.

After being thrown from the truck, I landed in a ditch—a mud-filled ditch, of course. I got to my feet, dripping; stagnant slime oozed out of my hair. It seems the harder I work to keep myself well-preserved, the faster karma comes back and smacks me.

The door to the truck cab popped open, and a stocky man with a black jawline beard swung out. His eyes burned like coals, and even from a distance I could tell he was hopping mad. He wore a trucker's cap, a red checked flannel shirt open to show his white undershirt, and jeans. He didn't seem injured, just furious as he stepped away from the wheezing and gurgling diesel engine that fought to keep running.

He stared at the ruined trailer, where a blackened crater and splintered wood surrounded the remnants of a slogan: "The Finest in Processed Lunches—Tolerated by Children for over Twenty Years!" On the image, a group of gaunt boys and girls looked dubiously toward the picture of their meal, which had been obliterated by the blast.

"They blew up my rig!" The trucker stalked back and forth, twisted his cap around backward, then, dissatisfied, twisted it back around front. "Out here on an empty stretch of highway? *They blew up my rig!*" He kicked gravel with his steel-toed boots, then looked up and saw me shambling toward him. "Did you see that?" Then he glowered, giving me a second look. "Where did you come from?"

"I was inside your truck," I said. "I'm Dan Chambeaux, private investigator."

The trucker blinked, still suspicious. "And I'm Earl—Earl Joe Bob, owner and operator of Earl Joe Bob Trucking." He scratched his beard.

"Say, what were you doing in that coffin? You weren't supposed to be in there."

"Ever hear those stories about babies being switched in the nursery?"

"Yeah," he said.

"I guess it happens with coffins, too."

Earl Joe Bob put his hands on his hips and swung his head from side to side, looking in dismay at his mortally wounded rig. Under the bright running lights, which could have given a Christmas tree on the Las Vegas Strip a run for its money, I saw "Earl Joe Bob Trucking" and a phone number, as well as government license number on the driver's door. He sighed. "At least the cab and engine are still intact. But damn—I'm liable for all this! And, hey, you weren't supposed to be in that coffin!" He shook his head again, stuck his thumbs into the waistband of his jeans. "What a mess."

At least the trailer hadn't caught fire, though some of the shards of wood still smoldered. "I think we were hit with a rocket launcher."

"It happens," said Earl Joe Bob. He went back to the cab, got some flares and reflective hazard triangles.

I realized that out here on this open and silent stretch of highway, under the stars and with no city lights in sight, we were much too vulnerable. This truck hadn't run into a random migratory rocket. I patted my pockets, looked around—I had lost my phone during the explosion.

"We have to call for help. Can we use your CB? Or a cell phone?"

Earl Joe Bob shook his head. "No, wouldn't be wise to use it."

I was exasperated. "Why not?"

The trucker narrowed his eyes at me. "Just can't."

I couldn't argue with that logic. I walked around the other side of the truck again, working my way back to the ditch, where I hunted around for my phone. The weeds were tall, and I splashed through the standing water. Mosquitoes fled from me—another advantage of being a zombie. I would have to write all the advantages down one day, just as a reminder.

Fortunately, the phone's screen light was still on, though my call with McGoo had been disconnected in the explosion. I smeared it against my muddy shirt, making a marginally clean patch, and was dismayed to see that my Angry Vultures scores had been wiped out. That was a problem I would have to deal with later.

I phoned McGoo, who answered right away. "Where are you, Shamble? What happened?"

"I'm on a road somewhere," I said, glancing around. "And I don't see one of those You Are Here X's." I told McGoo about the explosion, and that we were stranded. He promised to call in reinforcements right away.

"I'll see if we can track your signal through the cell towers," he said. "Maybe the truck has a GPS in the cab."

I ended the call and began making my way along the back of the rig, when I froze, hearing voices. I saw two figures approach the wounded truck. It was a starlit night, clear skies, a quarter moon. Zombie night vision is generally good, but I didn't need any supernatural powers to pick out the two young men. They wore camouflage jumpsuits—but light-colored desert camo, so they stood out plainly. They carried long rifles.

Since the side of the truck had been blasted open with a rocket launcher, and since these two men were approaching heavily armed, I decided it wouldn't be a good idea to wave my arms and hail them for help.

Earl Joe Bob spotted them as well, and bunched his meaty arms as he stalked toward them. "This wasn't the deal I had with Ma Hemoglobin! Which two of her boys are you—Moron and Imbecile?"

"No," said one of the young men. "I'm Huey, and that's Louis."

"Well, you're still Moron and Imbecile to me. You wrecked my rig! We were supposed to meet up at the Rest In Peace area down the road and make the transfer!" He spluttered, waving his hand at the crater in the side of his truck. "What kind of stupid—"

The two boys raised their rifles. Huey said, "Ma thought you might double-cross us, so we took matters into our own hands."

"You must be two of her human boys," Earl Joe Bob said. "A vampire wouldn't be that stupid."

"We'll show you stupid!" said Louis. He opened fire with his high-powered rifle. Not to be left behind, Huey shot Earl Joe Bob as well. The bullets slammed into the trucker's red flannel shirt, and he dropped to the ground.

I silently reaffirmed my wisdom in not waving my arms and calling attention to myself.

Now, as a detective, I solve cases, and I'm the hero in my own story. But sometimes heroes stick around longer if they aren't always … heroic.

I didn't know how I was going to get out of here, or how long it would take McGoo to bring in reinforcements. If this truck was on a cross-country trip to deliver a decoy into witness protection, McGoo could be miles away, even if he had been shadowing me.

With a jolt, I got a few more of my memories back: I did remember the idea of taking Sebastian's place in the coffin aboard the truck.

Meanwhile, Robin would take our nondescript and rusty old Ford Maverick, lovingly named the Pro Bono Mobile, with the scrawny blond vampire dressed in my fedora and a similar sport jacket, sunshades down, traveling across the state line to where he would be hidden in his new life. My ghost girlfriend Sheyenne was going to ride shotgun. Nobody would be looking for them. They would be safe. It would be a lark. I was the one under a narcolepsy spell in the back of a semi truck, a decoy. It should have been a long sleep for me.

Now, Ma Hemoglobin's two boys climbed through the blasted crater in the side of the trailer. My best bet was probably to climb back into the ditch and hide in the mud, but McGoo would never let me forget it.

Instead, I crept along the opposite side of the trailer. If I could make it to the cab, open the passenger side door, and climb into the cab, I was sure to find some kind of firearm, baseball bat, or tire iron that Earl Joe Bob kept there.

I heard Huey and Louis rummaging around inside the trailer, shining flashlights; I saw the gleam through splintered cracks in the opposite wall. They tossed aside a clutter of prepackaged school lunches. "The coffin's empty! He's not here!"

The other voice said, "I hate it when coffins turn up empty! But was it empty in the first place, or were we tricked?"

I made it to the front of the rig, yanked open the cab door—and of course the hinges screeched and groaned loudly enough to make any haunted house proud. The two Hemoglobin boys clambered out of the blasted trailer, brandishing their rifles, looking around.

"There he is!" yelled Louis.

"I see him," said Huey. They began sprinting toward me, running past the body of Earl Joe Bob, who lay sprawled at the side of the truck.

Earl groaned and sat up, shaking his head. "Dammit! You wrecked my rig *and* you shot me?" He sprang to his feet and flashed a set of ivory fangs.

I should have recognized earlier that he was a vampire. Many truckers who specialize in all-night hauls are vampires; they have no trouble staying awake, though they had to park in Rest In Peace areas and pull down the shades by dawn.

The two Hemoglobin boys turned white and spun around, raising their rifles again. Each managed to fire one more shot. This time, Earl Joe Bob merely flinched before lunging forward again.

"I thought you loaded the rifles with silver bullets!" Huey shouted.

"I thought *you* loaded the rifles with silver bullets!"

Earl Joe Bob was pissed.

Moving with vampire speed (earlier, I did mention that vamps can be quite swift and agile), he lunged forward and grabbed the young men by their necks, one in each hand. His grip was powerful, and he squeezed hard. I heard the loud double-crack as their necks snapped; it sounded like popcorn in a microwave bag. He tossed the two dead bodies on the ground—truly dead, because Huey and Louis had been two of Ma Hemoglobin's four human sons. (These days one or the other could still come back as an unnatural, but it wouldn't be anytime soon.)

Earl Joe Bob made a disgusted sound, brushed at his flannel shirt, looked down at the bullet holes healing in his chest. "I'm as much a mess as my rig is." He saw me hanging onto the door and flashed his fangs. "And where do you think you're going?"

The vampire trucker moved toward me. I held up my cell phone as if inviting him to play a game of Curses With Friends. "I already called in for help. The police are coming."

Earl Joe Bob scowled. "That doesn't give me much time, then. It wasn't supposed to go down this way." He straightened his cap, which sat askew from when he'd been gunned down. He sneered at the two Hemoglobin boys, who lay in their light camouflage on the ground, necks bent at improbable angles. "I hate dealing with amateurs. I've dealt with witness protection cases plenty of times, and I'm always available for additional 'enhanced disappearing' for a substantial fee. When I make people disappear, I really make them disappear."

I tried to move along the side of the truck; in a race, I could never outrun the vampire. "Isn't that a conflict of interest?"

"I don't lose any sleep over it," Earl Joe Bob said. "Pay is good, and I gotta earn a living."

I knew that he was going to have to get rid of me. I was the only one who could explain the mess around me, but Earl Joe Bob would make up some story of his own.

"We can be reasonable about this," I offered.

"Good idea." He lunged. I lurched—it was a much less fluid movement than his, but I did manage to evade the first pass. Earl Joe Bob slammed into the side of the trailer, shattering more wood.

"Careful about the splinters." My mind was racing. I could get one of the jagged spears and thrust it through the vampire's heart. In my imagination, it all worked out just fine, but in practice I wasn't quite the nimble athlete that I'd need to be for the scheme to work.

I did break off the long wooden splinter, lifted it—and Earl Joe Bob slapped it out of my hands. At least he got a splinter in his palm, and he paused to pluck it out. That brief respite gave me the chance to scramble through the blasted crater in the side of the trailer.

"Now I've got you cornered," the trucker said. While I shuffled and slipped among the debris of packaged school lunches, I saw his sturdy muscular form silhouetted against the starlit sky as he pulled himself through the hole. "Where are you going to hide?"

I hurled a package of Salisbury steak, which struck him in the center of the chest. Unfortunately, it wasn't quite the stake through the heart I required. The vamp trucker's eyes were glowing in the shadows. I could see him coming toward me. I nearly tripped backward over the coffin that had held me during my cross-country trip.

Police sirens howled down the highway, coming closer. Ironic, I thought: the cavalry was going to arrive much too late.

"At least we've already got a coffin to store you in," said Earl Joe Bob.

"Been there, done that," I answered.

He came closer, fangs bared, eyes glowing, hands outstretched. Earl Joe Bob was a burly guy, powerful enough to change one of his eighteen tires simply by lifting the rig and undoing the lug nuts with his fingertips. He could probably rip me limb from limb, stomp on any pieces still twitching, and then claim I'd been mangled in the explosion. McGoo already knew better than that.

"You haven't thought this through," I said.

The trucker laughed. "I could say the same to you—a vampire versus a zombie? The vamp will win, every time." He reached toward me.

That's when I pulled up the loose silver chains that lay draped over the coffin. I threw them onto Earl Joe Bob.

"Not every time," I said.

It was like Superman and Kryptonite—a real sight to see. Within seconds, the vamp trucker went from being a scary, overpowering opponent to a whimpering and helpless guy in a flannel shirt who squirmed under the chains.

"Awww crap!" Earl Joe whined. "That's not fair!"

Now the sirens were louder, and I could see the flashing lights through the hole in the side of the truck. Squad cars raced along the highway, followed by the state patrol. I was still undead and kicking, but I no longer needed them to rescue me. Still, I'd be happy to let McGoo handle the wrap-up paperwork.

As soon as the police climbed into the trailer, I waved McGoo over. He looked flushed and worried. "Shamble, you all right?"

There were shouts outside as other officers found the two bodies of Ma Hemoglobin's boys.

"Better than they are. And better than he is." I nodded to where Earl Joe Bob squirmed on the floor under the silver chains.

His cap had fallen off in the struggle, and I reached down and plucked it up. It wasn't my style—I much preferred the fedora, but that was gone for now, apparently on the head of a disguised Sebastian Bund. Since I felt naked without a hat, I settled the trucker cap in place.

I started rattling off the full story as an officer handcuffed Earl Joe Bob with silver-plated handcuffs. The vamp trucker spluttered and groaned at the way I described a few things, but he didn't deny any of the details.

"I'll cut a deal," he said. "Ma Hemoglobin is scary, and she's got four boys left. I'll turn State's witness. Put me into witness protection, otherwise I'll never survive until the trial." His eyes flashed, and he struggled against the silver handcuffs. "I know where all the bodies are buried—some of them more than once."

3

Back in the offices, Robin and Sheyenne were both in very good moods, having delivered Sebastian Bund to his official new undisclosed location.

"He was delightful company." Robin flashed a smile at me. "Did you know he used to be a singing barista?"

"Broadway show tunes," Sheyenne said. "That's all we talked about. He's a fan of musicals. Why don't you ever see musicals with me?"

"Because I don't like musicals," I said.

She gave me a spectral raspberry. "When you go out on a date, you're supposed to do something you don't like. That's how you show a girl you care for her."

"I'll keep that in mind next time we go out on a date." Our cases almost always interfered with our love life—and so did the fact that, as a ghost, she couldn't physically touch me, which made the intimate aspect of our relationship much more problematic. "Did we at least get paid for the case?"

"We got paid in satisfaction," Robin said. "That's our purpose here, to know that justice is done."

"Right." I turned to Sheyenne, repeating the question. "Did we at least get paid?"

She showed me a Chambeaux & Deyer invoice, on which she had merely written in capital letters: SERVICES RENDERED, no other details. "Officer McGoohan was true to his word." She pulled out a stack of other pending cases and floated ahead to place the files on my desk. "One more step in making the world safe for naturals and unnaturals everywhere."

"It's a start." I looked down at all the folders Sheyenne had gotten out, and I knew exactly what they were. Job security.

NAUGHTY & NICE

1

Santa Claus was an *unnatural*. That made perfect sense—I just hadn't thought of it before.

The jolly bearded guy in the bright-red suit came into the offices of Chambeaux & Deyer Investigations, desperate to hire my services. It's not often, I suppose, that Santa requires a detective—particularly a zombie detective.

"I need your help, Mr. Chambeaux," Santa said.

I extended my gray hand to shake his black-gloved one. "At your service."

I assessed my client-to-be. Santa carried a voluminous cloth sack over his left shoulder; it was limp and empty at the moment, rather than bulging with brightly wrapped gifts. His bloodshot eyes were as red as his suit. His cheeks were pale, and his face seemed less plump than the pictures I had seen on a million Christmas cards.

"It's a crisis." He looked around with haunted eyes. "I've been robbed!"

In the Unnatural Quarter, we see all sorts of clients. After the Big Uneasy, all manner of legendary creatures had reappeared: ghosts, vampires, zombies, werewolves, ghouls, and other creatures that go bump, growl, or thud in the night. Why not Santa, too? Somebody who can slip down billions of chimneys in a night—without incurring a single home-invasion charge—would fit right in.

"We'll do everything we can to help, Mr. Claus," said Robin Deyer, as she came out to greet the new client. "Is this more of a legal matter or an investigative one?"

"Oh-ho-ho, I definitely need a detective, and I came here because Mrs. Claus and I have heard about Mr. Chambeaux."

I was surprised. "We don't even advertise up at the North Pole. How did you find out about Chambeaux and Deyer Investigations?"

"Actually, we're local. My powers only manifest during the holiday season—it's not a full-time gig up in the cold. The rest of the year Mrs. Claus and I run a nice little bed-and-breakfast in the Quarter. Everybody around town knows the zombie detective to call when they're in a bind."

When I first moved into the Unnatural Quarter, I was a regular human P.I., trying to make a living like anybody else. I catered to clients who, though they sometimes looked like monsters on the outside, still had very human problems. Even after I got myself killed on a case, I climbed out of the grave and got back to work, still with Robin as my partner. Most unnaturals aren't even bothered by the bullet hole in the middle of my forehead, and I've stopped being self-conscious about applying morticians' putty to cover it up.

Sheyenne flitted up to Santa, beaming her gorgeous smile. "May I take your coat, Mr. Claus?"

Not only is Sheyenne extremely smart, competent, and efficient, she's beautiful on all counts. She's also my girlfriend. On top of that, she happens to be a ghost, murdered in the same case that saw me dead. But even through all that, we stuck together. It's a testament to the strength of our relationship.

Santa decided against removing his red coat. "No-ho-ho! It's part of my traditional image. The coat is made of magical material that keeps me comfortable no matter the temperature. That way I never have to take it off until the season's over. Traditions are important, and never more so than around the holidays."

Sheyenne leaned closer and whispered, "For the record, I never stopped believing in you."

He regarded Sheyenne with both wonder and mirth. "Strangely enough, I didn't believe in ghosts—until a few years ago." Santa sneezed, then turned back to me. "Mr. Chambeaux, I'm not going to kid you. There's more riding on this particular Christmas than ever before, and I'm coming apart at the seams. I need you to find my stolen property before Christmas Eve, or there'll be no joy to the world, no ho-ho-ho, no holly jolly, no Feliz in the Navidad, no Frohe in the Weihnachten, no Merry in the Christmas. You see how serious this is?"

"I think I do." I really had no idea, but I didn't want to look dumb in front of Santa Claus. "What exactly was stolen?"

"My list!" He was distraught—which was not at all the sort of attitude I expected from a man famous for his rumbling belly laugh and infectious good cheer. "My *list* of who's Naughty and Nice! Without that list, I won't know which houses to visit, which Johnny deserves a model train set and which one gets a lump of coal, which Susie deserves a doll and which one gets a boring sweater. If I can't figure that out, Christmas definitely won't be the most wonderful time of the year."

"Don't you keep a photocopy?" Robin asked. "Or an on-line backup?"

Santa was horrified. "And break Christmas tradition? Millions of children believe in me and the way I do things, just so. They have dreams about Christmas, and it's my responsibility to safeguard those dreams." He shook his head again. "If I modernized, there'd be an uproar—not to mention countless bugs in the system—and then you can bet the Easter Bunny would hack into my database and start grabbing my market share. No, everything's done by hand on a very long roll of parchment, the names of every single boy and girl written with a goose quill."

That must have been the world's largest two-column spreadsheet. "And how exactly was it stolen?"

"Someone broke into the offices of my North Pole headquarters. It's our busy season, all of my helpers doing double shifts, decking the halls, dashing through the snow. Our packaging department is a madhouse, full of complete sets of lords a-leaping, partridges, pear trees—and everybody wants five golden rings. We still have an overstock of last year's fruitcakes, and I don't know what to do with the figgy puddings. I was sure there'd be a demand for those again." He wiped a gloved hand across his forehead.

"It's very hectic. I was taking a break with Mrs. Claus. She had made a fresh batch of eggnog, and this time of year she spikes it rather heavily. I slept like a baby … and when I went back to the office the list was gone!" He tugged on his beard. "It had to be an inside job." He paced back and forth, scuffing his black boots on our all-weather carpet. "I checked with all the line supervisor elves and every single one of the toy builders. This time of year they work around the clock without even restroom or cigarette breaks. But everyone had an alibi."

"Could you have been targeted by Homeland Security?" Robin asked. "Or some other law-enforcement organization monitoring your research as to who might be on a Most Naughty list?"

"I can see why they might want that," I said.

"Not at all, I have a close cooperative relationship with government agencies, considering all that airspace I fly over—and my work has to be done in a single night, so I have no time to mess with clearances. I even let NORAD track me every year. No, that list is in the hands of someone who means no good, mark my words ... and no human could have gotten through my security. It had to be an unnatural."

He hung his head and seemed so sad that I wanted to sit on Santa's lap and give him a hug. He continued, "That's why I came to you, Mr. Chambeaux. If I don't get that Naughty and Nice list in time, I can't stop thinking about all those poor children who'll be disappointed, all those broken dreams, all those undelivered presents. It'll destroy their faith in Christmas ... and they just might turn out to be naughty next year."

I was determined to solve the problem. It's not every day you get a chance to save Christmas—and not just because Christmas only comes once a year. "Don't underestimate how relentless a zombie can be, Santa. I'll find your list. If I have any questions or developments, how will I get hold of you? Do you have a business card?"

"Much better than that." Santa reached into a pocket of his red jacket and pulled out a bright green ribbon with a jingle bell attached. "Just ring this, and I'll be there. Even if I'm otherwise occupied, I have an answering service that can get hold of me."

The pink had come back to his cheeks, and a droll smile lifted his lips. "Oh-ho-ho, if you solve this case, there'll be something very special under the tree—for all of you."

Relieved and encouraged, Santa slung his empty sack over one shoulder and prepared to go. He closed his eyes and touched a finger to the side of his nose.

When nothing happened, he looked around our offices. Finding no chimney, he chuckled. "Sorry, I've been so worried about Christmas being ruined, I forgot how I arrived!" He left through the front door instead.

2

Although I knew I might have to go to Santa's North Pole seasonal offices to see the crime scene, I decided to search in the Unnatural Quarter first, which was much more convenient. (Riding up to the Arctic for hours in a freezing open sleigh sounded worse than flying in a middle seat in Coach.)

I started with someone who kept a similar list—primarily a Naughty list.

Officer Toby McGoohan is a dedicated beat cop, but his penchant for telling off-color jokes to the wrong people had gotten him transferred to the Quarter. McGoo is also my BHF, my best human friend. We help each other on cases. We commiserate about life and unlife over beers at the Goblin Tavern.

I found him outside one of the Talbot & Knowles blood bars, which are frequented by vampires who need their daily caffeine and hemoglobin fix. Some fanged customers drink straight blood, while others go for berry-flavored blood frappés or, now that the weather had turned colder, steaming cinnamon-spice hot clotties.

"Hey, Shamble," McGoo said, tipping his blue cap. "What do you get when you cross a snowman with a vampire?"

"What?" I groaned in advance.

"Frostbite." He persists in telling me jokes. I haven't been able to convince him they're not funny, and he hasn't been able to convince me that they are. As a special favor, I did promise I would try to laugh at some of them. But only some. "What's new and exciting in your world?"

"I just picked up Santa Claus as a client. Somebody stole his list of Naughty and Nice kids."

McGoo's eyes widened. "Well, that's a miracle on ..." he glanced up, looking for a street corner, "32nd Street. If even Santa isn't safe from criminal activity, we are living in troubled times indeed. What does the list look like?"

"Long roll of parchment, millions of handwritten names. Two columns labeled N and N."

McGoo shook his head. "I'll keep an eye out, but we've got real problems of our own in the Quarter." He lowered his voice. "Kids are going missing, Shamble—a lot of them. We've received a rash of reports."

A vampire couple came out of the blood bar, chatting away. One held a to-go carrier with four cups of blood drinks marked with Type A (extra hot), Type O negative, and two with Type B positive (and a hand-drawn smiley face).

McGoo called, "Excuse me, can I see those for a second?"

The vampires turned, surprised. "What is it, Officer?"

"Your blood drinks. I want to show my friend something."

McGoo indicated the to-go cups, the first of which showed the printed picture of a young vampire boy who had been turned when he was maybe twelve years old. Big letters said "Have You Seen Me?" Printed below the photo were the vampire kid's name, pre-turned age, and last-seen data.

The second cup showed a zombie boy with an incongruous smile beneath his sunken eyes. The third was a scruffy-looking full-furred werewolf, and the fourth showed a human girl in Goth makeup wearing an off-the-shelf gloomy expression.

After he thanked the vampire couple, they left. I shook my head. "That's troubling, McGoo. I think I recognize the werewolf kid. He was part of the gang at the rumble a few months ago, Hairballs versus the Monthlies.

"Yeah, he's not the only rough one. Some of the missing children are straight off the Wikipedia page for Juvenile Delinquent. Not all of those photos were in a family album—a few are from mug-shot files."

"Some of the disappearances could just be runaways," I suggested. "Visiting some nice old lady's gingerbread house in the forest."

"For the record, Shamble, she wasn't a nice old lady—I worked on that case," McGoo said. "Not all of the missing kids have records. We've got grieving parents or foster-parents who want to find their missing little angels. I don't know if the cases are related, or just a coincidence."

"I don't believe in coincidence," I said, wondering if this might also have something to do with the stolen Naughty and Nice list. "But I didn't believe in Santa Claus either, and now he's my client. Let me know if you get a lead on my case. I'll do the same if I hear anything about the missing kids."

McGoo nodded. "The Quarter's getting nervous—put your mind to it, see what you come up with. You've got a lot of space in that big empty head of yours."

I tapped the bullet hole in the middle of my forehead. "A little extra space maybe, but it's not empty." I tipped my fedora at him and left.

My first order of business was to figure out who would *want* to steal the Naughty and Nice list, and what anybody would use it for. In order to brainstorm, I invited Sheyenne to lunch.

3

Being a ghost, Sheyenne doesn't eat, not even their special "ephemeral" plate, and I don't need much sustenance. (I've avoided brains, because I don't want to turn into one of *those* zombies who are an embarrassment to the rest of us.)

The Ghoul's Diner, though, was a place to hang out, and Sheyenne likes it when we go out on lunch dates. Strolling down the sidewalk toward the Diner, we free-associated. Sheyenne wore a bright smile as always, and those blue eyes could make a man's heart stop beating, or start beating, depending on which condition he started from.

I wondered aloud that maybe the Big Uneasy had made the Grinch manifest as well, but Sheyenne doubted he'd reached a worldwide cultural status similar to vampires or St. Nick. I disagreed, because I had grown up on the Grinch; still, I conceded that he seemed too obvious a cartoon villain.

I then postulated that the perpetrator could be a Lorax with self-esteem issues, upset that Arbor Day didn't have the stature of Christmas, Hanukkah, Thanksgiving, New Years … or even Kwanzaa, for that matter. I didn't know if Loraxes were real, either. I seemed to be in a Seussian rut.

A light dusting of snow came down, reminding me that I had to find Santa's list before Christmas Eve, or he would suffer a worldwide toy-distribution crisis. Festive decorations were already strung up in the streets of the Quarter: barbed-wire tinsel looped along windowpanes and awnings, colorful wreaths hung from nooses on gallows lampposts.

Before we reached the Diner, Sheyenne and I stopped on the street where crowds had gathered and traffic halted for an early holiday parade. And it sure wasn't the type hosted by Macy's.

Elves capered and danced at the front of the parade, diminutive creatures dressed in pointed floppy caps and bright red outfits trimmed with white flocking. The costumes resembled a traditional Santa's elf suit, but these were cheap knockoffs that fit poorly with seams showing and with some of the white trim missing.

These elves were not the cute, smiling, industrious workers who stocked Santa's shelves and made the North Pole a cheery, if formerly imaginary, place. No, these elves came from the G-side of the family, having more in common with gremlins, goblins, and gnomes—pointy, stretched-out features, gray skin, and long ears that looked as if they had gotten caught in industrial picking machinery. When they smiled like good elves should, they showed alarmingly pointed teeth.

Behind the prancing elves came a bizarre motorized sleigh crawling along at pedestrian speed so everyone on the sidewalk had an appropriate opportunity to wave. Palm trees adorned the back of the sleigh. On a big wicker chair sat an elf with all the usual elf features (from the G-side of the family), but he wore a white rhinestone-studded jacket, trimmed in Christmasy green and red. He had slicked-back black hair, sideburns that extended halfway down his pointed chin, big garish sunglasses, and oddly out-of-place blue suede shoes.

"You've got to be kidding me," I said to Sheyenne.

"He's for real, Beaux. That's Elfis—I've seen his ads. You know, 'Santa Claus is coming to town, but Elfis will get there faster?' He's a celebrity on the cable-access channels."

I'm a decent enough detective, but I can be clueless about pop culture.

Elfis waved at the crowd and picked up a handheld Vegas-style silver microphone. "Thank ya very much. Santa's got competition this year, boys and girls, naturals and unnatural. The holidays should be for everybody, not just kids who pass some arbitrary naughty-or-nice test. Even naughty kids deserve presents, don't they?"

From the sidewalk crowds, a smattering of natural and unnatural children cheered—kids who knew they were included in the Naughty column, no doubt.

"Santa Claus has had a monopoly on the Christmas season for far too long—but I intend to undercut his position. Elfis Industries has wider distribution, more fairness, and less discrimination. More transparency in holiday gift-giving! We're going to expose all those 'secret admirer' gifts for what they are. And no more bribery with milk and cookies. *Everyone* deserves a present, and I'm the one to give it to them. It's time to put the kitsch back into Christmas!"

His elves began handing out candy canes, traditional red-and-white striped ones, blood-red ones, and black ones. A witch dressed in a midnight-blue gown and pointy cap stood by her young son who looked as if he might grow up to be a powerful necromancer. The boy ran forward to take a black candy cane, but his mother scolded him. "I told you not to take candy from strangers!"

The boy pouted. "He's not a stranger, Mom—that's *Elfis!*"

"Oh," the witch said, and handed him back the cane.

The motorized sleigh rolled by, with Elfis in his sequins and sunglasses waving from under his palm trees. He called out, "Who needs the cold? I have nightmares about a white Christmas! Let it snow, let it snow, let it snow—but somewhere far away! Stick with me, and the holidays will have a warm and sunny glow."

After the parade passed, Sheyenne leaned close to me. "So that's why Santa is so worried. He's got competition this year. And if his rival does a better job satisfying the customers …"

"Then Santa Claus won't be coming to town anymore," I said. "We might have our first suspect. Elfis has a motive to sabotage Santa's work. I better go talk to him and find out if his intentions really are as pure as new fallen snow."

I could tell this case was going to spell T-R-O-U-B-L-E.

4

After Sheyenne and I had a quick lunch at the diner (pink slime was on special), I went off to continue my investigation.

The headquarters for the competitive holiday operation was an office building in front of a fenced compound of airplane-hangar-sized structures, no doubt where Elfis manufactured and stored all the toys he planned to distribute ahead of his business rival. According to Sheyenne, Elfis's ads promised delivery by Christmas Eve Eve.

The sign at the front entrance had giant letters painted like candy canes, surrounded by yellow suns: "North Pole South: We're Better Because We're Closer to the Equator." Around the doorway was strewn blue sand or fake snow, which seemed incongruous ... until I remembered "Blue Christmas."

When I entered the front door of North Pole South, I heard many busy bodies working in the back, but the reception counter was empty except for a fist-sized fake rock sitting on top of an index card that said "Ring bell for service." I picked up the stone and realized it was hollow. When I shook it, a tinkling chime rang out.

A female elf receptionist scurried out of the back, smiling sweetly with her pinched face. "I see you found our Jingle-Bell Rock," she snickered. "Very clever, don't you think? Elfis came up with it himself." She shuffled papers and handed me a temporary-employment application. "Looking for part-time holiday work? Many positions available."

I shook snow from the brim of my fedora. "That would be a conflict of interest. I've been retained by Santa Claus."

The receptionist's eyebrows rose. "I'll let Elfis know you're here." She took back the Jingle-Bell Rock and punched an extension on her phone. "He told us to expect an overture from Mr. Claus."

"Overture?" I asked. "I can barely hum a tune."

Elfis agreed to see me, probably out of curiosity; at least it got me through the door.

The chief elf's back office was bright and stiflingly hot. A large tropical mural covered the far wall. Wearing only a towel around his waist,

Elfis lay back on a chaise lounge under a pair of heat lamps that could have been used to keep food warm in a restaurant. Standing on either side, a pair of Egyptian mummies gently fanned him with palm fronds.

Elfis lifted his sunglasses and sat up to regard me. "Dan Chambeaux, Private Investigator ... that seems an odd choice for Santa, but I knew he'd send a representative before long. He has no option but to open negotiations. I suppose he wants to suggest some kind of merger and keep a token title for himself? Frankly I'd rather just buy his operations outright."

He waved for the mummies to back away. "Would you like some refreshment? I can get one of my boys to make you a mai tai or piña colada. Or, if you want to be more traditional, I have chestnuts roasting on an open fire."

Chestnuts weren't the only things roasting. "I'm surprised you keep it so hot in here," I said, tugging at my collar—and zombies don't perspire.

Elfis explained, "I want to change the paradigm of the holiday season. It's too cold, too snowy, too wintry. You really think shepherds prefer to watch their flocks in the snow? They'd rather be skiing. And if I want something frozen, I order a frozen margarita." He laughed, but it sounded more like heh-heh-heh than ho-ho-ho.

"Now then, let's talk about sending old Saint Nick into retirement. Here's my offer: I take over all his operations, but I let him keep his North Pole annex. He and Mrs. Claus get a nice pension, run their bed-and-breakfast, maybe do a few public appearances for old times' sake, but I license his likeness and the brand. I'm dreaming of a profitable Christmas."

"There's been a misunderstanding, Mr. Elfis. That's not why I'm here."

The elf slicked back his hair, adjusted his position on the chaise lounge. The mummies came forward again to fan him vigorously with the palm fronds. "Well, then, I'm all ears."

"Santa Claus hired me as a detective because something very valuable was stolen from him."

Elfis seemed completely uninterested. "Really? And what would old St. Nick find valuable? Can't he just wiggle his nose and make another of whatever it was?"

"It's more of a matter of administrative records gone missing," I said. "I'm investigating the theft."

Elfis snickered. "You must mean his list. Anal-retentive, if you ask me." He slid his sunglasses back down on his face, scratched his sideburns. "And you think I had something to do with it? Why in the world would I need a list like that? I explicitly *don't* discriminate. I give presents to all kids, without scoring them on social behavior. What gives Santa the right to make a subjective decision about who's Naughty and Nice? Judgmental jerk, if you ask me." He sniffed. "I plan to take discrimination out of Christmas gift-giving, make it equal for all. What would be my motive for stealing the list?"

I did have a theory. "You'd hamstring Santa's activities, make him look incompetent, while gaining brownie points for yourself."

"I don't have brownies, Mr. Chambeaux. I have elves. There's a difference."

"That doesn't address my theory."

"Look around you, Mr. Chambeaux. I'm sabotaging Santa's work by perfectly traditional means—undercutting prices, faster distribution, more transparency in my operations. I don't need a list for that."

One of the mummies served him a cool drink in a hollowed pineapple, complete with a colorful umbrella. "Thank ya very much." Elfis took a long refreshing sip. "Tell Santa if he wants to come to terms, I'm having a holiday special. His decision. Either way, it's time he faced some competition."

Elfis reached down beside his chaise lounge and pulled out a baseball-sized knot of thorny leaves, like a wadded tumbleweed studded with berries. "Here, Mr. Chambeaux—have a free sample. Part of my effort to put the kitsch back into Christmas."

He tossed it to me, and I caught it. "What's this?"

"Our new McMistletoe. Cheaper to manufacture, no preservatives needed, non-poisonous, non-habit-forming." He spoke at such a fast pace that my ears could barely keep up. "It's not intended to diagnose, prevent, treat, or cure any disease. These claims have not been evaluated by the FDA." He grinned. "But our McMistletoe is just as effective as real mistletoe. Try it out, you'll see."

I pocketed the mistletoe in my jacket's other pocket, because it didn't seem right to tuck it beside the jingle bell that Santa Claus had given me. "I'll try it," I said, though I doubted Sheyenne would be impressed.

5

I was already disturbed about the missing children McGoo was investigating, but I didn't see the actual pain until the Tannenbaums came into our offices.

Mrs. Tannenbaum buried her face in her husband's broad chest. "Our baby boy!"

Both of them were werewolves—the Monthly variety, so they passed for normal except on full-moon nights. They seemed like a nice couple with modest lives, middle-income jobs, probably had a home that was not extravagant but one they were proud of.

Robin hurried forward to comfort them. "Tell us what happened."

Mr. Tannenbaum pulled a wallet from his pocket and showed us a snapshot. "This is our son Buddy." The kid was of the full-furred persuasion, the type of werewolf who maintained a long muzzle, sharp fangs, moist black nose, and facial fur throughout the month.

"That's his school portrait," Mrs. Tannenbaum said with a sniff. "He was just about to graduate sixth grade." Sheyenne flitted in with a tissue for the grieving woman.

I studied the snapshot. Buddy Tannenbaum's black lips were curled in what I assumed was a smile, but might have been a snarl. What kid didn't make a goofy face when sitting for a school portrait? "Not much family resemblance. Adopted?"

Mrs. Tannenbaum snuffled loudly. "He came from an abused home, and we took him in. Poor Buddy! We wanted to show him all the love and affection he deserved. But one day after school, he didn't come home to do his chores."

Her husband continued, "He often gets preoccupied with friends—he has a strong social life. And what's a chore or two around the house? No need to bother the boy with them. I can do the vacuuming and take out the garbage while my wife cooks dinner."

"On the night he disappeared, I made a fleshloaf with tomato sauce and onions. Buddy's favorite!" Mrs. Tannenbaum wailed, which came out as a trailing howl. "We had to eat it ourselves. We had leftovers for two days."

"Two days? Your son vanished and you didn't report it for two days?" Robin shot me a look, and I saw that furrow of concern on her brow.

"We thought he might be staying at a friend's house," said Mr. Tannenbaum. "He sometimes does that. We try not to be overprotective. A boy needs his space and ... a wolf has to run free."

"Can you find him?" Mrs. Tannenbaum said. "We didn't want to go to the police because ... because we want to keep his record clean. He's going to go to college someday, and it's really a private matter."

"You can count on our discretion, Mr. and Mrs. Tannenbaum." I doubted Buddy's disappearance was unrelated to the other children who had vanished.

"Can you give us the names of his friends, or places where he liked to spend time?" Robin asked.

Mrs. Tannenbaum considered. "He likes to hang out at the comic-book shop. Just Dug Up Collectibles, I think it's called."

"I know the place," I said. "I've been there."

In a fit of nostalgia, I had gone in to browse some of the old comics I'd bought and guarded so lovingly when I was a kid. One day, while tidying up my room, my mom gave them all to a thrift shop, and they sold for a nickel apiece before I could run down there to save them. A few months ago, when I looked in Just Dug Up Collectibles and saw the outrageous prices those issues were now selling for, I left the shop in despair and never went back....

"Is there anything else I should know? Anything that might help?"

The Tannenbaums looked at each other, as if uncomfortable, hesitant, then both shook their heads.

Sheyenne whisked in and made several color photocopies of Buddy's photo before returning the snapshot to Mr. Tannenbaum, who lovingly tucked it back into his wallet. "I'll also submit this to the Talbot & Knowles blood bars," Sheyenne suggested. "They can include it with the other photos of missing children."

Mr. Tannenbaum looked uncomfortable. "I'd prefer to keep this out of the public eye."

"We already talked to the blood bars," snuffled Mrs. Tannenbaum. "They said they were overbooked for the next two months until ... until ..." She began sobbing.

Mr. Tannenbaum completed the sentence. "Until Christmas." He patted his wife on the shoulder. "Please find him soon, Mr. Chambeaux. We have very important Hanukkah traditions, and Winter Solstice, too."

She sniffled again. "The holidays just won't be the same without our dear Buddy. Please find him, Mr. Chambeaux. Such a dear, dear sweet boy."

6

"That kid is an unholy terror!" said Adric the comic-shop owner. He barely glanced at the picture of Buddy Tannenbaum. "He and his friends are monsters—and I don't mean that in a good way."

The wall behind the counter was plastered with autographed 8 × 10s of Adric posing with D-list celebrities. He was a gray-skinned, pot-bellied zombie, not nearly as well-preserved as the special variant-cover issues he kept bagged-and-boarded on high shelves. His complexion showed some signs of putrescence as well as fresh acne, which made him doubly unfortunate; although the undead suffer from numerous physical maladies, few are afflicted by zits.

Adric wore a powder-blue *Star Wars* T-shirt with R2-D2 and C-3PO on the front, and it was much too small for him. I deduced that he'd bought the shirt when he saw *Star Wars* first run in theaters; in the years since, his body had enlarged considerably, though he probably told himself that the shirt had shrunk.

Adric handed me back the photo. "That kid and his friends are always in here stealing things, vandalizing, harassing customers, and of course never buying anything. A bunch of deadbeats and undeadbeats."

I frowned. It seemed Buddy Tannenbaum was not the upstanding young werewolf his parents imagined him to be. "He's gone missing. When was the last time you saw him?"

He snorted. "I kicked out the whole wild bunch two weeks ago—caught them shoplifting one time too many."

I had another thought. "So, does that mean you keep a list of, say, who's naughty and who's nice?"

"Nah, this is a comic store. We get all kinds in here. That Buddy Tannenbaum and his friends, though—they'd definitely go in the Naughty column."

As he talked, Adric used a box-cutter to slice open a cardboard case of new arrivals like an eager coroner working on his favorite autopsy. He opened the flaps and began pulling out shrink-wrapped Christmas ornaments, clumsy-looking figurines of werewolves, vampires, scaly demons.

Frowning in disgust, he held up a crudely painted vampire with red marks smeared across his face. "Look at these! My customers want quality. The catalog said they're hand-painted, but this looks like it was finger-painted, or *claw*-painted." He shook his head. "Maybe even *flipper*-painted."

Adric dug into the box, pulled out a larger figure, a well-muscled werewolf in a cop uniform, holding an enormous Magnum pistol. "Does this look like Hairy Harry to you?" The rogue lycanthropic cop from the UQPD was something of a folk hero, even though he'd retired from the force.

"I wouldn't pay a premium for it," I said. I noticed the figures were labeled *Elfis Originals! Collect Them All!*

Adric kept pulling figurines out of the packaging, then rolled his eyes as he lifted out six genuine Elfis figurines, each wearing a white sequin jacket, brushed-back black hair and sideburns, and big sunglasses. "What? I only ordered one of these."

Next, he removed a larger box showing a scaled aquatic gill-man labeled "Special Limited Edition Creature! (Comes with free lagoon!)." With his stiff zombie fingers, Adric pried open the package, removed the scaly figurine along with a tiny black plastic basin. Apparently, the user was supposed to fill it with water.

"Special Edition? Ridiculous! Look at this: 'Limited to 1,000,000 Units.' How the hell does that make it *collectible*? I'll be lucky to sell six ... well, five, because I'll keep one for myself."

I tried to get back to the reason I'd come there. "Have you seen any of Buddy's buddies? Anyone I could talk to? His parents are distraught."

"No, and good riddance. Maybe they all ran off to join the vampire circus." Adric continued setting out the Elfis Originals holiday ornaments. "Mark my words, his parents will have a lot more silent nights this way. Just imagine what a handful that werewolf kid is gonna be when he hits his teenage years and hormones kick in."

He looked up at where two young zombies were pawing over back issues of *The Crypt-Keeper's Funniest Capers*. The zombie teens had their mouths open and they moaned in laughter at the panels.

Adric yelled, "Hey, you! Be careful with those—you get decaying flesh on any of the pages, you bought it."

The zombies looked up at him, moaned, then went back to the comics, noticeably exercising greater care.

I picked up a fine-print catalog listing of the Elfis Originals ornaments and collectibles and pocketed it for future reference. I thanked Adric and left.

7

When Santa Claus returned to our offices, he looked even more anxious than before. His face was sallow, almost jaundiced; his flowing white beard looked scraggly, with a thin brownish stain from where he'd been hitting the pipe a little too often. He had lost enough weight that his red jacket was gathered in folds around his waist with his wide black belt cinched tighter. I saw that he'd even punched a new hole.

"Usually when I visit, people set out milk and cookies for me." He sounded disappointed, beaten down. "I'll be glad to get back to running the bed-and-breakfast, but I have my duties first. I can't do my rounds without that list of Naughty and Nice." He slumped into a chair beside Sheyenne's desk and let out a sigh. "I tried to write a new one from memory, but my mind isn't what it used to be—too many bitter cold nights out in a reindeer-powered sleigh. I won't kid you, Christmas Eve is a hard night—a real nut-cracker. After it's over, I crawl into bed and sleep for a week."

"My accountant says the same thing about Tax Day," I told him.

Santa adjusted his floppy red cap. "I haven't heard you jingle my bell, and time is running out. It's beginning to look a lot like a screwed-up Christmas."

"I've been investigating," I reassured him. "Particularly your rival Elfis. He makes no secret of the fact that he wants to take you out, but he insists he doesn't need your list to do it. What can you tell me about him?"

Santa's face fell, as if his heart had shrunk three sizes that day. "That elf deserves a lump of coal in his stocking on Christmas morning. Unfair business practices, inferior materials—do you know that his silver bells are made of cheap aluminum?" He frowned again, let out another sigh. "I try not to think ill of people, but I'd like to take a thick candy cane and go thumpety-thump-thump on his head. He's ruining traditions by taking away the incentive for children to be Nice. Just look at the rude manners in chat rooms on the internet."

My heart went out to him. "I'm looking into his North Pole South operations, and Robin is studying his business practices. I haven't found any evidence that he arranged to steal your Naughty and Nice list, but I'll keep digging."

After rummaging around in the kitchen, Sheyenne flitted into the main room, carrying a plate with three stale chocolate-chip cookies and a glass of milk. "Look what I found for you, Santa!"

He brightened. "'Tis the season to be jolly—so I'll try my best." He pulled a paper ticket from the pocket of his red jacket. "Could you validate this for me? I've got my reindeer and sleigh parked on the roof."

"Of course," Sheyenne said, and stamped his parking ticket.

Santa took the rest of the cookies "for the reindeer" and slipped through the door just as Mr. and Mrs. Tannenbaum hurried in. They looked anxious, and my heart sank, wondering how I was going to tell them that their darling Buddy wasn't the sugarplum they believed him to be. If the young werewolf was getting into so much trouble, how could the parents not know? Were they willfully oblivious to the fact that their angel came straight from the dark side?

"We weren't entirely honest with you," Mrs. Tannenbaum said, then looked away shyly. "We have something else that might help."

Her husband said, "I convinced my wife that we needed to give you every detail if we want our Buddy back. Our son is more important than our shame and embarrassment."

"We thought you might be able to solve the case without it, and then we wouldn't have to admit ... admit—" Mrs. Tannenbaum's lower lip quivered. Her eyes flashed golden, and I could see a hint of werewolf coming to the fore.

"Buddy's given us difficulties before," Mr. Tannenbaum admitted. "He's an unruly kid. I think it comes from his full-fur blood. Trouble in school, trouble with vandalism. He's even run away from home a few times."

"But he always comes back," Mrs. Tannenbaum interjected. "He's a good boy at heart."

I asked, "Do you think there's any possibility that he's just run off again?"

Both Tannenbaums shook their heads. "Not so close to Christmas. He would have waited to get his toys first. He's a troublemaker, but he's a greedy troublemaker."

I didn't know if that was the best kind or the worst kind. "The information doesn't help a great deal at the moment, but I'll keep asking around."

The Tannenbaums looked at each other. "Oh, that's not what we meant to tell you, Mr. Chambeaux. We were reluctant to say anything about what we did because ... because, well, it's not exactly legal."

That's never a good phrase to include in a sentence. I braced myself.

"We had to do something because Buddy ran away so often. So, the last time we took him in to the vet ..." Mrs. Tannenbaum swallowed hard, then lowered her voice. "We had a tracking chip implanted in the base of his skull. Nothing anyone would notice, mind you, but ... just in case."

I perked up. "A tracking device? Then we can pinpoint his location right away!"

"Yes," said Mrs. Tannenbaum. "Do you think that might help you find him?"

I slapped my forehead, and it made a hollow popping sound from the bullet hole there. "The cases don't solve themselves," I said, "but I do need all the information."

"The tracking signal has a very limited range," Mr. Tannenbaum said. "Quite discreet, but not terribly useful. Still, if you get close enough …"

The Tannenbaums looked sheepish after they gave me the secret frequency and serial number of the tracker. "Just bring our little boy home, please? That would be the best present we ever had."

8

When we began our search, I decided to take police backup—McGoo—just so I could say I was being sensible. I didn't want to go overboard, though, because there was a better-than-even chance Buddy had just run away with his juvenile delinquent unnatural pals. Still, if Buddy's disappearance was connected with the other missing kids, McGoo would want to be along.

Then Robin insisted on joining us. With such a three-pronged approach, how could we not be prepared to solve any problem?

She had frowned in disapproval when she heard about the implanted tracker chip, claiming that it violated the civil rights of an underage werewolf. But McGoo had seen enough troublemakers in his work, and he was more inclined to try the "terrified straight" approach. Robin finally conceded that if the tracker meant we could reunite the full-time fuzzy kid with his once-a-month fuzzy parents, then all was for the best.

With the tracker's frequency and serial number, Robin downloaded a free but highly rated Track Werewolf app for her smartphone. She bundled up in a wool coat, and we all set off into the snowy night to find Buddy, leaving Sheyenne in charge of the office.

We wandered around the Quarter for a frustrating hour, following false signals (a garage-door opener and a universal TV remote control). I was beginning to think that we might not pick up the tracker's limited-range signal until after we had already found the subject in question. We were lost and frustrated; what had seemed to be an easy solution was turning out to be a headache and a waste of time.

Then Sheyenne called us and saved the day. She had found an update for the Track Werewolf app, which dealt with certain bugs and user issues and increased sensitivity. Once Robin installed the update, we found a strong signal. We were closer than we thought.

The signal led us straight to the tall smokestacks and gigantic toy warehouses behind Elfis's North Pole South complex.

Holding her phone, Robin took the lead, guiding us along the chain-link fence to the back service entrance of the gigantic manufacturing warehouses. The temperature was dropping, and fluffy snowflakes drifted down. Not a creature was stirring, not even the ones that usually stirred at that time of night.

Approaching the back guard gate, we found two burly golems wearing security guard uniforms. Their clay bodies were stiff and hardening in the cold, but one perked up. "Do you hear what I hear?"

The other said, "Do you see what I see?"

Now alert, the golems prepared to block our way, both of them focusing on McGoo's uniform, the dark blue police shirt, trousers, and cap. "That looks good on you," said one of the golems.

"We both wanted to be cops, but couldn't pass the tests," the other explained.

I knew why, but I didn't embarrass them by pointing out the reason.

McGoo said, "We're searching for a missing child, and we have reason to believe he's inside one of the warehouses." He held out a copy of Buddy's picture.

"Kids just can't stay away from toys," said the first golem.

Robin held up her smartphone, showing the app. "And we have electronic evidence he's in there."

The golems were again intrigued. "Is that phone one of the new models?"

The other said, "Does it have Angry Vultures on it? Or Curses with Friends?"

I knew if the golems started playing games on Robin's phone we would never get past the gate. "We need to have a look, bring that boy back to his parents."

The first golem had a stony expression on his clay face. "Sorry. We can't let you inside. Elfis is very strict."

The other golem looked intimidated. "He sees you when you're sleeping, he knows when you're awake, he knows when you've been bad or good." In tandem, they shook their smooth clay heads and pointed upward. "Security cameras."

Time for Plan B. I removed a folded sheet of paper from the inside pocket of my jacket and showed it to the two golems. "We have a duly authorized search warrant to enter the premises, signed by Judge Hawkins herself. This grants us unfettered access to all parts of the North Pole South warehouses so we can find and rescue the young man."

The first golem guard took the sheet of paper and studied it intently, while Robin shot me a questioning glance. She craned her neck to see what the guards were looking at. McGoo could barely keep the smile off his face.

The other golem took the sheet from his partner; they both had frowns on their clay faces. "All right then. We're security guards, sworn to uphold the law." They opened the chain-link gate for us. "Go on inside. I hope you find what you're looking for."

Robin was perplexed, but she glanced down at the blinking light on her Track Werewolf app. Buddy was definitely close, inside the big factory building ahead of us. With his best I'm-an-authority-figure gait, McGoo marched away from the guard golems. Robin hurried alongside me. When we were out of earshot, she asked, "What was that all about? When did you get a search warrant?"

"It wasn't a search warrant," I said. "It's the fine-print listing of Elfis Originals I took from Just Dug Up Collectibles."

McGoo worked at the warehouse door; it was unlocked. "Golems can't read," he said. "At least most of them can't. That's why they couldn't pass their UQ Police Department exams. Good work, Shamble."

Robin was astonished. "Then we got in here under false pretenses, and I have real ethical problems with that. We're trespassing."

"We're rescuing a missing child," I said. My boundaries were a little more blurred than Robin's, but I did manage to get things done.

Robin was about to continue her objections when McGoo opened the loading dock door. The dark, noisy factory hangar was worse than the worst New Year's Day hangover. It was a true holiday of horrors.

9

I doubted children opening their gifts on the morning of Christmas Eve Eve (if Elfis and his minions delivered on time, as promised) would want to know where their presents really came from.

We were seeing the ugly side of holiday cheer: appalling labor conditions, thick smoke, clanging hammers, grinding gears, and jets of steam venting from pressure valves. Foul water trickled out of rusty pipes overhead. A labyrinth of rattling conveyor belts rolled toys along to packaging lines. Sparks flew and blazing fires roared out of open furnaces fed with black coal that poured from supply hoppers in the ceiling. A separate set of conveyors dumped defective metal toys into a smoldering furnace. It was as if the Island of Misfit Toys had an active volcano.

Robin looked around in horror, shocked by what she saw. McGoo's face was stormy with anger.

Most appalling of all, though, were the kids shackled to the assembly line, hunched over the conveyor belts, red-eyed, dirt-smeared, waifish. They toiled at assembling dolls, painting action figures, stuffing collectibles into boxes. There were werewolves, zombies, ghouls, even human children, all looking dejected and haggard.

As I scanned the faces, I recognized many of the kids featured on the Have You Seen Me? pictures from the Talbot & Knowles blood bars. I saw one gray-furred werewolf boy, mangy and yet somehow still cute, chained to a station where he was applying black button eyes onto Raggedy Ann dolls. Either he was confused by the instructions, or the dolls catered to an entirely different type of unnatural, because he sewed three eyes on each doll.

"That's Buddy Tannenbaum!" I said.

The boy heard me even over the factory din. He turned, his tongue lolling out of his mouth, and his eyes lit up upon seeing us. He dropped the doll onto the dirty factory floor and leaped toward us, but was brought up short by silver shackles that bound his wrist and ankle.

"I'll be good! I promise!" he yelped. "I won't be naughty anymore. I don't want to be on the list!"

Robin was ahead of us, grim and determined. "We'll get you out of here, Buddy. Your parents hired us to find you."

"My mom and dad? But Elfis said they didn't love me anymore."

"Of course they love you," Robin said. "Parents love even naughty kids."

A steam whistle blew. More coal dumped out of the feeding hoppers, and the furnace burned brighter.

Then the elves came—evil elves, and ugly enough that they might have been disowned by even the G-side of the family. They carried cattle prods painted like cheery candy canes; others brandished icicle spears that dripped in the intense heat of the factory floor.

McGoo and I drew our guns and stood next to Robin. The ten elves closing in didn't look afraid of us at all. Too late, I realized that they were just a distraction.

Two other hench-elves stood up from behind the conveyor belt and hurled snowballs at us—icy snowballs with rocks in the middle. Cheater snowballs. (I did say they were evil elves.) Their aim was supernaturally true, and with one hail of hard snowballs, they knocked the guns out of our hands.

Then the hench-elves closed in, wielding icicle spears and candy-cane cattle prods. They overpowered us, shoved us to the factory floor, and used tough strands of satin ribbon to bind our wrists. We were going to have a black-and-blue Christmas. An evil elf even slapped a coordinating stick-on bow on each of us before they herded us toward the back of the factory.

"Elfis is going to want to see you," said one of the guards.

"Oh, by gosh, by golly, that was on my Christmas wish list," I said, which earned me a jab from one of the cattle prods. Since I'm a zombie, it takes a lot to shock me, but the experience was still unpleasant. I was more worried about McGoo and Robin, who could indeed be permanently damaged.

Elfis was at a raised supervisor's station near the warmth of the big furnace, sitting on a high director's chair with a small worktable beside him. Black dust from the coal hoppers left a gritty film on everything, but somehow it didn't affect his white sequined jacket or his blue suede shoes. He was perusing a rolled parchment filled with names—countless names, sorted into two columns, one marked N and the other one marked N. He muttered to himself as he used a large goose quill pen to check off names.

"Naughty ... yes, got that one. Naughty ... yes. Naughty ... we have a very high success rate." Then he sneered at a line, crossed it out vigorously with the nib of his quill pen. "Somebody slipped up—this kid's in the Nice column! People tend to notice when *nice* kids go missing." A supervisor hench-elf scurried off to rectify the error.

Elfis picked up a bullhorn and began shouting toward the factory floor. "Listen up, kiddies! I have plenty more applicants to choose from, so if you want to be promoted in my criminal organization, you've got to produce, produce, *produce!* Only the best can survive this boot camp—also known as the Holiday Season! If you work hard, you'll be real henchmen by Easter." Elfis then started to laugh. "We're going to put that damned bunny out of business, too!"

He slid his sunglasses up on the bridge of his narrow nose as his fiendish hench-elves pushed us forward. He seemed surprised to see us. "Mr. Chambeaux and friends—have you come to negotiate on Santa's behalf again? Well, it's too late. I've already got the holidays sewn up in a body bag, and now you'll never stop me."

When all else fails, when things look grimmest, I like to state the obvious. It puts villains off guard and usually gets them talking—too much. "You said you didn't have Santa's list of Naughty and Nice. That was dishonest."

He held up a long finger. "No, that was *misleading*. I said I didn't steal the list in order to earn brownie points or to make Santa look incompetent. I stole it strictly for my own purposes." Elfis waved the parchment, showing us the long list of names. "It's a recruitment tool, like a screening folder for job applicants. Santa already identified the *naughty* children for me, the ones suitable to become part of my operation."

"But you put them to work as slave labor," Robin said.

Elfis shrugged. "Well, they are naughty. Even criminals need to know the consequences of their actions. You do the crime, you pay the time. Community service for *my* community."

I struggled against the satin ribbons binding my wrists. It reminded me of my childhood, trying to snap the ribbons so I could open my presents. Now, as then, the ribbon had supernatural strength.

Elfis leaned forward, opening both of his hands to warm them at the nearby furnace. The conveyor belt continued to clatter, dumping defective toys into it, plastic ones as well as metal. "It's so nice to be warm for a change. And you three will be all toasty, too. I'm afraid I can't allow my plans to be foiled—or tinseled. Into the furnace with them!"

The hench-elves swept forward like a blizzard of evil. Even though I'm a zombie, I had no desire to be cremated. And speaking for my two human friends, I knew that neither Robin nor McGoo wanted to tour the interior of the furnace either. I had to get us out of there.

Zombies, for all of our fragile bodies and flesh that's prone to decay, have very strong teeth. Some zombies use them for ripping into flesh and bone; now I discovered that my teeth were excellent at cutting Christmas ribbon. I tore into my colorful satin bindings, snapped the ribbon—and I was free.

But I couldn't fight all those armed hench-elves. Thinking of only one thing that might save us, I jammed my hand into my jacket pocket and grabbed the loop attached to the emergency jingle bell.

It wasn't much of a jing-jing-jingle—but it was enough to summon Old Kris Kringle.

The flames in the furnace brightened, then made a coughing sound. Black smoke swirled out, and with a whoosh of hot air Santa Claus slipped down the smokestack and made his dramatic entrance. The conveyor belt came to a screeching halt as the jolly guy in the magic red suit (which also proved to be non-flammable) emerged from the furnace like something out of *The Lord of the Rings*. He planted his gloved hands on his hips and bellowed, "Ho-ho-ho! Who's been a naughty boy?"

Elfis nearly jumped out of his skin and scrambled down from the director's chair so rapidly that his sunglasses clattered on the floor. With the empty cloth sack over his shoulder, Santa stalked forward like an avenging angel—and not the type that goes on top of a Christmas tree. He spotted his lengthy rolled-up list on the worktable and seized it, holding it up like a baton. "You have gone too far, Elfis. And now you'd better cry, because Santa Claus is coming to get you."

The hench-elves were panicked. They dropped their candy-cane cattle prods and icicle spears and cowered. Their teeth chattered as if they had gone caroling naked on a cold winter's night and no one was offering wassail, or even hot cocoa.

Elfis tried to run, but Santa quickly caught up with him. I couldn't believe how fast the old bearded guy could move, but he had to have a secret power if he could hit millions of households around the world in a single night.

McGoo held up his bound wrists for me to bite the ribbons. Now *that* was showing a measure of trust! "Good plan, Shamble."

"I call it Santa ex-Machina." I picked bright green satin out of my teeth, then turned to free Robin as well.

Santa had cornered Elfis by the big coal hoppers, and the evil elf had no place to go. Santa didn't need any help, but I was part of this, too— and I had a bone to pick with anybody who wanted to throw me and my friends into a furnace.

Next to me, one of the cowering hench-elves still had a sack filled with the icy rock-filled snowballs. I grabbed one and hurled it with perfect aim, proving that not all zombies are disoriented and uncoordinated. My snowball shot struck the release latch on the coal hopper just above Elfis's head. The trap dropped open, and Elfis looked up just in time to see a black avalanche dump down on him. He was buried under lumps of coal.

Robin, McGoo, and I rushed over to Santa, who gazed with satisfaction at the mound in front of him. "Coal is what Elfis deserved … although I'd hoped he would turn his life around if given the chance. Such a disappointment."

"You knew Elfis beforehand?" I asked.

Santa nodded. "He was one of my toy laborers, assigned to my workshop for community service, but he escaped, broke the rules of his North Pole parole. I was going to report him, but not until after the holiday season was over. It's a busy time of the year, you know."

We heard a groan, then a stirring. We moved the coal blocks away to reveal an Elfis now entirely covered in black dust. He plucked in dismay at his ruined jacket. "I guess I won't be having a *white* Christmas."

Santa unslung the sack from his shoulder, tugged it open, and strode forward. "Here comes Santa Claus."

Elvis scrambled backward when he saw the yawning sack. "No, Santa! Please! No!"

"Naughty children get what they deserve." Santa snatched Elfis, stuffed him into the sack, and cinched the opening shut. The captive kept squirming, but could not get out. Santa tucked his rolled up Naughty and Nice list under one arm. "Thank you all. I'll start checking these names, see who deserves to be sentenced to the North Pole for a few years."

"*Sentenced* to the North Pole?" Robin said.

"Oh-ho-ho, this list doesn't just show me who gets presents and who doesn't. The naughtiest of the naughty have to help me spread holiday cheer. Parents write me, too, you know. 'Dear Santa, please help me with my child who keeps acting out.' We have a community-service program up at the Pole, where naughty children can learn good behavior by doing good works." He had a twinkle in his eye. "There's a long waiting list, but our success rate is remarkable."

"Except for Elfis," I said.

"Some nuts are harder to crack than others, but a few days of shoveling out the reindeer stables usually makes them a little more cooperative."

Moving with supernaturally swift footsteps, Santa stalked around the factory floor, grabbing the cowering hench-elves one by one and stuffing them into his sack, which was obviously much larger inside than it was on the outside. It needed to be. How else could it hold a world's worth of toys?

With the bulging, squirming load over his shoulder, he turned to Robin, McGoo, and me. "I'll let you free the children." He turned to the shackled waifs on the now-still production lines. "Ho-ho-ho! Have you all learned to be nice instead of naughty?"

A chorus of the enslaved kids affirmed that they had indeed learned their lessons. Some, including Buddy, even volunteered to do community-service work up at the North Pole—after they recovered back home with their loving families.

Santa went to the coal furnace, shifted his heavy sack. "I won't forget you on Christmas morning, Mr. Chambeaux. Or you either, Ms. Deyer, or Officer McGoohan. And now, Merry Christmas to all, and to all a good"—he pushed down his black glove so he could double-check the time on his wristwatch—"a good night." He tossed the squirming bag ahead of him into the mouth of the furnace, touched the side of his nose, and vanished up the smokestack.

"Elfis has left the building," I said. "But the kids are still here."

The three of us spent the better part of an hour freeing the natural and unnatural children from their shackles. When Robin unlocked his chains, Buddy Tannenbaum threw himself into her arms. "Thank you, thank you! Can you take me back to my Mom and Dad now?"

"You'll be home for Christmas," I promised.

For a lot of families, it would be a happy holiday season, except perhaps for those who had ordered their gifts from Elfis Industries and were expecting delivery by Christmas Eve Eve....

While McGoo called for backup to shut down the factory and secure the crime scene, Robin took down names and developed a plan to reunite the kids with their parents. I called the Tannenbaums directly, and Buddy's parents rushed right down. It was a wonderful reunion, with the werewolf kid nuzzling his parents and promising he would be good.

10

It was Christmas morning in the Chambeaux & Deyer offices—and we found surprise gifts waiting for us, brightly wrapped in colorful paper with holly leaves and berries, wreaths, and little snowmen. Since we didn't have a chimney, Santa could only have delivered the presents by breaking-and-entering, but I wasn't going to press charges.

"Looks like Santa was true to his promise," I said.

Grinning, Sheyenne brought the gifts into the conference room. "If you can't trust Santa to keep a promise, who can you trust?"

I hadn't put anything on my wish list, but Santa Claus was supposed to know exactly what a person wanted or needed. I had to admit I was curious.

"You first, Robin." I nudged the thin, rectangular box with her name on it. As a lawyer, Robin tried to remain cool and businesslike, but I could see the sparkle in her brown eyes as she tugged the ribbon aside, and politely worked at the tape. When she couldn't get it unwrapped, she used a letter opener to slash the paper with all the finesse of a well-practiced serial killer.

Inside was a single yellow legal pad and a sharpened No. 2 pencil. Her excitement dimmed, though she remained smiling. "I can certainly use these. And not every lawyer gets to use a pencil and legal pad from Santa himself."

"There's a note," I pointed out.

Robin pulled a slip of holly-fringed stationery from behind the second yellow sheet, skimmed the hand-written note, then read aloud as her smile grew. "'I don't normally give magical gifts—I don't want to establish a present precedent, but I am so grateful for your efforts. After checking my list and the footnotes I made throughout the year, Robin, I know that your work delights you more than anything else. This special legal pad will never run out of paper, and the enchanted pencil will take notes for you so you can have your hands and mind free to concentrate on your client. Ho-ho-ho, best, S.C.'"

Robin's smile was wide. "I can't wait to try it out!"

Excited, Sheyenne picked up the box with her name on it. She used her poltergeist abilities to undo the bow, pull the ribbon aside, and then, giggling, ripped the wrapping paper to shreds. She opened the box to find an envelope inside—with both our names written on it.

"It's something the two of us can use, Beaux!" With luminous fingers, she opened the flap of the envelope to find an embossed, official-looking certificate inside. "Oh! An all-expense-paid romantic weekend for us at the cozy North Pole Winter Wonderland Bed and Breakfast! Off-season only, it says."

"Now that has definite possibilities," I said, imagining a wonderful time away with my girlfriend. We would have to be creative to overcome the supernatural difficulties that precluded us from touching, but I was up to the challenge.

"Open yours, Dan." Robin handed me the very small box with my name on it.

Judging by the size, I thought it might be a new pair of cufflinks or a tie clip, but who was I to doubt Santa's wisdom or imagination? Zombie fingers are not the most adept at unwrapping small gift boxes, and Santa's elves had used way too much tape, but I managed.

I opened a hinged, velvet-covered box to reveal a small plastic cylinder labeled "Magic Lip Gloss. Use Sparingly." I wasn't disappointed so much as confused, not sure what Santa had been thinking. "Lip gloss?"

Sheyenne made a delighted sound and snatched the tube out of the box. "I think it's for me, Beaux—and that means it's for you." She popped off the cap, extended the lip gloss, and applied it to her widening smile. "A special film for my ghostly lips that might just allow a kiss...."

She leaned closer, but I told her to wait. "Just a minute, let's do this right." I slipped a hand into my jacket pocket and withdrew the wadded and prickly tumbleweed ball of the McMistletoe artificial substitute that Elfis had been trying to bring to market. I raised it up over my head. "This is supposed to be as good as mistletoe."

Robin was skeptical. "With all the quality that we've come to expect from Elfis Industries?"

Sheyenne's lips glistened invitingly from the magic lip gloss. Under the McMistletoe, she came very close, and her ectoplasmic lips brushed against mine. Yes, I definitely felt a warm tingle.

"I think it works just fine," she said.

LOCKED ROOM

1

When a harpy tells you to do something, there's no room for discussion.

As a zombie private detective, as well as a regular customer at the Ghoul's Diner, I had plenty of experience with Esther the harpy waitress. She had been a client of mine, seeking to get rid of a bad luck charm that a customer had left her as a tip for the awful service Esther usually provided (if "service" is a word that even applies in that situation.)

Esther had a hawkish face, a raptorlike demeanor, and a vulturelike personality. Her curled iridescent feathers looked like straight razors that had been mangled in a mail-sorting machine. With her glittering eyes, she could shoot a sharp glare at anyone who looked at her the wrong way, and Esther considered almost any way "the wrong way." Her mood swings were best measured on the Richter scale.

Nevertheless, she was a client of Chambeaux & Deyer Investigations, and a paying one. In the Unnatural Quarter, where monsters tried to make quiet, normal lives for themselves, I'd had far worse cases before.

Late this afternoon, Esther had called our offices demanding—because Esther was incapable of making a mere request—that my ghost girlfriend Sheyenne and I meet her out in the Greenlawn Cemetery for the grand opening of a very special new crypt.

"It's imperative that you're both there," Esther said in a voice that made fingernails on chalkboards sound like sweet music.

As our office administrator, Sheyenne already knew about the case. "I'm surprised you want me along, too. Dan is our private investigator. I often help out on cases, but—"

The harpy cut her off. "Stop arguing with me! I need a zombie and a ghost. Be there."

We'd had a quiet day wrapping up cases and waiting for new ones to walk through the door. Robin Deyer, my human lawyer partner, had left town to visit her parents for their anniversary celebration, so it was only Sheyenne and me in the offices. I wouldn't normally leave the place unattended, but I had my phone and I didn't expect this would take long.

Besides, who was going to tell Esther she couldn't have what she wanted?

The Greenlawn Cemetery was a nice place, as far as cemeteries went, with well-tended lots, mid-range tombstones, and used crypts for rent or for sale. The flowers were replenished regularly, and a park and recreation area for new tenants had been added as part of an urban beautification project. After being killed during one of my cases as a human detective, I had been buried here, and then I clawed my way back out of the earth, cleaned myself up, put on a change of clothes, and got back to work. Yes, this place held fond memories....

As Sheyenne and I arrived at the cemetery, I wore my usual sport jacket with its stitched-up bullet holes and my traditional fedora, that didn't quite go low enough to cover the exit wound in the center of my forehead. I looked fairly decent—maybe even handsome enough to accompany my vivacious blonde, blue-eyed ghost girlfriend. Sheyenne drifted along beside me through the lanes of tombstones, ectoplasmic and glowing, too beautiful to touch (which was a good thing: since she was a ghost, I couldn't touch her anyway).

We found the harpy standing next to the impressive new crypt, which looked like a private fortress with thick granite walls and massive columns that conveyed an ornate but unwelcoming appearance. I wasn't surprised to see a broad-shouldered and bare-chested minotaur standing next to Esther. Yes, the classical architect would want to be there for the grand opening of his special new tomb.

With a loud snort, Percy Minotaur, Sr. adjusted the golden ring through his blocky nose. "Thank you both for coming."

The door to the crypt was wide open to show an austere, cold interior, dimly lit by high narrow windows.

"Where is everyone else for the celebration?" Sheyenne asked.

"We only need you two," Esther snapped, and gestured with a feathered arm. The harpy had an odd and unsettling feminine appearance, a sexiness that at first attracted men, then made them ill as they realized exactly *what* they'd been attracted to. "You're here to test Elspeth's tomb. There's no time to waste."

"How is your sister's condition?" I asked. "Any change?"

"No, still terminal." Esther sounded disappointed. "And still no closer to it."

The minotaur invited us through the open door of the tomb. "Allow me to show you the finer points of the new construction. It is magnificent, as usual."

Sheyenne and I entered the tomb, though there wasn't much to see— an open empty vault with stone walls, stone floor, stone ceiling. The narrow slit windows at the top of the wall were thickly barricaded. The harpy's hard face curled in a smile as she saw me looking at them. "Those are so my undead sister can look out like a sad kid on a rainy day ... if she ever dies, that is."

The tomb walls glistened as if coated with some kind of thick varnish ... or maybe saliva. "A special anti-ectoplasmic preventive coating," said the minotaur architect. "One of the special upgrades Esther requested."

In the center sat a raised slab on which the resident's body would lie in repose. "Is this where you'll place your sister's coffin?" I asked Esther.

"Coffin? Hell, no! Why buy a fancy coffin? Who's going to see her in here anyway? She can just lie on the slab."

"I take it that's why you didn't waste money on interior decorating, either?" Sheyenne asked.

"Why would I waste money like that on Elspeth? This damned crypt is already costing enough arms and legs to make a body-repair shop happy! And it's all his fault." She snorted at Percy, who snorted right back.

"Great work doesn't come cheap," said the minotaur. "This crypt is my finest creation so far. It is beyond a masterpiece, because I've already produced a masterpiece, and that's just a beginning. Elspeth's tomb will be—"

Esther cut him off, "Will be *serviceable*, I hope."

"It looks secure," I said. "Impressive."

"We'll see about that," said Esther.

She and the minotaur slipped back outside the crypt, and before Sheyenne and I could ask any questions, the minotaur flexed his muscles and swung shut the massive door.

The harpy had just enough time to say, in her shrieking voice (which could cut through stone blocks), "I sincerely hope you never get out. Ever!"

After the slab sealed, we heard the loud clang of the massive bolt slamming into place.

2

When the harpy had first contacted us about her sister's ailment, I couldn't be sure if she was angling for sympathy or something else. She preened herself in front of Sheyenne's desk. "Elspeth is dying, and she's been doing so for a very long time—an unconscionably long time!"

"Oh dear," Sheyenne said. "I'm sorry to hear that."

"Don't be sorry for her—be sorry for me! I've had to put up with all this."

Esther's sister suffered from a debilitating mange—a lingering illness that made her linger ... and linger ... and linger, like something out of a heart-wrenching movie of the week, but not at all poignant. Esther had been tending her, reluctantly, for some time.

"Elspeth was obnoxious even on her good days—I got all the charm in the family." Esther clacked her teeth together and curled her fingers so that metallic black talons extended from the tips. The harpy family must not have gotten a large share of charm to start with.

"Eslepth won't let anyone see her because the mange makes her revolting. I told her no one would notice, because she was revolting before she caught the disease—but she doesn't believe me."

"You certainly have a bedside manner," Sheyenne said.

Esther fluttered her feathers. "I always wanted to be a doctor, except that I can't stand sick people. They're so needy."

I wished Robin were here, because she was always good at handling difficult clients. "Is the mange contagious?" I asked.

"Always thinking of yourself, Mr. Chambeaux!" Esther snapped. "You have nothing to worry about—zombies can't catch it."

"Actually, I was thinking about you," I said.

Esther flapped her arms, extended her plumage, inspected the small pinfeathers in her underarms. "What, do you see any symptoms? I douse Elspeth with bleach every day, as therapy—but if she's infected me, I'll pluck her naked, then tar and feather her all over again!"

I tried to calm her. "Just asking a question. I didn't notice anything in particular."

Sheyenne turned on the charm, which I knew hid her acid annoyance. "And how can we help you at Chambeaux and Deyer Investigations, ma'am?"

"I'm having a new tomb constructed for my sister, a special monument with many added features, designed to my exact specifications. I've got to make sure it's done on time—and properly. There's no room for error."

She withdrew blueprints and spread them on Sheyenne's desk, unceremoniously knocking aside the other papers and folders for our pending cases. As far as Esther was concerned, no other pending cases were as important.

"I've hired the greatest architect to build thick walls, reinforced windows, and an unbreakable door, with a few external decorative flourishes that will make the tomb fit in with the other ones in the cemetery. They have covenants for landscaping and exterior design."

Looking at the blueprints, I was impressed. This massive structure would certainly stand out among the ostentatious crypts and memorial markers at Greenlawn Cemetery. I understood what she was thinking. "It'll be like the great pyramids of Egypt."

Esther snorted. "No—more like Alcatraz. Once I'm finally rid of my sister, I'll seal her up inside there. If she stays dead, then fine—but a lot of people don't stay dead anymore."

Since I had come back as a zombie and Sheyenne came back as a ghost, I said, "Yes, we're well aware of that."

The harpy strutted about our offices. "Elspeth is just too mean to stay dead. Once she goes, I don't want to deal with her anymore. If and when my sister comes back, whether as a zombie or a ghost, I want her sealed up where she can't bother anyone again. *Ever.* So, I have to be sure that tomb is undead proof." Her eyes glittered at me and Sheyenne. "That's where you two come in."

3

A private investigation agency has to take cases of all kinds, but some are more unpleasant than others.

We were sealed inside Elspeth's fortress-like crypt, but I had no intention of staying there. As Sheyenne drifted in front of me, her faint glow illuminated the austere vault. Her blue eyes sparkled, and so did her smile. "It's not so bad, Beaux—we're getting paid to be alone together in a very private place."

"I'd rather take you to a coffin-and-breakfast of our choosing." I walked to the solid stone door, pressing my hands against it, tentatively using my strength. I knew it wouldn't be easy to break out of the tomb, but I had to start somewhere. I pressed hard, felt no movement—the old immovable object and irresistible zombie conundrum. I felt around the crack with numb fingers, but couldn't find any latch or self-release button on the door.

Partly due to Robin's recent legal efforts, laws had been passed requiring all crypts to have emergency-release locks, since you never could tell when someone might wake up and need to get out. But Percy the minotaur had not built this tomb to code.

I pounded on the door, hard, but that did no good. My cold flesh didn't even make a satisfying thump. I wondered if Esther and Percy were still waiting out there, amused, trying to see how quickly we could escape from this trap.

"If you're that anxious, I'll just slip through the wall, undo the latch, and open the door," Sheyenne said. "It's handy to have a ghost around."

She drifted in front of me, gave me an air kiss. As a traditional ghost, she could flit through any solid object, and her poltergeist abilities allowed her to manipulate inanimate objects.

She gathered speed as she headed toward the stone wall. Normally she would've melted right through without a sound; instead, I heard an alarming wet *smack*, and Sheyenne's beautiful form flattened out as she pushed and pushed against the stones. It was a very strange sight. I heard a thrumming as she continued to push, growing more and more flustered. Her form was distorted into a strange blob-like female outline, plastered against the impenetrable wall. Finally she withdrew, recomposed herself, and hovered in front of me, shaken.

"That's not what I expected," I said.

Sheyenne ran her ghostly fingers on the surface. The glistening coating sparkled faintly with an afterwash of her spectral impact, and I remembered the protective film that the minotaur architect had applied throughout the interior of the tomb.

She sighed. "Maybe this case is going to be more difficult than we thought."

If Esther's sister came back from the dead, she would return as a zombie or a ghost; therefore, Esther had instructed the architect to design a tomb that was proof against either one. A ghost harpy sounded even more unpleasant than an everyday harpy. And a *zombie harpy* ... well, I didn't even want to go there.

Zombies were strong and persistent, but it wouldn't be hard to build thick enough barricades to contain a shambler, even a well-preserved one like me. A ghost was more difficult to contain permanently, but this new anti-ectoplasmic film seemed quite durable and effective.

"Esther must really be worried about her sister harassing her from beyond the grave," I said.

With increasing persistence, then frustration, Sheyenne flung herself against different walls of the crypt, then the ceiling, even the floor, but she couldn't get through. She drifted up to the narrow windows, hoping to find some chink there, but the reinforced panes remained sturdy. The anti-ecto coating was everywhere.

When hiring us to break out of this unbreakable crypt, we hadn't established any kind of time limit. That was my fault for not thinking through the parameters. Robin always chastised me for entering into agreements without my lawyer partner vetting them first. Live and learn ... or, live, die, come back from the dead, and still miss the point.

I yanked on the raised stone coffin slab, and Sheyenne stood on the other side using her poltergeist powers, hoping we could uproot it, topple it, find a loose floor tile or something. No good. The slab and its base remained as sturdy as a redwood tree.

I removed my .38 from its holster, and Sheyenne looked at me, puzzled. If I fired the pistol, any bullets would just ricochet around the walls, but I had something else in mind.

I use the butt of the weapon to hammer the saliva-like varnish, pounding and pounding, but the film remained smooth, unscratched. "I was hoping to make a dent, chip away enough so that you could work your way through a chink in the armor."

She pressed her ghostly hand where I had been hammering, but couldn't find the tiniest nick. That stuff was tough!

Thinking the windows might be more vulnerable, I pressed up against the wall, reached as high as I could, and grasped the narrow sill. Pulling myself up, I raised my other hand and pounded on the glass with the .38. Again, the glass was armored, and the anti-ecto coating too thick. I didn't make a dent.

Back on the floor again, I tried to think the problem through. The cases don't solve themselves, but even with a hole in my head I can usually figure out a puzzle.

"Ah, of course!" I reached into the pocket of my sport jacket, removing my phone. "I'll just call somebody to get us out of here."

"That's probably cheating," Sheyenne said.

"The case agreement didn't preclude it."

Robin was far away and wouldn't be back in the Unnatural Quarter for days, but I had plenty of other friends in the Quarter I could call—particularly, Officer Toby McGoohan from the UQPD, my best human friend. I just needed to get him on the phone, and we'd be all done here tonight.

The phone said No Service. Of course. Esther and Percy would've thought of that and put in shielding. These days, almost everyone elected to be buried with a phone handy.

I sat down on the stone slab. "I hate to admit it, Spooky, but I think we're stuck."

4

Early in the case, Esther insisted that we meet her architect, as if we were challengers in a grudge match.

Percy Minotaur, Sr. was well respected in his field, not just in tomb design, but he had also studied with a man who claimed to be Houdini's ghost, working on a contract job for the Unnatural Quarter's prison system. Houdini's ghost and Percy developed specialized unbreakable prisons and holding cells for various unnaturals, demons, specters, and the like. Eventually Houdini's ghost was exposed as a fraud, that he was actually *Jim* Houdini, no relation whatsoever to the legendary magician. Jim Houdini was arrested, but before he could be brought up on charges, he had miraculously escaped and still remained at large.

Percy the minotaur's work, however, was quite remarkable. He had accepted Esther's commission to build an inescapable, unbreakable tomb for her sister, just in case. He seemed to relish the challenge.

Upon first meeting the bare-chested Percy, I asked him why he insisted on remaining shirtless all the time. Sure, he had a broad chest and decent biceps, but he wasn't going to win any Mr. Unnatural America contests, especially with a paunch showing over what should have been washboard abs.

The minotaur reached up to touch his big blocky head and his wide set of curved bullhorns. "Because of these. I can't ever pull a shirt over my head."

That made perfect sense, I supposed.

"How about something that buttons down the front?" Sheyenne suggested. "Maybe a nice Hawaiian shirt?"

Percy seemed embarrassed. "I never thought of that."

Esther stood in the architectural offices, impatient. "On with it. Just show them your portfolio." The minotaur displayed and explained photos of other buildings he had done, the façade of the Metropolitan Museum, several impressive tombs.

"My aim is to become the most respected, most widely known minotaur architect in the entire Quarter. I'm very bullish on my career."

He had spent a summer sabbatical at Notre Dame, considering how to create a fusion of Gothic cathedral architecture with typical Unnatural Quarter buildings.

"A developer wanted me to design tract homes in a new subdivision, but I would never stoop that low. A gated community is the minimum I would consider." With a fist he pounded his unspectacular chest. "My great works will endure the test of time. They'll last for millennia, like the pyramids."

"As long as they can endure a pissed-off undead harpy," Esther said. "That's all I care about. Better hurry up and finish the building."

"How long do you think your sister has left?" Sheyenne asked.

Esther made a disgusted sound. "She's been at death's doorway for years and years, but she just stands there on the welcome mat. How I hate it when she lingers. I wish she'd get on with her death, so I can get on with my life." She pointed a talon at me. "Your case, Mr. Chambeaux, is to test out the new crypt. My architect is confident, but I don't believe anyone. I wasn't hatched yesterday."

"What exactly do you want us to do?"

"You'll be locked inside. If you can escape, then you get paid. If you stay trapped in there until Elspeth dies—and that could be years and years—then the minotaur gets paid."

5

I had heard grim stories of trapped undead who were left to tolerate an eternity of unending boredom: vampires given the Jimmy Hoffa treatment, sealed in a coffin wrapped with silver chains and then sunk at the bottom of a deep cold lake, where the poor bloodsucker had to lie there without even a book to read or a digest of Sudoku puzzles. Or zombies that rotted and fell apart, unable to move ... but if the brain remained alive, did the inanimate decomposing pile of tissue just while away the hours pondering the meaning of life?

Now Sheyenne and I were stuck inside a sealed crypt. Nobody knew where we were, and the harpy certainly had no intention of letting us out.

Through the narrow windows, we watched night set in, then daylight again … and now night had fallen once more. Sheyenne's frustrated spectral glow was the only illumination to keep me company.

We'd been stuck in the tomb for more than a full day. After we had exhausted the first round of escape possibilities, neither Sheyenne nor I had any idea what to try next. Robin wouldn't come back to the office for another week. As soon as she found us missing, she would immediately know something was wrong, but she'd have no clue where to look for us.

Officer McGoohan would be concerned much sooner than that, but he wouldn't know where to look either. He'd file a missing monsters report, and he'd worry about me far more than he would like to admit—but that didn't mean Sheyenne and I were getting out of there any time soon.

For a while, Sheyenne let herself enjoy the quiet solace of the two of us together. We had all the makings of a romance to last throughout eternity, though I had never pictured our epic would all take place in a single room.

"Somehow I thought I'd have a more spectacular end than this, Spooky," I said as we sat together on the slab. "My first death was kind of embarrassing, getting shot in the back of the head in a dark alley, while trying to solve your murder." I had no reason to wear a fedora inside a sealed tomb, so I took it off, set it in my lap. "Now here we are, stuck, with no place to go, not even solving a case."

"You'll figure out something, Beaux."

"I suppose we can hope that Elspeth gives up the ghost soon, so they'll have to open up the crypt. But that's not the way I'd like to wrap up a case. After all my detective work, I never thought I'd be stumped by a locked-room mystery."

Sheyenne snuggled close to me so that her ectoplasmic body blended into mine. I wished I could feel something solid, but we took comfort in each other's presence nevertheless. Although death was no piece of cake, her afterlife hadn't been too bad. We had a good thing.

We reminisced about the times we had together, but I could tell she was growing agitated. Finally, Sheyenne flung herself at the film-coated walls and ceiling, again and again, becoming panicked. She smashed against the barrier, distorted her spectral body, then flew off to strike a different wall, trying to find some weakness in the protective film. She was like a moth, battering herself against a lamp.

I lurched to my feet and tried to catch her, but of course she slipped right through my grasp. I tried to calm her. "Hey, Spooky—let me think. I know you have faith in me, so let's work this through. Calm down."

"I don't want to be stuck in here anymore! I just want to get back to normal." Sheyenne slumped back on the slab and sat shuddering.

"Normal?" I said, cocking my eyebrow. "We have to break out of a sealed tomb that was built for a harpy by a minotaur, and then go back to work for a detective agency in a city full of monsters. Yes, let's get back to normal."

I worked my way around the sealed door again, looking at the corners, looking at the wall. Maybe I would notice a clue after all.

Sheyenne said in a depressed voice, "Looks like this tomb will stand the test of time, like the pyramids—just like that arrogant minotaur said."

"He's talented, I'll give Percy that. He did exactly what Esther hired him to do," I said. "But I didn't really see him as arrogant—just proud of his work. He intended for this crypt to be his masterpiece." Which was saying something, I realized, because we had looked at his architectural portfolio, all the great works he had already created. His masterpiece …

I sat up straighter, turned slowly around. An architect like Percy the minotaur took so much pride in his work—he would never leave a masterpiece unsigned. Esther wouldn't have let him make a big flourish, since she owned the crypt, had commissioned it for her own purposes. But Percy … I was sure he would have found some way.

"Let's look for initials," I said. "Comb every block. If that architect is the artist I think he is …"

Sheyenne didn't let herself show too much hope, not yet, but she flitted to the ceiling and scrutinized the stone crown molding, while I methodically—or as is fitting for a zombie, *relentlessly*—went from block to stone block, studying each one, looking for a signature or initials, hoping I'd find what I needed.

Finally, on a floor tile in the corner, back behind the coffin slab designed to hold the harpy's body, I discovered it. "Found it!"

The ghost swooped over, hovering next to me so that her lambent glow illuminated the initials: PMS.

"Percy Minotaur, Senior," I said.

"PMS," Sheyenne said, "could well be Esther's initials. But what good does that do us?"

I ran my fingers over the initials and felt the roughness. If my heart had been beating much, my pulse would've sped up. "Percy chiseled his initials in here at the last minute. He must have slipped in, pounded the letters, and then left before Esther could spot him."

With a fingernail, I tapped the chiseled letters, found a noticeable nick. "And he carved them right through the ectoplasmic protective film. The barrier is broken here, a chink in the armor." I smiled up at Sheyenne. "I've seen you slip through a keyhole when you needed to. Can you get through this crack now?"

She brightened—literally. "Even if there's only a little slit, I'll make it work."

Sheyenne bent over, concentrated, and extended her finger, sliding it through the tiny chisel mark of PMS. The rest of the crypt was sealed to her with the anti-ecto film, but she managed to push her spectral form into that tiny crack.

Her finger went first, elongating, then her entire hand plunged after it. She was gathering speed. "I can do this, Beaux." She flashed me one of those beautiful grins until she spun down and dove entirely into the chiseled letters. She disappeared through the floor tile with a faint *pop*, and her spectral light went out in the crypt, leaving me all alone in darkness.

Until she used her poltergeist powers to throw open the heavy bolt that sealed the door, cracking open the entrance to the crypt. I pushed as hard as I could, shoving open the stone barricade. I worked my way out into the humid miasma of the cemetery night.

Sheyenne was there waiting for me, smiling in triumph. I inhaled a deep breath, and it smelled like roses.

6

Proud and satisfied, Sheyenne accompanied me as we presented our bill to Esther the harpy for services rendered. Sheyenne insisted on carrying the paperwork herself. Somehow, I don't think she liked the harpy much....

Esther was meeting with Percy the minotaur inside his offices, going over landscaping concepts and shrubbery arrangements for the exterior of Elspeth's tomb. Esther was never in a good mood, but right now she was particularly unhappy to see us. Instead of welcoming us back, instead of graciously accepting defeat, her bird-bright eyes flashed like black lasers. She whirled to the minotaur, shrieking. "You miserable failure!"

"Now there's no need for that, Esther," I said. "You hired us to test the tomb. I'm sure he can make modifications." I wasn't sure I wanted to suggest improvements, though; no matter how awful Elspeth was—and harpies had their own separate category for "awful"—no one deserved to be sealed away like that for eternity.

"No! I want him to start from scratch and do it right next time—and I'm not paying you until it's perfect."

Percy snorted so loudly that the gold ring in his nose flapped and jangled. "This is bull!"

Sheyenne slapped our bill down in front of the harpy. "We, however, expect to get paid. We did exactly what we were contracted to do."

Esther shrieked, "You'll get paid when—"

"We'll get paid *now*, thank you," Sheyenne said. "You can take it out of your tips at the Ghoul's Diner."

Esther always provided abominably bad service, but she was so intimidating that customers were afraid *not* to leave a tip.

With a huff and a squawk, the harpy found a purse somewhere among her plumage and paid us. "This has been a lousy day. My sister suffered a relapse."

"Sorry to hear that," I said. "Is she getting worse?"

"No, a relapse of *health!* Looks like she might last after all…. This is the worst day of my life. And they keep getting worse and worse."

"There's always tomorrow," Sheyenne said in a flippant voice, and she drifted out of the minotaur architect's offices, with me following her.

As I closed the door, the harpy was launching into a long succession of nagging instructions, but this was no longer my case. "We should make it a general practice not to take harpies as clients."

"Sure, there were problems, Beaux," Sheyenne said as we headed through the bustling, colorful, and unnatural streets of the Quarter, "but I did get to spend time with you, and I like cases like that."

I stuck out my elbow, and she slipped her ghostly arm through mine. It was a charade, but we were good at it now. As we strolled along, other naturals and unnaturals saw how we were both positively glowing. They smiled at us, and we smiled back.

It was a good day to be alive, but, barring that, it was a good day for us to be together.

The Writing on the Wall

hat zombie wrote *FU* right there on the side of my store!" said Howard Snark, the human proprietor of Stakes 'n Spades, the only full-service hardware store in the Unnatural Quarter. He put his hands on his hips and fumed as he stared at the dripping spray paint.

Howard was normally a pleasant, soft-spoken man with salt-and-pepper hair, a full salt-and-pepper beard, and a salt-and-pepper personality. Standing there, I adjusted my fedora and inspected the graffiti. I could understand why he was upset, since his store had been defaced, but I thought he was misinterpreting.

"Actually, I think it says *FA*, Howard," I said. As a zombie detective, I have to pay close attention to details.

Beside me, my partner Robin leaned closer and nodded. "Dan's right. It's *FA*. Zombies don't have the best penmanship." She sounded apologetic.

We all stood together outside Stakes 'n Spades responding to the complaint, along with Officer Toby McGoohan, or McGoo. While walking his beat, he had apprehended the zombie tagger right as he was scrawling the letters with a can of lime green spray paint.

"It's still a violation," said McGoo, "regardless of the spelling."

The zombie graffiti artist looked dazed and confused, staring perplexed at the spray paint can in his grayish hands, as if he couldn't remember what he'd been doing.

Howard snatched the can away. "What were you thinking, Eddie? You're one of my regular customers. What did I ever do to you? I'm just trying to make a living here."

Howard had opened Stakes 'n Spades in the Unnatural Quarter because he saw an unfulfilled need. After all, monsters needed plumbing equipment, tools, lumber, nails, duct tape, and other building supplies as much as anyone else did. He had once lived in Silicon Valley, where many of his friends and colleagues became successful millionaires by working in software. Howard, on the other hand, had a vision that his own fortune lay in *hardware*.

When a rich, old aunt died and left him a modest inheritance, Howard built his store in the Quarter. Then, after he'd spent the entire inheritance, the rich, old aunt came back as a ghost and demanded some of the funds back. It could have been an inter-family argument with many consequences—legally speaking, the undead could sometimes reclaim their material wealth, depending on the amount of vagueness in the deceased's last will and testament—but, Howard and his aunt reached an amicable settlement. He gave her enough money to go on a retirement cruise with other ghosts, and he downsized his store slightly, but made it more profitable. Howard Snark had faithfully served the Unnatural Quarter for years, even becoming chairman of the Chamber of Commerce for a two-year stretch.

Now, McGoo stood with his report pad out, frowning at the zombie graffiti artist, ready to write a citation or make an arrest, whichever was necessary. "Well, Eddie, what have you got to say for yourself? You were caught red-handed."

Eddie looked down at his hands where some of the messy spray paint had covered his fingers in a neon-lime color. "I don't know."

He wasn't as well-preserved a zombie as I am, but he wasn't a horribly decaying shambler, either. His pants were slung low so that his waistband encircled the bottoms of his hips, while the waistband of his plaid boxer shorts was pulled high up on his back. Apparently, his demographic considers that sort of dress "stylish."

"What were you trying to write?" asked Robin. "FA ... what else?"

"I don't know."

McGoo took off his policeman's cap and wiped a hand across his freckled forehead. His reddish hair was rumpled. "I don't know why these deadbeats can't just take an art class." He looked up at me. "Maybe you can solve this one for me, Shamble. There's been a rash of incomprehensible graffiti in the last day or two. None of it makes any sense. You're the detective—can you figure out what goes through a teenager's mind when he does stupid things?"

"That's beyond the skills of the most talented zombie detective," I replied. "And I *am* the most talented zombie detective—or so I've been told."

"That's what you tell yourself, at least," McGoo muttered.

"Did the other graffiti writing make sense?" asked Robin. When she decides to work on something, Robin is intense and dedicated. When she'd gotten her law degree, she decided to help the unnaturals who needed legal representation. She and I have been partners for a long time, both when I was a human detective, and now that I'm a zombie detective. When you have a good working relationship, you keep it.

McGoo flipped back through his pad. "First time, two days ago, some zombie just wrote *HE*—and then never went further." He looked at me with teasing scorn. "You zombies don't have a lot of follow-through."

"Some of us have ADDD. Attention deficit disorder of the dead."

McGoo looked down at his pad, turned the page. "Another zombie scrawled *I'VE* on a brick alley wall. Another one just wrote *LP*, whatever that means."

"I don't know," said Eddie again, even though we hadn't asked him the question.

"Maybe he was inspired." On the street corner in front of the Stakes 'n Spades hardware store sat a long-limbed zombie artist with a set of multicolored spray-paint cans and a stack of shiny hubcaps. Goch was a marginally popular street artist who specialized in painting designs on hubcaps, then selling them to curious human tourists who came into the Quarter to see everyday monsters in their natural habitat. Goch claimed that he "found" the hubcaps, although more likely, they had been stolen from parked cars. He had very long arms and legs that he folded up like a spider's, and long hair that made him look like an aging post-mortem heavy metal rock star.

Now, Goch held a spray can in his hand as he swirled a jet of color around on the hubcap. "When the muse takes you, you gotta paint."

"Well, he doesn't gotta paint *my store!*" said Howard.

Eddie slouched his head and his shoulders as much as his pants slouched. "I'm sorry, Mr. Snark ... I don't know what came over me."

Howard let out an exasperated sigh. "Eddie, you're a good kid. All right, if you sweep up in the back, break down some boxes, and help run the store for a day or two, we'll call it even. I won't press charges—this time. I've got work to do. An entire new shipment of mallets and stakes came in, so we're having a special sale in honor of Bram Stoker's birthday."

Howard was always good at marketing.

McGoo put away his pad. "Doesn't bother me not to make an arrest. Less paperwork that way." He looked at me with gratitude. "I guess you didn't need to come out here after all, Shamble."

"We didn't come here for you," I said as Robin and I turned to go. "We're working on a case. We've been hired to see Angina, Mistress of Fright."

2

Despite her worldwide fame before the Big Uneasy, few people had seen Angina, Mistress of Fright since she'd retired from show business and become a recluse in the Unnatural Quarter.

She was a much beloved screamfest hostess, who had become quite a star on *Nightmares in the Daytime*, a monster movie double feature that had played first on a cable channel out of Chicago on Saturday afternoons before it caught on and spread around numerous syndicated channels.

With her scanty outfit, large breasts, and campy, as well as vampy, personality, Angina had become a cultural icon. Few people actually watched the bad black-and-white horror flicks she hosted; the audience was much more interested in her goofball comments, and her cleavage, during the breaks.

But when the breasts started sagging and crows' feet appeared around her eyes, Angina—whose vanity was legendary—retired from public life, preferring to be remembered as she was in her femme-fatale heyday.

Nowadays, though, with real monsters setting up shop and interacting with normal society, the demand for old horror flicks dwindled, so Angina had picked the perfect time to retire. And she found the right neighborhood for her retirement home.

Even though she chose the Quarter as her "unnatural habitat," Angina built high fences, barricaded herself in her house, and became a total recluse. She interacted with no one, had groceries and supplies delivered by golems who were sworn to secrecy. And she never left.

But recently an admirer, a dedicated fan, had engaged Chambeaux & Deyer Investigations to make contact with Angina. It was our job to make our client happy.

The Angina house was a rickety, bent-over affair (designed that way on purpose) with peeling wood siding, slatted shutters that hung askew on the windows, black shingles on the roof, a belfry complete with bats, seven gables close together. The house was surrounded by a brick wall topped by fierce-looking wrought-iron spikes and a dash of barbed wire (probably electrified). The rusty gate was padlocked shut. At the cornerstone of the brick wall, I saw the engraved notation, "Chas. Addams, Architect."

Everything about the Angina house looked rundown and dangerous—which was perfectly acceptable décor in the Unnatural Quarter, in accordance with the neighborhood homeowners' association covenants.

Just outside the padlocked gate I found a speaker and an intercom button. "Would you like to do the honors, Robin?"

I could see she was barely suppressing a giggle. "I confess, I'm a little nervous, Dan."

Robin had faced horrific monsters, fierce demons, and powerful black magic, but now she had butterflies in her stomach because she was actually a big fan of Angina, Mistress of Fright. She pushed the intercom button. "Hello?"

A loud, harsh, female voice burst out of the speaker. "Go away!"

"We're here to see Angina. We have a request—I hope you can help us out."

No answer—only dead silence.

My turn to push the button. "Is anyone there?"

"I want to be left alone!"

Robin's turn. She pushed the button. "We were hoping for an autograph, if it's not too much trouble."

"No trespassing!"

Robin and I looked at each other, and she seemed very disappointed. "A person has a right to privacy. We can't intrude if Angina doesn't want us."

Robin was always a stickler for the rules, which had worked much to our disadvantage many times. I've often found it more effective to apologize afterward than to ask her permission before I did any questionable activity.

I didn't give up so easily, though. "The cases don't solve themselves, and we have an obligation to our client to try everything possible. We've got to figure out a way."

Back at the offices of Chambeaux & Deyer, clients normally just walk through the door, whether it be a golem seeking justice for his comrades caught in an illegal sweatshop, or an opera-singing ogre who had lost his voice, or even human clients whose interactions with unnaturals hadn't gone well. (That happens more often than you might think.)

This time, though, we received our engagement letter via the mail. Jackson B. Hayes introduced himself to us as an avid collector, insisting that he was Angina's "number one fan!" Then he went on to reassure us that there was nothing obsessive about it, like Annie Wilkes of *Misery* fame, but that he really, really, really loved Angina. He had grown up captivated by her, watched every episode of *Nightmares in the Daytime* cinema, collected a Standee figure of her, posters on the walls. He had DVDs of her movies, VHS copies of her older ones, even Betamax copies of older ones still.

Jackson had sent us a black-and-white glossy photo, one of the beautiful head shots that showed Angina in her prime: alabaster skin and eyes with enough mascara and shadow to make an Egyptian sarcophagus jealous. The canyon of cleavage between her breasts was large enough and prominent enough that it could have been a national park, or at least a national monument.

"I desperately want to get this photo autographed," wrote Jackson. "It would mean so much to me."

So, he engaged Chambeaux & Deyer Investigations to break Angina's legendary reclusive barrier just long enough to get a signature. "And make certain it's an *authentic signature*. I've been duped before."

He described how he had purchased a signed photo from a collector on the internet, but because Jackson B. Hayes was an Angina expert, he recognized the forgery immediately.

"Angina always signed her autographed photos to her fans with a special exclamation point drawing the dot in the shape of a heart. She said it symbolized a stake going right into the fan's heart. So endearing! Since the photo I purchased had a normal exclamation point, I know it was fake."

Sheyenne brought the package to Robin and me. "Here's a new case."

"Sounds like an easy job," I said. "Everyone knows where the Angina house is."

Robin's eyes were sparkling as she began to gather our information, gazing at the beautiful black-and-white photo. "I'd really love to meet her myself."

I'd never seen my partner turn into a fangirl before. It was charming.

Sheyenne had used her poltergeist powers to dial the phone and let Jackson B. Hayes know that we would start work right away. All we had to do was get a minute of Angina's time.

Now, as we stood outside the imposing brick wall and padlocked gate, Robin clutched the black-and-white photo in its protective envelope. She wasn't sure what to do.

I pushed the intercom button again. "We won't go away until we see you, Angina."

The response came back loud and gritty. "Keep out! No trespassing!"

Robin pushed the button. "Please, we don't mean to be a bother, but—"

"I want to be left alone! Go away!"

This was starting to sound redundant. I pushed the button again. "Is this just a recording? Is there anybody in there?"

"No trespassing! Keep out!"

Robin looked at me, worried. "Maybe we could try again later. Perhaps a phone call? Send a package in the mail?"

"Zombies can be persistent," I told her.

"Not as persistent as lawyers," Robin said.

3

The Unnatural Quarter really got hopping after dark, when all the nightbreeds, vampires, and shadowy creatures felt their metabolisms rise. But it was after official business hours for Chambeaux & Deyer. I decided to relax with Sheyenne and watch a movie. Considering our Angina case, though, it was a work-related date.

Since my girlfriend is a ghost, she can't touch any living, or formerly living, thing, which makes it difficult to hold hands. She passes right through my flesh. But when she really gets into that spectrally romantic mood, she can don a polyester glove and make her grip feel almost lifelike. Since at times I can be almost lifelike, too, we make a good couple.

Sheyenne has been with me longer after death than we were a couple when we were both alive. Of course, our relationship and some unsavory acquaintances was what led to our respective murders in the first place, but neither of us let that dampen the post-mortem romance.

We sat in the conference room with a portable TV set and the lights turned down so we could watch a DVD of Angina, Mistress of Fright's *Nightmares in the Daytime*. The movie itself was an old stinker, *Revenge of the Grinning Skull*, whose effects were so bad the director must have gone home every night hanging his head in shame; the acting was so bad, the cast must have done the same; and the writing was even worse, so the screenwriter probably didn't bother to go home at all, for fear of facing his family once they'd seen the film.

But when Angina came on screen during the breaks, she was really something. The Mistress of Fright had a sparkle in her dark eyes, and she laughed so boisterously that sometimes her artificial fangs fell out—which she played for laughs, as well.

She groaned at a particularly awful point in *Revenge of the Grinning Skull*. "Angina must have gone out of her way to pick movies so bad that they would make her look good."

Her polyester glove levitated and I reached up to hold her hand. A fresh-popped bowl of popcorn sat on the conference room table in front of us, mainly for ambience, because a ghost can't eat and I usually don't have much appetite.

Normally, I would have gone to the Goblin Tavern to share an after-hours beer with McGoo, but that night I told him I had a date. "Must be nice, Shamble," McGoo had said. "You're dead, and you still get more girls than I do."

"Yes, that's me, McGoo. Always been a babe magnet."

"Me too. But I think my polarity is the opposite of yours. I just repel them."

McGoo was probably still walking the beat even this late at night; he didn't have much to go home for.

A few hours after Robin and I came back from our unwelcome reception at the Angina house, McGoo called to tell me that he had found more incomplete zombie graffiti scrawled on a wall in the Quarter. Another young zombie with the same intellectual capacity as Eddie had spray painted "*LLEN AND I*" before running out of steam.

McGoo had caught the deadbeat as he stood there looking at the can of spray paint in his hands. When McGoo demanded to know "Who's LLEN?" the zombie didn't seem to know. No surprise there.

Now, while Sheyenne and I watched the movie, Robin was burning the midnight oil in her office, poring over cases, studying legal precedents, writing up briefs. She's still alive but she doesn't have much of a life—except with us. I didn't want this talented young woman to work herself to death, but I knew that working on cases and hammering out briefs was how Robin chose to relax. She was more stressed when not working.

Robin came to stand at the door of the conference room, peeping in so she could watch the movie, too. "You're welcome to join us," I said.

She looked at Sheyenne and me holding hands. "I don't want to interrupt your date."

"You're not," Sheyenne said. "This is about as far as Beaux and I were going to get tonight."

"Always stuck on second base," I said.

Robin snagged the bowl of popcorn. "I will take this if you're not going to eat it. It smells delicious, fills the whole office."

She stood munching on a handful of popcorn, captivated by *The Revenge of the Grinning Skull*. "I remember this one!" When Angina came on, we all laughed aloud as a man in a rubber Creature from the Black Lagoon mask did pratfalls and fell into a half-full bathtub.

"Angina certainly has stage presence," Robin said. "With those looks, that body, she used to be quite a dish."

"And now she's just leftovers," I said. "No wonder she's a recluse."

Sheyenne said, "Maybe she just wants people to remember the way she was on screen. You never age there."

"Right," I said. "Like the Blu-Ray of Dorian Gray."

The phone rang. Even though it was after office hours, everyone knew that zombies and ghosts—and dedicated lawyers—worked all hours anyway.

Sheyenne flitted out of the conference room while I paused the movie. She didn't bother to use the door, simply passed right through the walls to get to her desk. Robin munched popcorn while we both listened to the phone conversation in the reception area.

"All right, McGoo, I'll send her right over. I'm sure Dan will want to come, too." After hanging up, Sheyenne flitted back to the conference room. "More trouble at Stakes 'n Spades. Goch, the hubcap artist, has been arrested, and he's demanding to see Robin as his lawyer."

I groaned. "What did he do?"

"Defacing private property, but he denies it. Said he's got to have Robin right away."

Robin set down the popcorn. "Sorry about your date and movie."

But Sheyenne understood. She always did.

4

It was the dead of night, but that's when the dead really got lively. At the hardware store, the streetlights were bright, and McGoo stood there flustered, disappointed, and at his wits' end.

Goch was in handcuffs, his long legs shaking so badly that his knobby knees knocked together. His colorfully painted hubcaps were strewn around, like a going-out-of-business sale for bad artwork. Several spray paint cans lay tipped over on the sidewalk.

Outside the hardware store, Howard Snark wrung his hands and shook his head. "I barely got the other graffiti cleaned off!" He shook his fist at Goch, who cringed. "Why can't you get a life?"

"Because …" said the zombie artist.

But Howard wasn't listening. "I am pressing charges this time, Officer McGoohan."

"I thought you might," McGoo said.

Scrawled in gigantic letters across the front of the hardware store, were the words "CAN'T GET."

It didn't make any sense to me. "CAN'T GET what?"

Robin stepped up to the artist, using her most understanding voice. "You've got us all confused, here, Goch. What does it mean?"

The zombie heaved a long sigh. "You don't ask what art *means*." He looked pleadingly at Robin. "It was the Muse—it must have been. I couldn't control myself. You have to defend me, Ms. Deyer. It's about artistic expression."

"I'd like to express myself all over your face!" Howard slapped his forehead. "I sold you that paint. I even bought four of your hubcap creations for my store—and this is how you thank me?"

When Goch trembled, his handcuffs rattled like the chains on a restless spirit.

Other unnatural spectators had gathered around—two vampires who had just come back from a nightcap at a Talbot & Knowles blood bar, a partially unwrapped mummy who was still in stitches from a show at a comedy club, and several slack-faced and curious-looking young zombies.

As Howard Snark and Goch continued to argue and McGoo wrote up the citation, one of the young zombie spectators shuffled forward, picked up a discarded can of pink paint, and walked over to the door of the hardware store. As we stared in disbelief, he started painting—right in front of us.

I lurched forward. "Hey! Stop that."

McGoo and I seized the arms of the disoriented young zombie who was moving listlessly like a … zombie. I grabbed the spray paint out of his hands.

He'd had time to paint the word "UP!" Oddly enough, the dot of the exclamation point was a cute little heart.

Howard groaned, exasperated. "What is wrong with you undead people?"

"*UP* with what?" Robin said to the dazed zombie. "You knew you'd be caught!"

"*UP* yours," Howard said. "You're going to pay to clean my building."

I paused and stared, though, looking at the words.

CAN'T GET and *UP!*

Then, I remembered the afternoon's new graffiti—*LLEN AND I*—and the incident that had called us here early in the day, *FA.*

The first graffiti McGoo had reported to me was just the word *HE*, but I recalled what else we'd seen. *I'VE* and *LP.* I was sure I was putting them in the correct order of how the graffiti had actually been written.

HE

LP.

"McGoo, it's a message. It all goes together. The graffiti is telling us something—and we'd better listen."

I felt a chill rush through my embalming fluid as I realized that the spray-painted letters spelled out that terrifying mantra so dreaded by senior citizens everywhere:

HELP, I'VE FALLEN AND I CAN'T GET UP!

"Who?" McGoo said, "Where? How do we respond to this? Shamble, you're onto something."

I pointed to the stylized exclamation point with the little heart. "It's Angina. And she's in trouble."

5

As we raced to the Angina house, I placed a phone call to Sheyenne. "Spooky, we might need you." She's always happy to help, and I seem to solve cases better when she's around. At least, that's what she says.

An emergency with a person potentially in peril took precedence over arresting a zombie vandal with a side career in hubcap painting. Besides, we knew we could always find Goch again, since he was a well-known street artist, not a particular flight risk.

Howard said, "I'll hold Goch for you in the meantime. Stakes 'n Spades has a full line of chains, padlocks, and rope."

Robin, McGoo, and I arrived at the Angina house, which looked even more corny and stereotypical under the full moonlight. Sheyenne joined us just as we arrived; she's a powerful poltergeist who is not bound by the restrictions of physical travel as are human cops, determined lawyers, or shambling zombies.

Remembering the imposing padlock that held the main gate shut, I had planned ahead and asked Howard for a sturdy set of bolt cutters. He showed me the options from his store, gave me a sales pitch about the craftsmanship and the warranties of each. I just took the biggest one.

McGoo punched the gate's intercom button. "Ms. Angina, we're here to help. Are you in trouble?"

"Keep out! Go away! No trespassing!"

"Sounds like she's fine." McGoo lifted his eyebrows. "Though not very friendly."

"It's a recording," I said. "Same words every time."

"She's definitely in trouble," Robin said. "We've got to do something."

I grasped the bars to rattle the gate, and I was shocked, literally, when sparks crackled through my body. I yanked my hands away. Fortunately, zombies don't have to worry about being electrocuted.

"She means business," I said.

Robin sounded desperate. "Given the evidence, there's a reasonable expectation that this person is in danger. If it's to do a wellness check on a person who hasn't been seen in a long time, we have sufficient cause to break in. We're on sound legal ground here."

I lifted the tool. "And I've got a big bolt cutter."

"There's an easier way." Sheyenne took a shortcut by flitting right through the gates. "At least let me switch off the current."

Once through the wall, she deactivated the electrified fence, and I used the bolt cutters to snap the chain. We pushed open the gate and raced up the flagstone walk that was artfully surrounded with scraggly weeds.

Sheyenne vanished directly through the front door of the vintage haunted house. And, since my ghost girlfriend had just gone inside, it was now, quite literally, a haunted house—but in the best possible way.

McGoo, Robin, and I ran up the rickety wooden porch steps, and we heard a loud series of *thunks* as multiple deadbolts were turned. Sheyenne pulled the door open with a loud nerve-jarring groan and hovered in front of us, pale and glowing, but her expression was distraught.

"We're too late," she said.

I went inside first, with my hand on my .38 in its holster. McGoo had already drawn his service revolver, though there was nothing threatening inside the haunted house.

Just a dead body.

The foyer of the Angina house was a large receiving hall, with two towering grandfather clocks, ostentatious furniture, marble tiles, a dramatic curving staircase. And Angina, Mistress of Fright sprawled at the bottom of the stairs on the marble tiles. Obviously dead. And for several days from the looks of her.

Even though we had just watched *The Revenge of the Grinning Skull* on Angina's *Nightmares in the Daytime,* I barely recognized the famous horror film hostess. Angina had retired from the public eye and gone into hiding years ago. I suppose the kindest way to describe it was that she "had not aged as well as a fine wine." Angina had gained another film hostess's worth of weight, and her lush, black hair had gone gray and fallen out in clumps. Her skin showed numerous age spots (other than the normal discoloration of having been dead for several days).

"I guess we didn't have to run so fast."

Then the air above Angina's body shimmered, and a figure appeared—an indistinct and barely visible image of Angina, like the ghost of a ghost, a watermark in the air. She was just a flickering afterimage, compared to Sheyenne's bright and intense ectoplasmic form.

"It took you long enough!" She was indignant, but her voice sounded as if it came from a great distance. "Didn't you get my message?"

McGoo and I looked at each other. Robin said, "Not right away. It wasn't clear."

The ghost of Angina let out a disgusted snort. "Zombies are lousy messengers."

In sharp contrast to the decrepit old, overweight, and age-spotted corpse of the Mistress of Fright, Angina's ghost looked as if she had stepped right off of one of her pristine DVD images: beautiful face, voluptuous body, fine skin tone, and bodily curves that went gently in and out rather than just *out.*

"You're a ghost, just like me," Sheyenne said. "Don't you have poltergeist powers? Couldn't you just walk through the wall and get out?"

Angina's ghost let out a metaphorical sigh. "I tried, but I couldn't walk through walls, and I don't have any poltergeist powers. Looks like I washed out as a ghost, just like I washed out as a serious actress. I'm weak, and I'm trapped inside this house, but I feel that I'm supposed to move on. I needed help."

I made the connection. "So you possessed those zombies to put out your message."

"Zombies are very poor conduits, but they were the only thing I could use. Undead slackers—they're hard to control for more than a few minutes at a time."

I tried not to sound testy. "Some of us are well-preserved zombies."

"And a lot of them aren't well-preserved at all," Angina snapped. "It was an ungodly challenge to get them to write down one or two letters before their attention would wander off somewhere. The whole thing took days!"

Robin nodded solemnly. "Yes, ADDD."

"I couldn't leave the house, and I was stuck here, fading away, like my career. But at least you finally came."

"We were too late to save you, though." Robin frowned.

"Oh, don't worry about that. It was quick—I tumbled down the stairs, and ... then I was a ghost. Besides"—she drew herself up, touched her breasts, ran her spectral hands along her spectral waist—"look at me! Quite an improvement, I'd say. That old body was quite a burden, and I'm glad to be rid of it. I like this much better.

"But after I died, I was trapped in this house, and I just couldn't figure out how to let anyone know." She glanced at Sheyenne, gave one of her signature Mistress of Fright winks. "Now, I may not be a poltergeist, but after all the movies I hosted, I remember damn well that ghosts can possess people—particularly weak-willed people. And who's more weak-willed than a zombie?"

I chose not to take offense at that.

"I just didn't realize it would be so tedious just to get one line right. Ugh, it reminds me of some of the actors I worked with."

"Well, we're happy to have found you now," Robin said. "We'll let you out of the house. Even as a ghost, you'll be welcome in the Unnatural Quarter. You'll fit right in. A lot of monsters watched your show, too. And ..." She seemed embarrassed. "I'm a big fan, too."

Angina shook her faint, spectral head. "Oh, I'm not going out there! I need to move on. I know I do."

Yes, the undead had become a common sight—vampires, zombies or ghosts—but not everyone came back for an encore. Some people died and stayed dead ... and they liked it that way. I was glad that Sheyenne had come back to haunt me, but Angina just felt trapped.

"Then I'm not sure I understand," I said. "What do you need our help for?"

"I died here alone, under violent circumstances. My body needs a proper burial before I can head toward the light."

"You sure that'll work?" McGoo asked.

Angina huffed. "Mister, do you know how many hundreds of horror movies I hosted? I've seen enough to know that's what you have to do."

6

The Quarter offered several services that could take care of Angina's needs, such as ghost-removal services and licensed "proper burial" teams with all the bells and whistles. There were budget plans and extravagant ones.

Angina, of course, needed to have the best.

Once released from her house, Angina had followed us out the front door, and now she hovered around the Chambeaux & Deyer offices, waiting as we wrapped up the details. Sheyenne described the ins and outs of being a ghost, but Angina wasn't really interested, since it wouldn't matter for long.

But I had other cases as well, and I always keep my clients' needs foremost in my mind. While we arranged for the proper disposition of Angina's corporeal remains, the real client who had started this whole mess—or adventure—was the autograph collector, Jackson B. Hayes. I wanted to wrap up that case while I had the chance.

I pulled out the black-and-white head shot that the fan had lovingly sent to us. "We were trying to get your autograph, Ms. Angina. That's why we visited you in the first place."

I showed her Jackson's letter, and faint fuzzy tears appeared in her translucent eyes. "I was always good to my fans."

"Is there any chance …?" I held up a pen. "An autograph would mean so much. Then we could close out the case."

Sheyenne drifted closer. "But if she doesn't have any poltergeist powers, Beaux, she can't scrawl her name."

"My penmanship was very neat," Angina said. "I would never scrawl."

"Maybe we could just get a photo of me holding up the glossy with you in the frame," I said. It was all I could think of.

Robin joined us. "She's very faint. I doubt the ghost image would even show up in the picture."

Angina, though, had a bright idea. "You're a zombie, Mr. Shamble. I could do what I did before. Hold onto that pen and empty your head of thoughts."

"That's easy enough for him," Sheyenne teased.

I couldn't let her get away with that. "Not when you're around, Spooky. I have lots of thoughts."

Robin was uncertain. "You want to possess Dan, so that he can write, just like the other zombies did with graffiti?"

"I can try," said Angina.

Whatever it takes to wrap up a case. I dutifully cleared my head, held the pen, and felt a strange presence enter through the bullet hole in my forehead, which was a very strange experience.

My hand moved of its own accord, flexing my wrist, limbering up, and then with a flourish I signed, "To my Number One Fan—Best Wishes, Angina, Mistress of Fright." For veracity, Angina possessed my hand and forced me to make the final exclamation point, complete with a cute little heart for a dot.

"There," Angina said. "See? A stake headed straight for the heart."

Robin witnessed the signature and signed a certificate of authenticity to verify for Jackson B. Hayes that Angina herself had autographed the photo. She also made a secondary notation that this was guaranteed to be the last signature Angina ever gave to a fan. Jackson would love that.

Within an hour, the proper disposal service had been completed, Angina waved farewell and then winked out of existence heading off to a better place where she hoped to find a new audience for her work.

After Angina vanished, I stood next to Sheyenne, who looked somewhat wistful. "I could've gone on at one time, but I stayed behind to seek justice, to find my killer ... and to hang out with you, Beaux."

I didn't know what I'd do without Sheyenne. Unlife was so much better with her around. "You're not going to leave me, are you, Spooky?"

She smiled and snuggled close. I felt a tingle, but little else. It didn't matter, I knew she was right there, and her presence warmed my cold blood.

"No, Beaux. I'm here on purpose, and I intend to stay. We've got a lot more cases to solve."

ROLE MODEL

1

C ome on, Shamble—it'll be fun," said Officer Toby McGoohan, my best human friend. He acted as if he'd gotten season tickets to his favorite sports team.

I was immediately suspicious, sure that this would not be typical police business. "I don't even know what a cosplay convention is, McGoo."

He had met me outside the offices of Chambeaux & Deyer Investigations, seemingly by happy coincidence as he walked his beat, but we both knew it wasn't an accident. He'd been waiting for me.

"Cosplay—costume playing. It's when people dress up as characters from their favorite movies, TV shows, comics, video games, whatever." He had looked it up online, so he considered himself an expert.

"Oh. Trick or treat for grownups." Every day in the Unnatural Quarter, I saw a parade of werewolves, mummies, vampires, zombies, ghosts, witches, and second-string monsters, so I wasn't going to be impressed by a few interesting costumes.

"A lot more than that. These people think they *are* the characters. It gets a little intense. And weird. And fun."

It didn't sound any stranger than my usual cases, and McGoo and I often helped each other out. "So why do they need a zombie detective?"

He seemed exasperated that I was spoiling his fun by being such a hard sell. "They don't *need* a zombie detective any more than they need a beat cop, but the hotel manager is nervous about having such big crowds—naturals, unnaturals, all those people running around in costumes. Thought he might need some extra security." McGoo flashed one of those grins that had, over the years, convinced me to do things that would get us both in trouble. "Besides, he gave us two free passes to the con."

He's a redhead with a round, freckled face and a rough sense of humor (to put it mildly). We've been friends for a long time, even back when I was still alive, and our friendship had survived me coming back as one of the walking dead. If a friendship can survive that, it can survive anything (though he still makes jokes about the unsightly bullet hole in my forehead).

My caseload at Chambeaux & Deyer Investigations was light at the moment, so I shrugged and agreed to go. I had already been to the Worldwide Horror Convention when it was held in the Quarter last year. I assumed this would be the same sort of thing.

So, that was why the two of us found ourselves in the lobby of the Motel Six Feet Under and Conference Center standing next to two clattery silver-armored cylons from the old *Battlestar Galactica* TV show. They gleamed and hummed, red optical sensors in their helmet visors drifting to and fro.

"CosplayCon security," one said in a vibrating synthetic voice that I could barely understand. He took his helmet off to reveal a young man with dark sweat-plastered hair. "Whew, those things get hot after awhile! Thanks for joining us, but I doubt you guys'll be needed. We don't expect any trouble. Everyone has a good time at the con."

As I looked around the lobby and common areas, I saw Klingons with wicked-looking bat'leths, masked ninjas with curved swords, *Star Wars* stormtroopers with heavy blasters, *Lord of the Rings* orcs with large battle-axes.

"How could there possibly be trouble?" I asked. "Nothing looks harmful at all."

"All the weapons are peace-bonded," said the cylon. When I gave him a blank look and McGoo didn't seem to recognize the term from his extensive Wikipedia research, the cylon security guard said, "Zip-tied. Everything's strapped down so the bladed weapons are perfectly safe. And of course the blasters are just molded resin props. The Jedi lightsabers are neon tubes." The cylon put his helmet back on and told us in his monotone robotic voice, "Have fun—and stay in character," then marched off with a clatter of silver armor.

Tables had been set up in the hall with volunteer staff doing their best to register attendees. This was the first year of CosplayCon in the

Unnatural Quarter, and they were glad for the added attraction of real monster attendees as well as cosplayers.

A banner over the registration area proclaimed "We are all someone else inside!" and the program book cover said, "Find your inner YOU!" as if this was a therapy session. Maybe it was—costume therapy.

At the motel front desk, a lone vampire clerk shook his head at all the costumes. He muttered, "Bunch of weirdos," then went back to a magazine he was reading. I didn't see why costumed fans were any weirder than the socially acceptable sports fans who put Viking helmets or cheese wedges on their heads.

Normally on a slow Saturday I might have walked around the Quarter with Sheyenne, or helped Robin finish paperwork on cases. Like any workaholic, I had "fun" by doing my job—solving cases and helping clients. It was my reason for living, in a loose definition of the term.

Over the past decade since their reappearances, unnaturals tended to gather in this section of the city where they were accepted, where they felt right at home. But they still had problems, just like anyone else. While most unnaturals lived perfectly normal everyday lives, some were criminals; others wanted a divorce; others needed to find lost family members. A detective working in the Quarter had the same sort of cases as a mundane detective on the outside, but the clientele was a little stranger.

Back when I was living, and trying to *make* a living, I'd partnered up with a young firebrand lawyer, and I had a good run, a successful business, before I was killed. But, as I said, I *like* doing what I do. So when I came back from the dead, I just got back to work.

In the Unnatural Quarter, being a zombie is no handicap to being a detective, though I insist on maintaining my physical appearance, bathing regularly, going for scheduled top-offs at the embalming parlor, even seeing to it that I receive my monthly maintenance spell. I won't let myself turn into one of those slobbering, shuffling embarrassments that make polite society turn up their noses at zombies.

I'm accustomed to seeing monsters in my everyday life, but I had to admit these costumes were amazing, even a little intimidating, when I started to think about the obsessive time and effort the fans had put into making them.

A squad of white-armored *Star Wars* stormtroopers marched past, representing the 501st Legion, led by an impressive black-caped and wheezing Darth Vader impersonator.

A group of Klingons had taken over the motel's woefully inadequate coffee shop and sat around the tables, pounding fists and demanding more coffee. They grew louder and more unruly by the minute, while a harried-looking mummy waitress tried her best to serve them.

A drunk furry fan was coming on to a full-furred werewolf busboy, who didn't know how to react to all the unwarranted and unwanted attention.

"See, told you this would be fun, Shamble," McGoo said. "Look over there, it's the Doctor. How many can you name?"

I looked around, but only saw a random assortment of eccentric-looking men. "Who?"

McGoo rolled his eyes. "Let's not get into the Abbott and Costello routine. Dr. Who. The first one there with short dark hair—he's the David Tennant Doctor. And the one with the scarf—you gotta recognize *him*—it's a Tom Baker lookalike, probably the most classic Dr. Who. And the one with the bow tie—Matt Smith."

Even after all this time, I was surprised to learn something new about my friend. "I didn't know you were a fanboy, McGoo."

"Not to this extent," he said, gesturing around. "But I've got a TV, and I am culturally aware."

One tall beanpole fan peered over the crowd, trying to reach the information table. Finally he gave up and just yelled, "What time is Van Helsing going to be on stage?" Some of the vampire attendees booed.

"Five o'clock in the main ballroom," yelled an unseen person from behind the desk.

Four skinny guys in clinging red shirts from classic *Star Trek* walked by, and someone yelled in mock panic, "Look out, it's redshirts!" I couldn't see why they posed any kind of threat; in fact, the tight shirts emphasized how scrawny their arms and chests were. If that was the kind of security available to Captain Kirk and crew, no wonder the old show got canceled after only three seasons.

For my own part, I wore my usual sports jacket with crudely stitched-up bullet holes and my fedora—it's my trademark, and what PI would be without one? McGoo wore his blue beat-cop uniform, and everyone seemed to think he was playing a part from an old police show. Several fans came up with very clever guesses from obscure programs that I hadn't heard of in years. One fan marched up with a sneer, poked a finger at McGoo's chest, and said, "T.J. Hooker—not Shatner's best," then walked away without waiting for a response.

Suddenly, we heard yelling from the mezzanine open area and the sounds of a growing altercation. McGoo glanced at me. "This is what we're here for, Shamble. Come on."

We ran up the stairs (and I use the term "ran" loosely, since my joints are stiff enough that it takes me a while to get up to speed). A group of rowdy Klingons yelled, "*Star Trek* is better!" One heavyset Klingon woman had the loudest voice of all.

Across the room, the 501st stormtroopers, who had made an uneasy alliance with costumed Jedi Knights and Mandalorian bounty hunters, took offense. "*Star Wars* is better!"

"*Star Trek!*" insisted the Klingons.

"No, *Star Wars!*" The intellectual debate continued in that fashion for a few more exchanges before the groups ran forward and clashed in an all-out brawl. The Klingons struggled to draw their bat'leths against the peacebonding ties. The stormtroopers punched and pummeled with a clatter of white plastic armor. The Jedi Knights lit their fluorescent-tube lightsabers, but were careful not to damage them.

Before McGoo and I could break up the fight, the group of redshirts rushed into the fray, trying to drive the combatants apart. Eventually, the Klingons brushed themselves off and the 501sters adjusted their body armor. Somehow, the only ones genuinely battered, bruised, and injured in the fight were the redshirts.

"You're right, McGoo. This is fun." I smiled.

Wandering about to get the lay of the con, we walked past large and small panel rooms, costuming workshops, and autograph tables featuring bit actors from long-canceled programs. One large room hosted a "robot smash" where model-builders pitted a remote-controlled R2D2 against a more ominous-looking Dalek. The two machines clashed, with the Dalek crying in a synthesized voice, "Annihilate, Annihilate!" while R2D2 responded with a series of incomprehensible but clearly rude beeps and squeals.

Primarily, though, people wanted to show off their outfits (or lack thereof, in the case of some of the very scantily clad barbarian princesses).

A hard-faced Asian woman wearing a COSTUME JUDGE badge blocked my way. As she ran her critical gaze up and down my appearance, she looked as if she'd had her sense of humor surgically removed. In an officious voice, she said, "I've seen one or two of you already at the con, but your costume isn't up to snuff." She clucked her tongue, then tugged on the front of my sport jacket. "Wrong number of bullet holes on the left. That exit wound in your forehead is at least a centimeter off. And that makeup is terrible. It should be blended more."

"But I'm the real one," I said. "I *am* Dan Chambeaux."

She rolled her eyes. "Right, keep telling yourself that. Getting into character is important, but you have to take the costume seriously, too. After a decade as a cosplayer, trust me I know what I'm talking about. If you're going to be a zombie detective, at least do it right." She walked off muttering.

Loud enough to slice through the background noise came a bloodcurdling scream—and not the good kind of bloodcurdling scream. We hurried toward the source, as did all the other attendees, as if the shriek somehow signaled free beer for everyone.

McGoo and I shoved our way toward a small second-floor panel room, but a crowd had already clogged the door. We tried to jostle people aside, but they reacted as if we were just fellow costumers. So, we got more aggressive and finally made it through the door.

A stormtrooper lay sprawled on his back on the floor—with a wooden stake protruding from his chest. It had been pounded right through the white armor plate.

A burly Klingon stood over him, raising both hands. His bronze skin was flushed and his mouth drawn back in panic. "I just found him like that!"

A young woman in the back of the room—a motel employee holding a pitcher of water for the next panel—screamed again for good measure, although her first scream had already accomplished whatever a scream could do.

By now, all the formerly brawling *Star Wars* and *Star Trek* fans had made their way to the crime scene. The man in the Vader suit came huffing up behind them all, gasping with real exertion that was louder than the sound of his respirator voice box. The stormtroopers reeled when they saw their murdered comrade. One of the troopers looked through the open door and cried out, "Oh, no! It's TK-9399!"

I asked, "You can tell that just at a glance?"

The helmet turned toward me. "Of course, look at the red shoulder pauldron. It's very distinctive. That's TK-9399 all right."

"Yes, I suppose it is." I turned and called out, "Is there a doctor in the house?" The David Tennant, Matt Smith, and Tom Baker Whos arrived, drawing sonic screwdrivers and looking eager to help. I revised my shout. "Somebody call an ambulance."

McGoo drove the spectators away. "Out of the way, all of you. This is a crime scene."

"I didn't do it!" yelled the Klingon, unable to tear his gaze from the body on the floor. "I didn't touch him!"

McGoo turned to him. "I'm Officer Toby McGoohan from the UQPD. I need to ask you some questions. What's your name?"

The Klingon composed himself and said proudly, "I am Ach-gLokh Heqht!"

McGoo had drawn a pad from his pocket, poised to take down the information, but didn't know how to spell it. "Is that a name, or are you coughing up phlegm?"

"That is how I got my name!"

"Ach-gLokh Heqht didn't do it!" claimed a loud and busty Klingon woman. "I was with him at the time."

"No you weren't," I said. "I saw you in the altercation up on the mezzanine just a few minutes ago."

"You would call me a liar?" The Klingon female strode forward as if she meant to tear my limbs off.

I've already been through having a limb torn off, though, and found it unpleasant. I backed away, trying to be calm. "Just stating a fact, ma'am. It won't do for an alibi."

The Klingons regrouped and tried to come up with something else. McGoo and I bent over the staked stormtrooper.

"Take his bucket off," called one of the troopers in a sad voice. It took me a minute to realize that he meant the helmet.

McGoo shook his head. "Nothing gets removed until the Coroner examines him."

"What if he's not entirely dead?" I asked. "Never can tell these days."

Though it went against normal police procedure, McGoo couldn't argue with that. "Right, Shamble. Better make sure." He and I carefully lifted off the victim's helmet without disturbing any other part of the armor.

Then we discovered an even greater surprise. The dead stormtrooper TK-9399 was a vampire.

2

The ambulance and the Coroner's wagon arrived together with a dueling set of screeching their tires in the motel's designated "Coroner" and "Ambulance" parking spot. (The two spots saw frequent use.)

McGoo had called for UQPD backup, and now half a dozen uniformed officers swarmed through the Motel Six Feet Under and Conference Center ... which was even more confusing because some of the cosplayers wore similar—some might say better executed—uniforms, including one dressed up as the T-1000 from *Terminator 2*.

The Klingons had commandeered the coffee shop again, where they demanded goblets of warm bloodwine to celebrate the life of TK-9399, whose soul had now gone off to some place called Sto-vo-kor ... which sparked a lively discussion as to whether *Star Wars* fans could even go to Sto-vo-kor, or if that was exclusively limited to the *Star Trek* franchise.

McGoo and I went to the Con-Ops room, just off the registration area. We met the pot-bellied and balding con chairman named Phil Somerstein. He looked bleary-eyed, harried, and overworked with management details. The murder of one of the CosplayCon attendees seemed just one more hassle he had to deal with.

McGoo said, "This is an active investigation, Mr. Somerstein. I'm going to have to impose a lockdown. The murderer is likely still in the motel, and until we've had a chance to talk to everybody, we'll need your help in insuring that all of your attendees stay put."

Somerstein wiped a sweaty palm across a sweaty forehead. "Officer McGoohan, you don't understand—this is *con weekend*. Nobody's leaving the motel, with or without a lockdown."

The elevator chimed, and the doors slid open to reveal two uniformed trolls from the Coroner's office. They wheeled a gurney on which rested the zipped-up body bag. They had placed TK-9399's white bucket on his chest like a memorial, and as they rolled the gurney past, the other 501sters stood in a solemn honor guard, their heads bowed. Darth Vader also hung his helmet, flicking off the respirator in a sign of respect.

One of the stormtroopers shook his white helmet. "He never stopped trooping."

The crime-scene techs had swarmed in with their kits, taking the necessary photos, although many of them spent too much time taking additional photos of sexy Xenas and Wonder Womans (Wonder Women?) who posed for the shots. The police detectives conducted interviews. Off in a quiet area they were taking statements from a Batman and an Indiana Jones.

McGoo looked overwhelmed already. "I may need your help with this, Shamble."

"The cases don't solve themselves," I said. "And you did promise me this would be fun." I was already starting to formulate a plan.

Ach-gLokh Heqht was the obvious suspect, and I've been a detective long enough to know that the obvious suspect usually isn't the guilty one in the end. Besides, if all these cosplayers were really into their characters, why would a Klingon kill someone by pounding a wooden stake through the chest? TK-9399 was a vampire, however, so the murderer's options had been limited. Still, I would have expected a Klingon to, say, decapitate him with a bat'leth and stuff his mouth full of garlic. Then I realized the white bucket would have posed a challenge to the garlic follow-up....

"I can help," said a cheery voice. "It's what I do."

I turned, and faced myself—or at least a reasonable facsimile of me. He extended his hand. "Dan Shamble, Zombie PI."

I was taken aback—he had the fedora, the bullet hole in his forehead (though shifted a centimeter closer to center than mine was), and his skin was pallid. His sport jacket had prominent stitched-up holes. His facial features even bore a strong resemblance to mine. "You dressed up as me?"

"It's an honor to meet you, Mr. Shamble. I've read all your books."

"They're not actually my books," I said. "Someone else writes them, and they're just loosely based on my actual cases." In fact, I found it embarrassing that Howard Phillips Publishing kept releasing comedic horror mysteries that featured the cases of a fictitious zombie detective, based on me. "Just as long as you remember that I'm the real one." I paused to consider. "I'll call *you* Fanble."

He seemed disappointed. "But I have to believe I'm the real Dan Shamble. It's cosplay. I'm in character. Cosplay means you *are* that character, not just dressed like him. It's all about finding the real *me* inside."

"Right. I saw the program book."

McGoo looked from Fanble to me and back to Fanble again. "Usually one Shamble's enough, but we have a lot of potential witnesses and a lot of potential suspects." He raised an eyebrow, as if about to give a test. "Hey, Fanble, have you heard this one? A skeleton walks into a bar, says to the bartender, 'Give me a beer ... and a mop!'"

Fanble managed to stay in character by not laughing any more than I did. McGoo has an unfortunate repertoire of bad jokes.

McGoo shook his head. "Yeah, Shamble, he's just like you." He started off down the hall. "Let me talk to the crime-scene techs to see what they found."

I nodded. "Meanwhile, I'll go meet with the stormtroopers, learn more about the victim."

"We're on it, McGoo," said Fanble. "The cases don't solve themselves."

3

After TK-9399 had been hauled away in a body bag, CosplayCon got right back into swing as if nothing had happened. The attendees waited all year for this event, and they worked on their costumes with obsessive attention to detail. They weren't going to let a simple thing like a murder ruin their fun.

I didn't know what to think about Fanble. He seemed earnest and more serious about being "me" than I was. He took great care to imitate my movements, my mannerisms. It was like having my own portable 3D mirror walking alongside me. I decided to accept the help, though. Two heads are better than one when trying to solve a case.

The 501st troopers were nowhere to be found. I looked around, frustrated. "How do you hide a bunch of fans in identical white armor or a tall man in a Darth Vader suit?"

Fanble responded, "It's our job to find out. We are detectives, after all."

As we walked down the hall, other con attendees gave admiring glances and complimented us on our realistic costumes. When I assessed Fanble again, I realized that the bullet hole in his forehead was in the correct spot after all. I must not have noticed it before. We looked like twins.

But the grin on his face made him appear immature and idiotic. Did I really look like that? "Don't smile so much," I said. "It's out of character." He immediately resumed a stern "I'm a PI and I'm at work" expression.

A young man impersonating Edward from *Twilight*—who didn't look like any real vampire I had ever met in the Quarter—asked us if we knew when and where Van Helsing would be giving his talk. Fanble gave him the Crown Ballroom number, then asked if "Edward" knew where we could find the 501st members. I wouldn't have expected a character from *Twilight* to pay much attention to *Star Wars* personnel, but the imitation sparkler directed us to an unused panel room that the stormtroopers had commandeered.

Fanble and I looked at each other. "Do you think they're discussing the case? Maybe working out a retaliation against the Klingons?" he asked.

"Maybe they're holding some kind of memorial for TK-9399," I said. We found the door and pulled it open without knocking. In detective school I was taught that it's best to surprise your suspects.

The surprise wasn't exactly what I'd intended, though, because we came upon a group of half-undressed stormtroopers. Definitely not something I'd ever intended to see.

"Oh, excuse us," I said.

Fanble added in a gruff, no-nonsense voice, "We're investigating the murder of a Mr. TK-9399."

The troopers had taken off their helmets and shucked out of their white resin armor. They stood around in skin-tight body gloves while they adjusted boots, butt plates, greaves, and shin plates.

"Come on in, but close the door," said the troop leader, who identified himself as TK-6370. "We've got an important troop in an hour, lots of exposure, lots of attention. We wanted to check our kits."

"I'm sorry about your fallen trooper," I said. "We're trying to determine who killed him and why."

The stormtroopers grew solemn. "Poor TK-9399. Even after he died and came back as a vampire, nothing changed. I've never seen a fan so dedicated. *Star Wars* is a way of life." That trooper identified himself as TK-7246.

Another trooper, TK-9754, said, "I'm going to miss TK-9399. Sure, he was a fan. Sure, he was a vampire. But he didn't let that change who he was. TK-9399 always used to say '*Star Wars* is my life, and now it's my unlife.'" He picked up a piece of white plastic and turned to the person beside him. "Help me with my codpiece, will you?"

The man in the Darth Vader suit flicked his respirator box on and off, fiddled with the sound effects, then unsnapped a compartment on his wide utility belt to remove a roll of menthol cough drops. "TK-9399 caused quite a stir by trooping as a vampire. He was an activist, even wanted to form an Unnatural Quarter garrison. He tried to round up *Star Wars* fans among the werewolves, mummies and ghosts." He tugged on his black gloves. "He thought it would be cool to have a real ghost Obi-Wan and Anakin, maybe even a troll dressing up as Yoda. TK-9399 didn't expect to cause trouble by expanding the fanbase."

TK-6370 chimed in (and I was proud of myself for remembering the name/number), "*Star Wars* is a pretty diverse universe. Think of the cantina scene, or Jabba's Palace. Gamorreans and Jawas, Twi'Leks and Trandoshans, Gungans, Ithorians—even Chiss and Khomms and Dathomiri."

TK-5794 snorted. "Chiss and Khomms and Dathomiri are from the Expanded Universe. I hear even Disney's dumping those now."

"They still count," insisted TK-6370.

"And don't mention Gungans. I want a Jar-Jar free convention," said another trooper; I was starting to lose track of the numbers.

"Point is, everybody gets along just fine. Why can't vampire fans and human fans share a love of *Star Wars*? But TK-10625 certainly didn't like it. He claimed it was ruining the purity of *Star Wars*, to which we all said, 'Excuse me, *Star Wars Holiday Special*?'"

"And *Greedo* shooting first? Like *that's* pure?" piped up another trooper, to a general groan of assent.

"TK-10625?" I asked, looking around.

"What really bothered TK-10625 was that TK-9399 had to wear a modified stormtrooper suit and armor once he became a vampire. Added sun protection so he could troop out in broad daylight as long as he wanted," said TK-5470. "But TK-10625 said the modifications made the armor an unofficial variant and therefore non-canon."

Several troopers groaned simultaneously. "Let's not get into the canon discussion again."

"But TK-10625 can be a stubborn and angry man. He didn't like the idea of an Unnatural Quarter garrison at all, and he made no secret about that."

Fanble stepped up. "Where is TK-10625 now? We'd like to talk with him."

"Not here," said TK-6370 with a sigh. "Just after the con started, he and TK-9399 got into a huge argument. TK-10625 stormed off, and we haven't seen him since. I was surprised TK-10625 agreed to troop at CosplayCon in the first place."

I glanced at Fanble, then looked at the troopers. "A huge argument? And TK-9399 was murdered right after that?"

The man in the Vader suit frowned. "Sure, but a lot of things happened right around then. I mean, the con was getting into full swing."

TK-5794 glanced at the wall clock. "Time's tight. Better get ready to troop."

TK-6370 nodded. "Happy to help with the investigation, but we've got to be on stage in a few minutes."

Fanble also looked anxious. "I have to go, too, Mr. Shamble."

"It's Chambeaux," I said. "You should know better. What's so important?"

"Van Helsing is about to take the main stage. Who wants to miss that?"

I had intended to miss it, but I let Fanble go, and he dashed off so he could get a good seat. The 501sters finished adjusting their armor components. TK-6370 said, "Buckets on!" and they all donned their helmets. I was now in a room full of identical stormtroopers (although one of them seemed a little short). The man in the Vader suit flicked on his respirator, seated his black helmet in place.

"What is this important troop you're doing?" I asked.

Between gasping breaths, his words garbled by the cough drop, the Vader impersonator said, "We're escorting Van Helsing in the main ballroom."

"And ... how can you tell each other apart?"

"We *are* supposed to be clones," said one trooper, and they marched out.

4

Out in the common area, a Heath Ledger version of the Joker was comparing notes with a Cesar Romero version of the Joker as the crowds made their way toward the ballroom, ready for the main event.

Since I was alone for the moment, I took a few minutes to call the office—not because I had any important pending cases, but because I wanted to talk to Sheyenne. "Sorry, Spooky, this was our date day," I said. "You would've enjoyed hanging out at this cosplay convention."

I could picture her ethereal spectral form as she sat at her desk in Chambeaux & Deyer Investigations. She would hold the phone, smiling, her sparkling blue eyes lighting up. "You always take me to interesting places, Beaux."

"Interesting ... right. This time a murder's gotten in the way. *Star Wars* fan dressed up in a stormtrooper outfit found dead with a stake through his heart. Turns out he was a vampire. We've got a Klingon as our main witness."

"Oh, another one of those," Sheyenne said. "Are we on the case?"

"I'm here helping McGoo. The motel's on lockdown, but no one seems interested in leaving anyway."

"Let me know if you need our help. Robin and I are here for you."

"I've already picked up an unexpected sidekick," I said, looking around for Fanble, but I didn't see him among the crowds. "I'll explain later."

After I said goodbye to Sheyenne, McGoo came up, red-faced and harried. "I tell you, Shamble, this is turning out to be a full-fledged cluster-frack."

"Cluster-frack? That's a new one."

"From the new *Battlestar Galactica*, Shamble. Get with it." He mopped his forehead. "Ach-gLokh Heqht has gone missing—and the rest of the Klingons aren't talking. He was our only suspect."

"We might have another person of interest." I explained about the internal dispute between TK-9399 and TK-10625.

McGoo looked interested. "All right, let's have a talk with him. Is he with the other stormtroopers?"

"Unfortunately, no. He's gone missing as well."

"How do you lose a Klingon and a stormtrooper in the same day?" McGoo asked, then looked at the chaos of convention-goers and answered his own question.

I said, "I'm going to the main ballroom to see Van Helsing's keynote speech. Since the man's known for killing vampires, it's worth a look."

McGoo, meanwhile, had to get back to the crime scene. The techs had promised some preliminary results.

I entered the Crown Ballroom, where hundreds of chairs were spread out—and everyone was occupied. I worked my way through the costumed and uncostumed fans, many of whom were unnaturals: curious zombies and werewolves carrying comic book issues and limited-edition action figures. A burly bent-over hunchback clutched a pack of *Magic: The Gathering* cards, and a mummy held a first-edition papyrus scroll covered with hieroglyphics that he claimed was the "real" ashcan version of *Action Comics Issue 0*, available only in Ancient Egypt. He was excited at the prospect of getting it signed by one of the ghost comic creators.

Vampires comprised the majority of the seated audience, apparently having a love-hate relationship with Van Helsing.

Over the ballroom PA system, loud music started playing the thunderous notes of the Imperial March. The audience applauded and booed simultaneously as the costumed Darth Vader strode out from backstage, his black cape flowing, boots pounding on the rickety raised platform, respirator chugging. He reached the podium, lifted his black gloves, and waited for the crowd noise to die down. In his best James Earl Jones impersonation, the suited Vader said, "Some consider me a bad guy, a person who took a walk on the dark side of the Force and enjoyed it. But I did get better in the end."

Several fans in the audience grumbled. I couldn't tell if they disliked his original villainy or his epiphany.

"My exploits are nothing, however, compared to the man I'm about to introduce. The greatest villain known to monsters ... the bloodiest serial killer in all of vampire history."

The crowd grew more raucous. They screamed, yelled, and hissed. The vampires in the audience rose to their feet, shaking their fists.

"CosplayCon is proud to present our special guest: For one day only—Honest Abe Van Helsing!"

Vader turned and extended an arm in a dramatic gesture to the curtains at stage left. The vamps screamed and roared, then werewolves joined in, and finally everyone in the audience shared in the hate.

With a clatter of plastic armor, the stormtroopers marched in as an honor guard around a man in a trenchcoat and floppy hat. He had a narrow face, long dark hair, stubbly beard. I wasn't familiar with this incarnation of the character, but he seemed to exude predatory evil and bloodlust. His eyes were close-set and blazing.

When Vader yielded the podium to the guest of honor, Van Helsing just stood there in silence, spreading his glare across the audience and basking in the anger he provoked. "Thank you for the warm welcome. It makes my blood boil, seeing all of you disgusting creatures out there. You think you're safe. You think CosplayCon is harmless fun."

A ghost in the audience yelled, "Boo!"

Van Helsing parted his trenchcoat like a lecherous flasher to show dozens of sharp wooden stakes tucked into his belt, as well as long knives and a bandolier of garlic bulbs across his chest. "I've only got an hour, so I'll just hit the highlights of my career. Let me reminisce about some of the scumbag bloodsuckers I've slain over the years. Ah, there are so many.... Good times!"

The vampires howled so loudly they sounded like werewolves.

"Dracula was the one I killed most often, but that guy's like a Timex watch—takes a staking and keeps on sucking!" He laughed at his own joke. A few audience members groaned. Van Helsing rattled off his favorite impalements, beheadings, or solar overexposures.

As the crowd grew angrier, I wondered if they remembered that this was just a guy in costume, a fan playing a character. Van Helsing seemed to be really getting into the spirit of his cosplay. *Find your inner YOU!*

Thinking of that, I looked around for Fanble, since he'd been so interested, in the speech, but I couldn't spot him in the packed ballroom. I did see a couple of other Dan Shambles, though not as well executed as Fanble's costume.

Even so, I realized that Fanble's preoccupation with me as an alter ego was nothing more than innocent fun. Van Helsing's role-playing seemed deadly serious. If this guy truly believed his mission was to kill vampires, and if he happened to find a vampire stormtrooper alone in an empty panel room, maybe he wouldn't have been able to resist.

I needed to find out if one of his wooden stakes was missing.

After the hour-long panel was over, the crowd filed out of the ballroom, while a few people rushed the stage to mob Van Helsing with questions and curses. Since I had a few questions of my own, I pushed forward, too. "Excuse me, coming through—zombie detective, coming through! Official business—zombie detective."

When I finally reached the front, fans were pushing program books at Van Helsing for him to autograph while cylon security guards tried to herd people into an organized signing line. When I was within earshot, I introduced myself, which got Van Helsing's attention. Although he had a grudge against vampires, other types of undead didn't knot his undies quite so much. "Are you aware there's been a murder here at the con, Mr. Van Helsing?"

"*Doctor* Van Helsing."

"Whatever." I decided to let him stay in character. "A vampire stormtrooper was murdered with a stake through his heart."

"Murdered?" Van Helsing raised his dark eyebrows. "If he was a vampire, wasn't he already dead? I'd call that house-cleaning, not murder."

The gathered vamps spewed more hatred, but Van Helsing ignored them. He looked me in the eye and said, "Vampires everywhere are fair game—even at a cosplay convention. They'd better watch out."

His comment was greeted by more venomous ire ... yet somehow his autographing line got even longer.

5

The initial report from the crime-scene techs did not contain any good news. McGoo let out a sigh. "Whenever I have a case like this, why can't we just turn up a simple clue and an obvious explanation?"

"Whenever you have a case like *this*? When do you ever have a case like this?"

"When I'm around you, Shamble, more often than not."

The crime-scene techs had dusted the wooden stake from TK-9399's chest, but found no fingerprints. McGoo tried to draw conclusions. "That means it could have been another stormtrooper—they all wear gloves."

"So does the Darth Vader guy," I pointed out, then attempted to remember whether the Klingon Ach-gLokh Heqht had worn gloves as well. "And so do the cylons. And so do half the cosplayers here. And why limit it to that? Many con attendees are unnaturals, and a lot of them don't have fingerprints at all."

"Yeah, I guess the lack of fingerprints doesn't limit the suspect pool by much."

As McGoo and I talked, two full-furred werewolves walked by, laughing and bumping shoulders. Each wore a Jayne hat, an odd-looking orange-and-brown stocking cap that looked as if it had been knitted by a blind but well-meaning grandmother. The two were immediately adopted by a group of similarly-chapeau'ed Browncoat fans of *Firefly*, the long-ago canceled show from which the style derived. I realized that everyone seemed to be part of one big happy fannish family. All fun and games, until someone gets murdered.

The Motel Six Feet Under was still on lockdown, with uniformed police officers at all doors, but the attendees didn't seem distressed, or even interested in leaving. As McGoo and I contemplated our next step, Fanble strutted up, looking as if he had just won some kind of costume contest. "I got a break in the case," he said.

McGoo looked at me. "How did he figure it out before you?"

Fanble adjusted the fedora. "Never underestimate Dan Shamble, Zombie PI. I had a hunch and, getting into character, I convinced the con chairman to let me see the registration records. He thought I was you." He nodded toward me, then continued his summary. "I discovered that Ach-gLokh Heqht and TK-10625 both registered under the same street name! They're the same person in real life."

McGoo looked at me. "Now that's unexpected."

Fanble nodded again. "Indeed. Crossover fandom doesn't typically happen."

I said, "The Klingon and the stormtrooper were our two most likely suspects. If they're the same person, then it sounds like a slam-dunk." I grudgingly added, "Good work, Fanble."

Fanble grinned before he remembered to get back into character. "The cases don't solve themselves."

"So what's his real name?" McGoo asked.

Fanble showed great pride as he revealed the identity of our likely perpetrator. "John Doe."

Just knowing the suspect's name didn't help much, though. We had no idea what John Doe really looked like, not that anyone really "looked like" themselves at CosplayCon. *Find your Inner YOU!*

If Ach-gLokh Heqht/TK-10625 knew he was wanted for detailed questioning, however, maybe he would hole up where he wouldn't be seen.

"Let's check with the front desk and get his room number," I suggested. "We might find some clues there."

The desk clerk stood behind the front counter, using it as a protective barricade against the costumed fans. McGoo meant business as he strode up and flashed his badge. "UQPD. I need you to let me into a room."

To show that I meant business, too, I held out my official private investigator's ID card. "Zombie detective. I'm with him."

Fanble flashed a fake ID, which, I had to admit, looked pretty good. "Zombie Detective II, Cosplay Edition. I'm with them."

The motel desk clerk, a rabbity little vampire who looked as if he currently regretted his choice of employment, fluttered his hands, mumbled, and turned the computer screen toward him. "And what name is it under?"

"John Doe," McGoo said.

The desk manager keyed it in. "Yes, we do have a John Doe. He's in room 1013. May I see your search warrant?"

McGoo smiled benignly at the officious request. "It's a … welfare check, not a search. We have information that someone may be injured."

"Oh dear, of course! I'll make you a duplicate key."

The three of us waited for an elevator. And waited. And waited. Each elevator stopped at every single floor. The doors finally opened at lobby level to disgorge a throng of cosplayers.

McGoo waved his badge and said, "Police business, we're commandeering this elevator." I pushed the button for 10, and we began to ride upward … but of course we stopped at every floor on the way up. Soon the elevator was jammed with imaginary characters. It was a relief to get off on the tenth floor.

McGoo pounded on the door of John Doe's room. "Police! Open up." When we received no response, he slipped the magnetic card into the key slot and opened the door. "Okay, we're coming in." Before entering, McGoo drew his revolver, and I pulled out my .38.

I was surprised when Fanble also pulled out an identical .38. "Is that real?"

"Part of the costume, for that added bit of realism."

McGoo frowned. "Shouldn't it be peace-bonded, like they said?"

He looked too much like me when he responded, "It would be if they knew about it."

Together, we entered John Doe's hotel room. The shades were drawn. A suitcase was open on the luggage rack. Clothes lay strewn around the floor and furniture, but the room was silent.

"Looks like nobody's home," McGoo said.

"Records showed that only one person checked in here." I glanced at all the clothes.

"Fans often share a room at cons to save money," said Fanble, picking up a long Dr. Who scarf draped over the back of a chair. "Maybe John Doe is more than one person."

McGoo bent over to inspect a half-open black suitcase that contained all the components of stormtrooper armor. "There's not enough normal stuff here, though. Only one suitcase of street clothes."

I found a complete Klingon outfit tossed roughly in the corner. Behind the chair, McGoo was startled to come face to face with a polished silvery cylon suit.

Fanble was amazed. "You know, we never did see any of those characters together at the same time."

"How could you tell?" McGoo went into the bathroom and studied the vanity counter—saw only one toothbrush and a set of basic toiletries. "No makeup here, no prosthetics or wigs. How did he manage that whole turtle head for his Klingon outfit, or the mop of hair for Dr. Who?"

As I went to the closet, I felt a sense of dread. Normally in the Unnatural Quarter you might find skeletons in any random closet, but this time I found something else. When I slid the door aside, I saw the complete Van Helsing outfit hanging there—the trenchcoat, the bandolier of garlic bulbs, the floppy hat, the belt loaded with wooden stakes.

And yes indeed, one of the stakes was missing.

6

TK-9399 had somehow made himself a target for either Ach-gLokh Heqht, or TK-10625, or Van Helsing. An intersection of motives. And if the killer had an entirely flexible murderous intent, then CosplayCon was full of potential victims.

We had to find John Doe—and soon. And among hundreds of disguises.

Fanble had had the bright idea to cross-check the registrations, discovering that the various suspect characters were all under the same street name. I had the equally brilliant idea of flipping that around: we could look up any registrations submitted by "John Doe" and find out what other characters he intended to play. Since we'd already found the Klingon, stormtrooper, Dr. Who, and cylon outfits discarded in the hotel room, John Doe had to be wandering around the con dressed as someone or something else.

As precious seconds ticked away, McGoo, Fanble, and I waited for the interminable elevator. Each time the doors opened, the car was going up, not down. Finally, when another upbound elevator opened on Floor 10, two of the costumed fans motioned us in anyway. "Dude," said a *Star Trek* redshirt, "you have to go *up* to go *down*."

So we rode the elevator up to Floor 14, then back down to the lobby (again, stopping at every floor). When we reached the lobby, McGoo bolted out, and the two of us zombie detectives—both the fake one and the real one—followed him to the con registration desk.

CosplayCon was in full swing, with attendees preparing for the evening's big masquerade, though I couldn't see how an official "masquerade" was any different from the rest of the day here. Natural and unnatural fans were grinning. Werewolves got their pictures taken with Wolverines and a too-scrawny-looking Thor.

We had a case to solve. I could enjoy the con after we captured the murderer.

The registration desk wasn't busy this time of day, since everyone already had their badges and set about to enjoy the convention (at least those who hadn't been murdered or were considered suspects). No one was going in or out of the Motel Six Feet Under because of the lockdown.

A woman sat behind the information table, happily knitting, while a forlorn cat sat in a zipped-up pet carrier beside her. The woman looked up. "How may I help you?"

"We need to cross-reference your database," McGoo said. "One of the con attendees, Mr. John Doe, registered as several different cosplay characters. We need to know the full list so we can track him down."

She frowned and set down her knitting close to the cat carrier; inside, the feline batted at the sidewalls, trying to catch the yarn. "Our computers are down right now, but fortunately, we rely on a more efficient analog system." She pulled out a large plastic recipe box full of colored index cards. "I have every one of the attendees listed here. I can look up your John Doe and pull out his entries."

I let out a sigh of relief. "How long is that going to take?"

"As long as it takes. I'll flip through the cards and pull them out."

"Aren't they organized alphabetically?" Fanble asked.

"No, chronologically. By date of registration." She began flipping through the cards one at a time, starting at the front. While we waited, I looked at the large banner at the doorway: "We Are All Someone Else Inside!"

Right, I thought. *And one of the people here is a murderer.*

A group of rowdy Klingons stormed through the lobby, chasing after a Captain Jack Sparrow who had insulted them somehow. A Mandalorian Boba Fett bounty hunter sneered at a colorful figure of Kenny from *South Park*, saying, "He's no good to me dead."

I picked up a spare program book at the registration desk. "Find Your Inner YOU!" Killing time, I flipped through the program listings. McGoo fidgeted, waiting.

Fanble seemed optimistic. "We're on the verge of solving this case, I know it—and I'm proud that I could help. Is there any better way of getting in character?" He grinned, then remembered his serious expression again. I had to admit, he was doing a decent job.

The registrar's fingers must have been nimble from her knitting. She flipped through all the cards quickly, pulling out every one that listed John Doe. "That's all of them."

McGoo, Fanble, and I turned as she spread the cards as if they came from a Tarot deck. "All these were submitted at different times, all registered to a John Doe. He's a very ambitious costumer." She flipped one down. "Klingon, name of Ach-gLokh Heqht." I was impressed by how well she pronounced the name.

"501st stormtrooper, designated TK-10625. And a Dr. Who—Tom Baker Incarnation—oh, we have several of those here at the con." She kept flipping down cards.

"Old series cylon, toaster variety." She pursued her lips. "Hmm. Honest Abe Van Helsing ... one or two of those at the con as well, but he claims to be the real one." She rolled her eyes, "Don't they all? And ..." She held up the last card, squinting down at it. "This is strange ... he's also dressed as Dan Shamble, Zombie PI."

McGoo looked at me. "What's that all about?"

A cold dread rose within me as I turned to look at Fanble. "You?"

Startled, Fanble raised his hands. His fedora was askew. "No, not me! How could think it was me? It was one of those other guys!" He shook his head as if having a seizure. "That was someone else! They were all someone else!"

"But you're the one who called attention to John Doe in the first place," I said, though I liked to think I would have figured it out myself sooner or later. "If you're the murderer, why would you put us on the trail?"

"Because that's what Dan Shamble would do."

McGoo pulled out his handcuffs, crouched, and prepared for a fight.

Fanble lurched away. His shoulders jittered, his arms flapped. His bullet-ridden sport jacket whipped about as he thrashed. His face blurred like melted putty, fuzzing, reshifting. He shook his head. "No, not me! Gotta stay in character ... all the voices in my head!" He clapped both hands to his temples, knocking off the fedora. "Too many personalities. So many expectations!" His features shifted, twisted.

After the cosmic upheaval of the Big Uneasy, just about every form of legendary creature had returned to the world, from basic garden-variety vampires, werewolves, et cetera, to the more exotic mythical beings, even including Santa Claus. After all my years of investigating in the Quarter, I was beyond being surprised when I figured it out. "You're a shape-shifter."

"That would explain all the different characters," McGoo said. "John Doe, you are under arrest on suspicion of the murder of TK-9399."

Fanble backed away, still twisting and writhing. Somehow, he found the energy within himself to snap back into character so that his features looked just like mine again. He reached inside his sport jacket and drew his .38—which I suspected was very real.

The con chairman, Phil Somerstein, ran forward with an angry and annoyed look on his face. "Hey! That's not properly peacebonded!"

A large number of cosplay fans had gathered in the main lobby, many in costume, everyone excited for the impending masquerade. They gasped to see Fanble wave his gun. He pointed the .38 at me again.

I took a chance, though. I saw how determined Fanble was, how hard he worked. His features were so eerily similar to mine it was like confronting myself in the mirror. Holding my hands up, trying to calm him, I stepped closer.

Fanble yelled, "Don't come any closer. I'll shoot!"

"I've been shot plenty of times."

Then the shape-shifter swung the gun toward the fans in the crowd. "Then I'll shoot *them*."

I took another step forward. "But if you're truly in character, as me, then you know I'd never shoot innocent people. Not humans, not unnaturals."

The crowd grew thicker around the tableau, redshirts, numerous incarnations of Dr. Who, Klingons, stormtroopers, cylons, Jedi Knights, Browncoats, Visitors, and countless anime, superhero, and videogame characters, even another faux Van Helsing, whose costume was much less impressive than the one I had seen on stage—the costume John Doe had worn.

And it wasn't just the cosplayers. The unnatural attendees from the Quarter were also caught in the crowd: real vampires, werewolves, even the dedicated mummy fan with his hieroglyphic Issue 0 *Action Comics* ashcan edition.

Fanble's .38 wavered. He swung it around the gathered crowd, then seemed to sulk like a marionette with the strings cut. "You're right—Dan Shamble, Zombie PI would never do something like that." He dropped the .38 on the floor, then shucked the sport jacket, stomped on the fedora—and his features began to morph in an extravagant transformation.

As the flaccid flesh, skull, and facial features reorganized themselves, Fanble shifted through Tom Baker, then into a burly Klingon, thrashed about, and finally settled on a powerful and murderous character, someone who would not hesitate to harm innocent fans: Van Helsing—Honest Abe, ruthless vampire serial killer. His eyes flashed, his dark hair writhed. He drew his lips back to expose his teeth in a glare. "I'll kill you all!"

But despite his facial features, he didn't have his full costume, didn't have his tools or props.

Before McGoo and I could bolt forward to seize him, though, my doppelganger lunged toward the crowd like a quarterback in a game. The fans yelled, trying to scramble away.

Then I saw where he was headed. Van Helsing leaped toward the other Van Helsing cosplayer, knocking him to the ground and ripping at the wooden stakes thrust into his belt. He drew back, holding up one of the sharp projectiles.

Trying to get away, the vampires in the crowd screamed, "Watch out! He's got a stake!"

Van Helsing's hands blurred as if they were rapid-fire crossbows. He hurled his sharp projectiles at random into the crowd, and somehow every stake struck and injured a *Star Trek* redshirt, all of whom dropped to the ground, bleeding.

Drawing my own .38, I yelled at McGoo. "As Van Helsing at least he's *human*. We can take him down."

Realizing his vulnerability as a human, Van Helsing blurred and took on a different form, sprouting fur and massive muscles. His face elongated into a fang-filled canine muzzle and he became a powerful bull werewolf.

I hesitated before I fired, but McGoo didn't. He drew one of his two service revolvers. "I'll just wing him," he said.

McGoo's shot struck him in the shoulder, which flung the shape-shifter backward to the floor of the lobby. He thrashed about like an earthworm on a hotplate.

"It's just a flesh wound. I was careful—Nothing to worry about."

The shape-shifter didn't react as if it were a minor injury, though. He wailed and spasmed, clearly dying.

"What did you hit him with, McGoo?" I asked.

"Uh-oh. Looks like John Doe picked the wrong cosplay creature this time." He looked down at his service revolver. "This is the one loaded with silver bullets in case I get in a shootout against unnaturals."

The shape-shifter moaned and jittered, shed his werewolf persona, and lay twitching—a formless thing like a store mannequin whose features had melted away, gasping out of a round toothless mouth.

He said something, and I bent close, still feeling a certain connection to the man—to the *being*—who had known and imitated me so well. John Doe gasped, "I couldn't stand the pressure ... I just wanted to be somebody ... to be *everybody*."

With a last writhing rattle, the shape-shifter lost even its featureless humanoid form and dissolved into a puddle of organic goo that seeped into the StainGuard carpet of the motel lobby.

I stood next to McGoo, and he shook his head. "I didn't mean to kill him. Now there'll be a lot of paperwork." He sighed. "I can honestly say I've never seen a shape-shifter before."

I turned to him. "How would you ever know if you had?"

The cylon con security guards came forward to help wrap up, and McGoo decided there was no further need for a lockdown. I realized that it was a good thing McGoo had coaxed me here in the first place.

I felt sorry for Fanble. He had been so earnest, wanting to be the best "me" he could be. I often wondered who I really was inside, just an undead guy who liked to solve cases—was that enough? I had a wonderful (if ectoplasmic) girlfriend in Sheyenne, a great partner in Robin, a true friend in McGoo. I didn't have a need to be anybody else. Zombie detective suited me just fine.

356

Phil Somerstein announced that the CosplayCon Masquerade would take place in fifteen minutes, on schedule. He called out, "Photo opportunities in the side hall."

McGoo looked at me, adjusted his cap, and I adjusted my fedora. Both of us had to remain in character, of course. "I told you this would be fun, Shamble. Thanks for your help solving the case."

"It's what I do," I said. Maybe I'd call Sheyenne after all. She might enjoy this with me. The event ran all weekend.

As people passed, Phil Somerstein handed out pre-registration cards for next year's CosplayCon. Almost everybody took one.

So did I.

BEWARE OF DOG

1

The snarling whirlwind of fur struck a quiet drinking establishment in the Unnatural Quarter just after happy hour. Rampaging destructive hairy beasts weren't all that unusual in the Quarter, however—especially on a Saturday night.

I wasn't there in person, since my traditional watering hole is the Goblin Tavern, but witnesses described a tornado of claws and teeth. Luckily none of the patrons—neither monsters nor humans—were injured in the howling and smashing, but the New Deadwood Saloon was going to need a complete makeover (which it had needed for a long time anyway).

Sheyenne heard about the incident on the police scanner, and only a few minutes later Officer Toby McGoohan called me to the scene. "Hey, Shamble, I could use your help."

A bar disturbance didn't seem like something that would require the services of a zombie private investigator, but McGoo is my Best Human Friend, and friends help each other out. "I'll be right there."

I tugged my fedora over the bullet hole in the center of my forehead (the formerly fatal wound that had left me a *zombie* detective instead of a regular detective) and donned my sport jacket with the prominently stitched-up bullet holes across the front. After tucking my .38 in its holster, I gave Sheyenne an air kiss (about all I could do with a ghost) and headed off to the New Deadwood Saloon.

The place had batwing doors and an Old West feel—not surprising since the proprietor claimed to be the ghost of Wild Bill Hickok and could produce photo ID to prove it (complete with an olde tyme black-and-white photo on his driver's license). Fake or not, he was a nice enough ghost with big handlebar mustache, leather vest, and bad ectoplasmic teeth from chewing too much ectoplasmic tobacco.

The proprietor had opened up the saloon shortly after the Big Uneasy, and, claiming to have mellowed over time as the world settled down, he now preferred to be called Mild Bill.

Now, standing outside the saloon and looking at all the destruction the hairy whirlwind had caused, the ghost put his hands on his hips. "Golly."

The wooden siding had been raked to splinters, windows smashed, one of the batwing doors ripped off its hinges, and the sign over the door knocked askew so that it dangled on one bent nail. The painted letters said NEW DEADWOOD SALON, with an extra "O" added by hand to correct the embarrassing typo in the last word.

McGoo was already there in his beat cop uniform, notepad out, jotting down the reports of several witnesses: a half-unraveled mummy who looked as if he had tangled with the wild hairy beast, but on closer inspection I saw that he was just naturally disheveled; a dapper vampire, whose tuxedo vest was mis-buttoned by one and who looked as if he had imbibed too much Type AB negative mixed with Scotch; and a befuddled-looking human tourist in a golf cap who had obviously followed the wrong directions from his GPS.

McGoo looked up at me and tipped his blue policeman's cap. "I already called it in, Shamble. A code 10623A, Monster on the Loose (Hairy Variety)."

I inspected the claw marks on the torn wooden siding, pulled out a few tufts of fur wedged in the cracks. "Nobody saw what it really was?"

"No, siree," said Mild Bill. "The thing was moving so fast—it tore up the place then ran off howling. Came in here like one of those Tasmanian devils you see in the nature documentaries."

"You mean in the cartoons," I said.

"Yeah, the animated documentaries. I watch them all the time. Somebody better catch it and put it on a leash."

McGoo pocketed his notebook. "We're on it, Mild Bill. It's not really my jurisdiction, but in the UQPD, the lines between animal control and law enforcement are a little fuzzy."

"Yup, that thing was fuzzy all right." The cowboy ghost looked at the damaged façade of his establishment. "Shoot, I've needed to get a new sign for years. You can't imagine how much ribbing I get for the Deadwood *Salon*. Next time I'll check the work before I hang the sign."

McGoo was clearly done with everything he could do here. "Can you help me out, Shamble? We better catch this thing before it causes any more damage."

He knew I'd agree. "Sure thing, McGoo. The cases don't solve themselves."

2

The monster shouldn't have been hard to track down, since a rampaging furball on the loose tends to draw attention. But no one saw the beast for the rest of the night.

Sometimes, though, an obvious lead walks right through the front door.

Next morning, I was in my office, looking over the files Sheyenne had put on my desk, while Robin met with clients in her office.

Robin is on a crusade to see that unnaturals receive justice, but despite the exotic clientele most of our cases actually turn out to be pretty mundane. This morning, she met with a bickering ghost couple who wanted an easy, no-fault divorce. Robin intended to file on the basis that the "till death do us part" vow set a quantifiable time limit on the contract, and therefore made the marriage of two ghosts no longer binding. I could tell from their squabbling—which Sheyenne and I heard even through Robin's closed door—that nothing about the divorce would be simple.

And then a real-life legend barged into our offices. He was a burly werewolf with thick dark fur starting to turn gray at the temples and around the muzzle. He wore a dark, shabby-looking suit and a thin black tie, something a government agent might wear, or a police detective.

Or a retired police detective.

Or a retired legendary, rogue cop who had become a folk hero in the Unnatural Quarter.

I had seen his furry face on the news, on a poster in the UQ Police Department precinct house, even on action figures and comics. It took me a moment to recognize him, then another moment to get over my surprise.

I lurched out of my office, embarrassed that acted like one of those stumbling zombies rather than the well-preserved one I prided myself in being. I extended my cold hand. "You're Hairy Harry!"

He bristled. "Yes, I am, punk." His clawed hands clenched into fists, and his muscles bulged in his suit, but then the low growl faded in his throat. "I don't like attention, especially after the ... incident." Hairy

Harry had left the police force under the shadow of scandal, something terrible about the death of his rookie human partner, but I didn't know the details. "I'm retired now, keep a low profile. Just want a normal life—but they won't leave me alone."

Beautiful Sheyenne levitated from behind her desk. "Could I get you something to drink, Mr. Harry? Coffee, tea, soda?"

"Got any bourbon?"

"Afraid not," I said. "I'm a beer man myself, and I do my drinking outside of the office."

Hairy Harry's bristly eyebrows rose. "What kind of private investigator doesn't have a bottle stashed in his desk drawer?"

"A zombie private investigator," I said. "How can I help you?"

"I came to you, Mr. Shamble, because you're a legend yourself—I figured you must be good with all those books about your cases."

"*Based on* my cases," I said, keeping my tone even. "Fictionalized."

"Right," growled Hairy Harry. "Most of the stories about me were fictionalized, too. Didn't stop people from believing them. Right now I need a detective, and even a zombie will do." The restless werewolf cop prowled around the reception area. "My pet hellhound is on the loose, and I need to get him back before somebody gets hurt."

Thinking of the snarling furry beast that had wrecked the New Deadwood Saloon, I thought that was a definite possibility.

Sheyenne said, "What's the hellhound's name?"

"Lucky," said Hairy Harry. "It's an ugly world out there full of punks and dirtbags. He must be lost and lonely." His glowing yellow eyes focused on me. "I want you to find him, Mr. Shamble. I'll pay whatever it takes—just remember I'm on a cop's pension."

"We can work out payment plans," said Sheyenne, who was always business minded.

"Do you think Lucky just ran off?" I asked.

Hairy Harry seemed offended. "A loyal dog like Lucky? He's my guard hellhound. I suspect foul play. Come to my house and have a look at the crime scene. His doggy door was jimmied open—some sadistic pervert nabbed him."

3

Hairy Harry lived in an old, quiet residential neighborhood with a lot of old, quiet, residential neighbors. His house was a modest brick rancher with aluminum awnings over the windows, shrubs that needed trimming, a small lawn that was mowed under duress, and a flowerbed that seemed to grow only dirt. I couldn't imagine a larger-than-life rogue cop planting petunias ... pushing up daisies was more likely. The back yard was surrounded by a chain-link fence, probably a place for the dog to run.

The werewolf cop's mood hadn't improved since he reported his stolen hellhound. On the way over to his house, I thought Harry might regale me with his exploits as a tough vigilante officer with a sixth sense for sniffing out guilt and "Jack Bauering" a confession out of a quivering suspect. What I'd heard through the rumor mill was surely exaggerated, but as I rode beside the feral, furry werewolf, I could imagine it wouldn't take much to nudge him into violence.

We went up the front walk, and he used a set of keys to work the locks on his front door—four deadbolts, as well as the lock on the regular knob. "Can't be too secure."

I noticed the large BEWARE OF DOG sign on the garage door, another one taped in the front window, and a third one on a stake pounded into the lawn.

"I made a lot of enemies when I was a cop, plenty of punks gunning for me with silver bullets. I've kept a low profile for years—I'm done with law enforcement. But a lot of the creeps I put away are just getting out on parole. Damn pussy liberal justice system! They should've all been fried in the electric chair, just because."

Instinctively, I avoided talking about politics or judicial leniency with him, although Robin would have jumped into the debate.

He swung open the thoroughly unlocked door and marched inside, letting me follow. Inside the dim house I could smell the musky scent of damp fur—either Lucky the hellhound, or maybe it was just an old werewolf smell. As he entered the front hall, Harry's shoulders sagged. "I always expect Lucky to come barking and yipping and slobbering all over me, but now the house just feels empty."

I could sense the obvious weight of guilt in Hairy Harry. I doubted he felt bad about all the criminals he'd put away, most of whom had confessed (though many were scarred for life after the experience). "Nice house, Mr. Harry," I said. I feel it's often good to start an investigation with an inane comment.

"It's just Hairy. I stopped being a Mister when I stopped being a cop ... after I lost my partner." Shuddering, he hung his head, and his tongue lolled out.

I wanted to ask him about the tragedy, but Hairy wasn't a warm and fuzzy sort of guy. More like prickly fuzzy.

On the mantel in the living room, I saw a large spiked dog collar as big as a basketball hoop. The bristling points were each as long as a sacrificial dagger, and a shamrock nametag dangled from the center. "Is that Lucky's collar?"

"Wow, your detective skills are impressive," he said with a sarcastic edge in his voice.

Trying to imagine the size of the beast based on the diameter of the collar, I thought the New Deadwood Saloon had gotten lucky, and I said as much. The werewolf growled again and slumped in a tattered plaid reclining chair. "I used to drink at that saloon, me and my partner, Amy ... though she wasn't old enough to drink. Mild Bill carries good sarsaparilla. Amy really liked it." His claws dug into the fabric arms of the recliner. "But that's all behind me now. I'm just a retired guy who wants a quiet life. Can't a man sit at home with his dog, do the crossword puzzle, watch the shopping channels and laugh at the stupid stuff people buy?"

"Did you have a routine with your hellhound? Did you take him to a dog park, walk him down the street where other people might have seen him?"

"Everybody loved Lucky and he loved everybody—didn't make him a very good guard dog, I suppose. I had an appointment to take him to the vet for some minor surgery, but now he's out there, all alone." His claws shredded the arms of the chair. "And *I'm* all alone. I need Lucky! I got him after ... after what happened to Amy. I don't know what I'd do without my dog."

"What happened to your partner?" I asked, then quickly added, "just in case it has something to do with your missing hellhound."

"I was three days from retirement when it happened," Hairy said with a distant look in his yellow eyes. "And Amy was a perky human rookie, almost to her twenty-first birthday, and she'd just gotten engaged to be married. Had everything to live for ... until we got into a bad patch, and I failed her."

He snapped his jaws shut, and he turned to glower at me. "That's got nothing to do with Lucky!" He sprang out of his reclining chair. "Let me show you his back doggy door." He strode through the kitchen to the back door, half of which had been replaced with a hinged trap door for a large dog to exit into the fenced yard. The doggy-door hinges had been removed, though, and the panel hung askew.

"What were you doing when Lucky went missing?" I asked.

"I was asleep in my reclining chair, self-medicated with a fifth of bourbon. It's the only way I can chase the demons away, the only way I can sleep. But when Lucky's here, I feel safe—and now I'm not safe. In a world where a hellhound guard dog can get stolen, how can anyone ever feel safe?"

On creaking knees, I bent down to look at the hinges, saw what looked like a smudge of tiny fingers near where the swinging door had been detached. I looked outside in the back yard, saw the four-foot-high chain-link fence that could never contain a large hellhound. "So, Lucky was well trained then?"

"Such a good dog." Harry slid the hanging trapdoor aside. "Some bastards slipped in and stole my Lucky." Rage seemed to boil out of him, and he slashed the air with his claws, but then he deflated. "Find him for me, Mr. Shamble. Before it's too late." He led me back to the front door. "I just might go rogue again."

I remembered the posters in the UQPD: the bristling werewolf cop with his enormous .44 Magnum filled with silver bullets. For the dognapper's sake, I had to keep Hairy Harry from becoming a vigilante.

I started formulating a plan in my mind. I would check the animal shelter just in case someone had brought in a stray hellhound, and the veterinary clinic where Lucky had been scheduled for surgery. Sheyenne could print up LOST HELLHOUND flyers and post them all around the Quarter.

As we stepped onto the porch, though, the werewolf snarled. I saw three figures two feet tall scuttling out of the shrubbery and dashing across the grass. Gremlins. Deceptively cute and innocuous-looking critters, not quite the same as the "don't feed after midnight" variety. These were landbound, not the type to sabotage airplane engines, although gremlins had been known to wreak havoc on unattended lawnmowers.

Hairy Harry bared his fangs and roared. "Get off my lawn!" The gremlins scuttled away in a blur, and I left, convinced that I definitely did not want to see Hairy Harry angry.

4

The first place to look for a lost dog—even a ferocious hellhound—was in the Unnatural Quarter animal shelter. It was a long shot, but I wanted to cover all the bases. Besides, Robin liked to look at the puppies.

Robin has a personality that makes her want to help the downtrodden, including oppressed monsters, anyone caught up in unfortunate circumstances; by extension, her compassion embraces lost animals as well. She's a beautiful young African American woman with a hard persistence when she's on a case and a dazzling smile when she's about to win. She believes in the Law and Justice (complete with the capital letters), but the real world doesn't always operate the way her law books describe, and sometimes I have to bend the rules to shield her.

The UQ animal shelter was a cacophony of yips and growls, snarls, hisses, subsonic vibrations, and smells that made even my deadened zombie olfactory senses ready to shut down in dismay. Robin was stoic about it, though.

The animal shelter had specific sections for reptiles, felines, canines, large arachnids, and "other." Some rooms were barricaded with heavy steel doors and reinforced bars; others had special spell wardings. A lost hellhound, no matter how large and ferocious, would've been the least of the animal shelter's worries.

Robin and I made our way to a reception desk staffed by a young human woman with round glasses, long straight hair parted in the middle, and a Summer of Love hippy peasant dress. She seemed unfazed as a skeletal gray-skinned woman (and I use the term loosely) harangued her. "Puppies!" she shrieked. "I want all of your puppies."

The woman's spiky black hair looked like a startled porcupine on top of her head. Her face was gaunt, all angles sharp, and her skin had a zombie-like pallor; I could tell she was a lich, but from the way she treated the kindly receptionist girl, I could think of at least two other lich homophones that would have been appropriate.

"I'm sorry, Miss De Ville, but we have no puppies available this morning," said the receptionist.

Robin and I both recognized the name at once. Coupe De Ville, a well-known undead socialite, who threw gala fundraisers that attracted the Unnatural Quarter's snootiest investors and philanthropists, though no one could quite identify which charities were the beneficiaries of such largesse. I suspected Coupe De Ville simply pocketed the donations to finance her lavish lifestyle.

Now, she pointed a long claw-like finger at the receptionist. "How can an animal shelter not have any puppies?" She swirled and glared at us as if we would join her in the shouting.

"Sorry, they're all gone as of late last night," said the poor receptionist.

Robin stepped up. "We were looking for puppies as well."

"Actually," I interrupted, "I'm trying to track down a missing hellhound that's been on the rampage." I withdrew one of our Chambeaux & Deyer Investigations business cards. "I'm Dan Shamble, Zombie PI. This is my partner Robin Deyer."

"I was here first!" shrieked Coupe De Ville in a voice that would've made a chalkboard cringe in anticipation of sharp fingernails.

"And you've been here for quite some time," said the mild-mannered receptionist.

The socialite's white fur coat was comprised of countless small swatches of fur—from skinned lab rats, hundreds of them. Robin frowned. "Are those lab rat pelts?"

Coupe De Ville whirled on her, flashing sharp white teeth in what she might have considered a smile. "*My* lab rats, from *my* laboratory." She said the word with an emphasis on BORE. "They displeased me."

"And why do you want all the puppies?" I asked. She didn't seem like a cuddly pet owner.

"For various purposes," said Coupe De Ville before turning back to the receptionist. "Now, why don't you have any puppies?" Her sharp claws scraped on the countertop leaving long gouges.

"We ... lost them all," the young woman admitted. "An animal activist group broke in last night, opened the cages, and set them free. They're gone."

Coupe De Ville looked furious.

"What about a hellhound?" I said. "Did you have any hellhounds?"

The receptionist looked at her records. "No, not in at least six weeks. Hellhounds tend to be adopted quickly."

"Which animal activist group?" Robin asked. "I know several of them."

"It was GETA. They left their calling card, graffiti scrawled a foot off the ground."

I couldn't figure out how the height of the graffiti letters would be significant, but Robin turned to me and explained. "GETA—Gremlins for the Ethical Treatment of Animals. Little guys that cause a lot of havoc."

"Gremlins as a species like to sabotage things," I said.

Coupe De Ville snarled. "Little terrorists."

Robin continued, "At first they were called GET-U, which stood for Gremlins for the Ethical Treatment of Unnatural-Animals. They liked the sound of the acronym, but in the end they disliked the hyphenate compound. Gremlins are inclined to sabotage, but they're sticklers for grammar and punctuation."

In a huff, Coupe De Ville swirled her white lab-rat coat. "Call me when you have more puppies." She stormed out.

I tapped my cold finger on the business card, sliding it closer to the receptionist. "And hellhounds. If you get any lost hellhounds, call me. I have a distraught client who wants his dog back."

5

After hours when I went for my usual beer on my usual bar stool at my usual place, McGoo was already there. He does a lot of business and pondering on that bar stool. During the day he caffeinates himself with sissy-sounding cinnamon lattes from the Transfusion Coffee Shop, and at night he takes the edge off with a pint or two of whatever is on tap at the Goblin Tavern.

Francine, the human bartender, took care of her patrons, most of whom were abuzz about what had happened at the New Deadwood Saloon. They congratulated themselves on choosing a less hazardous watering hole.

"Hey, Shamble," McGoo said, raising his pint. "You know why companies don't let zombies take coffee breaks? Because they have to retrain them afterward!"

So that was how the night was going to start out. It was no better and no worse than the usual. "I may be the butt of your jokes, McGoo, but you're just a butt." I stiffly maneuvered myself onto the bar stool.

I decided the best way to distract him from offering a second joke was to tell him my news. "Got a new client today, McGoo. Hairy Harry hired us to find his missing hellhound."

Officer Toby McGoohan has seen all sorts of things in the Quarter—and I do mean *things*—from resurrected corpses in beauty parlors, to necromancy spells gone wrong, to tentacled monsters in the sewers, and an evil elf trying to drive Santa Claus out of the holiday business. He took all those things in stride, but now I thought his eyes might actually pop out of his skull.

"You mean, *the* Hairy Harry? But he's retired. No one has seen him ... since the last time they've seen him. He's a legend. Every cop looks up to him, both naturals and unnaturals. He knows how to put punks in their place, and he doesn't take crap from desk jockeys. Hairy Harry single-handedly busted up dozens of crime rings, even a crime octagon once. He cleaned up the streets of the Unnatural Quarter ... until it all went south after what happened to his partner." McGoo hung his head. "He was never the same afterward."

I was about to ask more when the Goblin Tavern's door opened and two towering hairy creatures entered. At first I thought they were wookiees, but I knew that was impossible because wookiees aren't real. These two—one with matted brown fur and the other with a mottled gray and white pelt—were a Sasquatch and an Abominable Snowman, respectively. Their heads nearly scraped the ceiling as they walked around the bar tables, holding out a donation bucket and passing out leaflets.

They represented the Bigfoot/Yeti Visibility Society, "Yes We Do Exist!" They passed the patrons in the bar, holding out the change bucket, but no one seemed to notice them; they just continued their conversations. Since I'm soft-hearted (even if it's not a beating heart), I fished out a dollar and dropped it in the bucket. Robin, with her deeply ingrained sense of social justice, would have been proud.

McGoo looked up, startled. "What was that for?"

"A donation for the Bigfoots and Yetis."

He looked around and just glimpsed the two hairy creatures as they walked back out the door. "Oh, I didn't know they existed. I was thinking about what happened to Hairy Harry."

Francine brought me my own beer—I didn't even have to order—and I took a sip. "Tell me about Hairy's partner. He didn't want to talk about it, but I gather that her name was Amy?"

"Yeah, she was a rookie and he was the curmudgeonly old cop. Insisted that he didn't want a partner, that he always worked solo, but his chief stuck him with a young lady fresh out of the Academy, cute as a button. Officer Littlemiss. Hairy Harry never stopped being a curmudgeon, but she grew on him."

"I've seen that movie," I said. "In fact, several dozen of them."

"They were chasing a mummy mobster, Lenny Linens, who made a fortune selling counterfeit monster versions of classic Hummel figurines. Hairy Harry and Officer Littlemiss tracked him to the warehouse where he stored the black-market Hummels. Officer Littlemiss suggested calling for backup, but Hairy wanted none of that. The rookie wanted to use due process and arrest Lenny Linens so he could have a fair trial."

"I can guess how that went over with Hairy Harry."

"You'd guess right," McGoo said. "He didn't want the kid in the line of fire, so he told her to stay put outside while he broke into the warehouse. Hairy stalked the mobster through the warehouse, prowling along the dim aisles."

I felt a sense of dread. "I'll bet Amy didn't stay outside. She went in to help him, right?"

"Yes. I read the full inquiry—every cop does. It was a real cat and mouse. The two of them separate, tracking Lenny Linens—and when the mobster felt cornered, he started shooting. Shattered Hummel figurines everywhere." McGoo shook his head. "But that wasn't the real tragedy. Officer Littlemiss ran to flank the mummy while Hairy Harry bounded along the rows of boxes. Officer Littlemiss cornered Lenny Linens, told him to freeze, identified herself as UQPD.

"From the other side of the stacked boxes, Hairy Harry says all he heard was voices, then a gunshot. He opened fire with his .44 Magnum, blasted craters right through crates of vampire shepherd boy figurines and little werewolf riding hoods and cute baby witches with angel wings. Hairy Harry prided himself on shooting first and not bothering to ask questions later."

My heart was always a dead lump in my chest but now it felt heavier. "He shot Officer Littlemiss, not the crime boss?"

McGoo nodded. "When Harry realized what he'd done, he crashed through the shelves, pounced on Lenny Linens, and unraveled the mummy entirely. At the inquest, he said he was in such a blind rage he didn't even realize what he was doing. You know the rest of the story, Shamble. Big scandal, Harry booted off the force, couldn't live with himself, and just disappeared." McGoo lifted his beer in a silent salute. "We still consider him a hero at the UQPD."

I raised my glass to touch his, but I was already thinking about the case. "And now someone stole his hellhound."

6

The next morning as Robin met again with the divorcing ghost couple, I went to check out the veterinary clinic where Hairy Harry had made an appointment for Lucky. Fortunately, there had been no further incidents of a rampaging, ferocious beast the previous night, but it was only a matter of time. In the Quarter, it's always something.

Dr. Moreau's Veterinary Clinic (Sterilization Specialists) advertised "We serve all species, breeds, and dimensional aspects. Heightened security available upon request." As I approached the entrance, I encountered a small protest—actually it was a regular protest, but with small participants. A group of angry gremlin demonstrators, obviously members of GETA, marched up in front of the clinic. The gremlins looked determined, though with their diminutive size, not very intimidating. They carried signs, waving them in the air so that they came up to my waist, "Neutering is Nuts!" or "Protect Procreation!" or "Stop Spaying!" The gremlin at the end of the parade line carried a sign that said "Allow Alliteration!"

I dodged past them, careful not to trip on the socially-aware gremlins. When they yelled at me for crossing the picket line, I brushed them off. "I don't even own a pet."

"Want a puppy?" asked the gremlin carrying the "Allow Alliteration!" sign.

I wondered if some of the strays unleashed from the animal shelter had followed them back to their secret GETA headquarters. "Not at the moment," I said. "Maybe for the holidays."

I pushed through the door into Dr. Moreau's clinic, a place of stainless steel, reinforced windows, and surgical theaters. As I stepped up to the front desk, the nearest operating theater door swung open and a burly man in a surgical gown and mask strode out. He had rubber gloves covered with green blood. He wore large aviator mirror-shades.

"Mark down another success, Maria," he said. "You can tell Mrs. Johnson that her basilisk is spayed." He lifted his sunglasses. "And yes, these reflective shades work just fine. Good to know."

A surgical assistant in scrubs, with her hair tucked in a surgical cap, opened medicine cabinets and took out vials of antibiotics and de-wormers.

The receptionist marked down the successful surgery before looking up at me. "How may I help you?"

"Zombie PI. I'm here to speak with Dr. Moreau." I flashed my private inspector's badge and glanced at the veterinarian.

"Sure, what do you need?" said the big man. "Are those protesters still cluttering the front door? GETA is a PITA—Pain In The Ass! They don't understand the good work I do here. They want to protect the masculinity and femininity of unnatural animals, but who wants packs running loose? Have you ever seen a demon cat spraying to mark his territory? Or a hellhound in heat?"

I seized my chance. "A hellhound is what I'm here about, Dr. Moreau. Hairy Harry has lost his pet, Lucky, and I'm trying to track down all leads. I understand he had an appointment for some minor surgery here?"

"Oh, that one—I remember!" Moreau scratched his surgical cap. "We had already arranged security for the hellhound."

The surgical assistant finished arranging the bottles of medicine, took a vial of antibiotics, and headed for the operating room door. "I'll go check on the patient, Doctor."

He nodded absently, but just as she swung open the door, he extended his mirrored sunglasses. "Wait—"

But she didn't hear him in time. She walked into the operating theater where the freshly spayed basilisk was recovering. We heard a loud, terrified cry that turned into a bloodcurdling scream, then silence.

Moreau hung his head. "I lose more assistants that way. When dealing with unnatural animals, you have to take precautions."

I was worried. "Should we go investigate?"

"No, she's already turned to stone. Sometimes they get better, sometimes not. Nothing we can do." He turned to the receptionist. "Can we install more mirrors in the operating theater as a security precaution?" Then he glanced back at me. "Now where was I?"

"The hellhound, Lucky?"

"Yes, we were all ready, but Hairy Harry never showed up, so I canceled the appointment. We have a surcharge for that." He adjusted his surgical mask again. "I wish I could help you, Mr. Chambeaux. What's my next appointment, Marie?"

"A nightmare stallion in operating theater two, Doctor," she said. "To be neutered."

"One nightmare gelding coming up." Dr. Moreau took a large pair of bolt cutters hanging on the wall. "If I think of anything, Mr. Chambeaux, I'll call your office." Swinging the heavy tool, he went into the second operating theater.

7

The raging furry terror struck again that night, but instead of attacking a popular drinking establishment, the creature chose an odd target: an abandoned warehouse that had once been a laser-tag arena, "now featuring REAL DEATH RAYS!" The death-ray/laser-tag business had gone belly up though, probably because their clientele perished after only a few visits.

I met McGoo at the scene of the carnage. Claws and teeth had torn open the corrugated metal walls, peeling them aside like an orange. The windows had been shattered. Long silver claw marks looked like extended lightning bolts across the metal walls.

"Must have been the same thing that struck the New Deadwood Saloon," I said.

McGoo nodded. "You sure it's Hairy Harry's hellhound?"

"I can do the math, even though math was never my favorite subject. Any security cameras here?"

He frowned at me. "Who would be watching this place, Shamble? The squatters tore out the cams and sold them for parts a long time ago."

"Squatters? Does that mean there were witnesses?"

"No. They only sleep here during the daytime—a couple of trolls and a werewolf girl with a bad case of the mange. They were out panhandling when it happened."

"How does a wild hellhound just disappear, McGoo? Hairy Harry thinks Lucky was dognapped—but if that's the case, why would it go on random rampages?"

McGoo and I walked around the crime scene. "I put out an APB for a violent furry beast that's prone to ferocious destruction, and our tip line has been flooded. Apparently that's not a specific enough description in the Unnatural Quarter."

I looked up at the dilapidated death-ray sign, tipping my fedora back so I could see better. "An abandoned warehouse? An unlikely target. Why would a hellhound attack here?"

McGoo grinned. "I know something you don't know, Shamble—and if the monster really is Hairy Harry's hellhound, maybe ..."

"What?"

"Before this place was a death-ray/laser-tag arena, it used to be a warehouse—a criminal warehouse, owned by a mummy black marketeer. Lenny Linens." He grinned, and I caught on.

"This is the warehouse where Hairy Harry had his shootout? Where Officer Littlemiss was killed?"

"Win a prize every time, Shamble. Now that's a connection you can work with."

8

I felt guilty about laughing over someone else's misfortune, but it really *was* funny. Besides, Coupe De Ville had done very little to endear herself to the general public.

Walking on legs that were as thin and brittle as mummified sticks and adorned with sagging fishnet stockings, she emerged from a fancy boutique on Hyde Avenue. That's not an area I normally frequent, since uptown is too highbrow for me and most of my clients, but Hairy Harry and I were walking down the street when it happened.

The socialite lich wore an overabundance of unnatural bling: gaudy amulets, and necklaces of heavy moonstones that looked like eyeballs. She was haughty in her patchwork white coat made of lab rat fur, surrounded by a miasmic cloud of perfume from sampling every possible aroma in the boutique.

Coupe De Ville lifted her sharp chin as if she meant to cut the air and yelled for a taxi. Her severe face turned into a rictus of disappointment when a cab did not instantly appear.

That was when the rambunctious and militant GETA gremlins rushed out of an alley, yelling, "Puppy parasite!" and "Pet predator!" They carried plastic Solo cups full of scarlet paint, which they hurled at her. Several gouts only reached the lich's knobby knees, but one gremlin was exuberant enough to splash paint all over her rat fur coat. Then the gremlins dropped their empty plastic cups and raced away, laughing and cackling.

Under the best of circumstances, Coupe De Ville's voice was enough to make my skin crawl, and now her scream was enough to shatter glass. Fortunately, the jewelry stores and high-end perfume shops on Hyde Street all had reinforced windows to protect against burglars and, as it turned out, shrieking liches.

As she stood horrified at the red paint splattered over her, it really wasn't terribly funny—I know that. But Hairy Harry started chuffing first, and I couldn't help myself. It was good to hear the rogue werewolf cop laugh for a change.

He had been so forlorn and distraught ever since he came into our offices in search of Lucky. Sick of waiting around for news, he had begged to accompany me this morning as I walked the streets in search of clues. As a police detective himself back in the day, Hairy Harry knew the technique of "investigation by wandering around."

After last night's attack on the former black market Hummel warehouse, a place that had so many dark memories for him, Hairy Harry was in even worse shape. His lupine eyes were bloodshot, as if he'd been crying through the night as well as howling at the moon. He shook his shaggy head. "It's more important than ever that we find Lucky—before someone gets hurt." He suggested we go uptown. "Some rich types might want a purebred hellhound. You never know." I think he just wanted company.

Hairy was a rumpled, no-nonsense sort of werewolf, who, in his years of being a tough cop, had seen it all, then gone back for a second look.

He wasn't much for conversation, though. We had been walking along in companionable guy silence, not bothering to look in the store windows. I would have enjoyed the stroll more if Sheyenne were with me, even though we couldn't afford most of the things in stores like these. I couldn't pronounce most of the brand names, much less identify the type of merchandise they specialized in. I admit it, I'm not entirely sure I even know the definition of "couture."

Laughing at Coupe De Ville's misfortune didn't prevent Hairy Harry's cop instincts from kicking in. A werewolf cop can retire but he'll always be a werewolf cop. I controlled my laughter, too, as my detective instincts kicked in as well. "I want to talk to those gremlins. I keep bumping into GETA at every step in my investigation. They may be involved in the disappearance of your hellhound."

Hairy Harry's hackles rose. "Let's go."

Coupe De Ville was still waving her clawed hands in the air, looking in revulsion at the red paint that splattered her rat fur coat. She was in such a horrifying state that even well-meaning people didn't dare go closer.

I called out as Hairy Harry and I dashed past her after the gremlins. "We'll try to catch them, ma'am."

"But who's going to help *me?*" she wailed.

I gestured toward the curious onlookers. "They will." The crowd bolted as soon as I made my suggestion.

The werewolf cop put his nose to the ground, sniffed the discarded plastic cups, then loped off. "I'm on the scent."

I did my best to keep up with him. Fortunately, I stay in good shape, regularly working out at the All-Day/All-Nite Fitness Center, shambling along on their treadmills.

The paint-hurling gremlins were small but they could run fast on their little legs. Gremlins like to throw a wrench in the works, then dash away before they get caught—but they weren't used to being tracked by a werewolf cop and a relentless zombie detective (although my contribution to the pursuit was definitely secondary).

We never caught sight of the fleeing gremlins as they dodged from street to street, but Hairy Harry kept after them. As he ran along bent over and nose to the ground, his jeans slid down, letting me glimpse too much of his big hairy butt crack—not something I wanted to see, but I'd seen many horrific things before.

The werewolf cop slowed, sniffing harder. "We're close." He turned down a narrow side street, passed several unmarked tenement doors, then stopped at a low delivery door with a side mailbox labeled "GETA Secret Headquarters."

"This is the place," I said.

Hairy Harry snarled sarcastically. "You really are a detective."

As we approached, I drew my .38 just in case there was trouble. The werewolf gave my weapon a scornful glance, then withdrew his much more impressive .44 Magnum. Hairy Harry smashed the door with a clawed hand, then charged in. "Got you, little bastards!"

Inside GETA headquarters, the gremlins scrambled about in a panic. Several were washing up, changing clothes. They recoiled in alarm as we burst in, and several raised their hands in surrender upon seeing Hairy Harry's gun, which was about the size of their smallest member. One gremlin raised Neutering is Nuts! picket sign defensively, though a .44 Magnum blast would cut right through it as easily as it cut through a wall of monster figurines and one rookie cop.

I pointed my much-less-impressive pistol at them. "Caught you red-handed." Two of the quivering gremlins did indeed have red hands from spilled paint. "We saw you dump that on Coupe De Ville."

"She's an evil lich," said one of the gremlins.

"She wears fur coats. Think of all those poor lab rats," another gremlin said. "And she keeps adopting puppies. I think she eats them. They're never seen again."

The gremlin peeked out from behind her Neutering is Nuts! sign. "And she's not a nice person at all."

"GETA defends animals of all kinds, even the nasty ones," said the leader of the group. "We're here to stop the torture and the experimentation."

Another gremlin said, "And the neutering." His voice cracked in a high falsetto.

From behind a door in the back of the GETA secret headquarters, we heard a scuffle, a yipping sound, then muffled shouts.

Hairy Harry perked up his tufted ears. "That sounds like Lucky!" There was no stopping him as he boiled forward. Snarling, he swung his Magnum and blasted open the door to the back room. He didn't even bother to try the knob. The 44-caliber bullet blew the knob, the hasp, and half the door into shrapnel, then Harry smashed it inward.

Wooden steps led down to a basement, from which we heard excited barking and yipping.

I swung my .38 at the embarrassed and frightened GETA members in the main room, then I followed Harry down into the cellar of the secret headquarters. The basement was a wreck—not a chamber of horrors, but cluttered and ransacked ... as if it had been torn apart.

Hairy Harry immediately spotted the dog. "Lucky!"

Lucky really was just a puppy, about the size of a young German Shepherd. The small hellhound bounded forward, delighted to see his master. In his jaws, the puppy held a terrified and squirming gremlin by the scruff of the neck. The captured gremlin screamed for mercy, and Lucky dropped him on the cement floor, then bounded forward into Hairy Harry's well-muscled arms.

"I expected him to be a little bigger than that," I said.

"He'll get there," the werewolf growled. "Right now he's just a puppy with plenty of puppy energy." Harry tugged the ears and shook the dog's head back and forth as he cooed in a baby voice, "Isn't that right? Isn't that right?"

Lucky's tail wagged furiously, thumping against the open-frame cellar wall. Bored and rambunctious, the puppy had already ripped out the wadded insulation from the walls, knocked over boxes, spilled debris and laundry. I saw two other gremlins cowering in the corner, as if afraid the hellhound might want to play with them as well.

Lucky licked Hairy Harry's face, and the werewolf started licking him back. I grabbed the shaken gremlin that had been dropped from the puppy's jaws. "Why did you kidnap this dog? What did you mean to do with him?"

"We were saving him!" the gremlin cried.

The other cowering creatures came forward, struggling to find their defiance. "We knew about his appointment at Dr. Moreau's clinic."

"His master was going to have him neutered. That's a majestic hellhound. You can't emasculate a hellhound!"

The puppy barked and bounded toward the cornered creatures as they ran screaming for cover.

"He seems to be quite a handful," I said.

Hairy Harry glared at the gremlins. "And *you* want to handle a full-grown hellhound with too much testosterone? I suffer from the same problem. I love my puppy, and I'm not going to have him go through that."

"Save us," cried the gremlins. "Take the dog!"

Hairy Harry wrapped his big arms around the puppy and pulled him away from the terrified creatures. "Aww, he's just playing. That's what a puppy does. Maybe I should throw one of you across the room and say fetch."

The gremlins screamed and cowered.

"We should take Lucky and go," I said, trying to defuse the situation.

Hairy Harry glared at all of them. "You don't know how much damage you almost caused. Maybe you should try to understand the bond between a werewolf and his dog. I need my puppy."

Hairy Harry made sure his .44 Magnum was tucked in its holster, then he clapped his paws and made the dog follow him up the stairs. I swept my gaze across the cowering gremlins. Since Hairy was too distracted to remember it as he took his hellhound out into the streets, I said, "You just made my day."

9

Later that week, Hairy Harry called me back to his house for a visit. His voice sounded much happier, and his grin showed sharp teeth as he let me inside. "Things are back to normal, Mr. Shamble. Thanks for your help."

"Glad to have another satisfied client," I said. "So, Lucky was unharmed?"

He led me through the house to the back porch. "Yes, though he doesn't think so right now. I just brought him home from his appointment at Dr. Moreau's." He lowered his voice. "Snip, snip."

In the fenced-in yard, Lucky bounded around chasing leaves, although he was befuddled by the plastic cone around his head that prevented him from licking his new testicle stitches.

I thought of the enormous spiked collar on the mantelpiece back inside the house. "I have to ask. That collar is enormous, but Lucky is just a normal sized puppy."

Hairy Harry glanced back at the big spiked ring. "A dog can dream, can't he? Most people think *I'm* larger than life. I wanted my dog to be the same."

I thought I understood.

The werewolf cop leaned against the brick wall. "I feel so much more content now that he's back. Lucky calms me, keeps me at peace, guards me against my nightmares ... and all those memories." Hairy Harry hung his head. "Now that I've got Lucky back, the Quarter doesn't have to worry about some infuriated monster wreaking havoc anymore. Lucky's calmed me enough. I can handle the stress now."

I was confused. "Isn't Lucky the one that caused the damage to the old warehouse and the New Deadwood Saloon?"

Hairy Harry blinked his yellow eyes, then chuffed out in laughter. "No—that was me. When I have an episode, sometimes I go a little ... crazy. After what happened to Amy, and all the guilt and trauma I went through, I've been diagnosed with severe PTSD. I get flashbacks, panic attacks. They turn me into a wild beast. I can't control it. Lucky's my service dog, assigned to me as my best friend. It's therapy."

"That raging destructive hairy monster was you?" I asked, still trying to wrap my head around it.

"Lucky keeps me centered, calms even the worst flashbacks." On the back porch, he bent over and slapped his knees. "Here, boy! Come here, Lucky!" The hellhound bounded over, wagging his tail from the hindquarters on down. He didn't seem to hold the neutering against Hairy. The dog leaped up, placed his paws on his master's shoulders and slobbered all over his face.

Hairy Harry laughed. The dog let out a yip, and the werewolf responded with a loud howl. When they circled and started to sniff each other's behinds, I decided the case was solved and hurried back to the office.

ABOUT THE AUTHOR

Kevin J. Anderson has published 140 books, 54 of which have been national or international bestsellers. He has written numerous novels in the Star Wars, X-Files, Dune, and DC Comics universes, as well as unique steampunk fantasy novels *Clockwork Angels* and *Clockwork Lives*, written with legendary rock drummer Neil Peart, based on the concept album by the band Rush. His original works include the Saga of Seven Suns series, the Terra Incognita fantasy trilogy, the Saga of Shadows trilogy, and his humorous horror series featuring Dan Shamble, Zombie P.I. He has edited numerous anthologies, written comics and games, and the lyrics to two rock CDs. Anderson and his wife Rebecca Moesta are the publishers of WordFire Press.

IF YOU LIKED ...

If you liked *Dan Shamble, Zombie P.I. Zomnibus*, you might also enjoy:

Phule's Company
Robert Asprin

Prospero Lost
L. Jagi Lamplighter

Love-Haight Casefiles
Jean Rabe and Donald J. Bingle

Other WordFire Press Titles by Kevin J. Anderson

Alternitech

Blindfold

Climbing Olympus

Clockwork Angels: The Comic Scripts

Dan Shamble, Zombie PI Series

Dan Shamble 1: Death Warmed Over

Dan Shamble 2: Unnatural Acts

Dan Shamble 3: Hair Raising

Dan Shamble 4: Slimy Underbelly

Working Stiff

Gamearth Series

Gamearth 1: Gamearth

Gamearth 2: Gameplay

Gamearth 3: Game's End

Hopscotch

Million Dollar Series
Million Dollar Productivity
Million Dollar Professionalism for the Writer
Worldbuilding: From Small Towns to Entire Universes

Resurrection, Inc.

The Saga of Seven Suns, Veiled Alliances

By Kevin J Anderson & Doug Beason
Assemblers of Infinity
Craig Kreident #1: Virtual Destruction
Craig Kreident #2: Fallout
Craig Kreident #3: Lethal Exposure
Ill Wind
Lifeline
The Trinity Paradox

By Kevin J Anderson & Rebecca Moesta
Collaborators
Crystal Doors #1: Island Realm
Crystal Doors #2: Ocean Realm
Crystal Doors #3: Sky Realm

The Star Challengers Series

Star Challengers #1: Moonbase Crisis

Star Challengers #2: Space Station Crisis

Star Challengers #3: Asteroid Crisis

Kevin J. Anderson & Neil Peart

Clockwork Angels

Clockwork Lives

Drumbeats

Our list of other WordFire Press authors and titles is always growing. To find out more and to see our selection of titles, visit us at:

wordfirepress.com